VINTAGE MURDER

The Chateau Michel de Montaigne wine label reproduced on the front cover is used with the kind permission of the owner, Mme. C. Mahler-Besse.

Vintage Murder

A Robbie Cutler Diplomatic Mystery

William S. Shepard

Writers Club Press
San Jose New York Lincoln Shanghai

Vintage Murder
A Robbie Cutler Diplomatic Mystery

Writers Club Press
an imprint of iUniverse, Inc.

For information address:
iUniverse, Inc.
5220 S. 16th St., Suite 200
Lincoln, NE 68512
www.iuniverse.com

ISBN: 0-595-22413-X

Printed in the United States of America

This book is gratefully dedicated to the Foreign Service Nationals ("FSNs") with whom I have served, at the American Consulate General in Bordeaux and elsewhere. American diplomacy simply couldn't run without these dedicated employees, who are foreign nationals recruited to our career service from the countries where they live. In a diplomatic service which shifts American Foreign Service Officers from post to post every few years, FSNs provide local experience and continuity.

I want to cite four FSNs in particular: Mrs. Gillian Woehrle, Secretary to the Consul General in Bordeaux, Mrs. Livia Grusz and Mr. Johnny Haar, both Consular Assistants at our Embassy in Budapest, and Mr. Stelios Papadopoulos, Political Assistant at our Embassy in Athens. They all have had much to teach their American colleagues, and they did so with diplomacy.

Contents

Acknowledgments

I owe a particular debt of friendship to Alexis Lichine, a legend before I met him in Bordeaux. He was generous with his knowledge of wine, and a gracious host. I owe similar debts of friendship to many *Bordelais*, including Senator and Mrs. Jacques Valade, the wine estate owners of the region, the owner-publishers of the regional newspaper *Sud-Ouest*, and the surviving members of the French Resistance *CND Castille* network whom I met in the Dordogne.

I hope that my love for Bordeaux wine will prove catching, and that these pages will help others discover its treasures. Let me add that the locations in this book are all real except for Chateau Montmorency, Chateau St. Aubin and Chateau La Source. (There is, I discover, a Chateau St Aubin in the region, but it is not located at St Emilion where one scene is set in a fictitious estate of that name.) All characters are fictitious except for wine writer Ben Giliberti and Mayor of Bordeaux Alain Juppe, who make cameo appearances as the story begins.

The American Consulate General in Bordeaux was America's oldest consular mission. The first American Consul, James Fenwick of Maryland, was accredited by President George Washington in June, 1790 Over the centuries the Consulate General was only closed twice, first when war with France loomed at the end of the eighteenth century, and then again when the Nazi occupation spread throughout France.

The Consulate General was closed by the Department of State as an economy measure in February, 1996. Many including myself hope that one day America's oldest Consulate General will again open its doors.

Characters

Prologue:

Douglas Pryor, "America's reigning wine writer"

American Consulate General Bordeaux:

John Robinson "Robbie" Cutler, Consul
Stan Bartlett, Vice Consul
Ghislaine Martin, Executive Secretary
Claudine Auger, USIS
Guy Leblanc, Commercial Officer
Jean Deplace, Administrative Officer
Georges, Handyman-driver

Robbie's Family:

"Uncle Seth" Cutler, great uncle
Evalyn Cutler, sister
Minouette, a Siamese cat

American Embassy Paris:

Ambassador Ronald Adams. Pamela Adams
Elliot Hawkins, Deputy Chief of Mission. Marge Hawkins
Tim Everbright, Consul General Paris

Bordeaux Consular Corps:

Erika Lutz, German Consul General and Consular Corps Dean
Eduardo Dos Campos, Spanish Consul General. Elena Dos Campos
Richard Sanderson, British Consul General. Emily Sanderson
Georges Latouraine, Honorary Consul General. Suzel Latouraine

French Officials

Albert Demonthon, Prefect of the Aquitaine
Jean Claude Mauret, Prefect, Pyrenees-Atlantiques
Louis Armand, Sub Prefect, Bayonne
Jean-Luc Charasson, Prefect of Police
Jacques Moineau, Bordeaux Commissioner of Police
Jeanne Lhosmette, Mayor, St. Jean Pied de Port

American Official:

United States Senator William J. Etchevari (Dem.-New Mexico)
Jaime Etchevari, his cousin. Julie Etchevari

Sud-Ouest, a regional newspaper:

Jacques Lebrun, editor
Sylvie Marceau, reporter

Wine Estate Owners:

Yves Crespier, Chateau La Source
Charles de Tourneau, Chateau Montmorency
Claude de Monoury, Chateau St.Aubin, *Premier Jurat, La Jurade de St. Emilion*

Basque ETA:

Raul Izquierda. His nephew.
Alberto Aiguilar
Antonio Echurra

Prologue

Vintage Murder

This year's Bordeaux Vintage Dinner would be a special event, Robbie Cutler thought, nearly bumping into the nervous, scowling little man who bolted into the taxi that left Robbie at the Willard Hotel. Set in the cavernous oak walled banquet room of the historic Washington hotel, on Pennsylvania Avenue near the Treasury Department and the White House, the evening was a sellout. Robbie fingered his black tie nervously as he walked downstairs towards the banquet room. He was never quite sure that it wouldn't come unraveled. Still, he couldn't bring himself to wear a clip-on. What he didn't like were bachelor arguments with himself over details that never got resolved one way or another. He wished that he had brought a date.

The dinner would feature visitors from the Bordeaux wine estates, and a fine menu prepared by guest chefs. Eight renowned wines would be served from the most recent vintage now on the market, more wines than were usually tasted at these affairs, but that was what Pryor wanted. What Pryor wanted, he usually got. But that meant numbered wine glasses so profuse at each place that there was barely room for plates and silverware.

Douglas Pryor was America's reigning wine writer. Robbie had met him several times in Bordeaux, when the wine writer had visited either the region's wine estates, or the American Consulate General, where Robbie served as Consul.

"Hi Robbie. Some turnout, isn't it?" Robbie greeted Ben Giliberti, wine writer for the Washington *Post*.

"Good to see you, Ben. Yes, it's packed. Anything special going on?"

"That's what I was going to ask you, Robbie. There's word been spreading that Pryor has an announcement to make tonight. Something startling, his publicist tells us."

"I haven't read his columns for a while. But he's hardly the sort to do anything startling. It just doesn't seem in character."

"That's just it," Giliberti frowned. "It is out of character. That adds to the mystery. I got a personal call two days ago. She wouldn't add any details. From her tone of voice, I think she's as much in the dark as the rest of us. It's Pryor's surprise. The only hitch was that we couldn't write anything about it ahead of time. He made sure of that. Big mystery. But he's sure pulled in the wine writers."

He pointed over Robbie's shoulder.

Robbie turned and followed Giliberti's gesture. There was Frank Prial from the New York *Times* chatting with Gerald Asher from *Gourmet*. "Who's that fellow talking with Robert Parker?"

"That's James Suckling from the *Wine Spectator*."

"Come to think of it, what's Robert Parker doing here? Isn't Pryor his big rival?"

"Used to be," Giliberti agreed, "until Pryor stole his readers."

Robbie turned to admire a beautiful young woman on the arm of an older connoisseur. "Only at a Vintage Dinner would we notice the women after the wine writers," he said to Giliberti with a grin. Giliberti agreed, then left to compare notes with another writer.

Pryor would be introducing the main wines this evening. His approval spelled financial success. His sneer, which was more often seen, meant years of marginal operation for a winery. Robbie knew that since Pryor's widely read wine column had become successful, the pans had exceeded the plaudits. When Pryor had started his career, he had been more accommodating.

Those were the days when Robert Parker had been America's main wine writer. But Pryor had sensed that people were tiring of Parker's complicated system for rating wines, with scores ranging up to 100. He had simplified matters, with massive advertising and an A to F rating system. That's all you needed to know. Pryor had given a wine an A. Simple, and it worked. Parker lost readers, and Pryor gained them.

Champagne and *hors d'oeuvres* were passed freely, while the guests chatted and checked their tables on the posted seating charts, awaiting the open sesame of the banquet hall doors and the beginning of the Vintage Dinner. At length the moment came.

The room filled rapidly with formally dressed couples, all looking forward to a memorable evening. It was an expensive treat for many, but still, Robbie reflected, the wines alone could not have been purchased retail for the dinner's price. The wines had in fact all been donated by Bordeaux vintners.

That made commercial sense. As with similar Vintage Dinners that would soon be held in New York, San Francisco, New Orleans and Houston, this evening's actual purpose was the introduction of the latest Bordeaux vintage to an affluent and finicky public. The cost would be easily charged off to increased purchases of wines by the case if the vintage were a good one.

Robbie found his table, just next to the head table itself, and nodded to a wine grower from Bordeaux that he knew slightly while Pryor, at the head table, readied his notes. Then Pryor sauntered over to the rostrum to give his verdict for the first wine of the evening, a fine Pauillac first growth that his previous writings had now placed out of Robbie's buying range. He paused theatrically, cleared his throat, and surveyed the room and his fellow wine writers, with a forced smile that had a touch of acidity when he saw those writers whom he had bested for readers and for syndicated newspaper space.

Pryor was in a lecturing frame of mind. He had everyone's attention, and intended to take full advantage of it. "It took some doing," he began, "but for the very first time tonight, we're going to taste, and compare, the greatest wines from Bordeaux."

He cleared his throat. "I don't just mean the usual five first growths from the *Medoc* and the *Graves*," he said. "Lafite, Latour, Haut Brion, Margaux and Mouton. That's what you usually get at these dinners. That's because those estates have insisted that we only taste their five wines. But everyone knows that there are three other Bordeaux wines of the same quality, even though they weren't included in the 1855 Classification. So tonight, we're also tasting Chateau Petrus from Pomerol, and Chateau Cheval Blanc and Chateau Ausone from the other side of the Garonne River."

Applause. Whatever his secret was, he was milking it for the time being.

"And we're going to do it in the right order. No more of this nonsense of tasting wines in alphabetical order. Latour comes AFTER Margaux, not before it. It's TOO DEEP a wine. You CAN'T TASTE Margaux properly after Latour."

He was right about that, Robbie thought. But did he have to be so damned irritating about it?

"We're going to take four little trips tonight, around the great wine regions. That will help you to understand clearly my announcement later tonight. All in turn. We'll touch on the *Medoc* and the *Graves* first, and then go on to St. Emilion and to Pomerol."

He turned to a nearby table and added maliciously, nodding his head to a rival wine writer, "That's where Chateau Petrus comes from, you know."

"What a charmer," hissed someone at Robbie's table.

"Then, after we've savored these eight wines, I'll have a special announcement to make." Pryor underscored his comment with a stagey pause. Then, he absentmindedly fumbled in his pocket, and found a silver, antique pill box, with the initial P ornately scrolled on the cover. He extracted a pill, then tossed his head back and swallowed it with some water.

Turning again to business, he held up his wine glass ceremoniously and made a display, watched by all and imitated by some, of swirling the garnet liquid around in the glass. An expression of pleasurable anticipation flitted over his features as he sniffed the wine. Then he took a generous sip, swirling the wine around in his mouth before swallowing it.

Verdict ready, he cleared his throat a bit too loudly, the impatient schoolmaster demanding attention from unruly pupils. "This Pauillac..." he began.

The dinner crowd was too noisy. He started over again, voice rising to get attention. "THIS WHY-YN-NEHHHH," he gagged. Then gurgling sounds came, but no more words. His sentence ended in a screech.

Those who were still swirling their wine glasses in imitation of Pryor missed what happened next. But Robbie saw his contorted face and heard his astonished gasp of pain as Pryor tried to grab the rostrum to steady himself. Then he lurched forward, knocking over the microphone as he fell to the ground virtually at Robbie's feet. Pryor twitched spasmodically several times, and then was still.

It might have been a heart attack, but in the second or two that it took for a doctor attending the dinner to reach them, Robbie was able to catch a whiff of bitter almonds.

Decidedly, he thought, this was not a wine for a vintage connoisseur.

But it might do for an amateur sleuth.

CHAPTER 1

Bonjour Bordeaux

Robbie Cutler's late Saturday morning Air Inter flight from Paris to Bordeaux put him in a good mood after the sleepless night he had just spent on the TWA flight from Washington to Paris. The coffee was fresh, the croissants were hot, and the Normandy butter and nippy red currant jam were delicious.

Like a contented cat he tried to stretch—a mistake for a sleepy tall man in such cramped quarters—and hit his knee sharply against the jutting edge of the metal seat in front of him. Lucky for him that his overturned coffee cup was empty.

Robbie frowned and opened the newspapers. They were full of the death of Douglas Pryor in Washington three days ago. The Paris *Herald-Tribune*'s account of the murder seemed straightforward enough, factual, no embroidery yet. "Hmmmn, what's this?" The leading Bordeaux daily, *Sud-Ouest*, had frontpaged the murder in its Friday edition, the latest available on the plane, together with quotes from a number of the wine merchants of Bordeaux, regarding the "great loss that we all have suffered" with the death of Pryor.

"I'll just bet on that," he shrugged.

The article, by reporter Sylvie Marceau, also noted that the American Consul in Bordeaux, Mr. Cutler, had attended the dinner and witnessed Pryor's death.

He remembered that he was returning to post as Acting Consul General and reacted accordingly. Damn! Notoriety is one thing when war stories are being told long afterwards at the Foreign Service Club, but that wouldn't help him make inroads with the closed Bordeaux community now. Then he smiled. Loosen up, Robbie, he told himself. You're too young for that kind of posturing, thank God. Leave that to the older careerists.

Here's something interesting. Robbie saw that both papers also mentioned an upswing in Basque terrorism in Spain. There had been a series of car bombings along the coast, and written demands to local merchants for protection money. Perhaps it was time that he scheduled another visit to the French Basque region southwest of Bordeaux, to check things out for the Embassy in Paris. His visits were always useful, the Embassy said. Security police talked with him. Most people did.

Robbie scanned another article on the front page. "Tragic Wine Crop Loss." It was just a paragraph long. It seemed that an estate in the *Graves* had lost most of its cabernet sauvignon crop. After harvesting, the grapes had been pressed, and their juice siphoned as usual into enormous casks for fermenting. Then, a foreman must have misset the fermenting temperature gauges. The juice had simply boiled away overnight.

The loss was total, and wine being a blend, the estate would have to sell its merlot grapes to a local cooperative. What a shame, Robbie thought. Shows what drinking will do. They ought to be more careful whom they hire. The paragraph was accompanied by a photograph of the distraught estate owner.

Robbie folded the papers and put them in the pouch in front of his seat. His try for a quick nap before the Air Inter plane landed at Merignac Airport in the Bordeaux suburbs hadn't worked. Now there was just too much on his mind. The plane landed, he exited, walked to the terminal building, retrieved his luggage, and caught a taxi to his apartment in the old section of Bordeaux near the Garonne River.

Minouette, his Siamese cat, was waiting patiently in the apartment, sitting on the window seat of the living room that looked onto the *Quai des Chartrons*, the wine merchants' quarter where Robbie had managed to find a furnished apartment that was just beyond his housing allowance.

Well, what of it? As a thirtysomething bachelor, Robbie saw no reason to save. Time enough for that later, after he had married and started a family. The familiar rationalization had served him well. He had used it to justify his getting good meals, travelling business class, and starting a growing and selective wine cellar.

Robbie dropped his bag, picked up Minouette and stroked her fur. The purring animal was something of a minor celebrity herself in Bordeaux consular circles. Friends, particularly married women, would make a point of asking him "How is the American Consul, and how is your Minouette?" as though the Siamese were a character from a novel by Colette.

Those who didn't know that Minouette was a cat probably assumed that Cutler was harboring a mistress on the *Quai des Chartrons*. Well, why not! It was time that these obsessive Americans began to enjoy life a little, some might say. Clearly Minouette had not suffered by Robbie's absence. Friends had stopped by and fed her regularly, as planned.

Robbie went to his upstairs bedroom, unpacked, showered, put on a robe, and returned to the kitchen, where he made a drink and sandwiches. His twice a week housekeeper had done the shopping for him yesterday, as planned, so everything was fresh.

There was no mail to speak of, since letters usually came to the Consulate General. Sometimes he would get a card from a Brown classmate who had stayed with him at the apartment, sent from the next stop on a moocher's tour of Europe.

Robbie flipped through a few circulars, sent to the French equivalent of Occupant. Other than that there was nothing much, except for back issues of *Sud-Ouest* that he had missed during his brief home leave. These he scanned with more interest than he would have read the Washington *Post* back home. There was often a feature article about a town or castle or festival somewhere within the consular district, worth a drive to see.

Robbie sometimes wondered how much his choice of a Foreign Service career had been inspired by a desire to do as much tourism as he could, far beyond the broad brush of a two-week tour of the capitals. The seasons came and went. The best time of all was fall, the tourist season's end. The leaves dropped, the tourists went home, but he could stay, enjoying himself.

In short, he enjoyed his life overseas, and if the next promotion was delayed, well, leave that for the pushers and shovers. He would savor this life while it lasted.

Robbie read some more details regarding the Pryor murder, including the fact that no arrests had yet been made. In Saturday's paper, local reactions to the murder were given.

These ranged from official tut-tutting to the discreet French equivalent of "It served him right!" The former were due to the decorations that Pryor had received from a grateful Bordeaux municipality, anxious to improve wine exports after several disastrous harvests. The latter were, Robbie thought with a sudden grin, literally sour grapes, from growers whose wines Pryor had panned.

Robbie flicked on the telephone answering machine while he finished his sandwich, a nice baguette roll with fresh butter and Bayonne ham. Four routine calls, then a message from Sylvie Marceau of *Sud-Ouest* referring to the Pryor murder and asking him for reactions and an interview.

The last call had been left on Wednesday from the departing Consul General, Eric Johnston, Robbie's boss and the man in charge of the American Consulate General in Bordeaux. Johnston brought him up to date on a few routine, unclassified matters, confirmed his Friday departure from Bordeaux on reassignment, and reminded him of the reception being held by the Spanish Consul General, Edouardo Dos Campos, that very evening.

Other matters could await the opening of the Consulate General on Monday morning, when he would compare notes with Vice Consul Stan Bartlett. Robbie set his alarm, then slept for several hours before it was time to walk to the Spanish Consul General's elegant home for the reception.

The walk was a pleasant stroll in the fine spring evening. Flowers were plentiful in the *Chartrons* district, and from time to time Robbie paused to enjoy the odors of something wonderful and elaborate cooking for a neighbor's Saturday dinner.

"*Chartrons*" meant wealth and the wine trade. It was odd to think that this neighborhood had once been a Carthusian monastery outside the city. It was still called the *Chartrons*, after that monastery. Later, the district had housed the protestant merchants who shipped Bordeaux wine throughout Europe. The opulent main street was now named Rue Xavier Arnozan. Residents said that a Socialist mayor who had not been received by the area's old families had given it that unpronounceable name, out of spite.

That made no difference, for everybody still called both the street and region the *Chartrons*. As a matter of fact, two centuries ago the first American Consul General, James Fenwick, had built the elegant Hotel Fenwick there at the edge of the Garonne River. Too bad we still don't own it, Robbie thought.

The reception would provide an easy grazing dinner, and a drink or two that would help him get back to sleep and over the time difference from his flights more quickly. Of Dos Campos's hundred or so guests, perhaps thirty would be from the consular corps. There would be twenty or so officials from the Gironde Department and from the Bordeaux municipality. The balance would be in private business, which here still meant the wine trade.

Robbie glanced again at the invitation as he neared the door. The reception was being given for some Spanish academics. They were commemorating the painter Goya, who had worked and died in Bordeaux, in exile from the repressive Spanish court.

"Good afternoon, *Monsieur le Consul*," said the man just leaving the reception as Robbie arrived. He was surrounded by guards and by aides, and as always seemed the case to Robbie when he saw the man on television, his eyes seemed to twinkle from some inner amusement.

It was the Mayor of Bordeaux, Alain Juppe, the Gaullist politician who before the 1997 elections that had returned the left to national power, had also been Prime Minister of France.

"You seem to be in the news recently. I hope that you are back with us for a while. Are you enjoying your stay in Bordeaux?"

"Thank you, *Monsieur le President*." A nice touch that, Robbie thought. As Prime Minister Juppe had, after all, been properly President of the Council of Ministers. "I'm glad to be back in Bordeaux. It's like home. So much so that I've become a sports fan. I couldn't wait to read the latest soccer results to see how our Girondins were doing!"

Mayor Juppe, amused, rewarded Robbie with an invitation to sit in the municipal box at the soccer stadium whenever he wished. "Since the Bordeaux team has become 'our Girondins,' you must see a game as my guest!" Juppe had said. With a final bow to his hostess, the Mayor left the reception.

Robbie knew that this chance encounter was fortunate. Juppe also represented Bordeaux in the French National Assembly, and had to attend its sessions in Paris during the week. It was said that if you wanted to see him in Bordeaux, Monday was the best chance, or perhaps Friday. He often stayed home on weekends.

Edouardo and Elena Dos Campos, portly and well dressed, greeted him warmly. They were genuinely glad to see him. Either that, Robbie suddenly realized, or his sudden press notoriety had made him a timely conversational catch for this reception.

He was still early. The residence was not yet so crowded that the elegant Dos Campos furnishings could not be seen and appreciated. Robbie recalled his father, "Trip" Cutler, now a retired Foreign Service Officer, once saying that you could usually tell a lot from the state of a career diplomat's furnishings. How many moves they had made, and whether college tuition was being paid, for example, or whether a senior couple were empty nesters.

This was a proud and seasoned diplomatic home, with plush area rugs and opulent furniture to match, and money, lots of it. Robbie's own apartment, furnished in basic late graduate school style, was all organized clutter by comparison.

Perfectly matched sofas and living room chairs in Empire style, from the bee insignias in the pattern design to the hand-finished mahogany legs, were grouped near the grand piano. Robbie was amused that a representative of Spain would have chosen furniture from the period named for Spain's invader, Napoleon. Watching over it all from its perch on the grand piano was a signed photograph of King Juan Carlos to Dos Campos.

His hosts had, after all, a wry sense of humor.

There was just time to get a drink from a passing waiter before the friendly inquisition regarding Douglas Pryor's murder began in earnest. Which it did very shortly, led by Robbie's British and German colleagues, Richard Sanderson and Erika Lutz. Robbie repeated to them the details that he had witnessed at the Willard Hotel, resisting the temptation to embroider what he knew and had seen for the sake of improving the story.

Commissioner Jacques Moineau of the Bordeaux police joined the group, and heard what Robbie had to say with interest. Too bad he can't leave his duties at home, Robbie thought. Still, Moineau was a pleasant fellow, and had been useful to Robbie in the past, helping out with scrapes that involved American tourists, smoothing out things behind the scenes.

Moineau seemed to have as part of his responsibilities keeping a security watch out on foreign consuls living in Bordeaux. His short stature and trim little moustache recalled Claude Rains in *Casablanca.* He stated his concern over the failed wine estate. "I liked their wine," he said.

"Some think it's a shame that this didn't happen earlier," said a musical female voice from the entrance way behind Robbie. He turned around. It was Sylvie Marceau, the reporter.

Robbie knew her by sight, but now looked more closely as she approached. Trim and graceful, late twenties, perhaps a bit taller than average, she had auburn hair that framed her hazel eyes and dimpled chin nicely. She had a warm and inviting smile, almost a visible aura of friendliness, and, he was sure, a nice sense of humor. He couldn't quite decide if she was beautiful or just very pretty. It didn't seem important. The bizarre thought occurred to him that his parents would like her. She looked as natural as a picnic, and made you smile to welcome her.

Her dress was fashionable, Robbie thought, for a journalist, even a French journalist. He couldn't tell a Chanel from a Versace, but he did know that her dress wasn't off the rack at the local Prisunic department store. It surely came from one of those specialty shops along the Cours Clemenceau across the park from the Consulate General. She must not be living on her salary, he thought. She either had money, or she shared with him an instinct for living just a bit beyond her means. Unlike half the officers in his Foreign Service class, she was at home here, in this stylish consular reception. She didn't have to impress. She was naturally graceful, and she belonged.

"I just got your message, Sylvie," Robbie said, greeting her with a smile. "Sorry not to have gotten back to you earlier, but my plane just landed this morning. I'd be glad to talk with you about all this, but we'd better wait until I check into the office on Monday and see how things are going. Johnston has already left, so I'm in charge, for a while anyway, and I'd better take stock for a day or so."

She looked at him a few seconds too long before smiling in reply. He was a potential story, and as such she sized him up. His height was imposing, masculine and reassuring without being too tall. He was dark and moved with grace, probably like the cat everyone knew he kept as a pet. He looked too serious, too within himself, except when he tried to loosen up and make an awkward joke. Then despite herself she saw possibilities. Was he good-looking? He could well be. It was too early to tell. The canvas needed painting.

"Fine," she replied. "You check it out and get permission from the Embassy, *cher ami*, and then we'll have a talk. This story is not going away."

Robbie winced at her little dig, which was right on target. There was no way that he, as an American diplomat, could talk with a French journalist about a pending murder investigation involving the death of an American citizen without talking things over with someone at the Embassy in Paris. CYA, it was called. All the practiced bureaucrats did it. Was that what he was becoming?

The point of contact would probably be the Embassy's Consul General, Tim Everbright, a pompous timeserver who was in theory supposed to supervise the activities of Consulate General Bordeaux, as well as other American consular missions in France. But Everbright would be sure to give the wrong answer. He would say no.

Robbie made a mental note to call Deputy Chief of Mission (DCM) Elliot Hawkins instead. Robbie liked Hawkins, a savvy career professional who as number two at the Embassy ranked Everbright. The word in the career service was that Hawkins was mainly charged, like most DCMs, with keeping the Embassy's politically appointed Ambassador out of trouble.

Robbie wanted to go ahead and talk with Sylvie, and he thought that DCM Hawkins would see things his way. To put the best face on it, Robbie could say that all he knew was public knowledge anyway, and that he was sure that Hawkins would appreciate the importance of being on the good side of an enterprising reporter from the region's leading newspaper.

He could even imagine Hawkins's second take on their conversation, wondering what Sylvie Marceau actually looked like, after he had given permission and hung up the phone. Robbie decided to make her the horned rim glasses librarian type. Oh well, he rationalized, white lies were the oil that kept diplomacy gliding forward.

Robbie drew Sylvie aside and asked what she meant by her remark about Pryor. "Surely some wine makers had been put off by his ratings of their wines, but that wasn't enough reason to wish him dead?" he ventured.

"Come on, *Monsieur le Consul.*" Was he testing her, drawing her out? She knew that a shrewd person being interviewed often tried to turn the tables like that. He was intelligent and didn't lack a certain charm, this American diplomat. Some instinct told her to play along. "You know that he ruined many wine chateau owners by his scathing reviews, just as he made the fortune of others," she said. She caught sight of two men, who made her point. "Look at our friends Yves Crespier and Charles de Tourneau, for example, our Mozarts of the vine."

She gestured towards two men talking across the room. They couldn't have been more different in appearance. Yves Crespier, intense, short and brooding like a storm cloud, had worked up step by step to owning Chateau La Source in the *Medoc*, by sheer drive and determination. Charles de Tourneau, on the other hand, was a tall, fair and languid aristocrat whose family had owned Chateau Montmorency in the *Graves* region for generations. They seemed to be arguing about something. "That looks intriguing," Robbie said. "I wish I knew them well enough to interrupt."

Robbie remembered that *Sud-Ouest* had once staged a wine tasting. Their wine columnist had had an intriguing theory, that there could be, like perfect pitch for a musician, something approaching perfect taste for a winemaker. To test his idea, the newspaper had provided dozens of unlabeled wines. Many winemakers were conveniently out of town when the blind tasting was held. Crespier and de Tourneau had taken part. They had achieved nearly identical scores, virtually perfect, naming many wines and vintages exactly.

"You may be right about Pryor," he said. After the success of his first book on Bordeaux, the writer had turned his welcome into the region into a device for selling his newspaper column. All over the United States harassed husbands, before driving home from the office on a Friday night, searched at their favorite wine retailer for Pryor's latest recommendations. So did many others who wanted to appreciate wine more, make an impression, or display a bit of borrowed erudition over dinner. "And those two prove your point. I wonder if they are talking about him."

"Pryor may have been the most detested wine writer in Bordeaux," Sylvie said. "He was good at first, pointing out improvements that had to be made in winemaking. But then he started to play favorites in order to sell his wine columns. People who didn't know the difference took him at face value. Whole vintages were lost to unfavored producers because of a byte from Pryor's word processor. And his system is ridiculous anyway. Why does it make any sense to grade wine as A or C or F?"

"It doesn't," Robbie agreed, "but it's understandable. That's the secret. People got fed up with trying to figure out the specialized world of wines. Then along came Parker, and his scoring system. That helped. Pryor just made it much easier for everybody to understand. The fact that he is good on television, and comes across as someone who really knew his wines in detail, gave the customers even more confidence. Now you can see the 'A Buys' everywhere wine is sold."

Sylvie nodded again towards Crespier and de Tourneau. "There are two of his latest victims. That's probably why they are conspiring now. So all you will see here from wine producers is a sense of relief, properly masked of course. I wouldn't be surprised if one of them did him in. If the murder had happened in Bordeaux, after all, half of them would be suspects!"

That was perhaps precisely why Pryor had gone to his reward in Washington, Robbie thought. No wonder Sylvie wanted to talk with him more fully about that dinner at the Willard.

* * *

Later on, Consul General Dos Campos filled him in on the latest bombing outrages by the Basque terrorist organization, ETA. The initials stood for "Basque Homeland And Freedom" in the Basque language. Basque terrorism had a checkered history on the French side of the border with Spain.

The traditional Basque homeland straddled the border. A proud people with a rich history, many now seemed content with growing regional autonomy. Others still hoped for an independent Basque nation. Like the IRA in Ireland, the ETA had long been the violent and illegal expression of that aspiration.

For many years Basque extremists living in France had operated only across the border in Spain. Their unholy silent bargain with French authorities seemed to be that they would not stage bombings and killings in France. In return they would not be hounded by French authorities on their side of the frontier.

Those days had gone, however, in the latter part of President Mitterrand's second seven-year term, when French authorities began to cooperate openly with Spanish police, making arrests and even granting extradition for Basque prisoners back to Spain, which for a while had set off a new round of terrorism aimed at French targets.

The current French administration under President Chirac continued that policy of cooperation with Spain.

"It's the same old story," Dos Campos said. "We had hoped this terrorism was all over when the ETA offered publicly a cease-fire in 1998. Their murders of Spanish elected officials in the year before that had only alienated their support in the Basque community itself. But then, they started the killings again. Then after the tragedy at your World Trade Center on September 11, 2001, we had hoped that the ETA would come to its senses. But after a while, their violence continued."

He let out a sigh of regret. "So many missed opportunities. And now there seems to be a new phase. Stop by the office next week when you can. We'll compare notes in more detail."

Dos Campos seemed to think for a moment, and then added in a lower, confidential tone, "There may be something going on within the ETA. I can't tell for sure. It used to be that their leadership was solidly in control under Raul Izquierda and Alberto Aguilar," he said, mentioning two nearly legendary leaders of the ETA based in France. "Now I'm no longer so sure."

Robbie was grateful for the update. The American Consulate General in Bordeaux, which had the Basque country within its vast consular domain, tried to track Basque terrorist incidents, and keep the Embassy informed. That was probably, Robbie thought, the most interesting part of his job, checking out the scene on the Basque coast, in beautiful towns like St. Jean de Luz and resorts like Biarritz and Bayonne, as well as the picturesque interior, such as St. Jean Pied de Port, nestling at the foothills of the Pyrenees.

Robbie thanked his host and hostess and left the reception. It was a pleasant evening. and so he made a detour and stopped at a sidewalk cafe on the Place des Quinconces. The site of the medieval Chateau de la Trompette before it was hauled down during the Revolution, this was now said to be the largest open square in

Europe. Robbie enjoyed his coffee, savoring its sweetness and waiting for fatigue to hit him.

He realized that with Consul General Johnston gone, and a replacement Consul General not expected before the fall, that he would be in charge of the Consulate General for several months. Why not have a look at the mission from the point of view of the Boss? The idea amused him, and he walked the few blocks over to the Cours Marechal Foch.

He must have just missed them. The front door of the unguarded Consulate General building, a large townhouse that was rented from its French owner, was covered with red spray-painted letters.

Approaching the building cautiously to read the message, Robbie recalled that the last time this had happened was years ago, about the time that the American Consul General in Strasbourg had been gunned down with five bullets as he was leaving his residence. At the same time a splinter Middle East terrorist group had defaced this Consulate General door, also using spray-paint, with political slogans.

That had clearly been the work of political fanatics. This time the message seemed a bit more personal. It read, in French and in English, "Death To The American Consul."

It was signed by the ETA.

CHAPTER 2

Robbie Takes Charge

The Consulate General that morning was a study in controlled chaos. Chaos, because any change at the helm was bound to be a little unsettling, even without a terrorist threat. Controlled, because the dozen Foreign Service Nationals, non-American "FSNs" who actually provided continuity at the mission, knew their jobs well and did them efficiently.

Robbie entered the Consulate General and was waived through the inner security door by the guard. He glanced at the wall plaque by the staircase which listed every Consul General since James Fenwick in 1790. "Won't be in charge long enough to be listed," he sniffed. Then Robbie bounded up the stairs to the Consul Geneal's second floor office, which he had decided to take during the months that he would be in charge.

He greeted Ghislaine Martin, the bilingual executive secretary, a polished French lady in her late forties whose English businessman husband had died of cancer a few years earlier. Ghislaine was dressed for Monday morning in a trim, lightly patterned blue dress. Her only jewelry was her wedding ring and an unobtrusive set of gold ear clips. Everything seemed unobtrusive about Ghislaine. That helped her run the office.

Ghislaine had anticipated his move to the Consul General's office and set out the accumulated appointment requests and, in a reading file, the unclassified telegrams that had come to the Consulate General during his absence. "How was your home leave, Mr. Cutler?" she said before handling him the telephone messages. With Ghislaine, politeness was not routine. It was a good thing of its own. With others, Robbie might have waived off the question. He answered Ghislaine, however, filling her in briefly about his two week vacation (abbreviated due to the Consul General's sudden transfer) and of course the dinner at the Willard.

The question and answers had given Ghislaine information that would be recycled, Robbie knew from experience, into helpful suggestions in the future. Her approving nod seemed to affirm a working tone of confidence, and set the stage for the questions that she would now ask and the first instructions that he would now give.

Many thought that Ghislaine was the real key to the smooth functioning of the Consulate General. Robbie wasn't entirely sure of that. After all, he told himself, she had no access to classified information. Still, it embarrassed him when she offered him a cup of coffee, made in her adjoining office. He wasn't certain who should be making the coffee around here. Yet, her professionalism was a subtle goad to his own.

Ghislaine gave Robbie a brief rundown on the functioning of the Consulate General during the previous two weeks. "There was one interesting reception that Mayor Juppe gave. Consul General Johnston made a report, and asked me to mention it to you. You'd find that in the classified files. Aside from that, a fairly routine period. Lots of visa requests. The new Consular Assistant seems to be settling in well."

He then briefed Ghislaine on the action that he had taken after his discovery of the ETA's death threat. He had called the Embassy duty security officer, and been instructed to double lock all doors and windows and stay home on Sunday.

She touched her perfectly groomed hair involuntarily, as if deciding whether to hazard a personal note. "That must have annoyed you," she finally said with a smile. He smiled in return. This was as intimate a comment as Ghislaine would ever make. It meant that she knew they would work together harmoniously. "Yes," he said shaking his head, "I really enjoy my Sunday afternoon drives." Grounded by security, his Ford remained in a commercial garage not far from his apartment. He would look forward to visiting St. Emilion the following weekend.

"And you found Minouette well looked after?" Her voice trailed upward in real interest and concern. The reference to Minouette only needed a nod from Robbie in reply. She knew that if the animal had not been looked after well, Robbie would probably have mentioned that first, before even the ETA terrorists. These Anglo-Saxons and their pets! Even after her marriage, long residence in England and fluency in their language, Ghislaine still found herself amused by the English and their American cousins. She closed the door as Robbie entered the Consul General's office.

Robbie grinned. The cancelled drive had meant an extra hour's romp for Minouette, who had not had much company for the last two weeks. She hated seeing Robbie pack his bags, and two weeks ago had actually disappeared during the packing. Hearing a muffled meow, Robbie had opened his luggage, and discovered Minouette sitting on top of his shirts in a halfpacked bag! At least she had behaved herself, he thought, during his absence this time. Six months ago he had discovered, following a week's orientation trip to Toulouse and the Dordogne region, that the perfectly housebroken cat had disgraced herself on his best chair! Her favorite dry food, however, was not available in France, and so he bribed her good behavior after every trip by giving her some. So far it had worked. "Low animal cunning wins every time," he thought.

Robbie settled into his office. Once it had been an expansive sitting room for the wealthy Bordeaux family which had built this townhouse a century earlier. It had high ceilings, fine shuttered windows that overlooked the Cours Marechal Foch outside, and more space than his entire Georgetown apartment had contained when Robbie was assigned to the State Department. The walls looked bare now that the Consul General's certificates of service had been removed. Maybe, Robbie thought, he could at least put up his State Department commission, which now sported an attractive gold colored frame. That would at least give visitors the full John Robinson Cutler of Massachusetts effect.

He sat behind the large oak desk and skimmed the unclassified folders that Ghislaine had set out for him. The appointment requests would wait for a while. He sketched on a yellow pad what he wanted done first, and quickly reviewed in his own mind the steps he had taken over the weekend.

After notifying security at the Embassy in Paris, he had called Police Commissioner Jacques Moineau. Moineau had expressed interest and concern but then rather deflated him, calling Robbie back after visiting the scene personally.

Moineau said flatly that this sort of threat was not the ETA's style. "This targetting of Americans, and an American Consul at that, doesn't seem to fit the ETA at all. Why drag in Americans when their struggle is with France and Spain? It doesn't make much sense."

"But *Monsieur le Commissaire*, remember a few years ago, American owned property in the Basque coastal region was destroyed by the ETA. Perhaps there is a connection."

"*Ah oui, Monsieur le Consul.* We know that just recently, ETA attacks on the Spanish side of the border have targetted British tourists. Maybe they are trying to gain their ends by damaging tourist revenues. Who knows how these terrorists reason?"

Moineau elaborated. "But in one thing they have been consistent. They always leave a message in their Basque language. I wonder why they didn't do so this time. Perhaps you surprised them before they could finish?" It seemed to Robbie that Moineau, ever careful to worry a problem and consider alternatives, was arguing with himself. If so, his little sigh of annoyance meant that he had given up for the time being. "Never mind, I've already stationed guards around your Consulate General, and we'll double the patrols in your neighborhood."

For the record, Robbie had then reported the incident and his conversations and action taken, using a FAX machine in his apartment to notify the Embassy, all American Consulates in France (including his own) and the Department of State in Washington.

There had been no need to go over all of this with Ghislaine. She had already read his report. Robbie called Ghislaine over his intercom and she appeared in a moment at his desk, ready to jot down what he said on a steno pad. She looked at him for instructions.

This must be what is meant by taking charge, Robbie thought. He asked that she prepare the usual "take charge" cable to the Department of State announcing his assuming full responsibility at the Consulate General. From now on, all messages from the American Consulate General in Bordeaux would be signed "Cutler." He called a full staff meeting for two o'clock that afternoon (when the consular workload would have slacked off), knowing that she would spread the word immediately, and asked that the American Vice Consul come and see him when his visa interviews permitted. No rush, he added. She nodded agreement. There was an inner smile of satisfaction on her face that told Robbie that the "take charge" cable had already been drafted.

Robbie then asked Ghislaine to put in a call to Consul General Everbright at the Embassy. This was after all, Everbright's supervisory responsibility, and there was no point in Robbie's antagonizing him on his first day. "Following that," he said, "I'll decide on other calls, to Commissioner Moineau and perhaps to Sylvie Marceau at *Sud-Ouest*.

"She has already called twice this morning," Ghislaine said as she closed the door.

Robbie's musings were interrupted by the intercom. "Your call to Consul General Everbright," Ghislaine stated in matter of fact fashion, as though Robbie had been in the habit for months of placing calls through an executive secretary. He sat behind the large oak desk in the rear of his office and took the call.

"Welcome back, Robbie," came the blustering voice from Paris. "We hear you've had a warm welcome. What do the police have to say?"

"I thought I'd check in with you first, Tim," Robbie replied, scoring he thought a minor point, but one important to Everbright. "As you've seen, they're going to beef up security around the Consulate General and my apartment, but for now they are not sure that it really was the ETA. Frankly, I'm tempted to agree at this point. (That should ease the way for his later request to go to the Basque country.) But I'll touch base with the police later today, and keep you all informed of any new developments."

"Good. We don't want anything to go amiss when that CODEL goes to Bordeaux in a month or so. Keep us advised. I don't like surprises. And good luck with running the mission."

Everbright rang off abruptly, and Robbie turned to his reading file. What had Everbright been talking about? There hadn't been a Congressional delegation (CODEL) in Bordeaux for a year. Just his luck that one was now planned, even though Robbie rather enjoyed talking with prominent visiting Americans. They kept him current on what was going on back home.

Oh yes, here it was, a message from the Department of State, addressed to a number of posts in Western Europe, including Consulate General Bordeaux, this time as an action addressee, not just for information. He read that in six weeks' time, Senator William J. Etchevari (Democrat—New Mexico) would be visiting Bordeaux and the Basque region. The message asked for appropriate appointment suggestions.

Holy smoke. Etchevari was an icon here, the most prominent living Basque, the grandson of a sheep farmer who had emigrated from the French Basque region to New Mexico shortly after the turn of the century. The good news was that the Senator was coming to Bordeaux by himself, without even a staffer. That meant that he wanted his visit played down. That also meant that for the duration of his stay, his staffer would be John Robinson Cutler. Clearly, a return cable, and a classified one at that, should go out pronto with schedule suggestions for Senator Etchevari's visit. He'd better get on it. Maybe Stan Bartlett would have some suggestions.

The intercom buzzed again. "It's the Deputy Chief of Mission," Ghislaine announced, with a slight intake of breath.

"Good morning, Elliot," Robbie began.

"Welcome back, Robbie," Elliot replied. "Tim Everbright (Robbie could picture Elliot's sly grin) has just briefed the Ambassador and me about events in Bordeaux. We're both a little concerned about Senator Etchevari's visit. He had a lot to do with the Ambassador's appointment, and we don't take kindly to losing Senators. Keep us advised."

Robbie assured him that he would, and then, on a sudden whim, invited Elliot to visit him. "I'd love to see Marge as well," he added. "If you could come down for an informal stopover, and maybe stay at the apartment, I'll be able to put you in the picture. You haven't been here yet, and it would be good to see you." Rather to Robbie's surprise, Hawkins accepted immediately and said that he would get back to him later on timing for the visit.

Robbie had finished the reading file and was mostly through the accumulated messages when Vice Consul Stan Bartlett appeared at his office door. Their relationship had been an easy one, but clearly, Bartlett didn't know how to take Cutler's move into prime time, and the new office.

Sam's sudden appearance recalled to Robbie his whirlwind stops at the State Department before returning to post. He had conferred with the French Desk, and with Personnel, as well as the European Bureau's Executive Director. They had all brought up Stan Bartlett, to Robbe's considerable surprise.

"He's good and he's effective. No question about it." That's what they all said. It was what they didn't have to say that was so damning. "He's not one of us." Finally, as he was leaving Personnel, an assignments officer blurted it out. "You're lucky to have him, Robbie. Stan Bartlett is so conscientious, and not afraid to handle the really tough jobs. An unpolished gem, but a gem anyway. You'll have a good couple of months before we assign a new Consul General. By the way, what do you want next? Still Budapest?"

The abrupt change of subject brought a quick agreement from Robbie. Yes, he did still want Budapest, where his father had once served. It wasn't until he walked down the corridor that he wished he had said something positive about Stan Bartlett.

So Stan Bartlett didn't fit into the club. He wasn't soft spoken. When he was in a room, he actually took up space, unlike half the people in State Department meetings. You remembered him. You also remembered what he had to say, and the fact that he had said it. There really was a State Department type, and Stan Bartlett didn't conform to it. Well, neither had Dick Holbrooke, who had briefly served as a career Foreign Service Officer with his father in Viet-Nam. What did that prove? Not much, if you considered where Holbrooke had risen. A lot, when you remembered that Holbrooke had had to leave the State Department in order to come back in at his level.

Meanwhile, Robbie felt guilty, seeing Stan, that he had not stood up for him...and maybe put a question beside his preference for Budapest in the minds of those who would decide. I'm going to make it up to him, Robbie said to himself. This pigeonholing isn't fair and it isn't right.

"Come on in, Stan," Robbie said. "Tell me what has been going around here for the past two weeks. That was some welcome back that you arranged for the ETA to give me on Saturday night!"

Bartlett was pleased that their bantering relationship would continue. His expression exploded into a wide, likable grin. That was the expression photoed week after week in the fall sports pages several years back, when he had run halfback for Baylor. He had made the Associated Press second team All American his sophomore year. Then as his junior year began, an aggressive tackle had finished his playing career, and even left him with a slight limp. Still he had stayed on the bench and suited up for every game, at the coach's urging. "Stan Bartlett does more good for the team off the field than most players on it," his coach had said.

His Foreign Service oral examination had become something of a minor legend. Asked by the brusk examiners why he wanted to join the Foreign Service, Stan had simply replied, "Because this time, I want to make the first team." Everyone had understood the reference.

Bartlett came into the office and sat in front of Robbie's desk. He went over the routine business, most of which repeated what Robbie had already picked up from the reading file. He then outlined the classified message traffic, which was held in a safe in a locked room behind the Consul General's office. The classified message procedures were an improvement over the old days, when diplomatic pouches were routinely used. They still could be, but now classified traffic to and from the Consulate General was routinely sent over secure transmission facilities in the locked room.

"I've briefed Tim Everbright and the DCM about this ETA business," Robbie said. "There's not a lot to add right now, except that Police Commissioner Moineau yesterday made a point that troubles me."

"What's that, Robbie?"

"He pointed out that the ETA message on our front door here was not left in Basque, just in French and English. That's not their way. After all, they are nationalist extremists. Of course they would write in their own language."

"Maybe they didn't have time. Perhaps someone surprised them. You yourself, perhaps?"

"Moineau suggested that. It's possible, but, I don't know. It's just too pat. It redefines what happened and so removes the problem. Maybe so, but I'm not convinced."

"The police are following up, I suppose?"

"Yes. I should go and see him, today if he has time. And I'm calling a staff meeting for right after lunch. Meanwhile, Stan, you probably know already that we're going to be having a CODEL in six weeks. None other than Senator Etchevari. I'll tell our people about it this afternoon. Any ideas you'd have on his programming will be very helpful."

"Will do, Robbie. Now I'd better get back to the store. See you this afternoon." Bartlett went downstairs to the visa operation on the first floor, the only part of the Consulate General except the Information Service that routinely saw large numbers of the public. His thumbs up as he left Robbie's office told Ghislaine that he was pleased to be a valued and consulted member of the team.

Robbie stepped out of his office to talk with Ghislaine. He hated to buzz, or use an intercom. It just didn't seem right. He asked her to arrange an appointment with Commissioner Moineau for that afternoon, say three-thirty, after the staff meeting. In view of the impending CODEL, he wanted to get a better overview of the Basque terrorism problem.

She nodded agreement, or was it approval? Robbie had the feeling that he was passing a test. Then the phone rang. Ghislaine picked it up, and looked up at him, "Oh yes, *Mademoiselle* Marceau…." Robbie nodded affirmatively, retreating backwards into his office. Ghislaine suppressed a sympathetic giggle as he nearly tripped over his own feet.

"Yes, we have had quite a busy morning. Mr. Cutler is finishing a report to the Embassy, but he'd ask me to call you next. Hold on, and I'll buzz him for you."

He had passed the test. Ghislaine would cover for him with a white lie. Robbie picked up the phone. He was pleased, even jaunty. "Sorry I didn't get back to you earlier," he began. "The truth is, I haven't had so much juggling to do since my days as a breakfast cook at a Howard Johnson's restaurant near Providence my freshman year at Brown. If I ever see your President Jacques Chirac," he added, "at least we'll have a stint at Howard Johnson's in common."

Now, why had he done that? Strictly first date jitters stuff. He could see himself blushing. Good thing Ghislaine couldn't see him.

"*Monsieur le Consul*," she cooed, "thanks for the biographic background. I hope your Embassy has cleared your talking with me."

"I haven't even discussed it with them," he replied truthfully, kicking himself for having failed despite his best intentions to mention the matter to Hawkins. "What does your schedule look like for tomorrow? I'm afraid I'm all booked up for today already, first day back and all that."

"How about coffee at the Journalists' Club, say ten o'clock?"

"Eleven is better if that still meets your deadlines."

"No problem. I'm working on this for the longer term anyway. By the way, what do you make of this ETA threat?"

That wasn't said in her usual journalist's factual tone of voice. Robbie sensed a personal note. Of concern, perhaps? Or was this just a sympathetic tactic, to draw out the person being interviewed? He really couldn't say.

Robbie tried to strike the right balance between macho nonchalance (for his own safety) and concern (for effective French action against terrorism, in case this was for publication).

"That's up to the security experts," he replied. "I'm taking it seriously while it's being checked out." They rang off, and Robbie decided that it was time for luncheon.

Luncheons in Bordeaux tended to be either spartan or gourmet. Robbie's preference tended towards the former during the week. An omelet and *pommes frites* often did the trick, or perhaps a *croque monsieur*, a French take on grilled ham and cheese with a glass of chilled muscadet wine, if the weather was fine and a seat at an outdoor cafe available. He walked to the adjoining Place des Quinconces and saw that a fair, with a variety of rides, a Ferris Wheel, and games had settled in for a two-week stay. They would certainly be busy on the weekend.

Robbie settled for *pommes frites,* an Alsatian beer, and sausages, and enjoyed the bustle of the fair as the *Bordelais* on their luncheon breaks began to discover it. An outdoor luncheon was an excuse for a walk, in Robbie's opinion, and where better to walk than along the narrow streets and wider shopping avenues of old Bordeaux? Robbie finished his luncheon, and on an impulse walked across the Place des Quinconces, past the wine stores to the Place de la Comedie and the Grand Theatre, Bordeaux's opera house, an imposing eighteenth century building said to have inspired the Garnier Opera House in Paris itself.

The Place de la Comedie anchored Bordeaux's elegant triangle of shopping boulevards. There was the Allees de Tourny, a fashionable avenue to his right which angled sharply northwest from the Place de la Comedie to the Place de Tourny, meeting the Cours Clemenceau. The equally fashionable Cours de l'Intendance led due west from the Place de la Cornedie to the Cours Clemenceau at the Place Gambetta. That's probably where she does her shopping, he thought. Maybe it's time to do some of my own.

Robbie paused and then ventured straight ahead into the Rue Ste. Catherine, a long and unpretentious pedestrian shopping street which bisected the city on a north-south axis. It sported Bordeaux's first McDonald's.

He turned into the Rue Porte Dijeaux to his right, and entered a *Maison des Antiquites*. The store was an amiable collection of clutter, with some imposing armoires from the nineteenth century and perhaps even earlier, tables, chairs and sideboards from somebody's household earlier in this century or the last one, mirrors and pictures to complete a borrowed past, and various small decorative items of varying quality.

"*Bonjour, Monsieur le Consul,*" came the cautious welcoming voice of Rene Dupont, the antique shop's portly proprietor, manager, accountant and head clerk. He always looked slightly flustered, often with a few crumbs on his collar, as though he had just left a meal without finishing dessert. "Would you like to see our latest canes this afternoon?"

Robbie nodded. He had started his collection of canes at his first overseas post, the American Embassy in Singapore. It had been irresistible, a genuine Malacca cane, bought in Malacca itself, a city up the causeway from Singapore in neighboring Malaysia. Lightweight, flexible and trim, it was a reminder of the past, when Malacca canes had been part of an English gentleman's uniform. It didn't really matter that the wood could no longer be found in Malacca itself, and had come from northern Malaysia.

Now his collection included four more canes. Robbie thought of them almost as friends. They were a silver-tipped cane from the Budapest flea market (purchased during a summer holiday), an Abercrombie and Fitch black ebony evening cane with a hidden flask, an English nobbed blackthorn walking stick (which had raised eyebrows amongst the security checkers at London's Heathrow Airport when he had brought it back to France—after 9/11, come to think of it, surely they would never have allowed it on board the plane), and a pilgrim's staff from Rocamadour, a center of medieval pilgrimage near the southern Dordogne region.

Not one of the five had cost a lot, and Robbie enjoyed adding to his small collection or thinking of doing so. Monsieur Dupont led him over to the display of canes, and Robbie looked at them carefully. Most seemed rather ordinary, Sunday stroller sort of canes, some worn and others clearly never used at all, but there were some special ones.

Dupont showed him one, somewhat thicker than the others. Open the handle, unscrew the end, attach the firing piece, and you had a serviceable small calibre gun. The small tube in the hollowed-out handle even held a few lead bullets, and a fitted sectional ramrod which could be assembled and used, with cotton wads and gun oil, for cleaning the weapon after it had been fired.

Robbie was intrigued, but asked to see other special canes before making up his mind. He enjoyed just looking at the merchandise and had his favorite stores, but Robbie knew that to receive personal attention a purchase from time to time was necessary. Now seemed to be such a time. The drumroll of Monsieur Dupont's fingertips on the counter told him that.

"May I show you this cane? It's very rare, and quite unique." It was the store's rarest piece, a thieve's cane. This cane also unscrewed at the end, but in this case, a trigger mechanism and inner spring silently sent forth for several yards a wooden stick with a hook that clicked open at the end. "The cane," Monsieur Dupont said, "was used in a darkened theatre. The thief could sit several empty rows behind a lady with a purse. If that purse were placed on the floor, it could be reached and its top secured by the extended thieve's cane. Then *Voila!* With another squeeze of the trigger mechanism, the cane retracts to bring the purse back to the thief!"

The principle was not unlike similar devices that Robbie had seen used in libraries, where a handheld wooden tool with clamps at the end, expandable or retractable at the turn of its grip, was used to secure books that otherwise would have been out of reach.

Robbie, intrigued, glanced at a third cane.

This was longer than most canes, fitting Robbie's height nicely. It was a straight cane with, as an unusual feature, lightly indented grip markings on the handle portion. This one also unscrewed near the handle, revealing a slightly tapering steel blade, with an edge along its length, sharpened at its end. The weight and balance were excellent. Robbie could not resist brandishing it in the merchandise corridor, as Monsieur Dupont hurriedly retreated behind the counter.

Those moments of athletic glory at Brown were still worth savoring. Robbie had made the university's fencing team, and then been good enough at the sabre to win nearly all his matches, placing first in the Ivy League and second in the New England rankings. Not quite Errol Flynn, but good enough. Budget be damned, he must have this cane. He bought it on the spot.

The remembered days of athletic success felt good. He enjoyed walking back to the Consulate General, to all appearances just a man out for a stroll with a walking cane. It would be such fun to show this cane to Sylvie Marceau. He even imagined their conversation, and how that would lead to his telling her about his love of fencing. He greeted Ghislaine with a jaunty air. Back to business, she confirmed his three-thirty appointment with Commissioner Moineau. Robbie had just enough time to prepare some notes before the staff meeting began.

Led by Vice Consul Stan Bartlett, Robbie's staff dutifully trooped into his office. Following Ghislaine Martin were the dozen souls who saw to the effective functioning of the commercial, consular, administrative, and information service sections of the Consulate General. It was a self-contained diplomatic enclave centered in Bordeaux, but for four sprawling regions of France, it was the United States.

Robbie led off. He gave a pat little speech about all pulling together during his months of being in charge. He referred to the ETA threat, said that he had arranged for additional security coverage, that he had talked twice with the Embassy about the matter, and that he would be seeing Commissioner Moineau after the meeting. He then referred to the prospect of a visit by Senator William J. Etchevari, and threw the floor open for discussion, questions, and generalized show and tell.

The Information Service lady, Claudine Auger, squinted through her contacts and spoke up first. "*Monsieur le Consul,* I've scheduled several public cultural meetings downstairs in the conference room. If there really is a security threat, they ought to be rescheduled or cancelled."

"You're entirely right," Robbie agreed.

Stan Bartlett, beaten to the punch, said "I was about to make the same point." As the three members of his consular staff, who handled notarials, visas and American citizen services nodded in unison, Robbie promised to relay speedily to all concerned what Commissioner Moineau had to say.

Bartlett continued, "If the security angle is manageable, I've put together some suggestions for Etchevari's visit. He must visit the Basque region. That's probably why he is coming in the first place, but we should find out more from his Senate office. He should also come to Bordeaux. That would also give you, Robbie, a chance to pull together some people from the community for a reception or dinner."

Robbie liked the idea and signalled his assent with a grin. He could always use the now vacant but fully furnished Consul General's residence on the Avenue Carnot for a social function. Bartlett handed him a neatly typed, draft cable with suggestions for the proposed visit.

The commercial officer, Guy Leblanc, sporting a rather theatrical moustache, weighed in with a lengthy account of his last trip to Toulouse. "You've heard this before, *Monsieur le Consul*, but in many respects Toulouse and its region now eclipse Bordeaux from the commercial point of view. It's been a while since they have even had a high-ranking American visitor.

"As it is," he continued, "the *Toulousains* wonder why the Consulate General has not moved there. *Monsieur le Consul* should bear in mind that in six months Toulouse will be holding its International Fair. Several of our largest American firms including Motorola, General Electric and Ford will have booths. We should be there with an official presence."

Robbie agreed with him. How could he explain to this group of dedicated career employees that given State's chronic budget problems on Capitol Hill, they would be lucky in the long run to keep the Consulate General open at all?

Administrative Officer Jean Deplace assumed his usual air of intrigue. Ever the courtier, he had personally done what he could to beef up the Consulate General's security with existing resources. "Whenever possible, *Monsieur le Consul*, you should curb your habit of walking to appointments. There is, after all, an official car, and Georges, our young handyman, is a good driver."

When Robbie nodded agreement, Deplace mentioned a security circular that had gone to all European posts, regarding a short course on driving cars. It was designed for security purposes and even, to show the seriousness with which the Department takes the subject, provided fund citations so that scarce post funds would not have to be used.

"Excellent idea, Jean," Robbie said, agreeing in principle that Georges should take the course. The meeting ended, and all began to file out.

"Claudine, would you stay for a moment?" Robbie asked.

"I'm sure that you've seen the articles that Sylvie Marceau has been writing in *Sud-Ouest* about the death of Douglas Pryor," he began, when they were alone in his office.

"Yes, of course."

"Well, *Mademoiselle* Marceau buttonholed me at a reception that Spanish Consul General Dos Campos gave over the weekend. I'm seeing her tomorrow morning at the Journalists' Club. Tell me your impressions of her."

Claudine pouted a bit to show concentration. "She works hard after a story. I think sometimes she speculates a bit more than the facts would warrant, but she writes well. Do you want me to be present?"

Well, no, he didn't. This was a little sticky. Robbie blushed as he spoke, a little too fast. Well, what was done, was done. Time for a little confessional.

"You know, Claudine, I should have run this by you in the first place. But you know, jet lag, a terrorist threat, and a persistent journalist were hard to resist. I'll handle it this time, but I'd appreciate a file of all she has written on this before my meeting.

Claudine flashed him a very pretty smile before leaving the room. So *Monsieur le Consul* was up to something, perhaps?

She was replaced in the doorway by Ghislaine Martin, at her most somber. Ghislaine came into the office, an envelope in her hand.

"Excuse me, *Monsieur le Consul,* but this letter has just arrived in the afternoon mail. I thought that you would want to see it at once."

The letter had been sent to departed Consul General Eric Johnston from the United States the previous week. The printed return address in Washington was the Willard Hotel. Inked in above the address on the envelope was the name of the sender, Douglas Pryor.

CHAPTER 3

Message From The Beyond

Robbie quickly slit open the envelope and read Pryor's letter. Then he reread it several times, trying to see if it might relate to Pryor's death. It didn't seem to do so.

The letter was handwritten. It referred to Pryor's last meeting with the Consul General, at a wine dinner given by one of Bordeaux's leading regional wine fraternities six weeks earlier. Pryor mentioned his last calls on the wine estates throughout the region, and said that he was glad afterwards to have taken Johnston's advice for a brief vacation trip to Biarritz. It had been stimulating.

Robbie frowned. Nothing unusual about all that. Was he missing something? The letter then asked for an appointment with Consul General Johnston during Pryor's next trip to Bordeaux. He planned to be there later that spring, to sample again the previous calendar year's vintage, now blended and beginning the aging process in Bordeaux cellars throughout the region. "When we meet, I'd appreciate an update on the politics of the region," Pryor had added in a post-script.

If that was an afterthought, Robbie mused, why was the writing so bold? He could swear that had been the point of the letter. It was an odd request for the wine writer to make. He could be expected to take an interest in the effect of France's ruinous estate taxes on wine estates, yes. Everybody knew that families were being forced to sell their holdings, and that increased the numbers of corporations who ran wine estates in the region. A legitimate source of inquiry for a wine writer. But "the politics of the region?"

What on earth had Pryor meant by that?

It was time to leave for his appointment with Commissioner Moineau. Robbie asked Ghislaine to make copies of the letter. He decided to send the original back to Washington via special diplomatic pouch to be shared with the former Consul General. Perhaps Johnston could shed some light on this. Then the letter should probably be forwarded to the D.C. police.

Bordeaux police headquarters was a large and cheerless institutional complex on the Rue Abbe de l'Epee west of the Place Gambetta. He had made a courtesy call on Commissioner Moineau when he had first arrived at the Consulate General. Now, Robbie was glad that he had done so. Small courtesies did set a cooperative tone. Georges drove him to his meeting, and then went to enjoy a cup of coffee and his favorite sports newspaper at a sidewalk cafe while waiting for the return trip.

A police clerk showed Robbie into Moineau's spartan office. It was furnished with standard wooden furniture including an enormous desk, a lumpy sofa, and an unattractive bookcase or two. Robbie was amused to note that the chairs placed in front of Moineau's desk were low, so that a visitor would have to look upwards at the Commissioner. Not very subtle, Robbie thought.

There were some family pictures on a bookcase behind the sofa. There were no autographed pictures of politicians, but a large photograph of President Chirac hung over the desk. Robbie wondered if the same frame still held the banished picture of former President

Mitterrand behind the Chirac photograph. He decided that he didn't know Moineau well enough to ask.

Moineau greeted Robbie and waved him into his conference room. Robbie tried to remember the different French police entities, each with its own heirarchy and loyalties. Bordeaux and this region rated its own Prefect of Police, responsible to the Ministry of the Interior, who oversaw them all. Under the Prefect, Moineau headed the Bordeaux uniformed municipal police, and the plainclothes Criminal Investigation Department or CID, which investigated crimes such as murder.

The *Renseignements Generaux,* Robbie knew, was more clandestine. Also under the Ministry of the Interior (in Europe, quite different from the American Department of the Interior, with its emphasis on national parks and natural resources), the *Renseignements Generaux* was somewhat comparable to the FBI, investigating sensitive internal matters such as Basque and Corsican terrorism. For such a beautiful nation, France certainly had its share of whackos, Robbie thought. Well, we have them too, he mused. It took, after all, losers like Sirhan and Oswald to murder the Kennedys.

Commissioner Moineau greeted Robbie in his office, and introduced three other men who were sitting in. One, in uniform, was from the CID, while the other two, in plainclothes, represented the Prefect of Police and the *Renseignements Generaux.*

"We want to assure you, *Monsieur le Consul,* that we take any threats seriously. Should you wish it, we are prepared to grant you a police escort for the time being.

Robbie thanked him and said that he would report their cooperation to the Embassy. "Tell me first," he asked, "what you think of that painted threat at the Consulate General?"

"To be perfectly honest, it puzzles us," Moineau said with a perplexed expression. He turned to his colleague from the *Renseignements Generaux,* who gruffly added, "This is not their style. Americans are not their enemies. They have political objectives. Why compromise that with a threat against you? Particularly now, when Americans have led a military response to terrorism in Afghanistan? It ups the ante considerably, and that just doesn't make any sense."

Moineau added, "We have the matter under investigation. It is too serious and too specific to be a prank. But as a terrorist action...?" He threw up his hands palms upward in a Gallic gesture of incomprehension.

Robbie added, "Unofficially, I have to agree. The ETA wouldn't start targetting Americans in this haphazard way. That would be a serious change in their approach. I bet it would be announced first by their sympathetic political fronts in Spain, the way they usually do things. In the past, that's the way they have announced truces, and then broken them. Just spray-painting a challenge to my country on a wall makes no sense at all." The others nodded their heads in agreement.

He told the officers about his message from the State Department which had announced the visit of Senator William J. Etchevari. The *Renseignements Generaux* officer immediately knew that Etchevari was revered by the Basque people, and said so. The Prefect of Police's man started to take notes.

"A vague threat against an American Consul is one thing," Commissioner Moineau said. "A political assassination is quite another."

Thanks a lot, Robbie thought. His thought must have been visible, for Moineau reddened a bit as he continued. "We will want to keep very close watch on the Senator throughout his visit to the region, should his trip take place."

Robbie was intrigued that neither Moineau nor the other officers raised any objection to the visit itself. That was probably a political judgment, not their province, he thought. He could, however, now add to his own report their offer to be forthcoming on security during the trip itself, should it take place.

"Then you would not recommend against it?" he asked.

"There are no grounds to do so at present," said the representative of the Prefect of Police, rather too quickly for a bureaucrat. Oh well, Robbie remembered, the telex he had received had not been sent by secure means. That meant that it had also been seen by French authorities. They had had several days to form an opinion on the matter.

"I think we have another matter of mutual interest," Robbie said. "That is the murder of Douglas Pryor. I know it is the responsibility of the Washington police. However, I thought that you would be interested to know that Pryor had been planning another trip to Bordeaux."

Robbie handed over a copy of Pryor's letter. "Here is the letter that he sent just a few days before his death to Consul General Johnston. To me, the interesting thing was that he had requested a political briefing on the region. That hardly seems usual for a wine writer."

Commissioner Moineau nodded in agreement. He read the brief letter with interest, translated it word for word for the benefit of his associates, and gave it to the CID officer.

"And now, given the Etchevari visit, that threat—whatever it was, at the Consulate General—and Pryor's odd postscript, I'd like to get more detailed background on the Basque terrorist situation," Robbie said.

"We thought that might be of interest," Moineau said in his droll way. "Suppose we let our colleague from the *Renseignements Generaux* proceed."

"Some are surprised to learn about the Basque issue," the officer began. "But at a time when the Cold War is over, and Europe is uniting, there seems to be a countermove towards decentralization in fashion. The Basques have their cause, or at least some of them do. You are aware, *Monsieur le Consul*, that the Basque homeland, an ancient one, straddles the border between France and Spain."

He picked up a pointer from the conference table and gestured towards a map on the wall that highlighted the border region along the Pyrenees. "Three of its seven provinces are on the French side of the border, and four are in Spain, The main towns in Spain"—he stabbed the pointer towards the towns as he spoke—"would be San Sebastian, Pamplona, and Bilbao"—where we have closed the American Consulate, Robbie remembered—"for the provinces of Alava, Navarra"—Navarre, Robbie understood—"Vizcaya and Guipuzcoa.

"In France," he went on, "we would have St. Jean de Luz on the coast"—another jab with the pointer—"of course Biarritz and Bayonne as well, and a large stretch of the interior stretching to St. Jean Pied de Port near the border. These would be the three provinces of Labourd, Lower Navarre and Soule.

"You know, of course, that Basque nationhood has been the aim of some for generations. They have a motto in the Basque tongue that expresses it well...*Zaspiak-bat,* the 'Seven Which Make One.' Rather like your American *E Pluribus Unum,*" he said.

"Not everybody agrees with the objective, and certainly the terrorists are a minority," he added. "The Basque people are honorable and of ancient and unique stock." It suddenly dawned on Robbie that this officer himself was probably Basque. "They were energized during the Franco regime in Spain, when they thought that Franco was trying to root them out as a people, and turn their homeland into an industrial wasteland."

Surely the man was Basque. When he mentioned Franco and his policies, his hatred was palpable.

"It was during that period, before Franco died in 1975, that Basque agitation for their own homeland became more serious under the ETA's leadership," he said. "And it was also during that period that Basques from the Spanish side of the border began to use France as a safe haven. That went on for years. They carried out attacks in Spain, and fled across the border."

The officer noted that there had seemed to be an unspoken rule that no terrorism was aimed at targets within France. "That had changed for a while, however, in the 'eighties when during the second Mitterrand Presidency, France began an active program of cooperation with Spanish authorities, and began rounding up Basque terrorists, even allowing their extradition, when appropriate, back to Spain." Heads nodded, almost imperceptibly.

"Then came the GAL," he continued, "said to be the *Groupe Anti-terroriste de Liberation.* Have you heard of them?"

"Yes," Robbie said. "They carried out paramilitary actions on both sides of the border. It was thought at the time that they were perhaps mercenaries, hired by the population at large who were fed up with paying 'taxes' to support the ETA."

"As I am sure you are aware, *Monsieur le Consul,* the truth seems rather different," interjected the Prefect of Police's man. "There were lawsuits in Spain over the matter, and finally, the Gonzalez Government itself fell over the issue."

"Yes," Robbie said. "Now we know that the GAL was an extralegal group, probably started by the Spanish Government itself. That mercenary story was a cover story." Heads nodded again.

"The GAL had had some effect at the time in uprooting Basque extremists," the briefer continued. "But the price, in terms of murdered innocents and loss of confidence in government, was extreme."

"I remember hearing that they killed some totally innocent people, who were just in the wrong place at the wrong time. Some of that happened near Bayonne," Robbie said.

He could have added that in the propwash, the ETA seemed to have been given a new lease on life. Its terrorist activities on the Spanish side of the border seemed to have been redoubled, culminating in repeated attempts on the life of Spanish King Juan Carlos himself.

Robbie thanked the officers for their time and for their background briefing. He remembered the speculation of Eduardo Dos Campos about a changing ETA leadership. Should he mention that? No, better save that for talks on the Basque coast with those who were gathering raw information on Basque terrorist activities directly. Sometimes a bit of inside knowledge could lead to further revelations. The trick was to let peoplc think you knew more than you really did.

"Of course, I'll be following up as appropriate with other officials within the Basque region itself," Robbie said. "For now, I see no reason to recommend against Senator Etchevari's visit. I'll say so in my report. I'll also mention your offer of heightened, discreet security. Washington will be pleased."

"What about your own security, *Monsieur le Consul*?" asked Moineau as the meeting ended. Robbie considered that for a moment. Did he really want to sacrifice his privacy for security, all things considered?

"I appreciate the offer of special guards," Robbie said. "For the time being, let's leave it at increased patrolling around the Consulate General, my apartment and that of the Vice Consul," he thought to add.

He left Commissioner Moineau's office with another round of handshakes, and saw that Georges was waiting in the building's courtyard driveway to take him back to the Consulate General.

The next morning Robble walked briskly across the Place des Quinconces to the Rue Ste. Catherine, and took a side street to the left towards the river embankment. A block from it he entered the Place du Parlement, a handsome, open, paved square surrounded with seventeenth century buildings, many with fine grillwork and arcades, that Robbie found the most pleasing architectural ensemble in Bordeaux, and one that was just enough off the beaten track to have escaped the attention of tourists.

It also reminded him just a bit of New Orleans. Probably some of that city's first settlers had come from Bordeaux, he thought. The square was named for the Bordeaux Parliament which used to meet here, in a building that had been a royal seat of government centuries previously in the Plantagenet period when the Dukes of Aquitaine, Bordeaux and its sweeping southwest region, were also Kings of England.

The Journalists' Club was ensconced in leased quarters in one of the buildings on the square. It was Tuesday morning, and Robbie was right on time for his meeting with Sylvie Marceau. An early morning call to Elliot Hawkins had already cleared both his trip to the Basque coastal region and his interview with *Sud-Ouest*. Robbie swung his cane with a bit of a flourish and entered the doorway.

"Ah, *Monsieu le Consul*, I have a table over here." Sylvie was very attractive in a blue shirtwaist dress, that Robbie thought had gone out of style with Jacqueline Kennedy.

Well, if you can wear it, why not, he thought. He crossed the room.

"You are right on time. I've already ordered some coffee." It arrived as he reached the table and sat down.

This time she smiled. It was a delightful smile that seemed to light up her entire face and spread to Robbie's face as well. She looked at the cane, and her smile faded for a moment. "Not a touch of lumbago at your age, *Monsieur le Consul*?" She smiled again, warmly.

He opened the cane and showed her the blade. "Just seeing to your protection in this dangerous quarter, *ma chere demoiselle*." Then his face flushed as others stared at them.

"Actually, it's a secret vice. I collect canes." He did not elaborate. "Claudine Auger tells me that you have something new on the Douglas Pryor murder." His USIS assistant had briefed Robbie just before he left the Consulate General, while giving him the collected articles that Sylvie had written.

"Yes indeed, and all Bordeaux is going to breathe big sighs of relief. Your police have verified that Pryor's wine was not poisoned after all. It came over the Agence France Presse ticker just an hour ago." She was excited by her news and clearly wanted to share it.

Does she like me, or is that a trait of a good newspaper reporter, Robbie wondered.

"What have they found out?"

She leaned forward, as if to exclude the other working journalists in the room from what she was going to say. It was one thing for them to see that she was having coffee with the American Consul. It would be quite another to share her story and his reactions with the competition.

"The autopsy has been held, and the police have made an announcement. It seems that Pryor was poisoned all right, but not from the wine. His glass and the bottle were checked. Also, I'm afraid, all of the other bottles that the waiter had served for that first course."

Robbie winced at the waste of good wine, and expensive wine at that.

"They say that the poison was contained in a pill he had just taken. Pryor was asthmatic. He was in the habit of taking one or two 250 mg. pills every day. His allergist confirms that was the prescription. He may have taken another to ward off stress before public speaking. Apparently that was his habit. Some asthmatics do that. Others use an inhaler. Some do both. But Pryor's pill was a capsule laced with potassium cyanide. Death was fast."

"I know. I saw it. But how about an antidote?"

"The police were called, and your emergency service, but within minutes Pryor was already dead. With that much cyanide, they would have had to administer amyl nitrate virtually immediately, before they even got him to the hospital to pump him out. There just wasn't enough time to do even that," she repeated, shaking her head for emphasis and, Robbie was intrigued to note, with a touch of sadness. Did she know Pryor? Or did she have that much religious feeling?

Robbie scratched his chin. "I saw him taking what must have been that pill, but I didn't connect it at the time."

He paused and reflected, putting something together. "It rather reminds me of something that happened when I was in college. It was the late 'eighties I think. There was a rash of poisonings then. I don't know if they ever discovered who did it. The poisoner must have been nuts. He poisoned Tylenol capsules, and I think that they stopped making capsules after that, and even went to a lot of trouble to change the packaging."

"But this pill that Pryor took was a prescription, not a mass-produced over the counter product," Sylvie said.

She leaned towards him. "Wait a second. That series of poisonings might have given our poisoner the idea."

"Our" poisoner? Robbie thought. What a bizarre idea.

She continued. "It looks like anybody might have administered the poison by getting one capsule, substituting the cyanide powder for the asthma medicine, and then replacing it with the others."

"Do we know how many other capsules there were?" Robbie was getting intrigued by their little detective conspiracy. It sure beat "What's your sign?"

"He had enough for three months at a time. The prescription was American, and his doctor has confirmed that it was not a refillable prescription. It had to be ordered by the allergist each time Pryor was running out. This bottle was about two-thirds empty."

Robbie caught her drift. "That means, even if the killer fixed up his poison pellet when the bottle was just opened, the switch had to be made sometime within the last two months."

"Exactly. By the way, they also announced that one of the remaining pills had also been poisoned. They are trying to trace his travels now for the past two months. Obviously, he was here in Bordeaux, and I'm sure that he had also had tastings in Burgundy and elsewhere. He did enjoy his work."

Robbie nodded in agreement. "Furthermore, he was coming back here soon." He told her about Pryor's letter to Consul General

Johnston. "Oddly enough, this time he asked for a political briefing on the region. That was new, as far as I can gather."

He was immediately sorry that he had confided in her that much. Giving the police the letter was one thing. Blurting out its contents to a journalist was quite another. Better not compound his blunder by making something of it and asking her to treat the matter in confidence. Making too much of it would only increase the value of the tidbit in her eyes. Might as well keep to himself that gossip about an announcement that Pryor was going to make. He probably was just going to announce a new favorite wine, that's all.

At her request, he verified some of the details of the dinner, and the fact that he had directly witnessed what had taken place, at close range. He described the rather ornate banquet facility of the Willard Hotel, just down from the hotel's reception area off the Pennsylvania Avenue entrance.

"Too bad," she said. "Everyone in Bordeaux had been looking forward to the dinner being a success. There had been several years when the wine vintages had been just so-so. People had spent a lot of money updating their equipment. Now, the bills were coming due. An excellent vintage, played just right, would have done a lot to help the wine estates pay those bills, with spinoffs for the entire regional economy.

"Now at least the other vintage dinners can proceed as planned. The entire vintage wasn't lost with this one murder. I'm going to conduct a number of interviews along that theme. My editor, Jacques Lebrun, will appreciate that, I'm sure."

Robbie couldn't resist a dig. "Who knows," he said, "perhaps some public relations genius could turn the entire matter into a benefit." He could see it all now. "Solve the murder and win a weekend at the wine estate of your choice in Bordeaux!"

She nodded her head from side to side. Really, she'd have to do something about his sense of humor. She could see that at times it got out of hand.

It was time to go back to their offices. He thought about her leaving, and suddenly changed his mind about not confiding further in her. He couldn't help it. It was as natural as sunshine. "If you are interested in interviewing some of the wine growers, perhaps we might join forces. Something that Pryor said just before he died gave me an idea. I can't recall it word for word, but it was something about actually visiting the *Graves, Medoc*, Pomerol and St. Emilion regions on the ground. He seemed to be leading up to something. He was even going to make an announcement. Maybe retracing his steps could give us some insight into his murder. Anyway, I'm planning to drive through the *Medoc* on the weekend. Perhaps we could go together?"

She looked closely at him. He gave the invitation like a little boy who says his piece too quickly, deprecating his own words to devalue a possible refusal. It was charming.

He was pleased by her quick agreement.

Wednesday started off badly.

With the Pryor murder to look into as an excuse to visit some of the wine estates with Sylvie, and the ETA threat, Robbie had neglected office routines and the press of regular consular business. Even though the main tourist season with its influx of American visitors was months away, the Consulate General was buzzing and busy.

An American tourist was lost in a foolish mountain climbing jaunt by himself in the French foothills of the Pyrenees, just beyond Pau. This mid-spring period was the worst time for such an outing, as flash floods and abrupt weather changes made climbing dangerous, even for experienced athletes who knew enough never to climb alone. Robbie sent Vice Consul Stan Bartlett in the official car off to Pau. There Stan would get information on rescue attempts for the benefit of the climber's family.

Taking charge of the visas, Robbie conducted several interviews. The applicants listened to his cheerful talk, and everybody got their visas. He officiated at several notarials, affixing the official consular seal to legal documents that would be used in American courts, humming as he did so.

He had met with Claudine Auger, told her about his talk with Sylvie Marceau (but not about their plan to visit the wine estates together), and approved several of Claudine's suggestions for USIS activities involving cultural promotion activities in the region over the next several months.

The word spread throughout the office. *Monsieur le Consul* is in a fine mood today!

Then it was Guy Leblanc's turn. He gave Robbie a briefing on commercial prospects for American business in the sprawling Basque region, as Guy sought to weave a bonus for American commercial interests into the visit plans for Senator Etchevari. Frankly, outside the Toulouse and Bordeaux areas there weren't many. All the more reason, Leblanc argued, for Etchevari to make a pitch for investment on his return to the United States. "If Eastern Europeans who settled in America can help their old countries, why not American Basques?"

That made sense. Leblanc would back up his suggestion with a detailed commercial overview of the region and investment prospects. It might be good enough to present to Etchevari, if he expressed interest, and would agree to meet with likely prospects at home.

Robbie called administrative officer Jean Deplace, whom he had briefed upon his return from his meeting with Commissioner Moineau, for an update on Consulate General security. Deplace frowned at Robbie's decision to send Vice Consul Bartlett off with Georges and the official car for several days to the Pyrenees. "Better to have kept it here, *Monsieur le Consul*, for security reasons," he said gruffly.

Robbie could hardly argue with him. Deplace had a good point, but on the other hand, Bartlett didn't have a car, and those small towns in that region demanded mobility. It was the best of bad choices to make.

He had closed the consular section to the public for the afternoon, and, attempting to divide his time between consular and other duties, had the staff put up a sign that office hours for the public would be limited to the mornings for the next few days, owing to the absence of the Vice Consul.

Then Robbie turned to the urgent business of preparing reports for the classified pouch. Ghislaine had talked with Jean Deplace, who had arranged with the Embassy for a special pouch run. The purpose of the special pouch to Washington was to transmit the original of Douglas Pryor's letter under safe hands. But limiting the pouch to that one letter seemed something of a waste of resources.

And so Robbie wrote a classified, official-informal letter to his main contact in Washington, the French Desk Officer at the State Department. Such letters set forth matters that were in process, not completed enough for a final report. The Etchevari visit was worth the extra effort.

He put the original of the Pryor letter into the pouch with a routing slip sending it to the French Desk at the State Department, with a request to show it to former Consul General Johnston and then, at the Desk Officer's discretion (a nice diplomatic phrase when you were in fact ordering someone who outranked you in the diplomatic service to do something) to pass it to the District of Columbia Police Department's Homicide Division. He enclosed a personal note to Johnston.

Robbie made out the brief list of contents for the pouch, kept one for his records and inserted the original into the pouch itself, which he then tied, crimped and sealed with the consular seal. Copies of everything were filed down the hall in the safe in the Consulate General's secure room.

He took a call from a distraught American tourist, a lady of senior years whose long delayed trip to France had resulted in a medical emergency. Her husband was in the hospital, having keeled over from what seemed to be a heart attack while they were shopping in the city. They had both been passengers on one of the cruise ships that still visited Bordeaux from time to time, recalling Bordeaux's glorious shipping past.

The hospital was an excellent one, and Robbie was sure that they would do all that they could. "I'll check in personally this afternoon," he assured her. In the meantime, he arranged to have a consular assistant call immediately to see what further might be done. (He did not tell the tourist that the assistant, a very mild mannered and dapper gentleman, was the Consulate General's specialist in death cases, who arranged all necessary legal details in the event of an American dying in the region.)

Robbie had Ghislaine call a taxi for the railroad station, where the courier from the Embassy in Paris was coming to take his pouch. There were never enough professional couriers, and so from time to time, when a pouch run was necessary, a cleared Embassy officer who could spare the time and wanted a day trip was certified by Embassy security officials to make the trip.

Robbie's cab pulled up at the train station, and Robbie got out of the cab, clutching his pouch, and walked around to the driver's side to pay him the metered fare.

He never quite got there. Darting from the crowd leaving the station, a man ran up to Robbie, shoved him violently onto the cab door and grabbed the pouch. Then he ran with it at top speed across the avenue and into a side street, half a block ahead of his pursuers.

CHAPTER 4

The ETA Makes Plans

The bearded young man gloried in the mountain scenery, profligate beauty everywhere. Spring wildflowers were beginning to sprout near the mountain path as he effortlessly climbed the hill. Beyond, the majestic Pyrenees added dimension to this land. Westward, the Bay of Biscay gave sustenance to innumerable fishermen in a setting that had inspired generations of painters, musicians like native son Maurice Ravel, and of course patriots, like himself.

Here and there in the hills a Basque home wore white and red and green, colors that entranced the eye and blended harmoniously with the colors of the southern landscape. Such scenes filled the spirit with pride when beheld, and with hope when remembered from the prison cell. Not that that would ever happen to Antonio Echurra. Careful and given to suspicion, he was a prudent man. That is why he was late to the meeting of the ETA Executive Committee. He had scoured the hillsides before proceeding, and had spent the previous night reconnoitering each entrance to and exit from the meeting area. All was clear. Before the last meeting, he had had to wire an unauthorized car in the area with PETN explosives. The deaths that followed were necessary for those who breached ETA security, and set an example for others.

One couldn't be too careful. Too many of the ETA's patriot members and leaders had been taken in the past by the Spanish police or by their French accomplices. A raid near Pau the previous summer had picked up one of the old leadership, which had led to Antonio's selection for the Executive Committee.

Such arrests were an old story. They had also been decimated in 1982, just before the Barcelona Olympic Games, and now over 800 ETA members languished in Spanish prisons. ETA assassinations of municipal leaders in Spain in 1998 and then again in 2000 had offended public opinion and provoked a popular backlash. Even the Guggenheim Museum in Bilbao had given the Basque region new focus and pride The French and Spanish Governments continued to cooperate across their border. Antonio knew that more police strikes against the movement and its leadership might come at any time.

That is why he had called this meeting. Tactics and strategy had to be rethought, if their energies were to be refocused on their goal of an independent Basque homeland. Now they were on the defensive. They were not even viewed by former supporters as liberators, as they had been when the national enemy was the tyrant, Franco. Instead, they were seen by many in another light, as terrorists.

Also, there was a new climate of opinion regarding terrorism. The strikes against the United States by Osama bin Laden had awakened the Americans. The ETA had been sympathetic, but single-minded. Let *Al Qaeda* fight the United States. Their radical Moslem agenda was not the ETA's cause. It might even awaken Spanish memories of the *Reconquista* against the Moors, uniting Spanish patriotism in an anti-Basque effort. They had to remember always, Antonio had insisted, that an independent Basque nation was their goal, and that was why their struggle must continue. Antonio had won that argument, and the ETA bombings, following a brief pause after the 9/11 attacks against the United States, had continued throughout Spain.

But the ETA had problems, serious ones. Funds and recruits were beginning to dry up. Sure, they could always pull off a car-bombing operation, kill some police, and scare away tourists, particularly the cheap holiday British tourists who came counting their change for a few days at some uncomfortable guest house on the Spanish northern Basque coast. There was no trick to that. But did that really advance the cause? He suspected not. It was time for something much bigger.

He spotted the guards, unobtrusively posted around the mountain lodge. They were dressed as peasants, and did not stop their routine chores when they saw him, merely glancing up for surreptitious identification. One turned to relay a beeper signal into the lodge. But, Antonio noted approvingly, each had stationed himself in a position allowing cover and an excellent field of fire, while an approaching person faced the sun.

Good, we are learning, Antonio thought. He rubbed his beard in recognition, and grunted appreciatively. A return gesture from the bearded man ten yards up the hill to his right, in the clearing near the lodge, was his signal to proceed. So far everything was fine. He swung his *makhila*, a steel-spiked Basque cane, useful for climbing and for corralling animals.

A weapon by itself, some would say that the hardware installed by his friends, permitting the extrusion of a needle through the spiked end by a flick of the walking stick's handle, was overdoing it. But Antonio admired technology, and the security that the weapon and its concealed potassium cyanide cylinder provided. He had admired the Bulgarian umbrella episode in London a few years previously, and wanted the same capacity, with a traditional Basque touch, of course. His friends had been glad to oblige. Skill in fashioning blades was traditional in Damascus.

But it was his MBA from the Wharton School that was in the forefront of his thinking now. He had studied various business models, and the principle of cost effectiveness had struck him as on target. It was a guiding principle for businesses, and even for criminal organizations like the Mafia. Why, therefore, shouldn't it be heeded in their patriotic work?

For years, France had been a safe haven for the ETA. During the same period, expense money had been readily available through the revolutionary taxes that the ETA collected throughout the Basque region. Who, after all, would risk the reputation of being against the cause of the Basque nation itself?

Now the way was much harder. Antonio thought of the GAL, or "Antiterrorist Liberation Group." He often did. He couldn't help but think of them, every time he remembered his father and older brother.

"See you when we return from Bayonne," his brother had said. It was just going to be a routine evening for them at the sports bar, watching *pelota* on the television and making side bets. "Look after your mother, little student!" his father had said affectionately as he left. Prophetically too, it had turned out. The GAL gunmen waiting for them as they arrived at the bar had called out their names before murdering them execution style with handguns.

That had been his call to join the cause. Even before these murders, Antonio had never believed the cover story that the GAL had been privately recruited to protect merchants from paying their ETA taxes. No, that was absurd. And when the truth started to emerge, and the Gonzalez Government fell in Spain over the controversy, Antonio knew that he had to seek the liberation of his people, and avenge the murderers of his father and brother.

He struggled for self-control for a moment before continuing to the door.

Antonio was a new generation of patriot. First, like any craftsman, you must understand your trade. He grinned as he gripped his *makhila*. Then you must understand the benefits of new technology, and bring to the movement the thinking of an entirely new generation. For Antonio, a brilliant and disciplined student, that had led him eventually to the Wharton School in Philadelphia, and an MBA.

It also had greatly affected his thinking about the nature of their struggle, and effectiveness.

The others were old-fashioned, like pennyante terrorists of push-carts on the Lower East Side in New York before the Mafia had gotten organized. Here, the targets were too small, and the receipts were too paltry. Probably the one conditioned the other. How was it possible to mount major strikes against the enemies of Basque nationhood when the weapons at hand were so ineffective? He had to work through Raul and Alberto, then take over.

Real targets were properly defended. Getting at them required serious money. That was no longer available through the petty shakedowns of the past. And so, other methods were needed. With a proper, large scale cash flow, the movement would grow, attract new adherents, and become irresistible. They might start by a major military assault on the Spanish prisons that held hundreds of ETA comrades. Anything beneath that was merely the stuff of songs around a campfire, folklore for tourists, manna for losers.

The lodge door was opened just before Antonio arrived. He entered, and hugged the two men who waited for him within, Raul Izquierda, the grizzled elder leader of ETA, and Alberto Aguilar, the shy former schoolmaster The *abrazo* was a traditional macho gesture, true, but it also doubled as a body frisk. Antonio put his *makhila* on the table with the other weapons. Then he shook hands with two other men, who then left the room. By tradition no other persons were allowed to be present at a meeting of the ETA's three-man Executive Committee.

The Executive Committee as a whole had shared responsibility for operational issues, and for the ETA treasury and taxes that were levied on the Basque population. Each of the three, however, had his own area of specific responsibility as well.

Raul Izquierda, rural and suspicious, was a long-time militant. A large man of imposing physical presence, he wore a faded woolen shirt with suspenders over a pair of ancient and rather smelly farm trousers. Antonio knew him well. The challenge was to pry open his mind just long enough to change it. Raul ran the ETA's internal security, using it to secure warnings about those who would challenge his own authority.

Recruitment and training were Alberto Aguilar's responsibility. That seemed to follow from his schoolmaster background. So did his shirt, tie and crumpled jacket. Alberto was a slight man, whose cunning, Antonio thought, masqueraded for intelligence. The trick with Alberto was to make him think that he had come to your conclusion first. Then you had him. With sufficient inducements, loyalty could be assured. After all, he understood the importance of giving the soldiers something worthwhile to achieve, and the means to do it.

Antonio, with his broader background, was responsible for intelligence, and for liaison with other movements, in Europe and the Middle East. Today he wore a shirt and tie, like Alberto. At Wharton, he would have given them away for the homeless. Here, it was a subtle message of educational solidarity that was designed to flatter Alberto. Antonio had many such costumes.

"Coffee?"

"Yes, with milk." A steaming cup was poured and a moment of appraising silence followed.

Raul spoke first, his prerogative as the elder. He would not speak often, but when he did, it was wise to pay close attention. "What is this damnfool new idea of yours about money? We are raising enough now. Why change methods?" His narrowed eyes spoke their challenge. "We need changes like a bull needs tits."

Antonio leaned across the table. "The money being raised now only sustains a low level of activity. It is also levelling off. The people are beginning to doubt our seriousness. They remain afraid of retaliation and are now fearful rather than supportive. We need to regain their enthusiasm."

Alberto coughed nervously. He wanted to ask a question, but deferred while Raul's questions ran their course.

Antonio continued, pressing the point. "The initiative is no longer in our hands. Our enemies call the shots. It is that way that movements like ours wither and die.

Raul, foxy and cautious, slammed home a judgment. "You think we don't know that?" He shot a contemptuous look at Antonio. "Besides, our people know us. They know what we can do for them. They also know what happens if they fail to support us. But there are limits." He picked his nose reflectively, snorted and went on. "How do you think that we can squeeze any more money from them?" Antonio knew that Raul was within an inch of adding, "you smartass college boy!"

"I'm not sure that we can. On the other hand, look at our friends in the Middle East. They have their own worldwide network of wealthy individual supporters, and can strike at will. Even, as the world knows, at the United States. Their money gave them that initiative. We don't have that kind of financial base."

"So?"

"So we must develop a new one, or stagnate."

They were all cautious attention.

"What do you mean?" Alberto blurted out.

"You've seen the money that others have raised. The Airbus holdup in Perpignan in August '96, for example. That required a lot of careful work. But the results showed the payoff. Four minutes on the scene, and they made off with four million francs in used banknotes. Their only problem was how to dispose of the Brinks bags the francs had been stored in."

Raul was incredulous. "So you want us to hijack an airplane?" He was always literal-minded, Antonio knew. You had to spell it out for him, step by step. Then, if you were lucky, he caught on. Once he did, he wouldn't let go, and you had him.

"What I am saying is that others have raised money for their purposes by direct action. We have to consider new methods of raising money, serious money. The Bolsheviks in Russia and then the OAS in Algeria even robbed banks."

Raul fell into a ruminative silence, chewing his lip, oddly like the cattle he had once tended. It was Alberto's turn. "Is that an example that we should follow? They both failed, after all." Antonio nodded to the schoolmaster, showing off what everybody knew.

"We do not confuse the goal with the means. I leave that to bourgeois sentimental moralists. With an independent Basque homeland, in a generation nobody will care how it was made possible."

"I don't like it," Alberto began, but he was cut off by Raul's sharp glance and raised restraining hand. Raul was becoming intrigued.

"Hear me out," Antonio continued. "We need to raise huge sums of money. Without that, as the Americans say, we are stuck in the same groove."

This interested Alberto. "So you even disagree with what we are doing, our strikes against the enemy?"

"I don't think it is leading us anywhere. True, we are disrupting tourism in the southern provinces below the border. True, we are, but just barely, self-sustaining. But if we keep this up at this level we remain just an irritant. We are not an important liberation force for a Basque nation."

"Your suggestion?"

"We need bolder steps. One that occurs to me is an organized, coordinated military assault to free the hundreds of brothers now languishing in stinking Spanish prisons. Something like that would open eyes around the world to our struggle, and would fill our ranks with dedicated and experienced soldiers."

Alberto took up his train of thought. "Such a gallant strike must be well coordinated," he said. "It is not possible without a great deal of money. We need more and better weapons, and training from experts in their use, say in the northern Sudan. All of that is available. None of it is possible without serious money. We know that."

Antonio took a long drink of coffee, nodding approvingly while Alberto made his argument for him.

Raul began to savor the possibilities. "So what actions against the enemy do you want us to take?"

Antonio sensed the need for caution. He could only push so far at one time. It was far better not to stir up lengthy counter-arguments on operational matters. He instead launched into his carefully rehearsed remarks, for which he had prepared as he would have prepared a business case study at Wharton.

"I only say that we need more money. Alberto is absolutely right." Alberto beamed with satisfaction. "Those who have already paid for Basque freedom with their lives and liberty deserve that. If we do not have serious money, we are only repeating ourselves. That's stupid."

He took another long swig from the coffee mug, wiped his mouth with the back of his sleeve, and continued, as though the words had just come to him. "My friends, I make no recommendation on future strikes against the enemy. Such matters, after all, are for the Executive Committee to decide in the future, and we will do so together. I only say at this time that we must now consider new ways to increase our treasury, and that we must do so without further taxes on our own people."

There it was. This was a departure that would require careful consideration. Weighing its implications, Raul and Alberto lapsed into a lengthy silence, which Antonio did not interrupt. After a while they filled their coffee mugs, and moved on to other topics before returning to the issue at hand.

A recurring concern was recruitment, and they talked around that problem and its known contours for a while. Getting new ETA militants was becoming much more difficult, although sometimes heavy-handed reactions by their enemies helped recruiting. They all knew ETA militants who had joined not from conviction, but instead seeking revenge for a family murder or a beating from the Spanish police. Alberto added that he sometimes thought that the

GAL, in the long run, had furnished more recruits, like Antonio, than they had murdered.

Then Raul surfaced the underlying question. Peasant shrewd, he sensed that Antonio hadn't showed his full hand. "I suppose you have in mind a new source of funds for us?"

"Yes I do," Antonio answered firmly. It was always best not to display any doubts. "All of the details have not been worked out, but the opportunity is there, and it is not far from our own country. I refer to the wine regions of Bordeaux, which are rich with possibilities."

They gasped. "What do you mean, exactly?" This from Alberto, visibly intrigued.

"The region earns many hundreds of millions each year. Most of the wine estates even set their own prices annually. The demand for quality wines in a good year exceeds the supply. The best producers vary their prices according to what they think the market will bear."

Antonio took another gulp of coffee. "I've seen over the years that prices will rise sky high in a good vintage year. People want a certain wine. Price seems to be no object. They will pay for it At the same time, production costs remain relatively constant."

Antonio was warming to his subject. His professors at Wharton would have recognized their careful student.

"At the same time the wine producers are themselves vulnerable, financially overexposed. Almost without exception they installed expensive new equipment in recent years. Then several below average vintage years in a row reduced consumer demand, and their ability to meet production costs, let alone make profits. Notes are coming due for repayment, and may be hard to extend. Some are even selling out. That creates our opportunity."

Raul frowned. "You mean that we should go into the 'lending' business?"

"I'd like to think that we could. But that is far too risky, and we don't have the capital ourselves. If we did, we couldn't tie it up in that way. No. But there are other opportunities. The wine industry is, as I said, very vulnerable at a number of points."

Antonio ticked off his list. "Fermentation of grape juice at the first stage of wine production is carefully controlled by temperature gauges. These can be set to make the temperature rise too high, or to prevent cooling if the temperature is already too high. Either way would achieve the stane result, a ruined batch of wine, tasteless and cooked. That just happened to a wine estate in the *Graves* region. They are ruined."

He continued, the MBA in control of his material. "That method is the least labor intensive possibility." He looked at Raul's puzzled, grizzled face and translated. "It doesn't take many men or much training to learn how to break into a wine production facility and turn the temperature gauges."

Raul and Alberto were beginning to understand the possibilities. They listened intently.

Antonio continued. "There are other methods as well. Most require more effort. Casks can be adulterated or even switched. The last major scandal in Bordeaux wine was thirty years ago. Some producers actually adulterated their wines then with cheap Algerian stuff. Actually, just the threat to do so today would cause a major crisis of confidence, and disruption in the wine markets. That almost happened a couple of years ago, when one producer was caught putting too much sugar into his second wine The industry depends upon intangibles like trust, which can be broken."

Alberto raised a practical concern. "Why wouldn't the wine estates just increase their own security? Or go to the police, for that matter?"

"Some would, of course. Some wouldn't. The same sort of judgment we make now in deciding where to levy our revolutionary taxes would be needed there. Most producers would want to avoid scandal, or the suspicion of wine adulteration, at all costs. And a reasonable cost of doing business, paid for, after all, by the consumers long afterwards when the wine estates themselves set their annual prices for the wines that they sell, would be the security that we would provide."

Antonio leaned forward, warming to his subject. "All they would have to do would be to pay us for security, a legitimate item of expense, so that nothing happens to their wines. After some have hired us, others would feel compelled to do so. They needn't even be approached. They would come to us. All we would need would be an example or two from time to time. That would be all that would be necessary. Those who kept up their security contracts would have no problems. Any producer with sense would then have to weigh the possibility of a ruined vintage, all or part of the crop, against a legitimate expense, a cost of business that he could write off, or pass on to the consumer. Easy.

"If we are not greedy, and that is important, it should work. There are millions to be made here. I'm sure that a skilled accountant could even arrange to stash the money in an offshore bank, earning interest until we needed it. It's done all the time."

Raul and Alberto were intrigued. Raul, as elder, spoke for them both. "Perhaps we need a test case, to see if this scheme of yours really works. Could you arrange that?"

"Yes," Alberto added. "Can you find some wine estate with a nervous owner who would rather pay us a reasonable amount of overhead, as you put it, than face the uncertainties that you mentioned?"

Antonio played his ace. "In a small way, I have anticipated your request." He removed a parcel from his belt, opened it, and spread fifteen thousand euros in crisp new banknotes on the table. "Here is the proof, about one hundred thousand old francs worth, in the new euros, good everywhere throughout Europe. We don't even have to worry about foreign exchange regulations, thanks to the Common Market. Everybody has the same money now.

"This producer will not be disturbed for an entire year," he added. "His security is now guaranteed, and this sum, part now of his overhead costs, will be recouped easily from the final consumers when his wine is sold."

Their reactions told Antonio that he had won his argument.

CHAPTER 5

In Vino Veritas

Sylvie and Robbie met on Saturday morning at an outdoor cafe on the Place du Parlement. The sun shone bravely for late spring, warming their faces and making the rich, honey-colored stones of buildings facing the square seem to glow.

"These croissants are delicious. Have another one," Robbie said, passing the basket to her. She laughed to see that he had gotten some jam on his fingers, which she wiped clean with her napkin. He smiled and took a *pain au chocolat* and they drank their rich coffee with cream.

Robbie found himself telling her about what interested him at the office. Was she just a wonderful listener, or a skilled journalist who knew when to keep quiet when a source was talking to keep the flow going? Perhaps it was a bit of both. When she did speak, her spontaneity delighted him. She didn't talk at all like a diplomat, cautious with words, and that was a plus. He wondered if they would start finishing each other's sentences.

"Stan Bartlett, I've told you about him"—she nodded—"called in yesterday. He found that missing tourist in the foothills of the Pyrenees. Nothing worse than a slight concussion and a compound leg fracture after his fall. He's on the mend in a hospital there. His family's been called."

Why was he telling her all this? It couldn't be of any possible interest. And yet, her hazel eyes flashed interest.

Robbie didn't add that he had now read Stan's report, adding Stan's name to it in case any credit was forthcoming, and sent it to the Bureau of Consular Affairs in the State Department. That didn't ease his conscience entirely, but it helped some.

"Then we had an illness, an elderly American tourist whose wife had called the Consulate General. Turned out to be a case of prescriptions that hadn't been taken. The man had run out of his heart medicines. He weakened and fell down."

"It must have given his wife a real scare."

"Yes it did. It was a nightmare for her. They had saved for years to make the trip, and then this had to happen."

"What did you do, *cher ami*?"

That was progress from "*Monsieur le Consul.*" "Nothing much. I arranged a quick telephone consultation conference call between the tourist's physician at home, and the French attending doctor. They arranged a French equivalent for the American prescription. The tourist will soon be on his way."

"How nice that you can handle these things." She said it softly, reassured that he could be in charge when he had to be.

Robbie didn't mention that snatched diplomatic pouch, which had turned up on Friday morning. It was brought to the Consulate General by a dour security policeman. The pouch had been opened and the contents were missing. The pouch had been shoved into a public trash can a few blocks from the railroad station.

He had done a quick damage assessment. Probably this was just a theft, and the thief must be disappointed. He could only have learned something about preliminary security views regarding the Etchevari visit, and also would have seen Pryor's letter. Not much use to a snatch and grab artist, Robbie thought.

The real damage seemed to be the fact that an American diplomatic pouch had been compromised. Robbie was sure that the incident wouldn't count in his favor at promotion time. Oh well. He had e-mailed the text of Pryor's letter to former Consul General Johnston at the State Department. Then Robbie had sent a cable paraphrase of his Etchevari letter to the French Desk. That should tidy up the pouch theft, before the incident got out of hand.

One good thing was that the theft had not publicly surfaced. Sylvie was wonderful company, but no need to hand her a story that could put the Consulate General in a bad light. She saw he was mulling something over. Was it a girl friend back home? Better pull him back into their conversation. "So what is our program for today, *Monsieur le Consul*?"

He turned to her and smiled. "Well, you said that it was all arranged for us to go to Chateau Montmorency in the *Graves*."

"Yes. Charles de Tourneau is expecting us mid-morning."

"Then I thought, after luncheon we might as well see the *Medoc* wine estates north of the city. There is an evening reception at Chateau Margaux. Perhaps we could go together?"

"It sounds like a wonderful day. We can take my Citroen. But I'll have to stop by my apartment later and get a change of clothes for the evening."

He thought for a moment, and decided to trust her. Maybe together they could find out more. Would they be a team? "Actually, the day will serve a couple of purposes."

She looked at him appraisingly, out of the corner of her eye. He tried to continue, but then stopped, flustered, as if to say no, no, that's not what I meant. Her appraising look turned to crinkly amusement as she saw his discomfort. He actually was blushing! Then he went on.

"Just before he died, Pryor started to say something about the Bordeaux wine routes. He mentioned the *Graves*, the *Medoc*, then St. Emilion and Pomerol. I just had the feeling that it was tied up, somehow, to what he was going to say, and to what happened to him. Maybe we'll get some ideas on that from our drive. If not, well, it's a great day, and I haven't really been a wine tourist. This will give a nice excuse to do that."

They drove through the Place Gambetta, now a bustling square ringed with cafes, restaurants and movie houses, towards the Bordeaux outer perimeter beltway. Gradually the older sections of Bordeaux gave way to the suburbs. At Pessac they drove past Chateau Haut Brion, perhaps Bordeaux's most famous wine estate and certainly the oldest wine brand name in existence. Just across the avenue, in Talence, was La Mission Haut Brion, often a fuller wine than its neighbor.

Both estates were now owned by the American Dillon family, which had pioneered the use of new vinification methods for wine estates throughout the entire region. Robbie more than half suspected that his acceptance as an American official had been eased by the respect in which the *Bordelais* held the Dillons.

"What's your favorite *Graves* wine?" Robbie asked. Answering his own question, he added, "I really like Chateau Pape Clement." It was a rich, Falstaffian red wine, named for the medieval French pope who had once owned the property.

"I prefer Domaine de Chevalier."

"Ah, a connoisseur's wine. The red or the white?"

"Actually, both of them. They are made so carefully. You know, *cher ami*, if the estate were called a Chateau rather than a Domaine, I think the wine price would double. You Americans would pay that much, and then I'd never get to drink any," she teased.

"What other white *Graves* wines do you like?"

"There are so many that are good, and not very expensive."

"Yes," he said. "Sometimes I think that if wine buyers would spend more time pouring wine and less time pouring over charts, numbers and schoolboy scoring systems, they'd enjoy wine more and get taken less often. White *Graves*, for example. There are lots of good ones, as you say."

They found that they shared a taste for white Chateau Carbonnieux, a light dry wine made mostly from sauvignon blanc grapes, emphasizing current light drinking pleasure. More semillion in the mixture would make a fuller, better aging wine, like the three most acclaimed Bordeaux white wines from the Graves, Haut Brion Blanc, La Ville Haut Brion (made at La Mission Haut Brion), and the white Domaine de Chevalier.

"I've noticed that white Chateau Carbonnieux very often is the first wine served at dinners here."

"Yes," she said, "the trick is balancing flavors, and giving a refreshing taste without overwhelming what follows."

Not a bad rule for any first acquaintance, he thought.

* * *

Sylvie passed Leognan, made a turn, and drove through a leafy row of shade trees. There was no sign, and she had had to call for directions. It seemed that Chateau Montmorency was one of those rare self-sufficient estates which did not seek publicity through an active public relations staff. It was a home, an estate, and a vineyard, in that order.

Charles de Tourneau welcomed them personally to his estate, and was amused that they had taken several wrong turns before arriving. Elegant in white flannels and a blazer with English club insignia on the breast pocket, he reminded Sylvie of her promise that what he said would be treated for background use only, not for personal attribution. She nodded agreement.

For a languid-looking man, his question was unexpectedly blunt. "Do you want to see the estate first, or talk about this Pryor fellow?"

"Let's do both," Robbie and Sylvie answered together.

The three walked to a small knoll, where the outlines of the estate could be clearly seen. At the end of the entrance driveway, the residential manor was an imposing, rather formal three-story building. The property was a stunning ensemble of parcels of grape-growing areas, with here and there buildings that seemed to house the necessary implements of wine-making.

"Agriculture and architecture, each serving the other well," Sylvie said. De Tourneau nodded at the graceful compliment. Like most Bordeaux wine-growers, he believed in understated good taste—but not so understated that it passed unnoticed. They took in the view for a moment in silence.

Trucks near one out-building seemed to indicate storage, and a parking lot funneled to a carefully tended garden which in turn led to a building holding the visitors' tasting room. In between was a long, low-lying building that Robbie decided must be the aging cellar for the wines. It probably had several levels.

"This is where it all begins," de Tourneau noted with an expansive gesture. "Here we have the cabernet sauvignon acreage, followed by the merlot, and just over there"—he shaded his eyes from the late morning sun and pointed beyond a rise in the fields—"there is a nice small acreage of cabernet franc. That's just for our red wines."

"Those seem to be the three main grape varieties for red wines," Robbie noted, to keep their host talking. "Why is that?"

"Here in the *Graves*, as in the *Medoc* region, those are the three main grapes, with cabernet sauvignon by far the predominant grape used It depends upon the soil really. Over in Pomerol, to the east of Bordeaux, you'll find that much of the subsoil is very different, so they use merlot instead. You find clay over there. When it is planted in a clay subsoil, the merlot grape develops more lasting character and strength. That's the secret of Petrus."

He pursued his theme. "Here, the soil is largely gravel. That even accounts for the name of this wine district, the '*Graves*,' French for gravel. The cabernet sauvignon grows best in this gravel. We use merlot for richness and flavor. The cabernet franc adds finesse. That completes the blend here."

"What proportions of each grape do you use?" Sylvie asked.

"That's the great secret, and that is where the winemaker earns his salary and prestige. He becomes something of a symphony conductor, uniting the various elements together. The proportion varies slightly each year, and at Montmorency we would usually blend about 55% cabernet sauvignon, 30% merlot, and 15% cabernet franc.

"But every wine estate uses its own proportions. It varies according to tradition, what tastes best, which grapes (or parcels of grapes) did best over the growing year, and even the exact proportions of gravel and other subsoils. Over at Petrus in Pomerol, they use 100% merlot, but that property has a unique clay subsoil."

"I suppose it complicates the growing, having different grape varieties."

"Yes it does, *Monsieur le Consul.* Cabernet sauvignon is a late starting grape, so it is usually not affected by late spring frosts, which would ruin the cabernet franc. Merlot is very susceptible to wet weather, and lack of pollinization. We have to keep all three in balance, always keeping in mind their individual growing characteristics."

"So you are really raising three different grape crops simultaneously, to make one red wine?"

"Exactly, *Mademoiselle.*"

Robbie asked about the rose bushes that he saw at the ends of the rows of vines. "Do you do this just for the esthetic effect? It looks like a great deal of added work."

De Tourneau smiled. "Those roses serve the same function that canaries in cages used to serve for miners. When the canaries were affected by the bad air, the miners knew that they had to get out. Here, we know that rosebushes are susceptible to many of the same plant diseases that affect our grapes. So when, say, they are hit by mildew, we know it's time to apply Bordeaux mixture to the vines."

"What is Bordeaux mixture?"

"It's nothing very fancy, just a mixture of copper sulfate, chalk and water. Of course we also have various parasites, mites and so forth. They used to be handled with DDT and even arsenic, but most growers now use less toxic methods of controlling pests."

An interesting assortment of poisons, Robbie thought.

"What is important to remember is the obvious, so often forgotten, that wine depends upon grapes. It is an agricultural product, just like any other. And like any other product, a year or two of crop failure will put many of us into bankruptcy."

"That, I take it, is where wine reviewers come in."

"Precisely," de Tourneau nodded vigorously. "Now let's see the rest of the vineyards."

De Tourneau led them at a brisk pace down the knoll, to a stream that criss-crossed the property. "Along here we have the sauvignon blanc and on that rise, our semillion grapes."

The setting was fine and the weather perfect. Robbie turned to Sylvie. "What is it that Omar Khayyam asked, something about what could a wine merchant buy that was half so precious as the wine that he sold?"

"Rather poetic, *Monsieur le Consul.*" It was teasing this time, her use of his title. It was a studied formality, not something she would ordinarily say. He felt oddly reassured, a bachelor who had passed some early but crucial test of friendship. She had decided that she liked him.

He smiled back at her. "Well, maybe, but if I'd been born a Frenchman, this is what I'd like to do. I always rather envied a friend who went on to study oenology at the University of California at Davis. Then he found a job at one of the larger Sonoma Valley wineries."

Sylvie noticed their host seemed excluded from Robbie's reverie. Time to steer it back. "How is the quality of the vintage really determined? People say that it has to do with the weather," she said to him.

"That's largely true. Let me give you an ideal growing season here. To begin with we need rain, but not a great deal, and certainly not prolonged rain during the harvest, in September or October. That would dilute the grapes too much, although we have technical ways now to extract some of that excess water. So a very hot summer, with a warm, prolonged fall, what you call Indian summer, is perfect.

"Each phase of the growing season has its best weather profile, which we almost never see. But you will find the better the growing season, the finer the vintage. For example, the great vintages of 1961 and 1982 were almost textbook perfect growing years, very hot, with just enough rain. As a matter of fact, 1961 was the driest summer on record, and it even followed a cold spring. But the weather that followed was perfect."

"I suppose that it all depends upon where your property is located."

"That's right. It's the 'microclimate' that counts. You Americans have never understood, for example, that the 1983 Chateau Margaux is an even finer wine than their glorious 1982. That's because the growing conditions and rainfall in the Margaux region were somewhat better in the later year. Nobody can rely on vintage years, without taking account of the different regions, much less the quality of individual wine estates."

"Pryor gave both the 1983 and 1982 Margaux an A," Sylvie recalled.

"Exactly. They are both excellent, but very different. What does an idiotic system of letters—or numbers for that matter—tell you about wine?" De Tourneau shrugged his shoulders.

"I've seen lots of wine buyers in retail stores at home with their little plastic laminated wine vintage charts," Robbie said.

"Yes, I suppose they are of some help. But it gets to be ridiculous when the Bordeaux vintage year is the standard for everywhere else, *n'importe ou!* I've even seen buyers reject good Spanish *rioja* wines because it wasn't a top vintage year hundreds of miles to the north, in the Bordeaux region, when conditions might have been just perfect in Spain."

They walked down to the estate's wine processing facilities. De Tourneau showed them where the grapes, after harvest, were crushed, and the juice collected for the fermentation casks. "At Montmorency we leave the skins and pips in contact with the juice for a longer time than most," he explained. "That makes a fuller red wine."

He showed them the automatic machinery that could control temperatures in the fermentation kegs themselves. "This wasn't very widespread before the Dillons began to modernize their holdings at Haut Brion. But now we bear in mind that Pasteur wrote that entire vintages can be ruined if the temperature during the fermenting mixture rises too high."

"As happened to one of your colleagues not long ago. A ruined crop of cabernet sauvignon, I hear," Sylvie said.

Just for a moment, De Tourneau seemed to lose his composure. He hesitated. Something like fear crossed his face. "Yes, poor fellow. Probably saving money with unskilled laborers."

He recovered quickly, and continued, pointing out some gears on the wall.

"These levers are our insurance policy. They offer some control for the process, keeping the temperature at the right level. If it rises too high we can immediately send refrigerated liquid around the exterior of the fermenting vats. We've had to do that on occasion. In the past that wasn't possible, and entire vintages were lost during the fermentation process."

"But at Haut Brion, the fermenting casks are of stainless steel. Yours are the old-fashioned style, made of wood." Robbie gestured at the enormous, floor to ceiling wooden fermentation casks.

De Tourneau smiled. "It's possible to yield too much tradition to sell a product. This early contact with the wood of the fermentation casks helps develop the taste and maturity of the wine by adding tannins. Nobody has ever explained to me how stainless steel does anything for the flavor of wines. Alexis Lichine, of course, disagreed. We miss him."

They moved to the aging caves, where red wines were stored. De Tourneau went through the process.

"We have to be very careful at this stage. Notice that the barrels"—he gestured towards the closest of the extensive rows of barrels leading into the distance of the cave—"are all standing, with lightly stoppered openings so that we can constantly refill the barrels, allowing for evaporation. If we did not, the air space inside the barrels would be ripe for bacteria. So we keep the barrels filled.

"We also have to remove the lees from the barrels from time to time as the aging proceeds."

"These barrels look new."

"Yes, *Mademoiselle.* At Montmorency we only use the finest oak from the Limousin region for our barrels, and it is largely new oak for the first year. After two years we resell those barrels. The oak aging adds more tannins to the wine, supplementing those that the juice already has through contact with the skins and seeds, tannins which are absorbed during the initial fermentation. It is a mellower sort of tannin."

Sylvie asked, "So even the tannins vary? Why are they so important?"

"The tannins make the aging process of wine possible," de Tourneau replied. "They create a kind of structure within which the fruity taste of the grapes evolves, intensifies, and becomes"—he searched for just the right word—"magic."

They entered the second aging cave. There the refilled barrels rested for a second full year of aging, before the wine was bottled. De Tourneau explained the fining process. "It takes place shortly before the wines are bottled," he said. Here we do it the old way, using egg whites, which we put into the barrels towards the end of the aging process. This brings together minute suspended particles in the wine, which are collected under the winemaster's supervision and discarded.

"This results in the clear wine that you know. After bottling, it takes some years for more particles to form, and that is usually a sign that your wine is mature and ready for drinking."

"Those are the lees that we see in the bottom of the wine bottle?" Robbie asked

"Exactly."

A light dawned "So that's why we decant wines before we drink them, to get rid of those particles?"

"That's right. You pour the wine out of the bottle into a decanter, stopping the pouring when the particles come up. Sometimes a candle is used so that you can see the particles more easily. You stop pouring at the right moment, and they stay in the bottle. That decanting—which has the added benefit of letting the wine breathe and finally develop—before you finally drink the wine is like the fining we do here. If we didn't do that, the wine would not be clear. It would be full of those particles, and you wouldn't like it. All you are doing with your decanting is completing the process."

Sylvie had a question. "Are your white wines made in the same way?"

"It's a variation of the red wine process. The fermentation is done in smaller containers, more slowly to allow flavors to develop, and at lower temperature. We age the wines for a year, to preserve the fresh taste of the fruit, before bottling."

Sylvie and Robbie were then shown through the bottling facility, where half-bottles, bottles, magnums, and occasionally even larger bottles of Chateau Montmorency were bottled, corks inserted, and then the wines were put into colorful wooden casks for shipment around France and throughout the world.

The tasting room was next. It was immaculate, if a bit too much like a chemistry laboratory for Robbie's taste. He wondered if this was where they used to keep their pesticide chemicals. But still he liked the profusion of wine glasses at the tasting table, and the colorful cloth wine tapestry on the wall, which showed a grape harvest by medieval villagers. Here and there were some posters from the past, showing how the wine labels had evolved over the years.

"Try this white wine first," their host said as he poured some into their first glasses. "Tasting the red first would spoil the white for you, by masking the flavor of the lighter wine. That's why you drink white wines before red at dinner."

Sylvie tasted the wine and was delighted. "It's fresh, dry, pleasant. I like it."

Without comment, a second sampling was poured from another cooled bottle, freshly uncorked with a satisfying "POP!" before their eyes.

"If that was a Pryor A, this one is an A plus," Robbie grinned. "It's fresh but deeper, and velvety. It's the same wine, but richer."

"That is also our white wine, well aged for twenty years. That gives the blend time to develop and become richer. Some winemakers age their white wines in stainless steel instead of oak barrels. I don't think they will ever achieve anything like my white wine by doing so. Others, of course, disagree. That's a big argument over in Chablis, in Burgundy.

"Now I want you both to try something special."

He poured samples of red wine from six flasks into as many glasses for Sylvie and Robbie. As they sampled, de Tourneau explained the procedure.

"As we've said, all Bordeaux wines, almost without exception, are blends. You are tasting different samples of the three grape varieties that we use—cabernet sauvignon, merlot, and cabernet franc. Each grape variety has two samples—a sample from older vines, and one from more recently planted acres."

The variety was an education. Clearly whoever put a Bordeaux wine together had to have real creativity and judgment, to balance those tastes, and allow for their aging together.

Then de Tourneau uncorked a bottle and gave Sylvie and Robbie each a good measure from the latest vintage. "Don't forget to smell it first," he said. They did. It seemed to have a deep, rather fruity aroma, pleasant but not overpowering.

"This is what the wine is like when we have put it together," de Tourneau said. "Nothing is in there that you have not just tasted. The trick is in the proportions used."

Their compliments were genuine. "The wine is far better than its separate ingredients. This is a revelation." They felt like insiders and were pleased with themselves, with the tasting, with this fine red wine, and with the world in general.

"And now, I have a surprise for you," de Tourneau said.

The last glasses were then poured by their host from a separate flask. Robbie took a taste and hurriedly spat it out. "What is it? It's not really bad, but this wine isn't nearly as good as what we just had."

The wine was heavier, rather sweet, more alcoholic and cloying, a Rubens with a fat model. Sylvie nodded in agreement.

De Tourneau looked with new respect at his visitors. "This is the same vintage that you just tasted, but early in the fermentation process, it was adulterated with more fruity grapes from younger vines, and then more sugar was added, to make a headier wine. That is the taste that Pryor always preferred.

"They were called 'Pryor casks,' and your last sample was from the Pryor cask that had been prepared for his next visit here, in a few months. I'm ashamed to admit that we did it. But of course we won't have to use it now. That's better in the long run. So maybe his death counted for something after all. At least we can all go back to making honest wines."

Robbie was flabbergasted. "Was this a common practice?"

"Many wine estates resisted it. Those with well-established reputations could afford to do so. But finally, push came to shove. Who can compete in a profession that requires finesse, judgment and timing, against an army of wine buyers, each with their copy of Pryor looking for just the wine that he has said must be bought? Worse yet, who can stay solvent, in this most competitive and confusing profession, when a leading wine writer has said to buy wines from your competition instead? That's why many wine people detested Pryor. He kept rewarding his own taste.

"Finally, for a joke, one of our colleagues over in Pomerol who had received terrible reviews from Pryor concocted his own 'special' wine for Pryor's next tasting. He did what I did for the wine that you have just tasted. He fiddled with the fermentation process, adding more grapes from younger vines, and then more sugar. In other words, our colleague just decided to see if Pryor really knew his wines or not.

"The result was astonishing. Pryor went back and wrote a review that talked about the 'turnaround' at our friend's Pomerol estate. Sales took off when the vintage was bottled. It was an early Pryor 'discovery.' Of course, the vintage that Pryor had tasted never existed, and our colleague went on bottling his wine as he had always made it. He destroyed the cask from which Pryor had tasted immediately. Since Pryor's tastings are always from the barrel and since all wines evolve from there, he never knew the difference, and since our colleague always made his wines the same way, he felt vindicated. And his wines went from $15 a bottle on the American market to triple that price in one year. They cost even more now."

Sylvie asked, "Is making phony 'Pryor casks' widespread?"

"Many people started to do it. As I said, the entire thing started out as something of an insider's joke. But it really succeeded. Pryor couldn't tell the difference, and the pressure to join the charade became intense. If he dismissed your wine, you lost money for that vintage, and several years in a row might spell disaster.

"In the end, those who didn't do it, which remained the vast majority, and even those who did, all hated Pryor. Probably those who made up 'Pryor casks' hated him even more than those who did not. After all, they had compromised themselves because of him, they told themselves."

"Didn't Pryor understand that something was going on?"

"We don't think so. And let me add that nobody ever thought that Pryor was personally dishonest. He just didn't have a very refined taste for wine. But he was a master showman. You've probably seen him yourself at wine tastings, the studied glance, the pause for a pill from an antique silver case, then the deep sniff, another pause, eyes close, eyes open once more, then the sip, the theatrical spitting out of the sample, then the rolling eyes, as if searching for just the right adjective. What he really did was create some order from confusion, adding theater.

"For him, everything was precision and order. He put the different regions into columns that everyone could understand. Also he knew exactly what he liked. He was really a Beaujolais drinker. He liked fruity wines, with a touch of character, nothing very deep. He wrote well and clearly, and made sense—too much contrived sense some might say—out of these very different wine regions. His books were a success for that reason.

"Then he began to insist upon his own taste preference. That was not, after all, a very reasonable thing to do. Not all Bordeaux wines resemble each other. They are in fact very, very different. Even wines that are almost neighbors, like Lafite and Mouton Rothschild, do not resemble each other in the slightest. And the regions themselves have rather different, individual characteristics. That is part of the interest and the charm of wines, I always thought. But that was not Pryor's point of view. And his books kept selling and the money kept rolling in, which meant that he was successful. He liked some wines that weren't even produced at chateaux, just blended in a warehouse!" De Tourneau wrinkled his nose in disgust.

"In the end, if the winemakers of Bordeaux were enlightened enough to reproduce that special taste which he preferred, then he rewarded them with good reviews. Those who understood that taste and catered to it, prospered. But after a while, your wine writer had become the most detested man in Bordeaux.

"What happened to him didn't surprise me," de Tourneau continued. "He ruined lots of good people. I'm only surprised it didn't happen earlier. But now, I suspect that the police have more potential suspects than they will know what to do with, many of them in this region alone."

CHAPTER 6

Intermezzo

Stopping by her Bordeaux apartment to get a change of clothes for the evening reception, Sylvie carried on an argument with herself. She looked at one outfit in the mirror, holding it up. No, not quite the right color. She could, she supposed, have carried on this investigation for her newspaper without involving the American Consul. She had to admit, though, that having him along did make it easier. He opened lots of doors.

But having considered the matter from several points of view, she had earlier almost decided to proceed by herself for that very reason. Imagine having to lean on any official in order to get a story, and an American diplomat at that! She was self-sufficient, she told herself firmly. This excursion doesn't affect that one bit. On the other hand, he had opened up about Pryor, sharing what he knew. That was asking for her help.

This Robbie Cutler was rather nice. He was tall and friendly. His French was very good, and he wasn't stuffy, just shy. He might be fun to spend some time with while the story progressed. Here's the very dress. She put a medium blue long dress and a cashmere sweater into a carry-on bag, a pair of evening shoes, and a jewelry clutch containing her pearl necklace and earrings. Then she locked her apartment door and left the building to join Robbie, who was waiting outside in her car.

Sylvie counted herself fortunate to have a good reporting job at *Sud-Ouest*. It wasn't that the job was beyond her talents. No, it was actually just right for the time being, and a pleasure to work for the newspaper that had been the family's daily read for many years. But not many years earlier, and her reporting job would have gone to a man. She felt some obligation to prove herself to others, and occasional annoyance that she felt that way.

Her family had settled in Bazas, south of Bordeaux, where her father was a respected pharmacist, and her mother seemed to know everyone. Sylvia was an only child, and a much loved one. At the girls' *lycee* she had done very well, passing her national *baccalaureat* examinations with an outstanding score. Her literature, history and media studies at the University of Bordeaux had been an arduous pleasure.

On the side, and as a volunteer, she had written an occasional column for *Sud-Ouest*. She had gotten that job by inventing it, and then going to the newspaper and selling them on the idea. That might not have led to a permanent job, had she not done her homework well, known the editors and rewrite staff, and then been trapped inside a university building when a deranged student with an AK-47 had terrorized the university. Sylvie had telephoned her stories to the newspaper, and scooped everyone. On graduation she had her newspaper job, a paying one this time. She would make it a success.

That, of course, would also be thanks to the Blessed Mother, whose help Sylvie never importuned for special requests. That was probably because her devotions were addressed routinely, in good and in unhappy times, and not reserved for emergencies. Her parents knew that her spare time regularly included a trip to the shrine of Lourdes, in the Pyreneean foothills southeast of Bordeaux. They hoped that she would eventually find a good Catholic boy to marry and they saw no need to remind her of it, not yet. She saw them when she could, and telephoned when she could not.

Since the Pryor story had broken, her days had been very busy. It was, in fact, her first major story since joining the newspaper's staff.

She crossed the street and smiled at Robbie, putting her bag in the car trunk. It would be interesting to see what his apartment looked like. "*Monsieur le Consul,* let's skip that restaurant lunch. Wouldn't it be more fun to have a picnic along the way instead? There's no point in doing anything fancy when we've been tasting wine all morning. Let's do some shopping at that Felix Potin grocery store instead."

"What a good idea. Then we'll put it together at my place when I pick up my suit for the reception. And everyone calls me Robbie."

They had fun choosing just the right ingredients for the picnic. She picked out some fresh, thick crusted Poulain bread, of course more expensive than an ordinary baguette, but worth it. Bayonne ham, some fresh tomatoes from North Africa, a venison *pate*, several cheeses, some chilled Evian water and a bottle of the previous year's Beaujolais Villages completed their shopping. Then they went back to Robbie's apartment to freshen up and make the sandwiches.

Sylvie was pleased with the apartment. It wasn't at all the untidy mess that she had expected. It wasn't fussy either, but things were picked up properly and not strewn around. As Robbie looked for the picnic basket and some napkins and paper plates in the kitchen, she glanced about his sitting room. It was light and cheerful, with well chosen, floor-length light blue curtains along the windows behind the couch that looked out on the *Quai des Chartrons.*

There were only one or two magazines. Books seemed to be everywhere. They were on shelves, on the end tables by his couch, and there were several even on the cocktail table in front of the couch. Good stuff too, as far as Sylvie could see. There was a well-thumbed, matched set of Dickens that clearly wasn't just for show, and a recent French edition of the works of La Fontaine, both the *Fables* and the more bawdy *Contes.*

Also, she was intrigued to see that he was reading one of the Bordeaux novels of Francois Mauriac, to judge from the paperback volume left spine up on his cocktail table. What an odd thing for a diplomat to do. He seemed to be finding out about Bordeaux and its people by reading about them, rather than by talking with them and coming to his own conclusions. She really must tease him about that. No, better not do that, she reflected. Most shy people would prefer to be drawn out indirectly, rather than have their shyness pointed out to them.

An upright piano stood against the far wall, and set out on it was a selection of popular music from the Big Band era. Next to the piano was a writing desk and chair, with an expensive word processor, screen and printer. Bookends held correspondence to be answered, and probably bills. Next to the word processor were a FAX machine and telephone.

His furniture was serviceable, not fancy, and of good quality wood, she concluded. Pride of place was taken by a nineteenth century, French country *armoire* on the opposite wall. It was open, and contained a television set, a compact disc player and a stack of discs in their containers. Speakers were wired along the sides. Sylvie admired the *armoire* and wished that it were hers. Next to it, a brass floorstand held several canes.

There was only one painting in the room, a large riverside oil of Bordeaux that Sylvie seemed to remember from a show held a year ago at one of the galleries along the Cours Clemenceau. She liked the colors and the perspective, taken from the east side of the stone bridge, or Pont de Pierre, of the eighteenth century quayside buildings curving along the Garonne River.

A collection of photographs was arranged on a low shelf of the bookshelf nearest the cordovan leather armchair, near the couch. She supposed that armchair was probably Robbie's favorite perch. The pictures must be important to him, she thought, for the best way to glimpse them was to sit in the armchair.

There was an agreeable lack of signed photographs from politicians. Instead, here was an elderly man with a perky, amused expression, who had signed the picture "To my favorite nephew, Uncle Seth." Next to it was a group photograph of a fencing team, mostly wearing equipment and face masks, so it was hard to tell which one, if any, was Robbie. An elegant older couple beamed in a third picture. In a fourth, a striking, and pleasantly smiling, well-dressed young woman commanded by silent force of personality a group picture also containing, Sylvie noticed, both Uncle Seth and the couple in the third picture. A final photograph showed a frankly posing Siamese cat held by Robbie. This one had been autographed by an inky paw print near the edge.

Both originals made their appearance from the kitchen.

"Surely this is the famous Minouette," Sylvie said, as the cat meowed a greeting and jumped on the chair's armrest, wary and friendly at the same time. "I'm sure we'll get along well." She gave the animal a friendly pat or two, and was rewarded by a purr from Minouette and a smile from Robbie.

She followed Robbie towards his kitchen, where the picnic basket and various knives and forks had been laid out.

Along the way, Sylvie was surprised to see a signed Jean Cocteau lithograph, very chic, very 'thirties, in the small hallway that led from the dining room to the cramped kitchen. The dining room table and chairs and buffet were serviceable. They looked like they had come from somebody's warehouse. They were probably Embassy issue, Sylvie decided. Not so the nice barometer on the wall with a view of Nantucket Island. The table was set for one person.

Sylvie cheerfully took charge of turning their purchases into a luncheon, with rich Normandy butter and grainy Dijon country mustard completing the Bayonne ham sandwiches. Some glasses were added for the Evian water and the Beaujolais. Sylvie, having noticed instant coffee on the kitchen table, said quickly that there was no need to pack coffee. They could stop for some along the way.

Robbie opened a can for Minouette's dinner as Sylvie went upstairs to freshen up. It was a two-bedroom apartment, and seemed furnished with some care, sparingly but clean and well looked after. The bathroom had the usual French collection of contraptions that hissed and spouted water, that every American tourist wrote home about. The shower curtain featured, unnecessarily Sylvie thought, a profile caricature of Alfred Hitchcock. How disconcerting!

She couldn't resist a peek inside the medicine cabinet. It contained an assortment of shaving items, a minimum of French and American over the counter toiletries, aspirin, antacids and the like. There was a small collection of soaps from pricey hotels. She looked once more. There was no woman's emergency kit of perfumes, bath oil, eyebrow pencil and mascara.

Robbie carried the picnic basket and a foldover flight bag containing a dark suit, shirt and tie as they left his apartment. He locked the door, and they entered Sylvie's Citroen for their afternoon ride through the *Medoc* vineyards. On the windowseat looking out on the street, Minouette surveyed their departure regally.

⁂

They drove north of Bordeaux along the Garonne River, which imperceptibly became the Gironde, flowing north past Bourg and Blaye and Pauillac into the Atlantic Ocean. They turned right on Route D2, a small turnoff at Blanquefort, onto the main wine route of the *Medoc*, as Pryor had said and Lichine before him, a road worthy of dreams.

Margaux, St. Julien, Pauillac and St. Estephe, four capital centers of wine, each as famous as the *Graves* region that they had seen that morning. "I've been looking forward to today for a long time," he smiled. "Let's see what we can find out before the reception."

"I was interested, for a start, to listen to de Tourneau," she said. "Who could have known all that about Pryor? And did you notice all of the things that can go wrong, to spoil a wine vintage? Really, it's quite hazardous. All or nothing, and then you have to worry about wine reviewers."

She saw his quick interest, and it pleased her. She also liked his sheer excitement in being in the *Medoc*. "For me," she continued, "this route recalls Dr. Johnson's remark about London. When I am tired of the *Medoc*, then I will be tired of living, I think."

Driving north, Margaux came first, known for its rather elegant, almost perfumed wines. They saw Chateau Prieure-Lichine on the left. "Alexis Lichine was a friend of Dad's," Robbie said. "I'm sorry that his son Sasha sold the estate. Alexis Lichine once gave Dad the best wine advice I've ever heard. It was to trust his own taste, and develop it carefully. Lichine suggested buying three bottles of the same producer's vintage, say for example a 1995 Prieure-Lichine. Drink one, and make some notes on how you like it. Put the other two bottles away. Then drink the second six months later, and the last six months after that, making notes each time. Then compare your notes. That will do more to develop your taste, Dad used to say, than all the vintage charts put together. It's still good advice."

"That would put Pryor and his alphabet soup out of business," she said.

It was a reflex to stop the car and take a picture of Chateau Palmer. One really couldn't help it. And across the vineyards lay Chateau Margaux itself. They would be returning later that afternoon for the reception, but couldn't resist turning right off the coast road for a moment, to approach the property itself, and admire its famous Palladian architecture. If a movie set were ever needed in the *Medoc*, surely Chateau Margaux would be perfect.

The day was becoming a little warm for spring. It would be just right for their picnic. "Do you come here often?" he asked.

"Perhaps I should. I've never enjoyed it more." His sheer boyish pleasure at being there was catching.

Continuing north along the river road, they came to the next region, St. Julien, with its huge bottle shaped sign welcoming the traveller by the road. Many people said that the wines of St. Julien were of the highest general quality of any in Bordeaux. Certainly the estates seemed grand, and the wines offered a nice balance between the elegance of the Margaux wines to the south, and the robustness of the Pauillac wines just north.

They passed Chateau Branaire Ducru on their left, and the gorgeous residential estate of Chateau Beychevelle on their right, along the river. A side road to their left led to Chateau Gruaud Larose and Chateau Talbot, said to have been an estate of the last English High Constable of France when they still held this region in the fifteenth century.

They continued driving slowly north, so slowly that occasionally, an impatient driver behind them would beep a horn. No matter, for they were not in any hurry at all. Robbie wished that he could capture this afternoon on video and have its languid moments always for a reminder.

"Look, there is Ducru Beaucaillou," she said. "It's the finest estate in the *Med*oc. Just look at those superb porches, perfect for viewing the vineyards in front of the estate. I've heard that the formal gardens behind that swept down to the Gironde are superb." And then they came to the three Leovilles: Las Cases and Poyferre were on the river side, and Barton stood on the other side of the road. Formerly one great estate, the three had been separated by inheritance in the past. They were now rivals in quality at a level that few wines ever achieved.

Their excursion had taken about an hour, and it was time for their picnic. Sylvie pulled off along a side road and found some wooden chairs and a bench. They had a view of the Gironde and could also see Chateau Lamarque.

"So pleasant," Robbie said. "But I'm not sure that we're finding out anything useful about Pryor."

"Don't be too quick to judge. For one thing, we're concentrating on the most famous estates. One does. Does it strike you as logical that any of them would compromise their reputations by making phony casks of wine to influence a wine reviewer?"

"Put that way, no," he agreed. "They would have too much to lose. Let's take that logic one step further. Why would de Tourneau exaggerate? After all, he said the practice was widespread."

"He could have been exaggerating, to excuse himself."

The logic was very French. Robbie wouldn't have thought of that. "That's possible," he conceded.

"So we should be looking for an estate in trouble to confirm his story. Also, we shouldn't necessarily accept what he said at face value."

"All that sounds reasonable. Maybe we'll find out more at Margaux tonight. Tell me about Chateau Lamarque."

"This is one of my favorite places," she confided. "It has history and wine and the most original wine cellar you'll ever see, a real medieval dungeon where the bottles now are kept."

She told him about the picture gallery leading upwards along the staircase, where family portraits were hung. "One set is particularly fine. There is a young man, next to a young woman. Both are simply dressed, in shirts open at the neck. They seem to stare resolutely ahead."

"What happened to them?"

"They were aristocrats who used to own this property. During the Revolution they were arrested. When the Terror came, they were both condemned to death. Instead of the elaborate costumes that nobles were used to wearing, what you see in their portraits is what they wore when facing their accusers."

"So they died young, I suppose. Who got the property?"

"Robbie—use your imagination. The story didn't end quite there. By some miracle they both survived the Terror and the Revolution and regained this property."

"Where they lived happily ever after...."

"Wrong again. Freed from prison, they discovered that they had nothing whatsoever in common. Divorce was not possible, of course, so they lived apart after that. And now there they stare away from each other on the wall, side by side for all time!"

He smiled. "That's why I haven't married. You have to get it right the first time," he said, and wondered why he had said it. "Family history aside, they make a very nice wine here."

They set out their picnic and began to have their luncheon. It had become just sunny enough to be pleasant, no coats needed, with traces of a breeze from the river now and then.

"Your sandwiches are perfect," he said with real appreciation as the Bayonne ham and Poulain bread began to disappear. "Are you a good cook, too?"

"Are you always so politically incorrect? Really, *Monsieur le Consul*, I thought that you were from the land of liberated women and no stereotyping." She smiled at him as she teased. Her smile was worth her teasing. If only he had a video camera, he could capture that warm expression, corners of her mouth slightly pulled up.

"Actually," he began gravely, "you've guessed it. I am the last male chauvinist left on the American East Coast. That's why they sent me to France, so I wouldn't corrupt my fellow citizens. Why are you dodging my question about cooking? I thought France was the home of fine food, after all." He took an appreciative sip of the Beaujolais wine as she put cheese slices and butter on the remaining bread. They finished their picnic, and continued their slow drive through the *Medoc*.

Pauillac, the home of three of the five great first growths, Lafite Rothschild, its neighbor and rival Mouton Rothschild, and Chateau Latour, was a short drive away. There was so much diversity, and so many famous wine estates in this small area, that Robbie thought that a visit to Pauillac just by itself would justify a wine lover's trip to Bordeaux. Along the way, just north from St. Julien, Chateau Pichon Longueville Comtesse de Lalande, or "Pichon Lalande," stood on the right or Gironde River side of the road, facing its rival, Pichon Longueville Baron, once part of the same larger estate, across the road.

"They say that the best wine estates have a view of the Gironde," Sylvie said. Robbie nodded. "And there's one of the best of them all."

Chateau Latour was approached by a small country road just past Pichon Lalande. Sylvie drove down that road, past the immaculate rows of newly flowering plants, towards the Gironde River. The tower for which the estate is named was to their right, along with fermentation, aging and storage facilities, and the bottling center and touring rooms where tourists from all corners of the world saw videos on Chateau Latour and its history before visiting the other facilities.

Sylvie preferred the lighter style of Lafite, on those very rare occasions when she could afford to taste it. "It has always been an elegant, light wine, from the days of Madame du Barry and Madame Pompadour, who served it to their monarchs. Let's hope it stays that way. You see, I worry about the wine reviewers too, and how they can influence things."

For Robbie, Latour was the ideal wine, full of rich flavor and character, as unlike Lafite as any quality wine could be.

"Well, Pryor was right about that, anyway," he said.

"About what, exactly?"

"At the dinner, he said that vintage dinners are always wrong. They always arrange for Bordeaux wines to be tasted in alphabetical order, in English. That puts Latour before Margaux, a much lighter wine."

"He was indeed right about that. What else did he have to say?"

"He started to give a little lecture. I guess that was a habit with him. As I said this morning, he did mention something about the wine routes, the *Graves*, then the *Medoc*, St. Emilion and Pomerol."

Her silence became a question. She ran her fingers through her hair as she looked at him. He had a silent argument with himself, the diplomat versus the detective. The side that knew she understood detecting, and had already proved it, won.

"There's something else, Sylvie. Something I dismissed at the time. As you know, many major American wine writers were there. That was unusual. It seems there was word out that Pryor was going to make an announcement. He himself seemed to allude to it. But he never got to do it. The reports of his murder missed it."

His little-boy earnestness was endearing. What had she heard, that Robbie Cutler enjoyed mysteries and detection? Yes, and he had shared them with her, a reporter at that. He was a diplomat, used to keeping his secrets. But now, he had let her into his private world. They were partners, for today, anyway. There was nothing she could think of to say. Recognizing the moment without comment was the most intimate comment of all.

"It's so beautiful, Robbie, just perfect. I wish we had time to see it all today."

"Then we'll come back one day, just to see Latour?" Robbie asked.

She nodded agreement.

Just before arriving in the little port town of Pauillac they drove past Chateau Lynch Bages, a Fifth Growth in the governing 1855 Classification. Sheer nonsense, Robbie thought. Lynch Bages was a superior wine that would surely be upgraded should a new classification ever take place. That was not likely. And so Lynch Bages, the first wine carried in space by a French astronaut, had to settle for that distinction, and for its reputation as a well made, flavorful wine with depth.

Robbie managed a touch of nostalgia at Pauillac. "This is where the young Lafayette sailed to help our Revolution," he said. Sylvie was sure that if he had been wearing a hat, he would have removed it at as he made that rather theatrical announcement.

After the town of Pauillac, a confusing detour to the left took them first to Chateau Pontet Canet, which Robbie thought was one of the last great bargains left among the classified Pauillac wines, and then to the great estates of Mouton Rothschild and Lafite Rothschild. "If only we knew what we were looking for," she said.

Sylvie wanted to make sure that he knew about the art museum that had been assembled at Mouton Rothschild. Pottery, sculpture, tapestries and paintings, all the objects in the excellent collection had wine, its cultivation and enjoyment, as their theme. That clearly was another return visit that they would have to make. Sylvie tossed off the remark that Mouton always seemed to her like a deep, rich Burgundy wine rather than a Bordeaux. "But that," she admitted, "is hardly a criticism."

They entered the fourth region, St. Estephe, a rather different, hilly area whose wines seemed to many to be less rounded than those of Pauillac, requiring longer aging. They were delighted by the pagoda like gates adorning Chateau Cos D'Estournel. Many people said this estate was the finest St. Estephe wine, although Robbie had heard that Chateau Montrose, closer to the Gironde River on a hill that overlooking the river, was closing any quality gap.

For years, Chateau Montrose, itself highly regarded and classified, had been considered the "poor man's Latour," for it had something of Latour's great depth following many years of aging, and cost considerably less. However, recent high quality production had raised Montrose's price to the point where the old saying was no longer true. It was not a poor man's wine, if it ever had been. Still, it was a fine wine. So was the estate to which Montrose had once belonged, Chateau Calon Segur, the northernmost classified growth of the *Medoc*, and one of the very few wine estates which had retained exactly the same boundaries that it had had when the 1855 Classification was first made.

Sylvie stopped the car on a plateau which overlooked the Gironde River. This was Chateau Meyney, an unclassified wine of great distinction and moderate retail price. The view in all directions from the estate was spectacular on that fine afternoon, as Sylvie and Robbie could follow the coutours of the Gironde River as it looped northward towards the ocean.

Together they savored a shared silent moment as they got out of the car and looked at the vineyard and at the estate beyond. "Why doesn't this silly American take the opportunity to kiss me?" Sylvie thought. "If only I knew her just a little longer or better, what a perfect spot for our first kiss," Robbie thought.

They stopped for coffee at a cafe in the little town of St. Estephe. Robbie looked at Sylvie and said "Well, aren't you going to ask about her?"

"I thought that you would tell me when, and if, you wanted to," came the assured reply. "But she certainly is lovely. I assume that the picture was taken with your parents?"

"Yes, and it doesn't do her justice. We all get along very well. I'm afraid that the tortured American families one sees on stage aren't a model for mine. Not that anybody pays the least attention to me at home when Evalyn is around. But she is the nicest kid sister I could have wished to have. Perhaps you'll meet her when she visits me in Bordeaux in a few weeks."

"I'd be very pleased to meet her," Sylvie said, in what she sincerely hoped was a self-assured tone of voice. Suddenly she looked forward greatly to their reception at Chateau Margaux, and didn't really care if her enthusiasm showed or not.

CHAPTER 7

A Reception At Chateau Margaux

The beefy woman proprietor of the cafe smiled as Sylvie asked where she might change clothes. "*Par ici, Madame*," the woman said, gesturing towards a back parlor as she cast a quizzical look at Robbie. "*Plus tard*" ("Later"), Sylvie said, and then she blushed as the woman laughed and Robbie, redfaced, stared at the ceiling. When Sylvie emerged from the back parlor, fresh and neatly dressed in her dark blue ensemble for the evening, Robbie went in and changed.

Then he fished the reception invitation from his inside coat pocket and read it to Sylvie. "Erika Lutz, Consul General of the German Federal Republic and Dean of the Bordeaux Consular Corps, has the pleasure of inviting John Robinson Cutler, American Consul, to a Tasting Reception at Chateau Margaux." The invitation added that the wines were donated by the *Confrerie des Vins du Medoc*, a well-regarded regional wine promotion organization.

"I'm a member, come to think of it," Robbie said. "They made me a member shortly after I arrived here. The scroll says 'In Recognition of Eminent Services for *Medoc* Wines.' I remember wondering, 'How did they know?'"

"It must have been grand fun."

"Yes. It was at a citadel across the river. We all marched in wearing crimson robes. Then we walked to church for a ceremonial mass." He became serious for a moment. "You know, even the stained glass in the village church celebrated wine. You'd never see that in New England."

"You make New England sound rather grim."

"No. That isn't it. It's just different. I love wine, and the best is made here. And I'll never forget the three-hour luncheon that followed the mass."

"They did well to make you a member, Robbie."

Then she looked at the invitation. "It makes a lot of sense for the *Confrerie* to sponsor this reception," Sylvie said. "The point after all is to calm down any rumors regarding the vintage that may be floating around following the Pryor murder. What better way to do it than to give a reception and invite the entire consular corps?"

"Half the wine producers in the *Medoc* should be there. We've followed Pryor's routes. Now's a good chance to find out something, if there's something to find out."

"How are we going to do that?"

"I'll drop a hint or two, and see what comes back to us. That's part of the diplomatic game at receptions. It works for politics, maybe it'll work for us."

"I don't quite follow that."

"Sorry. What I mean is, when you want to know what Foreign Ministry X is up to, just assume a serious air and say to a colleague that you've heard that Foreign Ministry X is going to do whatever…say sell off monetary gold…then you wait and within the hour, often you'll be 'informally' told that Foreign Ministry X denies it, or sometimes 'Where did you hear that, in all confidence don't tell anyone else, the price hasn't been set yet and we don't want a run on gold to lower our price, the Minister will be SO grateful.' You know, stuff like that."

She laughed. "I had no idea diplomacy could be such fun."

Arriving at Chateau Margaux, they were greeted by Consul General Erika Lutz, who joined them for a photograph in Chateau Margaux's reception area, the black and white checkered floor supplying a formal backdrop.

Lutz had served ten years in Bordeaux. A single diplomat, her French was excellent. As she never tired of reminding her colleagues, "You may come and go, hoping for a promotion and your own embassy and the title of ambassador. I'll stay here as Consul General for as long as the German Foreign Ministry sees fit to honor my extension requests. Why leave paradise?"

Why, indeed? To Robbie, she had a good point. He found himself muttering to Sylvie, "She may have the right attitude, after all." His own Yankee work ethic and desire for advancement, strong and logical and consuming in the springtime of his work, pointed in other directions. In any event, the State Department would have other plans for him after a few years, he could be sure of that. Meanwhile, he would enjoy Bordeaux while it lasted.

"Is he arguing with himself or with me?" Sylvie wondered.

The picture was taken of Erika Lutz greeting them. The German Consul General was amused when both Robbie and Sylvie asked for a copy of the picture. "Certainly, my friends." So the American Consul may have found a *petite amie*. That was rather nice. She liked Sylvie Marceau on sight. She was stylish, like many Frenchwomen, but had a nice, unpretentious touch as well.

Robbie and Sylvie walked through the residence entry and down the rear steps to the reception area, where under shade trees, tables had been set up for the wine tasting. Waiters passed trays of light *hors d'oeuvres*. The weather continued very pleasant, with a slight breeze blowing up from the Gironde River from time to time. A good thing for, trusting fate, no tent had been arranged in case of rain. They would just move inside.

The reception was catered but Robbie noticed several members of the Chateau Margaux staff were on hand. The chateau and grounds had been lent for the reception. Still, it was best to keep an eye on things.

There was a small orchestra over by the trees, playing background music, light and semi-classical. The mix of Strauss, Cole Porter, Lehar, Offenbach and Margaux was just right, Robbie thought.

Erika Lutz left her receiving line duties and came over to talk with Robbie and Sylvie. "Tell me about your adventures at the Willard Hotel," she insisted, snagging some raw veggies from a passing tray. "Anything of interest happen that we haven't yet read about in *Mademoiselle* Marceau's column?"

"Nothing at present. But if you want to get to the bottom of this, the fact is that Pryor wasn't the most popular wine writer in Bordeaux. We've been out sleuthing together in the *Graves* and the *Medoc* to learn more," he replied. "We hear that many vineyard owners didn't seem to like him very much. He inspired as much fear of what he might write as anything else."

"Do you mean that he could have been murdered by somebody from Bordeaux? How dreadful. How delicious."

"It seems possible." Robbie turned to Sylvie, who filled Consul General Lutz in on what they already knew about the method of poisoning. Sylvie added, "And as the Americans say, there is good news and bad news. The good news is that the murder had nothing at all to do with the Bordeaux vintage."

Lutz interjected, "That's irrelevant if the public gets the idea that it did."

"Absolutely right. That's why the *Confrerie* is underwriting this reception, I gather."

"Of course. What's the bad news?"

"The bad news is that we seem to have a murderer at large who could be anybody in this region, or indeed in any of the French or Italian wine regions who considered himself savaged by Pryor."

"Thank heavens that Pryor never wrote about German wines," Lutz observed. "That eliminates us as suspects . . . for once," she added, nearly under her breath. "Enjoy the reception, for whatever reason we got the refreshments. Consular dues are staying the same this year." She mustered a broad smile, and sauntered off to the mansion to greet some late arriving guests, a great consular ship leaving tugboats in her wake.

"She really ought to be wearing a large floral hat," said Richard Sanderson, the British Consul General, who came over to join them. Then he turned somewhat red as his wife Emily, who happened to be wearing a hat that exactly fit that description, joined them as well. "What's that you are saying about hats, Dick?" she squinted at him.

"On you it looks grand, my dear," he blundered on. Sanderson's habit of blurting forth whatever came into his head was one of his most endearing qualities, although it wouldn't help his Foreign Office career. It was clearly time for Robbie to come to his colleague's rescue.

"We were talking about this Pryor business. It seems that Pryor was the least popular wine writer in Bordeaux. What have you heard?"

All business now, Sanderson nodded emphatically in total agreement. He had spent three years in Bordeaux, and seemed to know everybody. More than that, everybody seemed to know him, admitted it, and trusted him. He looked like just the sort of fellow, rounded and rather drooping like a plant that needed pruning, that you could trust with a confidence. He might not quite remember it if it had been worth forwarding to London, but he would remember you for having trusted him. The world was his club, and it was full of friends.

Sanderson had heard the same rumors about Pryor casks that Robbie had heard. Not that there was any official interest to any of this business, of course. A murder wasn't something a diplomat got mixed up in. Still, it made for some interesting speculation. "Not much expertise in Bordeaux wines myself, you understand. They all seem to taste about the same to me. Quite fine, of course, but now you take porter or ale, there is a man's drink. Emily, of course, would have a different point of view. I'm quite sure of that."

The orchestra began to play a medley of Andrew Lloyd Webber melodies. "Tuneful of course, but just a bit jarring in this setting," was Robbie's opinion. "You really are a romantic, aren't you, Robbie?" Sylvie said, making a discovery. He looked at her. Was that the first time she had used his first name, or just the first time he had caught her doing it?

Emily Sanderson prodded her husband, and they drifted off towards a tasting table.

Other consular colleagues nodded or exchanged a word or two. They were about half from the various career services, either ending their careers in Bordeaux, or hoping for a career boost from the experience of having run their country's consulate general. The other half were French citizens who were honorary consuls, appointed by foreign countries, and anxious for the social honors that their designations bestowed.

The honorary consuls varied in diligence and in ability. The best were helpful, and the least capable did no harm. The former represented their nations broadly, in matters ranging from the occasional report on matters of general business interest, to helping a business from that country find a representative in the region, to rescuing a stranded tourist. The latter probably, if pressed, could not have told you who was running the government in the foreign countries which had appointed and promptly forgotten them years before. All were colleagues. None made a franc or a euro from their activities.

It began to grow a little darker, and the mansion lights and lawn reception floodlights were turned on. Chateau Margaux's Palladian mansion set an elegant background for the reception. It was a beautiful sight, one that Robbie would remember long after he had left Bordeaux. He couldn't forget it. If he ever did, the chateau was etched on the label of Chateau Margaux wines, year after year, to remind him.

"What a shame that the topic of murder had ever come up in this beautiful place," he said to Sylvie.

"I know just what you mean. This setting, which makes lowered voices natural, argues that it should not, *mon ami*. Tell me, do you think Erika Lutz will rise to your bait. About our surveying wine chateau owners about Pryor, I mean?"

"Not directly, *chere amie*. But someone else will. I want her to spread the word that we are looking into the Pryor case, and how people felt about him. It's called fishing. We just may catch something before we leave."

"Should we try somebody else as well?"

"Probably not. We'll see. I think it would be a mistake to overdo it. We might lose credibility. Everyone loves a secret, particularly one that is spread by other people."

"Why were you so candid with Sanderson?"

"We just do with the Brits. Force of habit, and a good habit it is. We stick together." He thought for a moment. "From now on, let's just say that I was a witness to what happened at the Willard, and so naturally we're interested in Pryor. NOT that we're on the trail."

She nodded. "Shall we bring up the 'Pryor casks'? You did with Sanderson."

He thought for a mnute. "Sure. Why not?"

Champagne and fruit juices were being passed, and Robbie and Sylvie savored their second glasses of champagne. They decided that from to time while Robbie was talking with some of his diplomatic colleagues, she would have a separate word with wine estate owners.

"Then we'll compare notes," they agreed.

Sylvie found nobody who had a good word to say about Pryor. Most just kept silent about the murder. Some seemed relieved that the vintage could now be evaluated on its own merits, as they put it, rather than by Pryor's odd standards.

"Imagine marking wines with an A or an F," one estate owner said. "It's totally preposterous. So is any other marking system. We're making wines, not marking examination papers. You're French, *Mademoiselle.* You know that. Next thing you know, President Chirac will be handing out the *Legion d'Honneur* or the *Merite Agricole* to these scribblers. Anything to keep sales up!"

After a while she came back and stood by Robbie. "Not one other person admitted to knowing about a Pryor cask, much less having one," she sniffed. "I don't know whether to believe de Tourneau or not."

"Now that Pryor is dead, does it still make a difference? After all, now they will be destroyed. His death seems to remove a menace to the Bordeaux wine trade, provided that the vintage itself isn't somehow tarred with the scandal."

She frowned. "I don't think it is as easy as that. There is a lot of grumbling about scoring wines. Not that that is worth killing anybody over. Something else. There seems to be an atmosphere of caution, anticipation, not quite fear, almost 'who's next.' People are still very concerned. Yves Crespier of Chateau La Source was quite nervous. I think that he may talk with you. He was talking earlier with Erika Lutz. I saw them. He has something to say that he doesn't want me to know, I think."

Robbie's smile told the story. He was pleased. So now they really were conspirators!

"You've got good instincts. I'll check it out later. Look, the Prefect is here."

He was right. The Prefect, the highest ranking official in Bordeaux and the region of five departments that comprise the modern Aquitaine, was just entering the reception area. The Prefect's attendance at this reception meant that the Government itself was paying attention to reassuring the foreign wine buying public. France's system of prefects went back to Napoleon's idea of having resident high administrative officials answerable not locally, but to him. They remained the personal representatives of the President of France.

Prefects lived very well indeed, in mansions that often had been church property before the French Revolution. Robbie thought that if he had been French rather than American, he would have entered the career prefectural service, rather than the diplomatic corps. Why leave France, after all? Prefects, the top of the pyramid, were selected from a very fine cadre of career officials.

Robbie and Sylvie moved towards the first tasting table. Several wines from recent vintages, including a flask from the current vintage, aging in the cellars of the region, were offered. They took appreciative sips. "This is showing well already," he said. "It should sell for a good price. You know, one of my predecessors at the Consulate General, many years previously, spent some serious money on young wines of a very good vintage, and then had them stored in Bordeaux. He was in luck. Years later, when his children had grown up and started attending universities, he would cable from whatever part of the world he was then stationed in, with directions to sell off several cases of wine and wire the proceeds. That's how he paid for his children's education."

"Imagine having to pay for university," she replied.

"For heaven's sakes," Robbie said. "There's Elliot Hawkins, Deputy Chief of Mission from the Embassy in Paris, and his wife Marge at the next tasting table. Let's go over and say hello."

What was Elliot doing here? They filtered through the growing crowd and Robbie greeted the visitors, introducing Sylvie.

"Ah yes, the intrepid journalist. Your stories are causing quite a stir. Expect it won't be too long before a Paris newspaper or television station snaps you up," Elliot cooed to Sylvie, who beamed with pleasure, and then went off to chat with some of the wine growers. Elliot was in good form. You usually had to finish his sentences mentally when he was feeling chipper.

It turned out that he had in fact called. "You ought to check your messages at the office a bit more frequently, old sod," came the chiding reminder from Hawkins. "Marge and I were invited to come in Paris by the owners. The weekend was free, so we drove down. Didn't want to trouble you. We're staying at the Relais de Margaux, of course, just a stone's throw."

Elliot pulled Robbie slightly aside. "Would be good to have a chat, though, if you have some time tomorrow. We'll be over at St. Emilion for the afternoon. How about an early luncheon at the Plaisance?"

Robbie agreed to drive over and meet them for luncheon at noon. It turned out that they had arranged a tasting in nearby Pomerol for the early afternoon, and then would be driving back to Paris directly. Robbie looked forward to it. The Hostellerie de Plaisance was one of his favorite restaurants in the entire region. If they were lucky, they would get a window table and have a nice view of the scenic town while they enjoyed luncheon.

The Prefect, Albert Demonthon, came towards their table, escorted by Erika Lutz. Robbie extended his hand, and introduced Elliot and Marge Hawkins, using full titles all around.

"Ah yes, *Monsieur le Ministre*, welcome to the Aquitaine Region. I understand that your Senator Etchevari may be visiting us in a few weeks."

"Yes indeed, *Monsieur le Prefet*. Robbie here has been consulting with your security experts"—Demonthon, who already knew this, nodded his head in acknowledgement—"and while the visit is not yet confirmed by the Senator's office, we are certain that he will come. He should be spending most of his time over on the coast, I'd expect."

"Naturally. That's also part of my Aquitaine region, of course, but you'll be talking with my colleague over at Pau?" His slight inflection made the statement, directed to Robbie, a question.

"Certainly, *Monsieur le Prefet,* but Bayonne and Biarritz will be my first ports of call." That made sense, for that is where Robbie would speak first with security officials responsible for the Basque region. Their French department, the Pyrenees-Atlantiques, was headquartered in the mountain resort town of Pau in the interior.

"Security will be appropriate for the visit, *Monsieur le Consul,*" Demonthon said rather stiffly. "That won't be a problem. I hope that we'll have news soon about the disgraceful graffiti at the Consulate General. I can't believe, though, that that really was the ETA. It was not like them, and it certainly does not serve their interests. We suspect that more probably it was a local hoodlum, or some young people on a dare who had had too much to drink on a Saturday night. We'll continue to look into it, though, of course.

"Ah, here comes Commissioner Moineau. I'd better leave police details to him. I hope that you enjoy the reception and"—he turned to Elliot—"your visit with us, *Monsieur le Ministre.*" He turned and greeted the Sandersons.

Commissioner Jacques Moineau came towards them, saw Robbie and brightened. He looked more than ever like Claude Rains, Robbie thought. With a little formal bow Moineau acknowledged the introduction of Elliot Hawkins, then cheerfully announced that an informer had told police that afternoon that the pouch theft had in all probability been the work of a small time thief well-known in the local milieu.

"We had some luck," Moineau said. "Drinking at the bar of a seedy cafe near the railroad station, the thief had been bemoaning his luck. He was overheard by one of our police informers. The man was a purse snatcher who plied his craft in public places around the city. *Monsieur le Consul's* appearance with the pouch had looked like a good opportunity. It had seemed valuable, but the thief hadn't counted on being chased, and the fact that several *gendarmes* were on duty there. He probably had just enough time to cut open the pouch and remove whatever was inside. We found the pouch, but not the contents. I hope there was nothing of value, or important?"

Robbie agreed that was so. "What will you do with him now?"

"We've already taken him in. He will be put out of circulation for a while," Moineau said. "There is enough to hold him even without the pouch theft. Probably we'll offer him a deal if he confesses."

"That sounds fine to me," Robbie said. "It beats asking authority from my government to waive my immunity so that I can testify, then spending a morning in court. Congratulations on solving the theft. That ought to end the matter."

Marge had strolled off, and Elliot started in search of her. Then on an impulse he turned back to Robbie. "How's it going here?" he said. It sounded a bit forced.

"Just fine. I'm enjoying being in charge, frankly."

Elliot smiled warmly. "Yes, it's fun. But don't let your guard down too far, Robbie. Diplomacy can be a tricky profession. See you tomorrow."

Now what the blazes had he meant by that?

Robbie strolled around the reception, admiring the grounds of the estate, and the profile of Chateau Margaux, now in silhouette as the daylight ended. There were more invited guests than he had first imagined, and the crowd noise was now a pleasant buzz, punctuated from time to time by amused laughter.

Sylvie caught up with him. "How about a look about the aging cellars? One of the winemasters is giving a private tour for a few people, if you are interested."

She didn't have to ask twice. The tour included the fermenting cask area, and both aging cellars. The miracle was that the second aging cellar, which lay below the first, was set even below the water table itself. All *Medoc* land was low-lying, but here that was especially true. They had to establish special generators, and a private backup system in the event of a power failure, to prevent the cellar from collapsing due to the water pressure. It was a superior feat of engineering.

The cellars were spacious and elegant. The tour ended, as they had hoped, with a private tasting of several of the recent Margaux vintages. They liked the 1990 best. "What a sublime wine," Sylvie said. "It is so rich,—so elegant. You're going to laugh, but I seem to smell violets."

"Bravo, Sylvie," Robbie said with appreciation. "That's a Margaux characteristic. What a shame the wine costs so much."

Sylvie and Robbie emerged from the building and walked towards the mansion and the reception area beyond. They saw that tables had been arranged in the parking lot outside the cellars. A truck was being unloaded by several workmen, puffing away at Gauloises cigarettes as they worked.

Curious, Robbie walked over to the truck, and saw that cases of wine were the cargo, as well as boxes containing the colorful paraphernalia of their co-host, the *Confrerie des Vins du Medoc.* There were corkscrews, aprons with the *Confrerie's* initialled insignia, and paperback guidebooks to the region.

Behind the tables, women arranged reception favors of bottles of wine and souvenirs in cloth bags for the departing guests. "That's a nice gesture," Robbie noted appreciatively. "I hope that we get lucky with the wine."

"Typical American reaction," Sylvie teased him. "What do they say in the theater…'There are no small roles, just small actors.' These wines are *all* good. Some are less well known than others. But these are the wines that you should drink when you want something not fancy, but good and affordable. That is probably nine times out of ten, I'd guess."

"Bravo, *Mademoiselle*," came an unexpected echo. Guy Leblanc, the Consulate General's Commercial Officer, emerged from the shadows near the truck. "That is our biggest problem in the *Confre-*

rie, getting a larger market for our lesser known wines." Leblanc wore the *Confrerie's* ceremonial apron.

"I hadn't realized that you were also affiliated with the *Confrerie.* That explains those long luncheons, surely," Robbie kidded.

"As you say, *Monsieur le Consul.* The best way to understand what is going on in the commercial life of this region is to take part in it. One finds out a great many things. That's why I volunteer some time with the *Confrerie.*"

Sylvie's reporter instincts were aroused. "We've been finding that out ourselves. In fact, we've been told some unusual things today. What do you know about Pryor casks? Is that a widespread practice?"

"People talk about it. I've heard those stories. Frankly, *Mademoiselle,* I doubt that the story is true. It seems to me like something that people make up to explain away their own failures. Then, like any urban mythology, the story spreads. Everybody has heard it, but nobody quite knows someone who actually does it."

He hesitated for a moment and then continued on, struck by a new idea.

"Why not do a real story, *Mademoiselle,* about the nonexistent Pryor casks? You could interview all sorts of people, surface the myth, and then explode it. That would be a real help to the region. Something positive would come out of Pryor's death after all. And now, please excuse me. I've got to supervise this end of things." He gave a polite little salute and disappeared onto the truck.

"I should have thought of that," Sylvie said to Robbie. "Murder or no murder, that's worth a story. Let's rejoin the others at the reception."

The reception was beginning to wind down. Clearly Prefect Demonthon had already left, a signal to the other guests. Here and there, pockets of guests spun out their own conversations. These ranged, Robbie was amused to overhear, from an appreciation of the wines served: "...Very good quality, but last year's vintage was better..." to the latest political news: "...Horrifying, but what can one expect from politicians..." to the fate of Bordeaux's soccer team, the Girondins: "...Thank heavens they are on the move again in the First Division. They won again last week at the *Stade Municipal.* Beat Marseilles 4-1 this time!"

They stopped, recognizing some friendly faces Inevitably, someone asked Robbie about what Americans really thought of France.

Robbie gave his patented little speech. He tried to make it sound fresh and original, composed on the spot. Actually, the reason for the question always puzzled him. France was our oldest ally, and that meant something. Was this like a wife who had been married some years checking on her husband's affections? He always thought that if you had to ask, there were problems.

He soldiered on "...We admire French culture, but don't really understand it. The language is hard to learn, so we pretend that you don't want us to do so. Deep down, we probably think that you have mastered a secret that eludes us, how to live well and really enjoy the moment. We are still 'pursuing happiness.' You French seem to have found it."

Leaving the reception area, Robbie and Sylvie joined an impromptu pedestrian traffic jam as the guests lined up to receive their gifts. Shaking hands with each guest as they left were Guy Leblanc and Yves Crespier, President of the *Confrerie* and owner of Chateau La Source farther north in the *Medoc.* Crespier saw them coming and stepped out of the line. Nodding towards Leblanc, he said "I gather that you have been running down that legend of the Pryor casks."

Sylvie nodded in agreement, hoping that he would continue.

He was in a mood to make a point. His tone was settled and rather grim. "You know, I work hard, as my father and grandfather did before me, to make a good wine at a reasonable price. I don't like cutting corners. Anybody who would do that by faking a vintage tasting to get a favorable review from a wine writer is beneath contempt. We would certainly expel him from the *Confrerie*. I'm sure they would also do that in the *Jurade de St. Emilion,* or any other respectable organization."

"What would you make of somebody who claimed not only to know all about Pryor casks, but was prepared to use one?"

"*Mademoiselle,* such a person is probably making an inferior wine. Either that, or calling attention to himself for reasons of his own. Either way, do not take any such admission at face value."

He leaned towards Robbie. "*Monsieur le Consul,* we all regret that you have been threatened by the ETA. They are a disgrace to the great Basque people. I hope that you are taking the necessary security precautions."

Robbie was surprised. "Actually, the police have almost written that off as a drunken prank in very bad taste." He saw no need to share anything more with Crespier.

"The police can make mistakes. Anybody can. But you must look after yourself. And please come and visit Chateau La Source soon. It would be a pleasure to welcome you both."

Puzzled by these differing reactions, Robbie and Sylvie tried to sort out what they had heard during the day as they drove back to Bordeaux.

"First, de Tourneau swears that Pryor casks exist, shows us one, and says that the practice is widespread," Robbie began.

"Then Leblanc says that is all wrong."

"The Prefect tells me that Basque security is under control."

"And then Crespier claims exactly the contrary."

"None of this is exactly helpful in sorting out who killed Pryor," Sylvie added.

"Maybe not, but it sure made for a nice day in the wine country."

She dropped him off at the *Quai des Chartrons.* Minouette, who always seemed to know when he was returning, was waiting up, as usual. An international call from Uncle Seth, "checking up on my favorite nephew," could be returned in the morning.

Robbie dropped off to sleep with impressions of wine, picnics, Chateau Margaux, Sylvie, the ETA, and murder stirring in his mind, not necessarily in that order.

CHAPTER 8

Sunday In St. Emilion

St. Emilion was Robbie's favorite destination for a leisurely Sunday drive, and, he liked to imagine, his own private discovery. It was only an hour or so from Bordeaux, east across the Stone Bridge, with Libourne and its medieval arcaded market square the only town of any size between the two. An easy drive past St. Emilion were Bergerac and the Dordogne.

This small town, with its winding streets and stone houses whose window boxes exuded flowers, would be worth visiting for its old world charm alone. But St. Emilion, together with adjoining Pomerol, was a magnet for wine fanciers around the world. Thank heavens most of them never made the trip. Hilly, bordered on all sides by wine estates that protruded into the plateau surrounding the town itself, St. Emilion boasted a church that had literally been carved out of rock during the Middle Ages. That is where the *Jurade* held its ceremonies.

The wine order, *La Jurade de St. Emilion*, was founded by King John, brother of Richard the Lionhearted, in 1199. "Aside from Magna Carta, doubtless the best thing he ever did," Pryor had once written. Under it the burghers of St. Emilion were granted some self-governing authority, including the right to set the grape harvest dates each fall.

The modern day *Jurade* had been revived after the Second World War by a highly regarded local vintner who planned it during his years in a German labor camp. And now the town prospered, and each year *Jurade m*embers proclaimed the harvest from the King's Tower within the hilly town. They also, Robbie knew, held colorful membership ceremonies each year, about the time that Senator Etchevari was visiting. He made a mental note to check that out.

Robbie drove his Ford into the town, past the church in the upper town, and the colorful ruined abbey wall that served as a scenic vineyard backdrop, and parked. Elliot and Marge Hawkins had just arrived, and they came over to greet him.

"We can't go back to Paris without buying some wines. What would you suggest?"

Robbie gestured across the parking area to the exposition hall that served as a community wine salesroom. A bit early for luncheon, they spent a pleasant twenty minutes taking a look at the wines on display. Elliot selected a mixed case of wines. What a pleasure it was to have a good wine assortment at every price range, so near the vineyards that freshness and quality were guaranteed. One didn't even have to spend twenty dollars for a fine bottle of wine.

"I may just stay here for my entire career," Robbie said.

They left their purchases in their cars, and walked to the nearby Hostellerie de Plaisance. They were in luck, with a nice table that looked over the lower town and had a fine view of the vineyards beyond.

"I was thinking that the *Jurade* will be having its June membership ceremony at about the time that Senator Etchevari will be in town. Perhaps he'd enjoy being part of it," Robbie offered. Might as well show the visiting Embassy fireman that he could think constructively even in these surroundings.

"Good idea. I've heard it is one of the most colorful wine ceremonies in France." Robbie took that as a subtle go ahead to try to arrange including Hawkins as well. The Ambassador had been included in 1999, when the *Jurade* had marked its 800th anniversary, and Hawkins was next in line at the Embassy.

Marge Hawkins was relaxed and very pleased by the little town and the luncheon setting. It seemed to be just everything that Omaha, Nebraska had lacked, and had all that pretentious restaurants back home tried to copy. This was the real thing.

They shared a bottle of white Montmorency with their first course. Dry and fruity, it complemented their *Coquilles St. Jacques* perfectly. A medium St. Emilion red wine was next, fragrant and flavorful with their leg of lamb, asparagus *hollandaise* and roast new potatoes. There was enough wine left to go with their cheese course, taken from the tray, three cheeses each. Then the array of desserts proved irresistible despite the fact that they had all stopped being hungry half an hour earlier, at least.

Coffee followed, and then a second cup, served with a St. Emilion specialty, macaroon cookies. Robbie told them about his drive with Sylvie through the *Graves* and *Medoc* wine regions the previous day. That interested Elliot. "We're really looking forward to our visit to Pomerol after luncheon. It isn't every day that one gets to visit Chateau Petrus."

"That's true, but don't expect a real chateau. The priciest wine in the whole Bordeaux region actually comes from a holding whose 'chateau' looks like a small-sized Pennsylvania farmhouse. That has nothing to do with their wines, of course. But if you don't expect too much from the house, you won't be disappointed. The wine itself, of course, is great. So are the surrounding vineyards."

Robbie couldn't resist sketching for them on the back of a spare menu the location of some of the Pomerol and St. Emilion estates that were neighbors to Chateau Petrus. Elliot folded the little drawing and kept it for reference.

"Actually, we're all becoming more interested in wine questions, since this Pryor business," Elliot said. "Did you know him well?"

"No, just by sight, really. But I was at the Willard Hotel that night, as you know. Also, we got that letter from him at the Consulate General, mailed from Washington just before his death. As Moineau told us, the pouch has been recovered, and meanwhile I've sent a copy of the letter on to the D.C. police."

"Good. Send me a copy at the Embassy."

"I've been rather caught up in the Pryor case since my return. But it all seems to be calming down now," Robbie added.

"He visited with us in Paris during his last trip," Elliot said. "That was just after he had had his first, preliminary round of tastings here on the new vintage. He did some grumbling. Apparently it might not have been up to snuff. I suppose he was coming back to check out his first impressions."

"Careful, Marge," he said as she coughed, and signalled that a piece of macaroon cookie had gone down the wrong way. He gave her a slight slap between the shoulders, and she took a sip of water, and excused herself. The men rose as she left. "At least it wasn't a pretzel," Robbie said.

"What do you make of this ETA business?" Elliot asked.

"It puzzles me. I take it you mean the spray-painting at the Consulate. I find it hard to take seriously. Anyway, security for Senator Etchevari shouldn't be much of a problem."

"Yes," Elliot said pensively. "But watch yourself, anyway. They are an irrational bunch, the ETA." He tapped his glass several times absent-mindedly with his spoon before continuing. "I suppose poor reviews of the vintage would have been really bad news," he ventured.

"That would have been rough on the entire region," Robbie said. "After a number of so-so vintages in a row, everybody is hoping for a very good year. They all need it to pay off their new equipment.

"Plus, if you ask me, American wines are really beginning to eat into French markets. What comes out of California is of increasingly high quality. The French used to joke about it. They don't anymore. They must recapture those lost markets, or maybe they'll lose them for good. Gone is the time when an American Consul General could serve American wines at dinner, as one used to do here a few years ago, and have it regarded as a friendly act."

Elliot smiled in agreement. "I've heard that some producers down here even stand to lose their properties if the string of lackluster vintage years continues. Now there's a motivation if I've ever heard one, at least to produce a good quality wine, and to be furious if it gets panned."

Robbie nodded. "That's what I hear, too. By the way, have you heard of 'Pryor casks?'"

Elliot was all attention. Robbie told him what he and Sylvie had heard at Chateau Montmorency "That's odd," Elliot said. "We just had their white wine. I thought it was delicious. Why would they have to fake it for a barrel tasting?" Robbie nodded his agreement.

"Of course, some wine estates deny the whole thing," Robbie went on. "But with no more Pryor, they would deny it."

"Sounds reasonable to me," Elliot agreed. They rose as Marge returned. "Feel better, dear?"

"Yes, much better, thank you. How are we doing on timing?"

"No problem. We're due at Petrus in forty minutes."

"You can make it with no problem, provided you don't get lost on the small country roads. Here, let me show you." Elliot took out the map Robbie had drawn. "Take a close look at Chateau Figeac and Chateau Cheval Blanc on the way. They're the two best St. Emilion estates on the plain, away from this little town."

"Oh yes, and before we go, let me give you a heads up on a couple of items," Elliot said. "Tim Everbright will be coming down in a couple of days. He wants to check out the Etchevari visit." Robbie nodded in acknowledgement. It seemed a reasonable precaution from the Embassy's point of view.

"Also, there will be a Consuls General meeting at the Embassy just before the Etchevari visit. I'm sure that Stan Bartlett will be able to handle things for a couple of days while you join us. Ambassador Adams will want a first-hand report from you then. He'll also be reassured to hear what the Prefect told us last night about security. That alone was worth our visit."

"So is this view," Marge said, reluctant to leave it.

They stood, and the men divided the check, one-third for Robbie. "With two bureaucrats involved, let's have no nonsense about grabbing the check," Elliot said.

Marge smiled at Robbie and thanked him for his suggestions on seeing the wine country that afternoon. "Why don't you plan to stay with us in Paris?"

"Come on, Marge. Here's an eligible single young man on the prowl in the City of Light, and you want him to be respectable after hours?"

After that raucous interjection from Elliot, Robbie could only accept. "Besides," he tossed in, "My kid sister will be visiting Bordeaux just then, and I'm sure that she will appreciate your looking after me."

"Sure she wouldn't like to join you?"

"Ordinarily yes, but she knows Paris fairly well, and this is her first visit to her big brother's diplomatic post. She wants to visit some wine estates too. I'll mention it, but I suspect she'll want to spend the few days of her vacation in Bordeaux. Thanks for the invitation, though."

They left the restaurant. and Marge and Elliot waved goodbye as Robbie walked down the crowded small streets to the lower town. Why not check out some wine shops, talk with the knowledgeable clerks, and then while away an hour at a cafe before driving back to Bordeaux?

Something about the luncheon conversation wasn't quite right, but he couldn't put his finger on it. Come to think of it, why had Elliot invited him to join their lunch in the first place? It didn't seem to make much sense. Too bad Sylvie wasn't there. She could have figured it out, or perhaps just told him that he was imagining things.

Robbie drove slowly back to Bordeaux. He considered taking a detour for some sightseeing. Heaven knows there were plenty of great places to visit, like the Toulouse Lautrec estate, Chateau Malrome, on this side of the Garonne River. No, better have some down time to rest while he could. It would be a busy week.

He remembered Uncle Seth's call. Great Uncle Seth B. Cutler, actually, to give that family legend his full due. He smiled at the thought of being Uncle Seth's "favorite," and only nephew. Only grand-nephew, really. Robbie looked forward to speaking with him. Given the time difference between Bordeaux and New England, he would be just getting Uncle Seth before Sunday dinner, on his return from church.

Uncle Seth was a creature of habit, and that characteristic did not define him. Instead, it gave some shape to a career that had fascinated Robbie, and half the United States, for that matter. As a very young man, just before the Second World War, he had settled in inevitably at a private bank in Boston, just for a year or so, before being asked to join the Office of Strategic Services.

Operating out of wartime London, first as a liaison officer with British SOE and then on the ground in Occupied France and within Germany itself, Uncle Seth's full range of exploits could only be guessed at, or gleaned from time to time as survivors wrote their memoirs. He retained from that period a talent for high-level intrigue, and a way of viewing life as a precious diminishing resource.

Early on, he had realized that the life of a Boston banker no longer appealed. He decided not to accept the offer from Allen Dulles to help build the new Central Intelligence Agency that rose from what remained of the 0SS. Instead, Uncle Seth did the unexpected, and not for the first time. He chucked the active life, or at least his family thought he had done so, for a professorship of modern history at St. Mark's, a prestigious private boys' secondary school near Boston.

The school evolved, with Uncle Seth as professor, then Dean of Students, and finally as Headmaster, leading the way. St. Mark's broke all the old status, social and racial bars. Then young women were admitted, gradually at first, then in equal numbers. Under Uncle Seth's inspired leadership, St. Mark's became a model for secondary school education that other schools emulated, usually with a lag time of years.

In the process, Uncle Seth became nationally known, even gracing the cover of *Time* Magazine before becoming their Man Of The Year. He resisted numerous offers to join any political administration in Washington actively, although he did serve on commissions that sought to reconcile the national security with democracy. His retirement from St. Mark's was national news.

Now the journalists left him alone, which suited Uncle Seth perfectly. Let them think that he was out to pasture.

There wasn't any aunt to think about, and never would be. Robbie had once, as a very young boy, broached that taboo subject at a family Thanksgiving Dinner. "Didn't you ever want to marry, Uncle Seth?" There were gasps around the table, and a look of pain on Uncle Seth's face. Robbie had gotten up from the table and gone around to take the old man's hand. He stammered a heartfelt "I'm sorry, Uncle Seth," for whatever unknown hurt he had brought back to flickering life. Uncle Seth had rewarded him with a kindly smile, and the incident cemented their closeness.

Much later, Robbie's father had told him about the spirited young English girl, who had been captured and murdered in France during the German occupation. She was a member of SOE, the Special Operations Executive, created by Winston Churchill to "set Europe ablaze" during the Nazi occupations. Uncle Seth was then American OSS liaison to SOE in London, and they had met and fallen in love immediately. She had not survived the war. That was all that Robbie's father could tell him.

It was after that mission that Uncle Seth's reputation for reckless daring had grown. He tempted the fates as though to mock them and his own survival, leaving his liaison work for drops behind enemy lines, volunteering so often that senior officers from time to time gave him less dangerous tasks for his own good. But he had, after all, survived, and now there were generations of young men and women, former students whom he could regard as his children.

Robbie had wanted to learn more about the young woman, and what had happened to her. Now that his consular district actually included the Dordogne, where her mission had taken place, that had seemed possible. But somehow the time was never right, and he couldn't imagine how to get more details from Uncle Seth. No, the thing was impossible.

The spires of Bordeaux came into sight, and Robbie crossed the Stone Bridge and turned right, towards the *Quai des Chartrons*. He stopped his car near the Quinconces and bought a selection of newspapers and, after some searching, also found an open store where some fresh bread baguettes were for sale, and some dry catfood.

Then he drove home, parking the car in its assigned space in the parking garage, and walked to his apartment, newspapers, baguettes and bag of catfood under his arm. "Anybody would say I'm a regular Frenchman out for a Sunday stroll," he mused, pleased with himself. He resisted the temptation to walk past the Consulate General and check for new messages from the ETA.

* * *

After attending an early mass, Sylvie had spent the morning at the newspaper, first writing and rewriting her story, and then arguing with her editor when the story was killed. Gone were the days of wondering whether she would be hired as a reporter, or even whether she would be accepted once she started work. Now, she ruefully thought, she was like all the other reporters, having to put up with heavy-handed editorial interference. *Tant pis* that they owned the newspaper!

She had burst in on her editor, Jacques Lebrun, full of excitement with her story, and watched with curiosity which turned to concern and then dismay as she studied his reaction. Lebrun, a fortyish man, stylish and bred to Bordeaux, made it abundantly clear that he was not about to emulate Washington *Post* Editor Ben Bradlee. Bordeaux was not Washington, and the Bordeaux wine trade was not Watergate.

"You don't have one shred of usable evidence about these so-called Pryor casks," he had snorted. Her enthusiasm was stopped cold. She was about to give him a piece of her mind, but then his tone changed and she heard him out.

"I must say, though, that I admire your initiative. The murder, and your writing skills, are why I assigned you to the story. Keep at it and get me some solid proof, something I can use. But don't ask me to destroy the reputation of the wine industry of this entire region based upon what you've been told by one source who won't go public. That's not enough."

Sylvie went back to her desk and stared at her computer, typed in several questions for later follow-up, saved her story, turned off her computer, and left the office in the old section of the city.

Every instinct, feminine and journalistic, told her that she was onto something here, something important. Maybe a printed story could have flushed out even more. But Lebrun wasn't willing to take that chance. From his point of view he was probably right, she conceded. Still, it was galling to kill the story. It was more galling still to know that tomorrow morning, her routine assignments would start once again. That probably meant more sanitation workers' problems and transportation funding delays. *Merde*!

She walked over to the Rue St. Catherine and now, feeling quite put upon, entered the McDonald's and ordered a Big Mac and a coke. Where was it that Robbie had said last night that he was having lunch? Oh yes, the Hostellerie de Plaisance over at St. Emilion. It was a fine place with, she was sure, great cuisine. She envied Robbie. Probably never catch him in a McDonald's! Well, she would pursue that later.

Maybe it was time to look into that ETA threat, that everyone said was bogus. That might be a lead worth pursuing. She finished her Big Mac, walked back to *Sud-Ouest*, and spent several hours researching the newspaper's past coverage of Basque terrorism, taking notes. Nobody would ever accuse her again of not being thorough.

Robbie decided that he had definitely been neglecting Minouette. Or rather, she reminded him of that fact by a chorus of meows. He opened the new bag of dry catfood and put some in her dish. She strolled over, sniffed it, and looked up with disdain. He could almost hear her thoughts: "Couldn't you do better than that?"

He stroked her back and tail, and then let her chase a catnip mouse tied onto an elastic string. Everytime she came close, he pulled the string, while she pounced. Robbie remembered that the writer Montaigne had wondered whether he was playing with his cat, or whether his cat was playing with him. It was probably a bit of both. Then, tired, Minouette curled up on the couch and dropped off to sleep.

Robbie remembered a dinner that he had attended in the Dordogne the previous fall, to celebrate St. Hubert, the patron saint of hunters. On the grounds, as the hounds were blessed by the village priest, there had been a falconer holding one of the raptor birds. Robbie had been fascinated by the fierceness of the falcon's eyes. They seemed to match the temperament of the barons who had kept these birds of prey in the Middle Ages, independent, uncivilized, unruly and battle-hardened, graceful and savage at the same time.

Perhaps, Robbie thought, people and their pets resemble each other. There may be some evolution here. The early barons kept raptor birds. And now I have this Siamese cat! Minouette, as if approving this thought, yawned in her sleep. On second thought it dawned on Robbie that whether his pet was a fierce hunter or domestic pet did not depend, after all, on the point of view of the cat. She was certainly both.

The Dordogne made him think of Uncle Seth. Time to return his call. Now there was a man who could have kept falcons. He wondered if the idea had ever occurred to his uncle.

"Hello there, Uncle Seth. This is Robbie. returning your call from Bordeaux. I hope my timing is convenient."

"Yes, indeed. I'm just in from church. Boring, predictable sermon, but the music was nice. I hear that you have been having an interesting time in Bordeaux."

"Interesting" covered a lot of territory for Uncle Seth. It could have referred to everything from a well-performed concert to an earthquake.

"If you mean the ETA threat painted on the Consulate General door, it did give me the chills at first."

"I do mean that. There was a brief news account of that in the Boston papers. There weren't many details. I kept looking, but no follow-up stories. I thought I would call and inquire in case your parents saw it. I'll be seeing them tomorrow night for their anniversary, their fortieth, you'll remember."

Robbie gulped. He had forgotten, but now he would be able to call them on time, thanks to Uncle Seth. And also thanks to some catalogs from home, and a credit card, now he would also be able to call and arrange delivery of a suitable present. Late, but he would have remembered.

"The police say that it was probably a prank, if that's the right word. There was nothing in the Basque language, unlike previous ETA threats. I'm looking out for myself, but it's stretching things to say that this was a real threat from the ETA."

"I'm relieved to hear that. I don't take kindly to the idea of threats against my favorite nephew. National terrorist movements were never quite my specialty, but it did seem rather odd their targetting an American, and an official at that. Not quite their game, really. It could get them into a lot of trouble if they started doing that."

"That's right. The Police said that, too. Perhaps a prank?"

"Maybe, but I must say, it would take a very odd sense of humor to go painting an ETA threat on a Consulate General door. Particularly since 9/11. Perhaps there was a message there, but not from the ETA."

Robbie chewed on that for a moment. That possibility had never occurred to him.

"By the way," Uncle Seth continued, "I hear that Evalyn will be over visiting you in a month or so. The trip will do her good. Keep up your reading. I know Evalyn looks forward to seeing the wine country. Meanwhile, I'll be informally meeting with some friends at the old firm in a bit. You'll hear from me about the time that Evalyn arrives there.

This meant, Robbie understood, that Uncle Seth was far from satisfied with what he had just heard about the ETA episode. He was going to do his own private research, and let him know using their old book code if he turned up anything.

The book code was old-fashioned, of course, and there were more modern methods, but Uncle Seth preferred to stick with secure methods. "We won't use e-mail," he had once said, "if there is anything confidential. Half the intelligence services on the globe must now be tapping in, and making profiles of the correspondence. You may take that as a given."

Robbie continued their elliptical conversation. "That'll be fine, Uncle Seth. I'd appreciate it. If you're in Washington, by the way, I'd also appreciate any further details on the death of that wine writer Pryor at the Willard Hotel. I was there that night, you know. I'm afraid that the French Desk at State has priorities that seem more urgent than than letting their Consul in Bordeaux know about the investigation. Besides, it would raise my stock with a certain lady journalist here."

"Understood." Robbie could almost see the twinkle in Uncle Seth's eyes.

"By the way, Uncle Seth, do you keep a pet these days?"

"Why yes, still a German shepherd. Why do you ask?"

"Just wondering. And thanks very much for the reminder about my parents' anniversary. It had slipped my mind, one thing and another, and I'm pleased to have been reminded. Now I'll be able to call them and arrange delivery of something nice."

"Don't mention it. Glad to oblige." The Yankeeisms were a nice reminder of home. "And look after yourself. A little caution never hurts."

"I'll try. By the way, Uncle Seth, what do you know about Senator Etchevari? He'll be visiting here, so I'll be seeing a lot of him. He's something of a legend with the Basque people, as I'm sure you know. What sort of person is he?"

"A solid man, one you can trust. Liberal in the outmoded, good sense. You'll like him and, what's more important, he'll like you. He's quite genuine. Odd you should be asking."

"Why?"

"You're the second person within half an hour to call, and ask my opinion of Senator Etchevari."

"Who was the first?"
"The President of the United States."

CHAPTER 9

Welcome For A Senator

Typical dreary newspaper Monday morning! Sylvie stared at her rejected story, and at the notes that she had made herself the previous afternoon for follow-up. Then she began reading the newspaper's past stories on the ETA and Basque nationalism. Really, there didn't seem to be anything here that would warrant an American connection.

So why had the American Consul been threatened?

Jacques Lebrun, seeking to make amends in his courtly way for his abrupt dismissal of her story on Sunday, called her into his booklined office. "The latest leak from Mayor Juppe's office is a possible visit to the Basque region by an American Senator, William J. Etchevari." He coughed. "That," he added, "may be worth pursuing."

He was pleased that she had thought already to consult the files on Basque issues. "The official opinion is that there was nothing but a drunken prankster behind that spray-painting at the American Consulate General," he said. "I think that is probably right. On the other hand, it does give you an angle to follow, in connection with the Etchevari visit Why don't you look into all that with your friend, the American Consul?"

So Lebrun had been at Margaux after all! She would have been more surprised at his absence. His go-ahead was good news. It was an assignment of a major story. She would handle it well, justifying her editor's confidence.

Now she faced a tactical problem of a different sort. Robbie really should have called her yesterday, after their Saturday together. Impossible man! Now, should she wait for that call, or preempt it with a call of her own on this story? She decided to call Robbie and let him suggest a meeting.

Monday morning was not Robbie's favorite time. It always seemed as though some meeting was being held so that action could be said to be taken on a dicey bureaucratic matter. At least, that is how it often seemed during Robbie's recent tour of duty in the Department of State. While the meetings were being held, the real work piled up.

Here it was different. Here Robbie was in charge. With a small, good staff, and a lot of work to get through every week, Robbie liked to get on top of things and plan the week's activities. You could get a handle on things, and not be thrown off track by the unexpected.

His private phone rang next to his desk. It was Sylvie. Whoops! With everything that had happened yesterday, he had forgotten to call. But she didn't give him time to blurt out an explanation, much less an apology. Why did the word "apology" cross his mind, anyway? There wasn't any reason why he should apologize. It was not as if they were engaged, or anything.

"Hello, *Monsieur le Consul.* I'm calling you on newspaper business."

So they were back to being formal. She must really be annoyed. That was for sure.

"Perhaps we can have a little talk? My editor wants me to look into the ETA and the Basque issues." Well, that was technically accurate now, she thought. "No great hurry for the story, but I'm anxious to start my research. Anything new about the spray-painting at your Consulate?"

Robbie managed to stop her flow of chatter and put in a word of explanation. "Sylvie, sweet of you to cheer up my dreary Monday morning. I should have called you yesterday. Sorry, got caught up with my Embassy visitors. No, nothing new on the spray-painting. It's a police matter, really. I'm sure you'll find out the latest from them."

That was true, she knew, but entirely too abrupt. He was drawing back. Was that because they had gotten along so well? These men and their fears of getting close. Did Robbie Cutler have "bachelor" engraved on his forehead? He was sounding like it.

Why was I so abrupt? he puzzled. He thought he heard something over the phone. What could it have been, an intake of breath, or perhaps a barely audible, involuntary sigh? He felt alone. It didn't feel good. It was not where they had been, and not where he wanted to be. This was new to him, and he didn't understand. Better try the soft soap once again. It would be nice to see her, after all.

He decided to enlist her help. Why not? She was bright and knowledgeable, and he could use her perspective. Then he got angry with himself. Why was he making up excuses to see her again, and selfish ones at that? Was he that much of a confirmed bachelor? Did he really need his space that much? He saw himself for a moment as another Everbright, pompous and unhappy and suffused with rank. He shivered. What to do? A second or two yawned before them.

"Sylvie, let's talk about the Basque situation soon. Can't talk just now. Will it keep for a day or two? Now, sorry, I'm up to my ears in work. Hawkins from the Embassy told me over the weekend that the Embassy Consul General will be coming to Bordeaux soon, and I'll have to squire him around. He's a real bore, Sylvie, but he writes my annual report, so don't quote me!"

She giggled. That sounded honest, and the ice was broken. He had gotten around whatever negative feelings he had by making an excuse, projecting them on someone else. "Anyway, I'm going over to

Bayonne and Biarritz," he added. "You do some research while I'm over there, and then we'll compare notes."

She murmured agreement, very matter of fact so that he would not understand and she would not have to acknowledge to herself the sense of relief that she felt. They would continue after all. How and when would they get to the next stage? It was up to him.

Robbie remembered his conversation with Mayor Alain Juppe about attending a soccer match. The Bordeaux Girondins would be playing several matches at home this week. Sylvie was probably a fan. Let's see. He found the schedule in his top desk drawer and glanced at it.

"Say, I haven't seen the Girondins play this year. I see that they are playing Paris St. Germain later this week. Maybe we can get into the Mayor's box if you are interested."

She was.

"I'll call back shortly. I'll look forward to comparing notes with you. It'll be nice to see you again. I had a nice day Saturday."

"So did I."

As he put the phone down, Ghislaine brought him the unclassified office mail, which included a letter from the French Desk at the State Department. The District of Columbia police were investigating the Pryor murder, and no leads seemed promising, at least that they were talking about. Several clippings from the *Post* tracked what was public. They also noted that Pryor was well-fixed financially, and that in the past he had "worked for the Government," whatever that meant.

He clicked on his e-mail. There was a brief note from former Consul General Eric Johnston at the State Department thanking him for forwarding a copy of Pryor's letter. "His request for a briefing on the region mystifies me," Johnston wrote. "I didn't know him that well. The times that we had met were devoted to small talk when we weren't discussing the vintages and wine estates throughout the Bordeaux region."

Johnston could have been Consul General to those wine regions alone, Robbie thought. If he ever got out of the office, it was to go and see a wine estate. That was part of it, after all, but a minor part compared to the enormous region that the Consulate General served. The territory included all of Southwestern France, twenty separate *departements* comprising four regions, about one fourth of the entire nation. Interesting that Johnston had never talked French politics, which he knew well, with Pryor. That made Pryor's request all the more unusual.

The letter from the French Desk also included some preliminary thoughts on the Etchevari visit, received from the Senator's office. As expected, he would be touching down at Bordeaux, but would be spending most of his time in the Basque region, both on the coast, and the interior. He was coming without an entourage, and he would be receiving an award from the mayor of the small town which his ancestors had left to go to America many years ago.

Robbie called in Ghislaine, and set forth two trips to the Basque region. The first would be to the coastal area of Bayonne, Biarritz and St Jean de Luz. The second would be later, and would include the Basque interior country. That trip would also include a call on the Prefect of the Pyrenees-Atlantiques at Pau. In addition to his soundings in Bordeaux, the trips would give him a first-hand appreciation of security prospects for Senator Etchevari's visit.

That was also on the mind of Embassy Consul General Tim Everbright, who telephoned from Paris as Ghislaine left the office. As Elliot Hawkins had warned, Everbright was on his way. "I'll be arriving Friday on the morning Air Inter flight. Why don't you set up some appointments for that afternoon, and ask Ghislaine to book me at some convenient hotel in town? I've got plane reservations back on Saturday morning."

Robbie called in Ghislaine once again, and they planned Everbright's visit.

Robbie decided to request a meeting on security at the Town Hall. He told Ghislaine to stress that the Etchevari visit was the reason for Everbright's trip to Bordeaux. Ghislaine made reservations at the Normandie Hotel, and then made a note to call the Bordeaux hostess and shoe-horn Everbright into the dinner that Robbie was attending on Friday evening.

Robbie buzzed Ghislaine. He didn't want her to see his reddening face. "Oh yes, Ghislaine, and when you call the *Mairie* about the Everbright visit, would you please check with the Mayor's office? He told me the other week that I could have a seat in his box for the soccer match sometime. Could you find out if two seats would be available for the match with Paris St. Germain later this week? Many thanks."

She buzzed him back within minutes. "They are arranging a meeting for Mr. Everbright and yourself for Friday afternoon. And the Mayor's office will be pleased to share the box at the soccer stadium. That is Thursday evening."

Robbie called Sylvie. She was pleased. Since France's 1998 World Cup championship, the national obsession for soccer had been rejuvenated. They agreed to meet for a quick snack before the soccer game. The Paris St. Germain team always played well. It should be fun, a close match.

Rather pleased that he had handled matters with Sylvie so smoothly, Robbie turned in some relief back to the business of diplomacy.

Some things he had to handle personally, not through his staff. He made a preliminary call to the head of *La Jurade de St. Emilion,* whom he knew slightly. This *Premier Jurat*, Claude de Monoury, was an affable, chunky little man who owned Chateau St. Aubin, a well regarded St. Emilion Grand Cru.

"*Bonjour, Monsieur le Consul.* When may we have the pleasure of seeing you at St. Aubin?"

"Soon, I hope." That would give another excuse for an excursion with Sylvie. "I'm calling about the *Jurade.* Will you be having another membership ceremony this June?"

"Certainly, *Monsieur le Consul.* Every year we hold two banquets and have membership ceremonies, in June and then in September for the harvest." De Monoury's voice was a bit cautious. These ceremonies combined knowledge of wines with prestige for the organization, after all.

"I just found out that a distinguished visitor, Senator William Etchevari, will be in our region then. I don't have his itinerary yet, but I wondered if your new membership candidate list was quite full at present."

Etchevari was an international political figure, and de Monoury rose to the occasion. "I am sure that I speak for the *Jurade* when I say that Senator Etchevari would be a fine addition to our ranks. Is this an official request?"

"Not at all. I mean, not yet. I don't have his final schedule yet. We're just checking possibilities. I know that you admitted Ambassador Adams to membership recently. His Deputy, Elliot Hawkins, and I were talking about that at Margaux the other evening."

"There would probably be room for one more American. We try to spread out the foreign membership. Your Mr. Hawkins would make a fine addition too, I'm sure."

That was the thing about the French, Robbie thought. They didn't have to have the obvious spelled out for them. He thanked de Monoury for his help, and pinned down the date for the ceremony. Then he called in Vice Consul Stan Bartlett to go over a roughed-in preliminary schedule for the visit.

Claude de Monoury was glad that the American Consul had called. Ever since that shadowy, threatening conversation that he had had a month ago, he had not been sure what course to take. It had taken him a long time and great effort after all to bring Chateau St. Aubin back to its previously respected status. He didn't want to lose all that.

De Monoury had begun by hiring a first-rate winemaker, replacing the family retainer who had been more inclined to save face by cutting corners than to ask Claude's father for more funds to improve the wine. Then everything, it had seemed, needed replacement or repair, from the storage facilities to the fermentation casks.

One annoying and costly project had started with the renovation of his aging cellar. Distributors reported back that some of his bottles had a corky taste. His corks were first-quality from Portugal, so that couldn't be the problem. Analysis showed the culprit to be a chemical that had been painted on the walls of his aging cellar, to preserve the wood. It also, in the cool humidity of the cellar, had morphed to produce a chemical reaction that affected the taste of the wines. The cellar was redone.

For the past two years, a steady improvement in the wine was beginning to be noticed. The trouble of course was that they were not generally thought to be excellent vintage years, and so the improvement that had cost so much was bound to seem just incremental. That wasn't what was needed, if Claude's investment and gamble in the future was to be recouped.

No, he needed a banner year, heralded as such by the wine writers who seemed so important to everyone's future in the wine regions.

What he didn't need was the threat of terrorism.

It had come suddenly and unexpectedly. First, a telephone message, never repeated, to his private number, suggesting a meeting. The voice was menacing. It brooked no refusal, and de Monoury kept the appointment. Then, as he was leaving that secluded area of Libourne near the river without being contacted after an hour's wait, a printed note passed to him by a street bum directed him to walk to a public phone several blocks away. When he got there, the phone rang. It was the same muffled voice, and the instructions were clear.

The amount, Claude had to admit, was not substantial. He could easily afford the fifteen hundred euros every other month. What he could not afford was to have his wine hijacked, or his fermentation cask temperature gauges misfire, or for biological agents to be spread throughout his vineyards, or for lethal substitutions to be made for his routine chemicals.

The enumeration had made his blood run cold. Clearly his unknown caller knew the wine industry and its pressure points intimately. And in a strange way, that unknown voice had also inspired a sort of sureness that the ante would not be raised, ever, provided that payments were made on time as stipulated, by Claude personally, and provided that the matter was kept entirely secret.

"Think of our arrangement as a necessary security expense," the cold voice had said.

So Claude had started making the payments, and nothing untoward had happened. In a way that was reassuring. But he still wondered why he had been singled out (if he had been), whether other Bordeaux wine producers had also been approached, and why the man's conversations had been in English.

He was therefore relieved by Robbie's call, and pleased to be in a position to do a favor for several prominent Americans. That might be worth drawing on later. Claude had just a nodding acquaintance with most public officials, and virtually none with the Bordeaux consular community. Perhaps by cultivating them he would be able somehow to insulate himself from this protection scheme. It always helped to have powerful friends.

Monday morning planning meetings were a necessary bore, but Antonio Echurra was also preoccupied with the Etchevari visit. It was not possible that the world's most politically eminent Basque should return to the homeland of his people without the ETA becoming aware of that fact.

The question was what, if anything, they should do about it.

On the whole, the Executive Committee was inclined to just let the visit take place. Alberto cited comparable past visits to that effect, and Raul, cautious as always, feared the repercussions of any political move that might misfire.

The trouble was, Senator Etchevari seemed prepared to force their hand. A confirmed internationalist, and one of the very last self-professed liberals in the United States Senate, he balanced pride in the Basque people with a detestation for terrorism. He had also taken the Senate floor and delivered an address that had denounced the ETA in no uncertain terms.

"Violence begets more violence. How can we fail to condemn national terror when we see it, just as we condemn international terror that is aimed at our shores? The Basque people deserve better. They have been forced into witnessing a pattern of violence that can only get worse. Let the French and Spanish Governments, with our encouragement, celebrate Basque culture and foster teaching it in their schools." So had he spoken then.

Etchevari's shaggy mane was more nineteenth century than present day, but he could move people. That was the trouble.

Antonio, Alberto and Raul quickly agreed that Etchevari would not be personally injured during his visit. He was too much of a hero. Remember after all that the assassination of Lord Mountbatten had only served to discredit the IRA cause. It had backfired, revolting everybody.

They also dismissed kidnapping. "Too risky," Antonio objected. "Etchevari is bound to have extensive security from the French Government, and there would be a lot of shooting involved in any kidnapping attempt. We could end up with no kidnapping. and Etchevari dead. Besides, for what purpose would we take him? We'll get enough publicity from his visit if we play it right."

Raul nodded in measured agreement. "No reason to do him any harm," he grunted. Antonio was talking more and more at these meetings, his appraising eye seemed to suggest. Better watch this cub before he turns into a bear.

Alberto argued that the Etchevari visit could, after all, serve their purposes. "Let's use it. Why not? As a minimum, we can make our presence, and our ideas, known whenever Etchevari makes a public appearance in the Basque country. You'll see."

Antonio agreed. "Yes. You're right. There will be a multiplier effect." They looked at him, not understanding. "Media covering the event will then also have to report on our struggle. We'll turn his visit to our own purposes."

They turned to other matters, including organizing an ETA presence at any public events held during the visit, and leaflets to be distributed. Just like precinct work in an American Congressional campaign, Antonio thought. The main difference is that we are better organized.

He then gave a brief progress report on organizing the Bordeaux wine regions. Another chateau owner had seen the wisdom of writing off their security protection as overhead. So far, so good.

"Speaking of Bordeaux, one thing bothers me," Alberto said. "That business in *Sud-Ouest* about the ETA initials at the American Consulate General in Bordeaux. It hasn't come up again since they wrote about it some time ago, but I don't like it. We didn't do it, or at least, this Executive Committee never authorized it. It's a detail that bothers me. Somebody did it. Who, and why?"

Raul grunted his agreement. Antonio could see that they had talked the matter over beforehand. If they had not, Raul would have mulled the matter over as something to be considered anew. He would not have agreed to what Alberto had said immediately.

"What is said in Bordeaux is that it was a drunken, Saturday night prank," Antonio said. "Anyway, the police noticed that there was nothing written in our Basque language. So they didn't take it seriously. But I spend more and more time in that region. I'll find out more and then we'll all know exactly what happened."

Antonio had seen a veiled challenge to his authority, and had slapped it down sharply. Now, he had better produce results.

The meeting ended, and Antonio walked down the hill, *makhila* in hand. He regained his car, and drove an hour towards the coast, varying his speed and doubling back on routes taken several times. The meeting had gone about as planned. It was amazing how Raul and Alberto played into his hands.

Now it was time for a brief report. The fuller details could await his drop the next day, but at least he must give the signal for that now. Time enough to compose the report later. He pulled his car over to a service area, walked to a public phone, put in some change, and dialed a number. A bureaucratic voice answered. That never failed to annoy Antonio. Since it was taped, was it really necessary for the voice to sound so bored?

Antonio gave the standard signal for the drop.

Then he added, "The weather will be fine in the Basque region," and hung up the phone. As he walked away from the phone booth he added under his breath…"unless the traitor Etchevari forces my hand."

* * *

Later that afternoon. the Case Officer received the message, and made a call of his own for Antonio's report to be retrieved the following night. He then reported to the Station Chief.

The Station Chief's sense of relief was palpable. He lit a cigarette, smiled and dismissed the Case Officer. The report from Antonio had already been essentially conveyed. There would be no violence during the Senator Etchevari visit. All was going well. It was good to have a voice within the ETA Executive Committee, and worth the risks.

Then why was he having that familiar argument with himself? He snubbed out the cigarette, and then absent-mindedly lit another while the first still smoldered away in the ashtray, creating an unpleasant acrid smell that would get into his jacket and hair and raise questions in his wife's mind. "Can't you leave those places to more junior officers?" she would say.

He stubbed the smoldering cigarette butt and ground it out.

He was a very lucky man. He could talk with her and did, even about some subjects that he had been cautioned to keep to himself. She was part of it, after all, sharing his diplomatic cover. He didn't share everything. Not the secret reports and intercepts and the missions that he sent people on, to amplify what the Embassy knew from its usual diplomatic contacts. As to those matters, it was necessary and even prudent to check on what one was told, even if sometimes the press caught on and the mission backfired. That was a cost of doing business, and usually a negligible one at that.

At least, Langley had finally understood that "doing business" didn't literally mean "business." It meant government and national security. It was stupid to risk good assets to find out what the business competition was up to, even if that had been a new national priority for a while.

Other matters were undeniably worth it. He lit another cigarette and puffed away for a moment. Then he looked at the ashtray, saw the first cigarette still smoldering there, and stubbed it out. Antonio's report was a relief. It confirmed what they had already heard from open sources, and that was worth knowing.

That justified the policy of penetrating terrorist groups. It was very hard work and usually failed. But in this case, Antonio had come to them. They hadn't even needed an access agent as a go-between to recruit him. That was unusual. There was such a gap between terrorists and intelligence officers that usually such go-betweens were needed. But this fellow from Wharton had literally walked in off the street.

His motivation was credible and understandable. He didn't want money. He wanted to know everything the CIA could tell him about the GAL. He wanted to know who had killed his father and brother in 1987, the last year the GAL was active. In return, he would keep them informed of what was happening within the ETA.

The Station Chief had no illusions that Antonio was telling them all that he knew. There was no way that could be ensured. And in return, all he could do from time to time was drop snippets of information about the GAL, and hope that kept Antonio in the corral. Actually, everything they told Antonio might have been gleaned by a reasonably close attention to what was going on in open court, and in legal and political circles in Madrid and the French Basque region.

Antonio must know that now. He was probably just building credibility of his own, working towards more useful revelations from them. For the time being, it occurred to the Station Chief that Antonio was probably using this conduit the same way that he was being used, as a check on what he could find out by other means.

But recently he had been grumbling. He wanted more. He wanted to know about the GAL's killing squads, or at least, the names of people who could give him that information.

They had better continue to be very, very careful. Senator Etchevari was a key man in approving Agency appropriations, and a national security ally, whatever his liberal credentials for the public might suggest. Better to err on the side of caution where his safety was concerned.

The Station Chief knew that the CIA was split on the use of terrorists. Yes, it was an important national priority to get information from them. That is why they had been glad to use Antonio. But the policy had limits. Terrorists who were also murderers were beyond the pale. In early 1997, the CIA had even dropped 100 foreign agents whose hands were too bloody, a policy that was quickly and publicly reassessed after 9/11.

Antonio fortunately hadn't been on the list.

There was another aspect to this. What if Antonio slipped over a line and mentioned an operation that the ETA was planning? It hadn't happened yet, but it might. That was a variation of standard

Mafia technique in the old days. Let the new recruit carry out an execution to prove himself. Antonio might do that to test his contact, or to immunize himself.

It was the Enigma Problem, and there was no satisfactory answer to the dilemma. During the Second World War, the British through the captured Enigma Machine and their codebreakers had access to German military and diplomatic messages. They could not act on that information without revealing the fact that they had it. So lives had been lost.

What if that happened now? What if Antonio signalled an ETA operation?

The answer to that was probably a matter of scale. Protect the assets, even if innocent people were killed, unless it was a major operation. Then, go with the information and let the source be blown. But for the Station Chief, who might have to make the call, it was not a very satisfactory distinction.

The Station Chief listened once more to the tape that the Case Officer had brought him. The tone of voice that he heard was showing annoyance. There was an undertone there, that the Station Chief had heard in other cases, but never before from Antonio.

It was a sign of growing impatience The Station Chief wondered what Antonio had left unsaid, or what he might have muttered to himself as he left the phone.

Antonio had to be kept on the reservation, at least through the Etchevari visit.

The options were few. He couldn't finger Spanish GAL sources even if he knew who they had been. There was in fact really very little that he could pass Antonio and maintain any credibility. His autonomy didn't go very far. All Langley wanted was for the source to continue, at least, he was sure, through the visit of Senator Etchevari. They would never authorize assets to be compromised. But a bureaucratic shuffle might solve the problem.

It was time to discuss this once again upstairs.

❧ ❧ ❧

The Senior Officer listened to the Station Chief. He had brought not only a problem, but its potential solution, one that the Senior Officer had tossed out for consideration earlier.

It was time to rearrange the chess board, the Senior Officer decided. The visit of Senator Etchevari would furnish a good excuse to do that.

Bait and switch. Give him a name, but protect the man. Move him, even. That would keep Antonio on the reservation through the Etchevari visit. That was the important thing.

A few contacts back in Washington should do the trick. It was, after all, one thing to put a man in danger for a tactical purpose. It was quite another to keep him there. The bait would be offered, then snatched away once the Etchevari visit was concluded. Until then, Antonio would be concentrating on Etchevari. Yes, it should all work out rather well.

The Senior Officer looked forward to welcoming Senator Etchevari.

CHAPTER 10

A Trip To Bayonne

Robbie settled into his chair at the Chapon Fin Restaurant with pleasure and anticipation. He was twenty minutes early, and looked forward to this dinner with Eduardo and Elena Dos Campos, and Erika Lutz. The invitation from the Spanish Consul General made up for the fact that Dos Campos had spent the last few weeks in Spain. He had therefore been unable to talk with Robbie about the Basque situation, as had been promised. The German Consul General made the foursome.

At the Chapon Fin, Robbie thought, you could easily imagine that it was still the period of Napoleon III. The elaborate rococo decorations, and grotto effect, would have been kitsch if they had not been absolutely genuine. This used to be on the route from Paris to Biarritz, the summer residence of the Emperor and his Empress Eugenie. Tables were indicated where the famous of the period had eaten, from Sarah Bernhardt to Henri de Toulouse Lautrec. It was fun to recapture the atmosphere, and the service was discreet and prompt. You could almost hear Offenbach.

It was the food that brought out Bordeaux regulars to this restaurant in the Place des Grands Hommes, where streets named for seventeenth and eighteenth century luminaries, including Benjamin

Franklin, radiated from the square. In the morning, it was also a center for fresh foods, colorfully displayed. A good Bordeaux housewife would think that she was cheating her family if she did not buy her foods fresh at the market at least several times a week.

Erika Lutz joined him at the table. She approved Robbie's musings on shopping in this colorful square. "And certainly, for a diplomatic dinner, the food must be absolutely fresh," she said. "As a matter of fact, when you choose a date for the dinner, the next thing you do is to confer with the cook and learn what is fresh. Then the cook, the morning of the dinner, buys everything absolutely fresh. If something isn't available, you confer again and substitute."

Robbie thought that this was the way it had been in Bordeaux and other traditional cities for many generations, ensuring that everything always tasted fresh and delicious. He then wondered aloud whether any other method of giving a dinner constituted progress, and doubted it very much.

"You are becoming quite the European," she teased.

"Nothing wrong with taking the best from wherever you find it. Here are our host and hostess." The Spanish Consul General and his wife came into view like galleons, Robbie thought, proud, expensively dressed, and elegant.

The protocol was complicated, but well-practiced and smooth. Dos Campos kissed his German colleague's hand, and shook hands with Robbie, who then shook hands with his hostess, bowing his head slightly as he did so, and then Elena Dos Campos exchanged pecks on the cheek with Erika Lutz. Good thing there are just four of us, Robbie wryly thought.

They ordered *foie gras* with a young Sauternes wine, filet of sole with a white *Graves,* and *entrecote* of beef with a fine Pomerol, Chateau Petit Village. Dessert would tempt them later. True to habit, the Spanish Consul General began dinner with a *fino* sherry, and his guests followed suit, at his suggestion.

Turning to the diplomatic business at hand, Dos Campos told his guests that Madrid was concerned about the upswing in ETA violence in the Basque region of northern Spain. "They paused for a while after the attacks on your World Trade Center," he began. "We hoped there might be a solution. But no, they started once again. Nothing big quite yet. But they are beginning to frighten away the tourists once again. The tourists don't seem to be their target. Nobody has been killed, not yet. But that may happen. It is, as you Americans would say, the law of averages."

"And they are still targetting the Spanish Government." This, from Erika, was a statement, not a question.

"Yes, local officials in the Basque region, and national ones in Madrid and elsewhere throughout Spain, when they can. Although what they expect to gain is beyond me. They only repeat themselves, and after each killing, the public demonstrations against them are massive. It seems pointless. We hear that their recruiting is beginning to dry up. We still have hundreds of ETA soldiers behind bars, and so do the French.

Robbie asked, "Do you tend to rule out any IRA parallel?"

"Aside from the use of terrorism. For one thing, the national history is totally different. They are a distinct people with a distinct language, yes, but there is no history of independent nationhood, and there is no internationally exportable sense of grievance. Not like Ireland at all. Franco, who did persecute them, has been dead for decades. And the regional Basque government has lots of autonomy, real autonomy. That's also why the ETA through its surrogates always loses in regional elections. They just have no case, except violence."

Robbie decided to let it pass. The Basques were a proud, distinct people with a long history. "Independence" was another matter. But surely Dos Campos was right in his last point. It would be hard for the ETA to raise serious money, and without it, they were stuck with random acts of violence which seemed to get them nowhere.

"Is their problem one of numbers too?" Robbie asked.

"It seems to be. Without a massive increase in funds and recruits, they simply cannot do anything more than sporadic terrorism. As police methods improve—and as the governments concerned pay more attention to legitimate Basque issues in an intelligent way—the ETA is going to lose even more ground. So Madrid is concerned, of course, but fairly confident. What if anything do the French authorities make out of that spray-painting incident?"

"Very little," Robbie admitted. "Commissioner Moineau tends to think that it may not have been the ETA at all. It lacked their calling card, as you know. Nothing was written in Basque, and anyway, targetting me, or any third country official, doesn't seem to make any sense. For one thing, if their threat is real, there could be a question of an international response." That was as far as he could go. It wasn't up to a consular officer in the field to make national commitments for the United States, after all.

They took bites from the *fois gras*, which was lightly seared, and went perfectly with the unctuous Sauternes.

Robbie poised his fork in the air and directed a question at Dos Campos. "Before you left, you said something about their leadership, something about the leaders changing, or being unknown. Do I remember correctly?"

"You do. The ETA has a three-person leadership. It changes from time to time, for operational purposes, depending upon who is in jail and who is not. Two leaders, Alberto Aguilar and Raul Izquierda, are known and have extensive files. Now, though, their security must be improving. They wouldn't have gone a year without a third member of their Executive Committee. We don't know who he is, and neither do the French. That is worrisome."

The courses continued delightfully. The sole had been poached in a wine sauce, to which grapes had been added. The *entrecote* of beef was a great Bordeaux specialty. It involved searing the meat over twigs that were actually dried vines from a previous year's grape harvest. That was a pleasant custom, particularly for the outdoor barbeque cook. The seared flavor was delicious, agreeing very well with the rich red wine sauce. They drank their glasses of Chateau Petit Village with smiles of appreciation.

"It's just right," said Erika Lutz. "Very full-bodied and flavorful, a classic Pomerol."

"I only hope the tradition of quality continues," Dos Campos said. "Bruno Prats made this wine, but he has had to sell his holdings and move abroad. The taxes on estates are ruinous. If it keeps up, insurance companies will own many of the great wine estates. Will they be able to make something this fine, or will the pressure for the bottom line change everything?"

The conversation drifted to other topics, inevitably in a city where the Mayor had also been Prime Minister. The next run for the presidency, the splintered Gaullist movement, the National Assembly, wage and price policies, and the next generation of leadership, all came up for review. Diplomats often compared analysis and notes, like journalists who didn't want to get too far out in front of a breaking story, Robbie thought. Too bad their conversational style was so flat. Unlike hers.

As dinner was ending, Robbie mentioned that he was going to the Basque coast the following day. Might as well tell them why, since the news was really no longer a secret. He added, "Senator William Etchevari is coming for a visit to the Basque region soon, and I'm checking out arrangements for the trip."

"Is he an important man?" asked Erika Lutz, sensing a possible report.

"I'm sure Mr. Cutler would tell us that all American Senators are important," Dos Campos interjected. "This one, however, happens to be the most famous living Basque. He is also well regarded by the White House, I should add."

Robbie nodded, amused. Dos Campos must have heard from the Spanish Embassy in Washington some diplomatic gossip that the Department of State wasn't sharing with the field. He remembered his talk with Uncle Seth. Something was up, that was for sure. He said that initial security assessments were favorable for the visit.

Dos Campos replied that he hoped so. "If we only had the Old Guard of the ETA to deal with, that would be one thing. It is the unknown leader, that third person, who troubles me. Better continue to make sure that the security precautions are good."

Dos Campos now had something confidential, if not exactly classified, to report to his government, that he thought would justify the dinner's expense. They lingered over coffee and the dessert tray. Feeling expansive, Dos Campos then offered a round of cognac to his guests. Nobody turned him down.

Robbie walked back to his apartment after the dinner, so lost in thought that he almost didn't notice the pretty young woman on the corner whose beguiling smile promised a closer acquaintance. It wasn't exactly "*Tu viens, Cheri?*"—this was a chic district of Bordeaux after all—but the message was clear.

He was no prude. But this wasn't the time of the Empress Eugenie, either. Today's realities were uglier. Robbie never had believed that AIDS only affected homosexuals. Over the years he had discovered through the alumni grapevine that a number of his friends, both gay and straight, had died of AIDS, or SIDA as the French called it.

He had no intention of joining them. It was better to practice abstinence outside a committed relationship. Some took that as a New Englander's reserve. Perhaps it was. For his part, Robbie saw no reason for the Offenbach mood of the evening to change to a *danse macabre.* Neither was there any call for rudeness. "*Bonne chance, ma jolie Demoiselle,*" he replied with a gentle smile, and continued to walk home alone. Sometimes politeness was all there was.

❧ ❧ ❧

This was a perfect morning for a drive to Bayonne. If Bordeaux had a drawback, Robbie often thought, it was the constant humidity, particularly the cold dampness in the winter. They called it an Atlantic climate. It was a good thing that he didn't have asthma. The climate would have made it much worse.

The weather in Bordeaux seemed the very inversion of the monsoon season that he remembered from Singapore, his first diplomatic post. Somerset Maugham could make something out of that tropical rain.

Who could make anything out of cold damp weather? Probably Mauriac had done it best. He had written about the flat Landes area, through which Robbie was now driving. His novels described the closed, stratified Bordeaux society. Actually it hadn't changed at all, Robbie thought, but people still wanted to marry up and join it. Did that make Mauriac just an outsider, precluded from playing the game, like Graham Greene, jealous of American power and forever forced to write bitterly about it? Robbie couldn't decide. Perhaps the ruinous French estate taxes would change things over time, and Mauriac's Bordeaux would then vanish, speared by national tax policy as it could not be by literary insight.

He looked around at the countryside. The Landes region, a vast pine forest flatland, and one of the largest forests left in Europe this side of Poland, reminded him somewhat of the Georgia piney woods that he used to see from the windows of the trains that took him to Fort Lauderdale on spring breaks. That was a carefree time.

Robbie thought of his own family. He was glad that Uncle Seth had reminded him of his parents' anniversary. They had been pleased by his call on Monday. His mother thanked him for the gift box, which had been delivered on time after all. She didn't have to ask whether he had met anyone special yet. The subject was always tacitly there. His father sounded less depressed than usual, and as usual, very interested in Robbie's career, how he was getting on, and how he liked Bordeaux. Then his sister Evalyn, vivacious and pleasant, bubbled onto the phone.

"Hi there, Big Brother. I hope you'll notify all of the chateau owners that your very diplomatic sister is coming to visit you soon."

"That's already underway, Evvie." (He would have to remember, a week or so before she arrived, to have Ghislaine make a few calls.) "By the way, if you want to spend some time in Paris, I'll be out of here for just a day or two during your visit. Consul General confab at the Embassy. We'd be able to stay with the DCM."

Evalyn chewed this over. "No, I think I'll just relax in Bordeaux. This editing job has me reading manuscripts in my sleep. There ought to be something more stimulating for English majors to do. I'd really rather relax in Bordeaux if you won't be gone that long. Uncle Seth was here earlier. He says hello."

That meant that she had talked with Uncle Seth, and was intrigued with whatever the two of them were up to. Nice kid.

After a two hour drive, Robbie arrived at Bayonne on the Atlantic coast. It was an important administrative city, the *Sous Prefecture* of the Pyrenees-Atlantiques Department, whose main seat, or *Prefecture*, was in the interior, at Pau. It was also, with neighboring Biarritz, and St Jean de Luz down the coastal road, the heart of the Basque coastal region.

Ghislaine had scheduled two appointments for him in Bayonne. First, he would call on the Sub Prefect at his palatial office. Then, there would be an intelligence briefing from the *Renseignements Generaux* in their gloomy, anonymous upstairs headquarters set in a back street, nondescript building near the Bayonne Cathedral. Both were after luncheon.

Robbie glanced at the dashboard clock, and realized that he had made better time than expected. Why not enjoy the region just a bit? He decided to proceed down the coast road and have luncheon in one of his favorite small restaurants in the old Basque section of St. Jean de Luz.

He parked the car near the port area of St. Jean de Luz, near his restaurant on the rue St. Jacques. Too bad there wasn't also enough time for more than a glance at Ciboure just across the Nivelle River from St. Jean de Luz. That charming, largely residential coastal village, houses painted in various pastel shades, was the boyhood home of Ravel. It wasn't hard to imagine where the musician's sense of drama and color had come from.

Here color was everywhere. It was France and not France, Spain and not Spain. Robbie understood something of the pull of the Basque country whenever he visited this coast. Before going to the restaurant, Robbie stepped into the Eglise St. Jean Baptiste. This was surely the best known, and perhaps the most ornate, Basque church in existence, with a wall of decoration, galleries upon galleries of painted panels, a vaulted roof, and a gold altarpiece. Here Louis XIV was married to Maria Theresa, Infanta of Spain, in a marriage arranged by Cardinal Mazarin. After the couple left the church, their doorway was bricked up, never to be used again. The church was a brilliant sight, worthy of a great people. Sylvie would like it. Robbie wondered whether it was on Senator Etchevari's itinerary. It should be.

Luncheon was an informal delight. Bordeaux seemed absolutely straight-laced compared with this menu and the local wines, with their unpronounceable names. Robbie chose a delicious braised Basque chicken with olives, garlic and spices. A glass of local rose wine hit the spot after his drive. He wished Sylvie were there. He really did. Time for business. Strong coffee cleared his head for the afternoon's meetings.

The Sub Prefect of the Republic, Georges Armand, greeted Robbie warmly at his Bayonne office. It was a high-ceilinged suite of rooms. One walked the length of the inner office to join the Sub Prefect. A nice touch, Robbie thought. Much more subtle than Commissioner Moineau's device of having visitors sit in low chairs facing his desk. The mahogany furniture and plush rugs were in contrast to the required portraits of political leaders. Windows gave a fine view of the Adour River.

Armand, Robbie decided, was not going to be promoted further. He was a man in his late indeterminate fifties, still not a Prefect. Surely his consolation was that now he was a Sub Prefect in a grand location, with an elegant office and residence. That was rather like being Consul General in Bordeaux.

Armand went directly to the point. He plied Robbie with questions regarding Senator Etchevari's plans to visit the region and, with a respectful referral towards his superior in the heirarchy, the Prefect at Pau, said that he looked forward to the visit. That was it. He was pleasant, playing it safe. Of course Robbie understood that the power and authority were at Pau. But this wasn't getting him anywhere.

"So you don't see a real security issue, *Monsieur le Sous Prefet*?"

"Not at all. There is a Basque issue here, of course, *Monsieur le Consul*. But it is pursued lawfully. There are orderly demonstrations from time to time. Some Basque people still want their own *departement*, with their language as the official language, as President Mitterrand once promised. They march sometimes for this. It is all quite orderly."

This was tredding water. Robbie thought he might as well up the ante. After all, the Sub Prefect was himself at the political level. He was not dealing with the police.

"As you may be aware, *Monsieur le Sous Prefet*, Senator Etchevari has been outspoken on the subject of Basque terrorism. He has condemned the ETA, for example, in speeches on the Senate floor in Washington, even before the attacks on the World Trade Center in New York. He has continued to condemn the ETA since then, even if they do not seem to have the 'global reach' that President Bush targetted as part of America's War On Terrorism. In addition to his visit here, Etchevari is supposed to receive a civic award of some sort at the village in the interior where his family came from. I wouldn't presume to tell him what to say, but he is an outspoken man."

This was a different matter altogether. Robbie was sure that he would have a reaction in a couple of weeks, when he paid an official visit to the Prefect at Pau. While it was perfectly true that he would have no business advising a United States Senator what to say, he had every right to sound the matter out and to give a judgment on possible reactions. He whistled as he walked to his car and drove over the bridge, finding a public parking space discreetly near the office he was visiting.

His meeting at the *Renseignements Generaux* was as different from the talk he had just held with the Sub Prefect as was its setting, dark, hidden, anonymous and full of suspicion. He was not sure who was interviewing whom.

The shadowy men and women that he spoke with were perfectly polite, but they reminded Robbie of his occasional CIA contacts, taciturn and unforthcoming. They would answer a question if put to them directly. Nothing would be volunteered. That must come from the habit of compartmentalizing intelligence. Don't tell anyone who is not in the chain, and then only if you have to.

They agreed with Commissioner Moineau's assessment at the Chateau Margaux reception. The ETA spray-painting at the Consulate General was surely not the work of the ETA. That matter remained open.

"What about the ETA's leadership?" he asked. "I've heard that there is a third, unknown member of the Executive Committee. Will that affect Senator Etchevari's safety?"

They profiled Raul Izquierda and Alberto Aguilar for him. Now in hiding, both men had long records of ETA involvement and leadership. They were cautious and, in a way, predictable. Their enemy remained the Spanish Government, in order not to increase French incentives for arrests. They did believe that there was a third member of the Executive Committee. There were two reasons for that. First, there always had been, and as an organization the ETA proceeded by habit. There had to be three leaders operating in tandem at all times. For very short periods, a leader could be imprisoned and still function as leader, but that was not the way that the ETA liked to operate.

Listening to these *Renseignements Generaux* officers talk, Robbie was reminded of Uncle Seth analyzing Nazi field organization and procedures. He could still discuss and dissect their doctrine, and tell you how the OSS took precautions in Occupied France accordingly. You had to know the enemy and the way that enemy operated. In the same vein, he was sure that some of the most competent Marxist theoreticians had been CIA case officers at Langley.

A small man sitting behind the others then spoke up and gave Robbie the second reason. His voice was hushed, and the others strained to listen. Robbie guessed that he only spoke once, and you had better get it right the first time.

"We haven't fully answered your question. The truth is that we cannot. However, you should know, *Monsieur le Consul*, that the third man has a nickname, a *nom de guerre*, if you will. We have twice in recent months heard ETA soldiers referring to the 'American.'

"What that means, we are not sure There is no body of evidence to fill it out for us. It could mean very little. Perhaps it is somebody with modern American tastes, a touch of Hollywood, perhaps a collection of jazz music. Or it may be somebody who has lived in your country, maybe even with dual citizenship. But we don't like it. This unknown introduces uncertainty for us. Until we know who he is, we can't say for certain what policies the ETA may follow in the future. It is not in their interests to create any danger for Senator Etchevari. But we cannot be categorical."

This unexpected speech astounded Robbie. There was a real message here. He had better be clear about it.

"How are you going about finding the 'American?'"

"All the usual methods. He is twice as dangerous unknown. If only we knew which male Basques had spent considerable time in the United States during the recent past, say over the last six or seven years, that would help us enormously."

"What about French and Spanish passport records?"

"They are very helpful, as are the records, when they are properly kept, of returns to France and Spain. But they are not perfect. A Basque living in France, for example, might return to France from Spain after living in the United States. We might not catch that. Visa records would be more helpful."

Robbie chose not to take that as a direct request, but rather as a sounding out. "We will be having a meeting of Consuls General at the Embassy in Paris before long. I will mention this to the Ambassador and DCM then."

"They already know. They have not acted. I hope that if the matter comes up during your meetings, that you will help them see the value of cooperation." Robbie caught his breath and nodded. This was beyond his pay grade, but he could see their point. There was one last matter that he wanted clarified.

"Tell me something about the GAL, if you will."

They seemed prepared for his question. Another briefer, a young woman, summarized what had been publicly alleged about Spanish Government complicity during the 'eighties in what was said to be a private antiterrorist movement. As Robbie knew, the issue had brought down the Gonzalez government in Madrid a few years previously.

"Tell me what they did," he said.

"It lasted from 1983 to 1987. It began, stupidly enough, with the GAL picking up the wrong man, an innocent French furniture dealer. They let him go after 10 days, through the intervention of the Red Cross.

"Then the killings started. They may have used hired gangsters in some cases. It went on for four years. In the end, it was like your Chicago during the 'twenties. There were killings in public places, like cafes and bars. The death squads killed 27 people in all. Most of them were probably ETA, but that hardly excuses vigilante killings."

The *Renseignements Generaux* leader gave his summary. "I'm afraid that bitterness about the GAL gave the ETA something new to rally around. That may be part of our problem now. There have been some trials in Spain, but who exactly did what, and with what complicity, may never be known."

You mean revealed publicly, Robbie thought.

* * *

Antonio Echurra waited at the cafe on the side street in Biarritz, enjoying the late afternoon sun at a sidewalk table until it was time for his telephone call.

The latest drop had signalled there was a message for him. That had not happened in months. Messages, when he got them, were never in writing.

He went inside, and using a telephone slug, called from the phone booth in the corner. There was a brief exchange of recognition signals. Then came the message from his contact.

"The GAL did have contact men with the CIA. The last was a young officer named Cutler. He is now the American Consul in Bordeaux."

CHAPTER 11

Murder In The Medoc

Yves Crespier sat behind his desk at his office at Chateau La Source. He looked outside, and gauged the weather. It was not too cool for this time of year. That was a good sign. A frost now that reduced the budding of the plants before the grapes could form would mean a smaller fall harvest. It had nothing to do with the quality of the grapes that would be harvested.

Not all writers understood that. Look, after all, at the 1961 vintage, the finest since the war. Some had even written off that year, based on a spring frost. You would think that they would learn from experience. But Yves knew that if some grapes were lost, or failed to develop fully, stories around the globe would say that it was a bad wine year. What rubbish! At least Douglas Pryor had never made that mistake.

Yves was sure that he had now done the right thing. After two monthly payments, he had rethought the entire matter. Of course, it wasn't a great deal of money. The business could certainly afford it. That was just the problem. His unknown contact had after all assured him that the fees would never be raised. For some odd reason, if you could trust a thief, he seemed fairly certain that this man would keep his word. He had no idea how many others were also involved.

There was also his position to consider. As a leading *Medoc* wine producer, he should have been the first to resist this sort of blackmailing. No matter that they had tried to hide from him that he was one of the first who'd been approached. He could feel it. All the more reason to stop it now, right now.

There seemed to be nobody he could talk to about it. His wife would only worry, and take those worries to church, perhaps sharing them with the village priest. He had tried to sound out de Tourneau, at the consular reception. That hadn't worked.

Finally, he had decided not to make the third payment. Early that morning he had left a note without money in the agreed drop zone, inside a rock pile in a corner of his estate. The best communications were the shortest. He had simply typed on a sheet of Chateau La Source stationery, "I can no longer continue this charade," and signed the note. He knew that meant trouble. But that is what the police were for, surely.

Well, nobody could say that he had given in easily. He wished that the police had put two and two together much earlier, when he had spray-painted that message at the American Consulate General. That should have focused more attention on the ETA. If they had only done their job, it might have been more easily handled. Perhaps it still could be.

Come to think of it, that was the only strange part of the entire affair. Why had he been told who was getting the money? Probably they had thought that he would be more intimidated if he knew that. Well, they had been right about that. He was scared. And now, he didn't know whom to trust.

Better to make the matter public. That's why he'd urged the American Consul and that *Sud-Ouest* reporter to come and see him. They knew about these things. Perhaps a news story could blow the lid off this racket, without naming names. That way, he could still remain anonymous and protect his family.

There were no visitors to his wine chateau in the *Medoc* on this Friday morning. It was the off season, too early for tourists. That is why he had set this morning for the newspaper interview. They would not be disturbed.

He was checking a few invoices when the slim, dark man slid into his office, at twenty minutes after nine. Crespier did not recognize the man, and brusquely asked him his business.

"My business is your third payment," the man hissed.

"There won't be one. I won't pay blackmail any more to keep my property safe. You have no right to make such demands."

"Would you rather lose your crop? Who do you think can protect you from that? We can get this over quickly if you'll think it over and decide to be reasonable."

"I've decided to do what I should have done when you first started your miserable blackmail. I'm not paying anything more!"

"You are not a reasonable man, Monsieur Crespier."

Crespier stood up and stared at him. For anyone other than an ETA fanatic, Crespier's withering glance would have had its effect. But this man stood his ground, his eyes narrowing as he heard Crespier out.

"My family did not work itself up from sharecropping in the Lot et Garonne by being reasonable," Crespier said, voice so strained that his own family would not have recognized it.

"My father did not survive a Nazi labor camp by being reasonable. I will not be reasonable and let you destroy our wine estate. Now get the hell off my land!"

Antonio smiled sarcastically. He pulled out a small knife and, infuriatingly, began to clean his finger nails. "I'll give you one more chance," he said softly, aiming for control.

"That's about all you'll be able to do, once the newspapers print what they know about your protection racket."

That got his visitor's attention. "You'd never dare."

"You don't think so? Why do you think that reporters from *Sud-Ouest* will be here any minute? I'm only sorry that I didn't go to them immediately."

Maybe he could bargain. Why not try? Crespier spoke quickly. "Leave right now, and I'll give you a break. I won't describe you, and I won't say you've been here."

Antonio's nonchalant pose was over. Now he was at full attention. Crespier had just raised the stakes. This was more than an ordinary collection now.

Crespier picked up a can of spray paint on his desk. "Talking with the press would have been a better way to handle the situation than this one was. Too bad I couldn't have written the message in Basque!"

Antonio exploded in fury. So this explained the fake ETA message spray-painted at the American Consulate General! This Crespier was responsible, and he had no cards left to play. Antonio took his revolver out. "Get away from your desk," he barked. He rifled Crespier's desk drawers.

Then he smiled once again, and gave a nervous little titter that had frightened his own ETA colleagues more than once. He had found Crespier's own weapon hidden in the desk drawer. It was loaded. This would all work out after all, even if a knife was more satisfying.

Antonio put away his own revolver, raising Crespier's. "Any last words?"

Crespier moved his right hand reflexively to his heart, to begin the Sign of the Cross. But he couldn't finish. Antonio shot Crespier in the head with his own revolver. Then he took the Chateau La Source letter from his pocket. Using Crespier's typewriter he added a contrite, one-sentence confession to the Pryor murder, just above Crespier's obliging signature.

The noise of a car approaching the estate's long driveway distracted him. Perhaps that was the reporter that Crespier had been talking about. Now he had to finish quickly.

Antonio carefully pushed Crespier's slumped body back into his desk chair. He double-checked, and found that Crespier had not been reaching for a hidden revolver. That simplified things. Any policeman would have read the scene as clearly as if he had been a witness, if Crespier had had one revolver in his hand and another in his jacket. This was the *Medoc*, not the Wild West.

Antonio pressed the revolver into Crespier's right hand and the letter under his right forearm, and left the office.

It was an easy matter to circle the building and avoid the newcomers. He stalked through the fields and regained his car, which he had parked half a mile away.

He congratulated himself on having thought of a plausible explanation for killing the first wine estate owner who refused to pay. The newspapers had said that they were all suspects in the Pryor murder. Now they would have Pryor's killer. With any luck Crespier would be blamed, and the investigation would stop before it really got started. Really, Crespier was turning out to be worth more dead than alive! Raul and Alberto would be pleased.

Antonio chuckled again as he drove slowly away. The Pryor murder would be sufficient reason for Crespier's suicide. It would also put the others in line. Nobody would dare back out of making their monthly payments, with Crespier dead.

Even better, he could now tell Raul and Alberto that he had discovered the man responsible for spray-painting the ETA's initials at the American Consulate General. That matter was now closed.

For a tight spot, it was working out rather well.

He was halfway back to Bordeaux when he remembered the can of spray paint. He cursed himself for not taking it. It could link Crespier with the spray-painting at the Consulate General, and raise questions. Well, *tant pis*! Too late now. It was a worry about a trifle.

Spray paint was a common item, after all. He had seized the initiative, and that was what counted.

Crespier, reviving for a moment, dropped the revolver. He propped himself up and desperately tried to seize the can of spray paint. If only he could spray the initials ETA on the white-washed walls of his office! The effort was too great. He collapsed before he could do so.

He felt at peace. Through a long tunnel he saw a light, and then he saw his father once again on the other side of the tunnel. He told his father about the workmen who were even now in the fields, attending to the vines, cutting where needed and marking the progress of the budding. If only the frost wouldn't come now, this would be an abundant crop. That was the thing about wine. Each season was new, with fresh hopes. His father nodded understanding, smiled and extended his hand.

Last night had been a nice, relaxed evening, Sylvie thought as she drove to the *Medoc*. She and Robbie had gone to the soccer stadium to see the match between the Bordeaux Girondins and Paris St. Germain. The Girondins, which had been one of the best teams in France, was again a contender for the First Division title. Paris St Germain, once the class of the league, was still a dangerous team. It had promised to be a good match, and it was.

Mayor Juppe wasn't there, but his box was nearly filled with cigar smoking municipal councilors. Mid-field, high enough to see clearly everything that took place on the playing ground, but not set apart from other fans (and constituents), the box was a great place to watch the game and to be seen. The crowd had been in a mellow mood, boisterous but not rowdy, refueled by beer and snacks.

Sylvie had enjoyed herself, and Robbie had loosened up too. "*Bande de cons!*" she had shouted when the visiting team scored a goal.

She looked at Robbie and blushed, really blushed red like a schoolgirl. He gave a mock bow and flourish, "*Comme vous dites, Mademoiselle,*" he said, laughing his agreement.

They finished the game with more laughter than she could remember in ages.

And the game had ended in a 2-2 tie, all in all a satisfying result, since the Girondins had to make up a 2-0 deficit in the fading minutes to achieve the tie.

Driving back, he was all business again. They had talked about the ETA. Robbie told her about his trip to the Basque coast He even shared with her speculation about the new ETA leadership. That was news, and a welcome confidence. Sylvie told him that she was starting her own research with a call on Yves Crespier at Chateau La Source in the *Medoc*, following up on his invitation at the Chateau Margaux reception.

That was where she and her photographer were driving now

The evening had ended with a chaste kiss when Robbie dropped Sylvie off at her apartment. I wonder what a real one with him is like, she wondered.

Neither had been aware that their evening from start to finish had been shadowed by a coldly methodical man, a human raptor who made mental notes on his prey as they watched the match.

Sylvie neared Chateau La Source, her aged Citroen chugging along in the morning sun. Now it was time to compose herself and rehearse a few questions for Yves Crespier. She shifted mental gears just before thoughts of Robbie became an obsession.

A few moments later, Sylvie entered the driveway of Chateau La Source. The office was to the right in a secluded copse of pine trees. She parked the Citroen and with her photographer went to the door. There was no answer to her knock. They were right on time, so they should be expected. Perhaps they should wait inside. It was a bit chilly after all.

Sylvie tried the door. It was open.

She saw Crespier's body immediately, sprawled behind the desk, blood still fresh, not yet beginning to congeal. So that report that she had taken for a backfire as they neared the estate was a bullet. Of course, it was the shot that had killed him. There were papers on the desk, and a revolver near his outstretched hand.

Sylvie tried to focus on the room and its layout. It didn't entirely work. She just made it back out the door before throwing up. Then she forced herself back inside.

"Don't touch anything," she told herself and her photographer. Moving towards the desk, she could just read the letter pinned under the dead man's arm. She called her editor, Jacques Lebrun, and the police, in that order, on her cellular phone. Then she told her photographer to take pictures throughout the office.

The police arrived forty minutes later. By that time she had already dictated the next day's front page story to her office. And what a story this would be! They had arrived just after the suicide of Yves Crespier, well-known wine estate owner, and President of the *Confrerie des Vins du Medoc.* There was a signed confession to Pryor's murder. The motivation was surely revenge for the poor reviews that Pryor had given Chateau La Source, which had brought the estate to the brink of financial ruin.

She left it to the police to sort out the means and the opportunity for Pryor's murder. It was a sad business, but now the police could tidy the loose ends.

Robbie also had nice memories of his soccer match date with Sylvie. It made the day that he was now spending with Tim Everbright almost bearable. Actually, old Everbright was an affable sort, provided you treated him with the deference he thought was due. He proved that once again when the official car pulled up in front of the Consulate General. Everbright walked briskly to the car, opened the door and plunked himself down on the right-hand side of the rear passenger compartment. That was where the ranking general would sit, by protocol.

Robbie and Georges looked at each other over the car, hunched shoulders in amazement, and grinned conspiratorially. Then Georges drove them through town, down the colorful Rue des Ramparts from the Place Gambetta, to their meeting at Bordeaux's Town Hall, or *Mairie*, on the Place Pey Berland. On a fine day with a light afternoon schedule, this was one of Robbie's favorite lunchtime walks.

The Place Pey Berland was anchored on the west by the *Mairie*, which was the eighteenth century Palais de Rohan, an elegant mansion which before the Revolution had been the palace of the Archbishop of Bordeaux. In the center of the large public square stood the St. Andre Cathedral, with its old bell tower.

The Jean Moulin Resistance Museum, also in the square, was named for a national hero, the only French prefect to defy the invading Nazis, follow General de Gaulle into exile, and then return to France as a leader of the Resistance. The displays were riveting, including a mock-up of Jean Moulin's resistance headquarters, and an actual boat that was used to smuggle refugees across the English Channel from Brittany.

This beautiful square was not always peaceful. Robbie told Everbright as they arrived that in October, 1996, a bombing attempt on then Prime Minister Alain Juppe's life had been made at the *Mairie*. The bomb had been placed behind an ornate staircase, the same one that Juppe's predecessor, former Prime Minister Jacques Chaban-Delmas, used to race up when he was well into his seventies

"The bomb ripped through Juppe's outer office and caused damage on three floors of the structure. Fortunately the Prime Minister had left for Paris a few hours earlier, and there had been no casualties. As the French Government expected, that Corsican separatist group, the FNLC, claimed responsibility for thc bombing attack

"A nasty business it had been, and a real shock to the *Bordelais* that their elegant *Mairie* could be successfully attacked by terrorists," he added.

"Let's hope that doesn't set a precedent for the Etchevari visit," Everbright said. "After all, here we are much closer to the ETA's base of operations than the FNLC was to Corsica."

Georges left his passengers in the courtyard, which was now guarded by both uniformed police and special security forces. Their identifications were briefly checked by an official from the Mayor's office, who then accompanied them inside.

Everbright pontificated a bit at the start of their meeting, which was held in a spartan second floor conference room. "We've all got to make sure that security is first-rate," he pompously announced to the trained professionals whose job it was to ensure exactly that. Then he lapsed into silence.

When Etchevari's visit was first considered, the security question had been the main concern. Was it likely that he would be an ETA target? The judgment had been that he would not, and now the Senator would soon be on his way. The issue now was implementation of a plan to make sure the visitor was safe, without cramping his movements unduly.

A dour little security official in plainclothes set forth the parameters. Provision had been made, he said, for discreet surveillance throughout the Etchevari visit by cross-trained security forces, and also for crowd control where possible.

"We're not providing rooftop snipers, checkpoints and the like," he concluded. "That would defeat the purpose of your Senator's visit."

He didn't go into an assessment of the ETA itself, as the *Renseignements Generaux* officers had done earlier. These were operational security men, not intelligence officers.

Robbie nodded in agreement. Elaborate precautions would isolate Etchevari, and exaggerate the ETA's importance as a security threat. Media spin artists grasping for a news story would then make the security arrangements the news story rather than the visit, putting both the French Government and the visitor on the defensive.

There remained the question of coordination. Robbie looked at Everbright, to see if he was going to comment. No. That meant that he could do so without fear of a negative comment in his annual efficiency report for taking the stage.

"Thank you so much for your help," he told the French security officials. "You are absolutely right. There has to be a balance. I'll coordinate with the Senator. I'm sure he will be grateful for your concern, and the professionalism of your security officers." They smiled and formally shook hands.

Riding back to the Consulate General with Everbright, Robbie said that the best thing to do was to allude discreetly to overall security arrangements in his pre-visit wrap-up cable. The French were on the right track, and any needed adjustments could be made later.

"Now I know the players, and how to contact them." He looked again at the business cards he had been given. "I'll get into any needed specifics with Senator Etchevari once he's on the ground." Everbright, relieved of responsibility for the decision, nodded in agreement.

"Would you like to meet with the staff?" Robbie asked.

"Not enough time. I'll do that the next visit. Just have Georges drop me off."

They left Everbright at his hotel to freshen up and go shopping before dinner. This really was going to be an easy visit after all, Robbie decided. He meant the Etchevari visit.

Their dinner was at an elegant eighteenth-century town apartment overlooking the park. The setting was a near match for the

Mairie in both period and formality. Robbie thought that he recognized several Boucher watercolors on the walnut interior walls along the entrance hall. Electrified crystal chandeliers lighted their way to the drawing rooms. The electricity was an intrusion.

The furnishings were comfortable old money, very old money, and that pretty much summed up Georges and Suzel Latouraine, their hosts. Equally at home in Bordeaux and London, the Latouraines seemed more English than the English. Their children were definitely BCBG, "*bon chic bon genre*" as the French put it, or "Sloane Rangers" as the Brits would say. Robbie wasn't sure, but Park Avenue probably was the American equivalent. *Vogue*, anyway.

Their host was a wine merchant, as his family had been for generations. Many years previously, a Latouraine who enjoyed city life more than agriculture had sold his wine estates to concentrate on the wine trade itself. It had been an astute business move, at a time when wine shippers had controlled the markets, even bottling the wines themselves.

Georges retained his family's shrewd appreciation of the soil and combined that quality with sound business acumen. The thought crossed Robbie's mind that if Georges were a poker player, he would be a good one. The nation that had chosen him to be its Honorary Consul General had chosen well.

The wines were superb, Robbie thought. He would remember them for years to come. In Bordeaux, the subtlest compliment was to serve a vintage wine produced by a guest which was considered marginally better than the wine the host had produced that year.

Latouraine started with oysters from the nearby Arcachon Bay, with a recent white Chateau Carbonnieux. The wine was crisp and clear and superb, Bordeaux's answer to Chablis.

Then with the beef *tournedos*, a Chateau Pichon Longueville, Comtesse de Lalande 1988 was served. It was an interesting choice. Not as overpowering as the 1982, it was a fine wine which had come together perfectly, the harsh tannins long receded to marry with the still fresh fruit of the grapes. The result was a superb blend that matched the meat course well.

Latouraine saw Robbie's quizzical look, and guessed that the wine had surpassed his expectations. "*Monsieur le Consul*," he said, "a wine properly aged is like a bride on her wedding day, perfectly beautiful." Robbie smiled his appreciation. "It makes little difference that her sisters may be more beautiful," Latouraine continued, in full flight. "They may also be at an awkward stage. That's what your wine writers, with their little charts and points and scorecards, miss entirely. See what you think of the wines to come."

Latouraine loved his food and hoped his guests did too. Next came the cheese course, and with it, magnums of Chateau Figeac 1975. The flavorful St. Emilion from a full-bodied year was a different taste entirely, and it complemented the cheeses well, rich and oozing flavor. Magnums of wine aged more slowly, and the result had been worth the wait. This wine made the dinner a memorable occasion.

Then came a rare treat, a bottle of Chateau Lafite Rothschild 1928. "I didn't decant it at all. It would have lost its flavors too soon," Latouraine explained. Robbie raised the small, hand cut glass, whose facets gleamed reflections of the candelabra on the table, alternating that light with the deep garnet colored wine that the glass held. He sipped the wine. It was well-made and flavorful, flavors receding but still there, elegant and memorable. It reminded him oddly of an old dance card found in a family album. When he thought to taste it again half an hour later, it was water and odd remnants, all gone.

Suzel loved being a hostess. Tall and attractive, dressed to the nines and high strung, she still lived in her family's aristocratic past whenever she had an appropriate audience. Tim Everbright fulfilled that role this evening. Somehow, attempting in his blundering way to feel his way into the politics of the region, he had made a comment about the French Revolution.

"Murderers!" she hissed. Then she told the family story of her elderly ancestor, hauled in a cart to Paris to be tried before a court of ignorant jackals, along with real peasantry, the retainers who had retained their loyalty.

Her eyes flashed with rage by the table's candlelight. "Your famous revolutionaries killed more peasants than aristocrats," she pronounced. The emotion was so vivid that it could have happened yesterday. For Suzel, perhaps it had.

There was an awkward silence, broken at length by Jacques Lebrun, Editor of *Sud-Ouest*, detained at the newspaper, who had slid in inconspicuously as the oysters were being served.

"Well, at least in our day justice is late but seems to be working its course. As you'll read in tomorrow's *Sud-Ouest*, the Pryor murder seems to be solved. Our reporter found poor Yves Crespier slumped over dead at Chateau La Source earlier today. She also found a signed confession to the Pryor murder. So it seems that there was a Bordeaux connection after all. No need to go into the details at dinner. Surely the police will verify everything in due course."

Robbie was stunned. Obviously it was Sylvie who had found the body. Poor kid. She must be in shock. He must call her immediately. Damn! He didn't have her number with him. He couldn't be a total idiot and ask Lebrun for the number. Well, the dinner party would soon break up. He'd call her from home. She probably wouldn't want to talk about this, so soon. No matter. He'd invite her to drive with him to the Resistance Memorial ceremony on Saturday.

There was a gabble of comment around the table. Everyone knew and liked Crespier. They also knew that Pryor had recently panned many of the wine estates of the region, including Crespier's Chateau La Source. Unexpectedly, Tim Everbright then made the remark they all later recalled.

"What an odd thing to happen, and how unnecessary. Why, during his last trip to Paris, based on his very preliminary notes from his last visit here, Pryor had told us that he was looking forward to a return trip to Bordeaux to test again the latest vintage. He said that he hardly believed it."

Everbright now held the entire room. He picked up his glass of wine and continued. "Across the board, Pryor told us that he thought that last year's vintage was the very best for Bordeaux since this wonderful 1982." He swirled his glass of 1975 Chateau Figeac, took a sip, and went on.

"Virtually everybody had made excellent wines, he had said. It was clear that was what he was going to write if he had only lived to do so. He said that chateau after chateau, the wine was a delight. He even said that we should consider buying futures in these wines, before the prices went up, which they would be sure to do. The pattern of excellence was clear for the vintage and it was unmistakable.

"So I just have to wonder," Everbright mused, "just why any wine estate owner would want to kill someone who was going to write a tribute like that to the entire Bordeaux vintage?"

The dinner party was left to ponder that anomaly as the waiters served the dessert with 1967 Chateau d'Yquem.

CHAPTER 12

Montaigne's Tower

They drove slowly in Robbie's Ford. Sylvie wanted to replace what she had seen with new impressions, and talk about anything rather than the murder scene. But she had to exorcise that picture first from the forefront of her mind, and talk about it because she had to, and because Robbie had gently asked her to. "You saw the article," she said. "It was even worse actually being there. Horrible." She shivered. "Lots of blood and no dignity. The pictures that *Sud-Ouest* wouldn't print get it right. But nothing really important was omitted."

Then, to change the mood, "Tell me about this ceremony and your part in it, *cher ami.*"

"It's called representation. It's a big part of Foreign Service life, and I love it," he said. "Not just the little stump speeches that I give and listen to. I like the ceremony, the celebration of something that had been worth doing, and I like the chance to show the flag."

"Not to mention," she grinned, "the receptions you attend."

Really, he had better start exercising.

It was a clear Saturday morning, perfect for the annual ceremony at the Resistance Memorial. They turned left on the small country road after St. Emilion, just before Castillon. So much concentrated history in such a small area, Robbie thought. Not five minutes earlier Sylvie had pointed out the little side road that took one to the chateau of Michel de Montaigne, author of the *Essays*. And it had been at Castillon that the English had lost the concluding battle of the Hundred Years War in 1453, literally outgunned by French artillery.

They arrived at a clearing, an open field surrounded by forest, marked with a sculptured wall, like a gate swinging open. This field dividing the *departements* of the Gironde and the Dordogne had also marked the boundary between Occupied and Unoccupied France during the early years of the Second World War. It was across this field that the Resistance network had slipped downed Allied airmen on their way back to England.

Each year, a commemorative ceremony was held for the Resistance group that operated here, the *CND Castille*. They had started in 1940 at a nearby chateau, a group of determined men who planned Resistance activities before France had even fallen, or de Gaulle had flown from Merignac Airport to England.

Robbie remembered some of their code names: Aramis, Champion, Espadon. These were heroes of Uncle Seth's generation. He must remember to call Uncle Seth and give him an account of the morning's ceremony. He made sure that the American wreath sent by Jean Deplace was one of the eight wreaths carefully guarded by the serious young man who was coordinating the ceremony. The young man was in turn watched by a much older man, probably a relative and certainly a veteran of the Resistance, who was seated near the wreaths.

An official wearing a ceremonial sash greeted him. "Ah, *Monsieur le Consul*, you are late." Robbie, early as always for official ceremonies, was puzzled. The man continued with a sad smile, "We hoped that you Americans would be here in 1939, you see. Then perhaps this would not have been necessary."

He shook hands with Dick Sanderson, representing Great Britain, and their Canadian colleague. In a new gesture well and truly marking the end of the Cold War, a Bordeaux wine merchant was even there as Honorary Consul for Russia. Erika Lutz was not there, of course. Bordeaux Mayor Alain Juppe was represented by his Deputy Mayor, and Robbie also recognized Albert Demonthon, Prefect of the Gironde, and his counterpart from the Dordogne.

There was a small crowd, and at the front row, all proudly disdaining to sit in the folding chairs that had been provided, stood the the spindly group of white-haired, aging lions who had saved French honor here. Sylvie joined the spectators while Robbie took his place with the other officials for the ceremony.

A trumpet call, an order to attention by the honor guard, and then Robbie, Dick Sanderson and the Canadian Consul General and Russian Honorary Consul walked slowly towards the wall, with the Deputy Mayor, the Prefects, and the President of the *CND Castille* Association. Just before stepping forth, aides handed the commemorants their appropriate wreaths. When they reached the wall, Robbie saw the commemorative plaques which had been donated years earlier, when the memorial had been enlarged and rededicated.

The plaque that had been posed by the American Consul General of the time recited what had been said after the Civil War battle of Chancellorsville, "Uncommon Valor Was A Common Virtue." At the center, another plaque noted that on that spot was buried an urn of ashes from the death camps. Sylvie had told him during their drive over from Bordeaux that the urn had been deposited there by General de Gaulle's niece, herself a survivor of Ravensbruck.

Robbie listened to the introductory prayers and the reflections of the *CND Castille* Association President, then on cue he stepped forward and deposited the wreath on behalf of the United States. Almost involuntarily, before stepping back into line he saluted the memorial and its meaning.

The dark man staring at him from the sidelines seemed out of place.

Robbie, sensing that he was being stared at, turned around briefly, but didn't notice anyone in particular. Probably just my imagination, he thought. I must be getting a little jumpy. Then he remembered that Commissioner Moineau earlier had said something about reinforcing his security detail. The man (if indeed there was one) was probably just a security officer stuck with Saturday duty, for himself or perhaps one of the ranking French officials here. Of course, that was it. Best not to trouble Sylvie with such speculation. She'd only be concerned, he hoped.

A *vin d'honneur* followed, in a nearby school. This was an inescapable part of French life, Robbie knew, apparently satisfying some deeply felt need for ceremonials.

At last, after shaking hands with all of the officials in attendance, Robbie spotted a very shaken-looking Charles de Tourneau. He seemed a bit out of his territory over here in the Dordogne. Robbie walked over, shook hands with de Tourneau and said hello. So did Sylvie.

"I hadn't expected to see you here."

"It's a family tradition. My father was a member of the Resistance, operating out of this area."

"So was the father of Yves Crespier, if I remember rightly."

"Yes. They were comrades then. The interesting thing is that neither knew that the other man was a part of the same network until after the war."

"That's probably what made the network so hard to penetrate and betray," Sylvie ventured. "They were able to keep things separate. People only knew what they had to know."

"That's still true, I hear, in intelligence work," Robbie said. Uncle Seth would like her, he decided.

He was struck that the fathers of two very different men, the aristocratic de Tourneau, and the earthier Crespier, had been united by the fight against the Nazis. The Resistance sometimes brought people together across all sorts of boundaries. Sylvie left them to speak with the Deputy Mayor.

"I was very sorry to hear about Crespier," Robbie said. "I didn't want to mention it in her presence. She found him, you know. It is still unbelievable that he would commit suicide, let alone murder…even if he had been injured by Pryor."

De Tourneau looked uncomfortable. "I suppose that we have to believe it now. A great tragedy for his family, and a real loss to all who value quality wines."

Only in France, Robbie reflected, could the tragedy of a suicide to the surviving family, and the loss for the wine trade, be put on the same emotional plane. He was sorry to have raised the matter, and after a moment's awkward silence was pleased that Claude de Monoury had walked over to see him.

"*Ah, Monsieur le Consul* how are things going? We're looking forward to a wonderful ceremony at the *Jurade.* Have you sorted things out with Senator Etchevari and Mr. Hawkins from the Embassy?"

He was stunned, as they shook hands, to realize that de Monoury was passing him a note. Fortunately, Robbie retained the presence of mind to simply pocket it, as de Monoury had obviously intended, and keep the conversation light.

There had been another exchange of cables, he said, and Senator Etchevari had confirmed interest in joining the *Jurade de St. Emilion* during his swing through the region. So had Elliot Hawkins from the Embassy. "Might as well sign up now. I won't be able to afford those fine St. Emilion wines once we're posted back to Washington," Elliot had chirped when Robbie had raised the possibility of his joining the order.

Since the only commitment was to drink some of the finest Bordeaux wines, don a ceremonial robe, repeat some formulas about wine, and then attend a gargantuan lunch, it would be a treat for both. Robbie thanked de Monoury on their behalf.

Please join us for the ceremony, *Monsieur le Consul.* Bring a friend, too, if you would like. I'm sure that you will like the luncheon. My own 1995 wines will be featured." That really would be a pleasure, and Robbie accepted.

"Bring what 'friend' where, *cher ami*?" Sylvie had rejoined him just in time to hear de Monoury's final words. There wasn't even any incentive to tease her. He just wanted her to enjoy the *Jurade* luncheon with him, and was pleased that she immediately accepted.

* * *

Robbie went out to his car to read the note in private.

"Meet me at four o'clock this afternoon at the Tower, Chateau Montaigne. Come alone." That was all it said. Robbie read it hurriedly as he waited for Sylvie. That gives me two problems. First, do I meet him? Well, it's just too intriguing to pass up. And he is, after all, doing me a favor with the *Jurade.* But he said to do so alone. So do I leave Sylvie in the dark about this?

Sylvie solved his dilemma for him. She came out to the car and he put down the window. She leaned in, pouting her annoyance.

"What's the matter?"

"Nothing. Just the office. They beeped me to say that I've got to spend some more effort on this story for the Sunday edition. That's what comes of giving feature writers vacations. I'm going to interview more of the people here, and then catch a ride back with the photographer. I'll be working late for the Sunday edition."

She frowned, then smiled again.

"If you are lucky," she teased, "I may mention you, *Monsieur le Consul.* I might even spell your name correctly!"

Robbie leaned over and kissed her. Then he drove on to Castillon. He would have enough time for a decent lunch, and still make it back to Chateau Montaigne before four o'clock.

❧ ❧ ❧

The private road was deserted. First Robbie drove a mile or so through woods, and then a valley, scenic and hidden, greeted him. The road ended with a sharp left turn up a small hill, near the top of which was perched Chateau Montaigne. The little hamlet itself, appropiately enough, was called Saint Michel de Montaigne, and it was just five miles from Castillon.

Robbie drove onto the property itself, a long country avenue bordered with trees, and approached the chateau. The privately occupied residential section was in front of him. Robbie had been there before. The property was owned by the family of one of his colleagues, the Honorary Consul General of the Netherlands. They produced an excellent wine, whose label displayed the chateau's famous Tower.

He parked his car. There were few other visitors in the Tower, judging from the cars already parked. It was a quarter to four, and so Robbie walked around the left side of the castle, to survey the valley panorama from the castle walkway.

Montaigne had been one of his favorite writers in college. He had substituted reason and measured judgment for chaos and hatred. Robbie remembered that Montaigne was a royal councillor who had left public life for years to retreat to this country estate and write. The composer of the *Essays* was a wealthy man, born here, whose father had been Mayor of Bordeaux five hundred years ago. So had Montaigne himself, in a time that included plague, devastating wars of religion and insurrection.

Much like our own century, Robbie thought.

On this hill overlooking the valley, there was an illusion of calm. It was striking that this peaceful oasis adjoined on one side a monument to the French Resistance, and on the other, the battlefield where English claims to France were decisively checked.

He walked back to the parking area, then through a gate on his right, which led to the public area of the chateau. There, along a wall, were two towers. Robbie paid his entrance fee, and received a ticket which was immediately taken from him again by the ticket seller, torn in half, and returned to him once again.

He entered the courtyard and climbed the first stairs to his right, past the former chapel, then to what had been Montaigne's living quarters, and finally to the top floor, the writer's library. It was exactly four o'clock.

The room had three visitors already there, an English couple on holiday, and Claude de Monoury. Since de Monoury did not greet him, Robbie decided to put on his tourist mode while the couple was still there.

That wasn't difficult. It was a fine Renaissance room, all dark wood and beams, with a window or two where the view, which was excellent, might be admired. The beams, Robbie noticed, were decorated with maxims that he struggled to decipher, with what remained of his schoolboy Latin and Greek.

Some, like the famous Greek "Nothing in excess," were easy. He soon gave up on the others. But it was interesting all the same that Montaigne had surrounded himself with symbols of moderation and reason. Robbie was reminded of the prayer before study of St. Thomas Aquinas, extolling similar virtues, which was inscribed at the saint's burial place, the Jacobins Church in Toulouse.

After an eternity, the English couple left. The men listened for a moment, to make sure that they would not be disturbed. Nobody came. De Monoury came over to Robbie with a worried look.

"Thanks so much for coming, *Monsieur le Consul.* I'm sorry to have been so mysterious about all this, but I didn't know where else to turn."

"Glad to help if I can. What's the matter?"

"I don't even know where to begin. Actually the whole business is embarrassing. I'm in a real mess, and I don't know how to get out.

Maybe I can't. But I thought you could suggest something. Certainly you may know more about this than I do myself. Perhaps you can even help me with some other pieces of the puzzle. It's too much for me to handle any more by myself."

De Monoury looked tentative, as though he were sorry on second thought that he was there at all. Robbie half expected him to throw up his hands, and leave the room without even telling him just what was the matter.

"*Monsieur le Consul,* I must have your word that this conversation is just between the two of us. At least for now." Now de Monoury looked frightened, and his voice reflected his fear.

"If you'd rather not go through with this..."

"No. But you may be sorry I talked with you at all. I can't help that. But I do need to know that this talk is between us."

"You have my word on that. Nobody even knows that we are meeting."

De Monoury was visibly relieved by this reference to the Consul's friend, the reporter from *Sud-Ouest*. So he hadn't told her about this meeting after all. That gave him the extra courage he needed to go ahead.

"The truth is, *Monsieur le Consul*, that I'm being blackmailed. He said that he would kill me if I told anyone."

"What do you mean, 'blackmailed?'"

"The word was badly chosen. I haven't done anything wrong. But he says that my wine crop will be destroyed if I don't pay him his protection money."

"Who is he? Why did he start this with you?"

"I have no idea. He just called, like that, out of the blue, several months ago. He asked for money. It wasn't a great deal. And I didn't get the feeling that he would raise the sum that he was asking. He seemed to have things carefully planned."

"What does he look like?"

"No idea on that either. I've never seen him. Our contacts have been entirely by telephone. He called me to set things up, and then to tell me how to proceed. Once a month I leave money for him in a prearranged place. Any problem, and I leave a signal for it to be done the following week. So far, all has gone smoothly. Then you and I talked once or twice, and I thought that maybe you could help. Now, another monthly payment is due next week."

They were interrupted by the sound of people coming up the stairs. De Monoury froze, and Robbie walked slowly over to the far wall, his guidebook in hand.

A noisy tour group of children entered the room, led by their teacher, a Catholic nun in full kit, with sweeping black gown, wimple and an amused expression "Now children!" seemed to be her usual mode of expression.

Several of the more studious ones looked hard at the inscriptions in the beams. To Robbie's annoyance, the class egghead started translating them, better than Robbie had done. Annoying child. Eventually they trailed out of the room, again leaving just Robbie and de Monoury.

We can resume our talk now, Robbie thought. His mind went for a moment back to a legend he had heard in Istanbul, when his father was Consul General there. The legend had it that an Orthodox priest had been serving mass at St. Sophia in Constantinople when the city fell. He was said to have walked into the wall when the Muslims entered the church. The legend also had it that he would walk back out of the same wall and resume the service precisely where he had stopped, when Constantinople, now Istanbul, was again Christian.

"What made you think I could help?" Robbie asked. "It sounds strictly like a matter for your own police to handle."

"Ordinarily I'd agree, of course. But he did say that he, or his people, I don't remember which, have police contacts and would know if I tried to bring in the police. They would retaliate immediately against my family."

"They?"

"Yes. He makes it sound as though he is backed up by others. Many others. But which others, who they are exactly, I don't care to know. I can only tell you that from the voice, this man is a fanatic, cold-blooded, highly intelligent, and not quite all there. I believe him when he says that he would retaliate against my family."

He had one further point to make, and paused before doing so. Robbie was about to ask what all that had to do with him, when de Monoury slowly continued.

"*Monsieur le Consul,* perhaps you will know how to proceed, or whether this has happened to others, and what the police may be doing already. If they are investigating, then you could be in touch with them, and it needn't involve me and my family directly."

His speaking pace grew slower and more deliberate. "You see, *Monsieur le Consul,* the man is an American. All his calls to me have been in American English, fluent and without the trace of an accent. I think there must be some American gangsters beginning to muscle in on the Bordeaux wine trade, and I appeal to you to help."

Robbie was flabbergasted. He sputtered that he was on excellent terms with the *Commissaire de Police*, and that Moineau had never mentioned to him anything about American criminals in the region. He couldn't even think of any American citizens in jail throughout the entire area! The idea was preposterous. Clearly the man was speaking English just to throw people off the track. "You must go to the police immediately," he said. "This is something that only they can handle."

"Then I'll just let it go for a while," de Monoury said sadly. "I can't take the chance of my family being hurt. He won't do anything while the money is being paid regularly, anyway. Don't forget to keep this our secret."

He left first, and when Robbie entered the courtyard a few minutes later, de Monoury was nowhere in sight.

* * *

As he walked into his apartment, the telephone was ringing. Robbie crossed the room quickly and answered it. On the line was Uncle Seth.

"Hello, Robbie. I've been making a call or two, and I've been hearing some odd things. How much longer are you supposed to be in Bordeaux?"

"Another year, I guess, depending upon whether or not I take home leave directly from here, or go to another post overseas. Why do you ask?"

"It was something one of my friends in State dropped the other day. He said that you might be moving on fairly soon. It sounded to me like a more immediate possibility."

"Well, let's see. I did stop by Personnel before returning to Bordeaux, and confirmed that I wanted language training and assignment to Hungary next. It's nothing immediate. Unless, of course, someone will be transferred out of Embassy Budapest ahead of schedule and they have a priority vacancy to fill. I've still got a year to go here, after all."

"That must be it. He probably got it wrong. Usually did, as I recall. Interesting that you would want to go to Budapest."

"Yes. It's a good idea to have a real specialty in the Foreign Service, one that the political appointees won't want to grab when ambassadorships are decided. Anyway Hungary has always interested me, particularly as you know the Hungarian Revolution of 1956. It would be fascinating to serve there."

"And your father would be pleased, I think."

There was an awkward silence. Robbie's father had served in Budapest as a young Foreign Service Officer. He never really talked about it, but his service there had not helped his career. Quite the opposite, it seemed.

Robbie was uncomfortable and changed the subject. "I sent you the newspaper articles on the suicide of a wine estate owner here. That seems to account for the Pryor murder after all. The man was probably despondent."

"How convenient."

"You mean that you don't believe that explanation?"

"Not necessarily. It may very well be true. I merely say that it is convenient, and perhaps what the police should be looking at is two murders, not one murder and one suicide. Obviously the Pryor and Crespier deaths are related in some way. The interesting question is whether they were done by the same person, or arranged by him. If not, murder number two must have come as a complete surprise to murderer number one. His reaction would be interesting."

Robbie tried to digest all this. Uncle Seth continued. "Crime never was my specialty, really, but I was taken by the pictures that you sent, that were part of the article. Take a close look at them, and you'll see what I mean."

So Uncle Seth was being inscrutable again. That meant that he was spinning in his mind some intelligence connection. Perhaps that explained the other "odd things" that he had been hearing. Robbie suspected that he would learn more on that subject during Evalyn's visit.

"I was going to telephone you anyway, Uncle Seth, or send another letter. You would have been interested by my day today. I joined others at a commemorative ceremony for the French Resistance near Castillon. The group was the *CND Castille*."

"We knew them and relied on them. They were so precise that at first London thought that it was a German plant. People were sent to Switzerland to meet with them and sort that out."

"What sort of intelligence did they supply?"

"Mostly ship movements in and out of Bordeaux. Actually one of the most helpful operatives was a manual laborer, a young man of limited intelligence, what we would now call handicapped, really.

The Germans never paid any attention to him at all. But he could keep an accurate count, and he had a reliable memory. And he was a true French patriot."

"How effective was the group?"

"Very." Uncle Seth searched his memory. "As I recall, their intelligence led to the tracking and destruction of at least a dozen Nazi submarines, and many more cargo ships. More than that, they also helped some Allied airmen to escape. Really, they were a fine group of patriots. I hope that most of them survived, although it doesn't seem too likely."

"I also heard that the father of Yves Crespier, the suicide, had been a member of the group."

"Alain Crespier? I remember him. A very tough, responsible man. Fearless by the ordinary understanding of the word, by which I mean that he controlled the fear that we all often felt very well. Not everyone can do that. I can't imagine a son of his a suicide. Acorns not falling far from the tree, and all that."

"I talked with some of the survivors after the ceremony, at the *vin d'honneur*. One woman told me that the Nazis sometimes staged phony air drops of their own people, supposed to be from London. Then they could round up the Resistance people at the drop zone."

"We heard about that, and tried to change the recognition signals often, to protect our people on the ground. We didn't always succeed."

"I've never seen such fear in a person's face as I saw today in that woman's eyes, as she told me her story." Robbie could have added the look he had seen on de Monoury's face, but resisted. He had given the man his word, after all.

"I can understand that. By the way, Robbie, I assume that you are not being negligent about your own security?"

There was a brief silence on Robbie's end of the line, so Uncle Seth pressed the point. "Remember your Montaigne. Moderation and order in all things. Don't go taking any foolish chances."

Robbie grinned. "I guess that means I should carry my new swordcane more often. No, really, I'm fine. And the local *Commissaire* promised me some extra protection. I spotted someone on duty today."

"Glad to hear it. But you might doublecheck to make sure."

Robbie shuddered. No wonder Uncle Seth was a survivor. Robbie hoped that he also had that quality. He was beginning to suspect that he might need it.

CHAPTER 13

The Last Redoubt

It was good to get out of Bordeaux from time to time, Robbie thought as he drove his Ford south. Beautiful city and all that, but sometimes you just have to get the fresh point of view that only the countryside has to offer.

At the Consulate General, security was improving at the Embassy's prodding. Administrative Officer Jean Deplace was pleased that the official Consulate General car was being replaced by an armored limousine. Georges had gone to Germany to pick up the new car and take a week's course in offensive driving. He would learn all of the driving habits that a careful driver was not supposed to have, but needed in order to save passenger lives from terrorists. It couldn't be helped, and would be worthwhile in the long run. And certainly Georges had to have that training before Senator Etchevari's visit.

It wasn't a very interesting drive down through the flat Landes country and Mont de Marsan to the Basque interior, but the scenery picked up near Orthez, and of course St Jean Pied de Port, his destination, was a vibrant postcard of colors. It was a Basque town, the capital of one of their seven districts, Lower Navarre, and it remained the gateway to the Pyrenees and the pilgrim route through Spain.

He arrived and drove to the Town Hall, past stone bridges over the Nive River. The streets of the little town invited walking. Basque red, white and green colors were everywhere, adding to the feeling that a festival must be in preparation. Beneath the town's French veneer, something older was apparent. It was from this town that Senator Etchevari's family had come to the United States. St. Jean Pied de Port would be the site of his most important stop, with a public speech. They would welcome home their friend, the grandson of all those who had left for the greater world.

Mayor Jeanne Lhosmette was ecstatic about the visit, and bubbled on about the arrangements. "Don't worry about any trouble, *Monsieur le Consul*. We're so honored that Senator Etchevari will be coming here. We'll issue a town proclamation. It'll be a grand day indeed."

"Senator Etchevari is known for being outspoken."

"So much the better. That is a Basque characteristic."

"Does he have any relatives left in town?"

"Indeed he does, a family living in a house near the Rue des Ramparts."

"Has Senator Etchevari remained in contact with them?"

"Not really, Christmas cards, that sort of thing. I know they would be honored to see him when he comes."

Nice touch that, Robbie thought. It will be like the return to ancestral Ireland of President Clinton, or President Reagan, for that matter. He took the names of the family and their address, promised to keep in close touch with Mayor Lhosmette, and went off on a walking trip of the city, cane in hand.

On a whim, he decided to visit the Senator's relatives. He walked along the Rue des Ramparts, admired a fine view of the old city, with its shuttered, colorful Renaissance-era houses and then turned off to their side street. The balcony of their two-storied home near the river gushed flowers and welcome.

He was in luck. Jaime and Julie Etchevari, a couple about his own age, were at home about to have a late luncheon. Robbie was welcomed and shown to their table. Colorful hooked rugs covered most of the burnished wooden floors of the small dining room. Julie substituted the good china from her upright mahagony armoire as she served.

"Nothing fancy, *Monsieur le Consul*. We didn't know you were coming, of course."

"You are more than kind, and I am intruding. But Mayor Lhosmette had given me your name and address, and so I came by to see if you were home." The home cooking was spicy and delicious. The wine was cool and refreshing, a fine contrast.

He continued, "Have you been in close touch with your cousin, Senator Etchevari?"

"From time to time." Clearly Jaime Etchevari was the family spokesman. "We are very proud of him, of course. All Basque people know of him. Nobody else has risen so far. Everyone is pleased that he will be visiting the Basque lands, and especially, of course, our town. It would be nice if he had the time to see us as well."

"I'm sure that he would want to do so. You'll be meeting him anyway, of course, when he gives his speech."

"He is a proud man who is not afraid to face the truth. I hear that he has talked about terrorism elsewhere."

Interesting, Robbie thought. Jaime Etchevari is raising the very topic that concerns me. Better hear him out. "He has been outspoken. What would you like him to know, before he comes here, about Basque issues?"

"There is nothing we can teach him about our people. He is a leader, after all. But maybe he hasn't heard everything about the extremists, the ETA. They are growing stronger. There is cause for fear."

"Why do you think they are becoming stronger?"

"We hear that there is more money coming in. From where, I could not say. There is talk of more recruits for an armed struggle. People are confused, but they are getting excited at the same time. That is all that I hear."

"Your cousin will be speaking here publicly, as you know. What should he say about Basque issues, and the ETA?"

"Tell him not to be afraid of the truth. The Basque heritage is a source of pride. Our history and our language should be taught to all of our children. Some people, including our mayor, favor a Basque *departement*. I like that idea, too. But an independent Basque homeland is a pipe dream. If it is possible, it can never be achieved by terrorism. I know that Senator Etchevari shares this view. He must tell the truth as he sees it. We will be proud of him, I know."

Robbie sensed that this was a long speech for Jaime Etchevari. He had probably rehearsed what he would tell his cousin if he ever got the chance. Sensing that he probably wouldn't be able to do so in person, he had just enlisted the American Consul to do it for him. Fair enough.

Now it was time to drive on to Pau. Robbie would have preferred to take a side trip, across the border, but there just wasn't enough time. Pamplona and St. Sebastian were not very far away, across the Pyrenees. Throughout the Middle Ages, pilgrims had converged on St. Jean Pied de Port on their way through France to Santiago de Compostela. Modern pilgrims increasingly did so once again. Robbie wondered what that might be like.

And just fifteen miles away, south along the mountain road leading from St. Jean Pied de Port, was Roncevaux. That was the first stop in Spain of the pilgrim's route to Compostela. It was also the location in the eighth century where Charlemagne's outnumbered rear guard under Roland had fought desperately. According to the *Chanson de Roland*, the enemy was the Saracen, and Roland had long since become a French national hero, like St. Joan of Arc. But Robbie knew that modern scholars believed that Roland's enemy had been the Basques.

❧ ❧ ❧

Jean-Claude Mauret, Prefect of the Pyrenees-Atlantiques, was an amiable, well spoken man. He welcomed Robbie at his official residence in Pau.

"I was curious about the portrait in the entrance hall, *Monsieur le Prefet*. I seem to have seen the man's picture before, but I can't place it."

"Very perceptive, *Monsieur le Consul*. That is Lieutenant Norman Prince, an American pilot with our Lafayette Escadrille in the First War." Robbie nodded in recognition. He had seen another portrait of Lieutenant Prince at the Harvard Club in New York. Prince was an icon from another era.

The Prefect elaborated a bit as they entered his study and sat down by the fire. "When Pau was rediscovered and became fashionable in the early years of the century, many English families had homes here. I don't know how many still do. There were a few Americans here, too. By the way," he said interrupting himself, "did you know that Wilbur and Orville Wright even had a flight school in Pau?"

Robbie had not known that.

"Yes, the Bearn Aero Club still recalls that school. There is more than *bearnaise* sauce here! Perhaps that is where Norman Prince got the idea of becoming a pilot, who knows?

"This was the Prince family home. They formally deeded it to the Government of France after the First War. The condition was that the portrait of Norman Prince always be displayed in the entry hall. We are honored to do so."

Robbie brought Prefect Mauret up to date on plans for Senator Etchevari's visit. "All of it, of course, except for the St. Emilion stopover will take place in your *departement*, in the interior and along the coast."

"I shall be pleased to welcome the Senator personally."

"I have been told that there will be increased security for his visit," Robbie volunteered. "Senator Etchevari is not only a prominent Basque, and an American, he is also quite outspoken, particularly on the subject of terrorism."

The Prefect answered slowly, in a measured way. "Yes, I've been told that. I even hear that he will be giving an outdoor public address at St. Jean Pied de Port."

Robbie nodded.

"Senator Etchevari has every right to his opinions. Of course, he is our guest, and would respect French opinion on the matter. We believe that Basque separatism is a bad dream. But sometimes I think that we need to do more to reassure the Basque people that we respect their culture and contributions to France, and that we will protect them from any extremists. And there is also the question of a separate Basque *departement*. However that, of course, is a matter for President Chirac."

"I think there is no question, *Monsieur le Prefet,* that Senator Etchevari does not back Basque terrorism. I'm not sure of his exact position, if he even has one, on the question of a Basque *departement*. But I can understand the sensitivity. Look at the political problems that President de Gaulle caused years ago during his visit to Quebec when he called '*Vive le Quebec libre*!' to the crowd."

Prefect Mauret smiled at the comparison.

"He most probably will do what he has already done in speeches before the United States Senate. He will condemn terrorism, and the ETA specifically, in this very region."

"He will be right to do so," Mauret said. "And we will be right to make sure of his protection. I know that he will not be a demagogue on the issue."

"That is not his style."

"Then he may well be making a fine contribution to ending terrorism, and the welfare of his people during his visit here. I will look forward to meeting him."

Left to his own devices after the meeting, Robbie sat at a cafe near the Boulevard des Pyrenees, an esplanade with a superb view of the Pyrenees and their foothills. It was easy to imagine families taking that stroll in the early years of the century.

On a previous trip he had seen the chateau of Henry IV, the first Bourbon monarch, who ended France's religious wars and was thought by many to be her greatest king. Now he spent an hour visiting the birthplace of Charles Bernadotte, now a museum to the marshal of Napoleon who became Charles XIV, King of Sweden.

Official chores now done, Saturday and Sunday were free, an excellent opportunity to see some of the grand sights of the Pyreneean foothill region. Usually, Robbie would have driven immediately to Lourdes, in order to avoid driving after dark. But tonight, he had planned a special treat, dinner at Chez Pierre on the Rue Barthou in Pau. Nobody goes to Lourdes for the food, after all.

Not many Americans knew the restaurant, which was a good thing, Robbie thought. With just a few tables, and a deserved star in Michelin, he had been pleased that Ghislaine had managed to secure his reservation. He had a single malt Scotch in the bar, deferring to the Scottish decor.

When it was time for dinner, Robbie enjoyed his *poule au pot* with three separate sauces. It had to be ordered in advance, and this chicken was as succulent as any from Bresse in Burgundy. No wonder Henry IV had promised his subjects a chicken in every pot, centuries before any American politician had used the phrase.

This was delicious, elegant in its simplicity, rich with flavors. Robbie promised himself that the next time he came, he would have a steak with the chef's famous *bearnaise* sauce. After all, this is where it originated. He was really being sparing, he told himself. In Edwardian times, both dishes would have been eaten at the same meal, with more courses added.

And now, Friday night, the weekend lay before him. Vice Consul Stan Bartlett was taking the duty at the Consulate General. Asceticism didn't appeal to Robbie. The sensual pleasures suited him very well. He liked a good meal, a warm fire, fine music. It was annoying not to be able to enjoy a good smoke, but he let that pass. He was for the moment a confirmed bachelor isolated in his contentment; too self-important to be lonely, too sated to reflect on his selfishness, and too satisfied to notice the athletic man at the corner table, half hidden behind an afternoon sports newspaper, who was just beginning his meal as Robbie's ended.

Saturday he would devote to Lourdes, and then to St. Bertrand de Comminges. He would stay overnight in the picturesque town of Foix in the Ariege Department. Then, on Sunday, he was looking forward to visiting the Cathar fortress of Montsegur, the last redoubt of a group of devout, schismatic believers, Christians who had been the victims of an officially sanctioned Crusade.

Then, there would just be time to drive through the Pyrenees to the little nation of Andorra for a brief visit, before the long drive back to Bordeaux. A lot to do, but Robbie thought, at just the right pace for a memorable weekend.

Robbie paid his bill, and drove the new highway to Lourdes from Pau, looking forward to his weekend in the mountain fastnesses that had inspired so many for so long. Perhaps he was searching for something in the guise of tourism. If so, that cover was perfect, in this beautiful region.

Lourdes was, as usual, filled with tourists. That didn't bother Robbie. He liked the idea that so many people hoped for truth here. He wasn't even put off by the souvenir vendors who ringed the church area itself, where they were forbidden. He spent a few minutes picking out a postcard or two, and looked quizzically at the replicas, said to be filled with water from St. Bernadette's miraculous spring. He tended to picture Jennifer Jones, who had played Bernadette on the screen, as the saint.

Lourdes, of course, was one of several sites where a miraculous visitation had come to ordinary people in the nineteenth century. There had been similar reports in Germany and in Spain, and perhaps other places as well. The battle between secular and religious authorities was a familiar one. Sometimes, as at Lourdes, they had even changed sides. Lourdes had received sanction, while others had not. That was perhaps one of those mysteries. Meanwhile, the fact that people wanted to come was surely a good thing.

Robbie had always been interested in religions. He had studied comparative religions at Brown. Perhaps his interest was due to his namesake, John Robinson, the pastor of the Pilgrims. But Robbie usually felt more kinship with Isaac Robinson, John's son, who had actually made it to New England, and who had been expelled from his offices in the Plymouth Colony for pleading tolerance for the Quakers. He liked the fact that Isaac, a founder of what became Falmouth on Cape Cod, had also kept a tavern there.

Robbie entered the church area. He felt isolated in the crowd. They were, after all, Roman Catholics, and he had slipped away from his Congregationalism. Odd how even a diplomat trained in cultural empathy still carried his own cultural baggage around like a shield. He would have felt less awkward in a Buddhist shrine in the Himalayan mountain region, not expecting any similarities with his familiar beliefs, and not receiving any. Come to think of it, the Valley of Kathmandu, which he had once visited, rather resembled this region in its ability to inspire faith.

The plaza and basilica were filled. He was glad that he had left his cane in the car. That would not have been right to bring here. It was a weapon, after all.

Turning his head, he could see the remnants of the inevitable *chateau fort* that had guarded this region, and now looked down on the basilica, there to accommodate the many thousands who came. Surely it would have been a grand setting for the concerts of the Easter season, now ended. It was a far cry from his New England ideal, the wooden, spired church on the village green.

Robbie joined others at the spring. Here it was easier to understand, and participate in what was familiar. The faces of the others were mirrors of belief and hope. Robbie wondered what his own face expressed. Surely something better than the dark cynicism of that fellow at the fringe of the crowd waiting for a sip of the spring water.

Abruptly he left the spring and the plaza, walking up an adjoining hill past the Stations of the Cross, life-size sculptures marking each stop on this Pyreneean version of the Via Dolorosa. They were good, and Robbie was intrigued to note, had been made by Hungarian craftsmen before the First World War.

He thought about all this during his cafe lunch, and as he drove southeast to St. Bertrand de Comminges. Then he thought of Sylvie Marceau. He wondered if she ever came here, and what her thoughts might be. He assumed that she was Catholic. In France, "The eldest daughter of the Church," that was almost a given.

Perhaps he should have asked Sylvie to come with him. She might have enjoyed meeting him here for the weekend. Then he smiled at the idea of a shared weekend visiting religious sites. Get a grip!

He drove on through the mountains.

The setting at St. Bertrand de Comminges was even more striking than that of Lourdes. Perched on a hilly location, its ancient history stretched back at least to Roman times, for according to the tradition, Herod himself was exiled here.

Ramparts enclosed the cloisters and cathedral, much of it Romanesque from the eleventh and twelfth centuries. Robbie was intrigued to note a Bordeaux connection. Bishop Bertrand, the man who became Pope Clement V and had owned the wine estate in the

Graves region known now as Pape Clement, had finished the cathedral's construction in the fourteenth century.

The open walkway by the cloister framed the surroundings perfectly, an archway here, a carving there, or a glimpse of the Pyrenees. It was comforting to realize that this, too, was the precise faith of his fathers in the era that it had been constructed. He felt content and at peace, almost alone in contemplating the beauties of St. Bertrand de Comminges. Just one other visitor, a man wearing a hat and raincoat, was loitering near the cloisters, guidebook in hand.

Then the mood changed. Tourists again! A busload of noisy urban pilgrims descended from their coach. Robbie sought refuge within the cathedral, but the calm had been shattered. Like invading carpenter ants, they spread out everywhere. There seemed to be even more tourists coming. Robbie could see yet another bus coming to join this one. Worse yet, this one seemed to be full of what promised to be extremely noisy children.

Robbie drove the scenic road to Saint Girons, and then to Foix, settling in for the evening at the Hotel Lons. Ordinarily, he would have been glad to prowl around this old town on the Ariege River, rich with history with its own ruined castle, its visual testimony to a rowdy, picaresque medieval past. With a long drive in store for the next day, however, better make it an early night. He did not stir from the hotel, reading a guidebook of the region and of Andorra before going to bed. At least he was sure to be alone with his thoughts at Montsegur.

Antonio knew that remote Montsegur, still isolated from throngs of tourists, would be the right place. Shadowing the American Consul all day had not been difficult. As he had thought, however, no real opportunity had presented itself. There had been tourists everywhere.

He looked forward to handling this by himself, face to face. He smiled with anticipation. Then he frowned, his mood changing. It was odd that the Consul was still driving his own car. It was a detail, but details counted. Was this a trap? *Eh, bien.* No driver, and no armored car. That made it easier. If his contacts were having any second thoughts about their revelation, they were moving too slowly. That was always the case with governments. They were ponderous. He held the initiative.

The Consul's chance remark to a waiter had led to Antonio's choice. Montsegur fit his plans perfectly. This must not be done anonymously. Vengeance for his family against the GAL and its American ally was a personal matter. The American Consul must understand. That was not possible in a crowd. As a symbol for the martyred Basque nation, Montsegur was perfect. So was the Basque *makhila* that he would use.

Antonio thought a bit about the future. He would see what this Senator Etchevari had to say before deciding what to do. Contingency plans were his specialty, after all. The priority of course was not this intruding American Senator, but getting ETA men out of their Spanish prisons, by whatever means.

If only he didn't have to handle so many things personally. Well, that would not be the case much longer. For now, there was Raul's nephew, eager to make his mark in the future leadership. That was a start. Once Antonio was in control, others would obey his commands willingly. But that took money, and careful planning.

Meanwhile, there was one more errand to handle. Antonio used a public telephone near his hotel in Foix, and called the home number of Jacques Lebrun, Editor of *Sud-Ouest* in suburban Bordeaux. This was a practice that his friends in the IRA had used with success. It was worth trying now.

"Monsieur Lebrun?"

"*Oui.* Who is calling?" Lebrun was entertaining at home this Saturday evening. He expected interruptions from time to time, from the newspaper, but this voice wasn't a familiar one.

"This is the ETA. The code word is 'Navarre.' I repeat, the code word is 'Navarre.' That will remain the code word until I change it. I will be calling you again soon." He hung up.

Lebrun was shaken. The caller sounded genuine, his voice calm, deliberate and cold. Lebrun recalled that the IRA's use of code words to authenticate their bombings across the English Channel had been an established practice. He also knew that such calls, with short deadlines, were often given just before public bombings. That meant that journalists who received them had only a short time to notify the police, and try to minimize loss of life. The practice carried with it a form of blackmail on the publication of IRA demands. But Lebrun then grimly recalled the call that had led to a building being evacuated…to the public square where the bombs had been set.

So that pattern was now spreading to France!

Lebrun's first call was to his publisher. His second call was to Police Commissioner Jacques Moineau. Then he returned to the dining room and his guests

The short drive from Foix to Lavelanet, and then another five miles or so south to Montsegur, was perfect on this crisp Sunday morning. Robbie recalled the history as he drove. It wasn't hard in this evocative landscape, hills left as hard-edged remnants as former seas and steady glaciation had worn away softer rock formations over the ages. The knobs that were left, called *pogs* locally, were perfectly isolated. Montsegur had been built on such a hill.

The Cathars, Robbie remembered, were a schismatic Christian sect, which had flourished in this region of France some eight hundred years ago. Their ruined fortresses, of which Montsegur was one of the last to be taken, still haunted the Ariege landscape like craggy ghosts. Their doctrine had intrigued Robbie in his comparative religion class at Brown. He had promised himself to visit this region upon his assignment to the Consulate General at Bordeaux.

A series of events had led to their last stand here, in 1244, against the invading crusader force initially commanded by Simon de Montfort. The siege had lasted a full nine months before the defenders, penned into their impregnable fortress on the hill, had surrendered. Just before the end, according to tradition four of them had carried the Cathar treasure away. There was no record of what that treasure might have been. Some variants of the legend referred to the Holy Grail itself.

Upon surrender, the two hundred and five heretics calmly descended from their fortress. Not one converted. All had walked into a gigantic funeral pyre, which had then been torched, burning them alive. Robbie arrived at the meadow beneath the fortress, where this had taken place, the *Prat dels Cremats.* He read the inscription in the Occitane French on the plaque that marked the site: *"Als cathars als martirs del pur amor crestian."* He silently meditated on their fate. He almost envied them the sustaining power of their belief.

Montsegur was an impregnable fortress for the thirteenth century. Clearly, Robbie imagined, the siege artillery of the time had not been up to the task of reducing the fortress. But it was not difficult for a reasonably fit hiker to climb this hill. It was at most a few thousand feet, not a real challenge for a determined White Mountains hiker. Still, his cane was useful, as an aid to keep his footing.

The fortress resolutely stood witness, despite the efforts of the elements, and villagers who over the centuries had pillaged its stones for construction of their own homes. It was glorious from below, Robbie thought, but it must be spectacular seen from above. A small plane or helicopter would be the perfect way to see it. What remained was a triangular courtyard ending in a rectangular tower, like a stone ship whose tower, or *donjon,* looked forward like a nineteenth century whaling vessel.

Robbie entered the courtyard.

The attack came so quickly that at first he was only aware of movement from his left, along the courtyard's inner wall. A man was bearing down on him with what seemed to be a spike. Instinctively, Robbie met that weapon with a sweeping parry of his cane. The attacker seemed disoriented as Robbie twisted off the cane's protective shell and assumed the trained fencer's semi-crouch, in profile towards his enemy. The man picked up loose gravel with his free hand and shoveled it towards Robbie's face as he prepared to lunge again. Robbie stopped the man's lunge with an agile parry, and then began his own attack forwards, across the courtyard lengthwise, towards the tower. The man parried him vigorously but with too much force. He was strong, but no match for a trained fencer.

Suddenly the man gave another lunge and he and Robbie gradually spun around, changing directions. Robbie, his back to the tower, lunged, wounding the man in the left upper arm. Then his sword cane caught the *makhila* in a sweeping circle as the wounded man lowered it, loosening his grip. It was a textbook *prise de fer* using the man's momentum against him, and the *makhila* was flipped in a long arc over the side of the fortress wall.

The man screamed with rage and pain. Desperate, he picked up a large stone and threw it at Robbie, catching him full on the chest. Then he backed through the narrow courtyard entrance and ran down the pathway, to the astonishment of devoted tourists that were swarming up the pathway, just arriving for a commemorative Sunday morning service in the Montsegur courtyard. By the time that Robbie, stunned, had tried to stagger away from the fortress ruins in pursuit of his attacker, he was surrounded by this puzzled and solicitous group.

CHAPTER 14

The Sweet Taste of Sauternes

Stunned, Robbie picked himself up. He was bathed in a cold sweat, hardly aware of the tourists who were helping him to stand. He rested for a minute, said no thanks to offers for help, and unsteadily started down the trail to his car.

Fifty feet or so from the summit he saw a long, thin metal cane with a fringed knob a few yards from the trail. It looked like his attacker's weapon. Robbie went over to get it, and nearly passed out while bending over to pick it up. This was tougher than he thought. Then he remembered about possible fingerprints. He had no idea whether his attacker had been wearing gloves or not. He picked up the cane lightly by the middle and gingerly carried it to his car, holding his own cane under his arm. He put both in the back seat, and sat down in the car and tried to think.

There was no sign of anybody else, except for the tourist group's bus. Even their driver seemed missing. He had probably made the climb with them. Robbie was exhausted. He tried to think it through. Thinking, like his breathing, came in short spurts. Of course he couldn't go on to Andorra, as planned. He should just drive back to Bordeaux. That was it. Then the Foreign Service instinct to report a new development kicked in. Better tell somebody first what had happened. Robbie got on his car phone and called Vice Consul Stan Bartlett.

Stan's cheerful "Hi boss. I hope you're having a great weekend…" faded as he heard Robbie's dulled recitation of what had happened. Stan was a quick study. He knew without being asked that he had to take charge, and he did so.

"No, Robbie, you're NOT driving back to Bordeaux, not right now, and not in that car of yours. You don't sound like you are up to it. And for another thing, you don't even know if that killer is waiting someplace along the road to try again."

That made sense.

"Look, Robbie, remember that I was down there a while back on that consular errand. I know the local officials. I'm going to get hold of the Prefect at Foix. I think that you should drive there. It's not very far. Are you up to it?"

"Yes." Robbie was glad not to have to think things through.

"Then drive to the Prefecture. I'll call the Prefect. I'll tell him to get hold of his CID. Then I'll get hold of Georges. We have the armored car now, just what you need. He's just back, and he'll drive you back to Bordeaux tonight. It'll be a wait, of course, but it'll be safer. I'll call Paris. Should I also call your family, or anybody here?"

"No…I'll arrange all that later. And Stan…'ask' the Prefect, don't 'tell' him."

"You've got it, boss."

"And Stan…thanks."

"Anytime, boss."

Stan's plan worked well. Robbie spent the afternoon at the Prefecture in Foix, made a statement to police investigators, and led them to the two canes in his car. He was called by Ambassador Ronald Adams from the Embassy in Paris expressing concern, a nice thing to do, Robbie thought. No need to trouble his family. They couldn't do anything but worry, and the danger seemed to be past.

While he was at the Prefect's phone, Robbie called Sylvie Marceau. "Please come over this evening, when I get back to Bordeaux," he said. He was relieved to hear her voice. She seemed worried to hear how he sounded. "I'll be there," she answered.

Late in the afternoon Georges arrived in the armored car. Robbie slept on the back seat most of the long way home. There were police stationed outside his apartment door in the *Chartrons*. Georges drove up to the door, and stayed in the car while the police came to the car to escort him to the door. Sylvie Marceau was with them. Robbie went inside with her and locked the door.

"Now I know what combat is like," was the first comment that came into his head. He didn't have to continue. She led him to the living room sofa and held him tightly, embracing him until his tension eased and he could talk.

"Now I know what it is like to nearly lose you," she said.

They went upstairs and undressed. The moment was natural before it became erotic. She had been beautiful clothed and was lovely nude. They kissed and held each other and sometimes even cried a little, whether from release or joy neither could have said. There was only love to feel and receive and share.

Downstairs, Minouette didn't seem to mind Sylvie's presence. A happy master meant more treats, after all.

Commissioner Jacques Moineau greeted his visitors at his office on the Rue Abbe de l'Epee. His foul mood showed. Chastened, they sat at his conference table. There were Jacques Lebrun and Sylvie Marceau of *Sud-Ouest*, Robbie Cutler, and representatives from both the Prefect of Police and the *Renseignements Generaux* A police artist and a CID inspector completed their group.

There was a lot to tell. At Moineau's request Lebrun led off, describing the telephone call that he had received.

"What time did you receive the call?"

"It was about nine o'clock on Saturday evening. We were in the middle of dinner when the call came. I left the table to take the telephone call in the next room."

"What was his voice like?"

"It was a rich, deep voice, one might say a trained singer's voice. But it was icy cold. It was not the voice of a reasonable man. However, it sounded to me like the voice of an educated man. But a fanatic. It made me shudder."

"Did he have any sort of accent?"

"There was no regional accent at all. He just said that he was from the ETA, that there was a code word, and that the code word was 'Navarre.'"

Robbie asked what the importance of a code word was.

Lebrun answered him. "The IRA used to do that. They were authenticating their work, so to speak, in order to get their message across. They would call, give the code word, then say that a bomb will explode soon in such-and-such a location. Then the police would try to evacuate the area as soon as possible."

"Has the ETA ever done this before?"

"Not to my knowledge." Lebrun thought for a moment and then added. "He also said that he would be calling back soon. He hasn't done so yet."

Sylvie asked if "Navarre" meant anything in particular. The *Renseignements Generaux* man answered. "There is of course the Basque connection. 'Navarre' has been used as a Basque regional name. It means the region in Spain around Pamplona, while 'Lower Navarre' is the region on our side of the border around St. Jean Pied de Port."

Commissioner Moineau puffed on his pipe. He commented, "Also, of course, King Henry IV was the King of Navarre, and united France and Navarre. Since he was from Pau, that is more evidence that the man who attacked the American Consul was the telephone caller."

Another puff. "The records of the PTT, Monsieur Lebrun, show that the call you received at your residence that night was made from a public phone in Pau."

Moineau continued. "Suppose you tell us what happened at Montsegur, *Monsieur le Consul*."

Robbie told them about his impromptu duel. "He lunged at me suddenly. I only had enough time to react. He is strong, but fortunately, not a trained fencer. And by sheer luck"—he thought of Uncle Seth's warning—"I was carrying my sword cane. After the initial lunge had failed, he was at a disadvantage."

"So you wounded him."

"Yes, in the shoulder, I think."

"We have the sword cane that you gave to the police in Foix." He turned to the CID man. "We are having it tested it for evidence. The man's dried blood should produce DNA samples."

The CID man nodded agreement. "Of course, *Monsieur le Commissaire*."

At Moineau's request Robbie gave the police artist as good a description of his attacker as he could recall. Then Moineau gave a little summary. "This may or may not validate the ETA threat against you that was on the Consulate General door, *Monsieur le Consul*. But as a working hypothesis, it seems inescapable that the phone call to *Monsieur* Lebrun, and the attack on you, were from the same man. He may have even been planning to call *Monsieur* Lebrun again after the attack on you, *Monsieur le Consul*.

"As a matter of police security, *Monsieur* Lebrun, I think that none of this should be public for the time being." Lebrun nodded. He knew that the full story would create a sensation, and that his newspaper would carry it exclusively. Besides, Moineau could enforce his order by judicial decree easily. It was best just to cooperate.

"We will meet again at my call. Please keep in close touch with the *Commissariat*." Heads nodded agreement.

The *Renseignments Generaux* officer intervened. "There is also the matter of the weapon that your attacker used, *Monsieur le Consul.*"

"I wondered about that. Why didn't he use a handgun? It would have been more efficient, to say the least."

"The weapon was distinctly Basque, a *makhila*, or steel-tipped walking stick. Perhaps he wanted your death to make a statement for his Basque cause. Would you know anything that would shed any light on that possibility?"

Robbie was mystified. and said so. "I'm just glad that he didn't use a deadlier weapon."

The CID man gave a little cough. "Your confidence is misplaced, *Monsieur le Consul,*" he said. "The tip of the *makhila* that he used contained a sort of hypodermic. Despite the jarring it took from being struck over the wall and landing on the slopes, there were still trace poisons that we recovered on the weapon. We have already analyzed them. The poison was deadly. Had his lunge succeeded, *Monsieur le Consul*, or had you not handled it with extreme caution, you would not have left Montsegur alive."

The workdays passed in a flurry of preparations for the Etchevari visit. Informed confidentially of the attack on Robbie, the Senator, a ranking member of the Senate Select Committee on Intelligence, became more anxious to visit the Basque region than ever. Cables flew back and forth, firming up details for his visit.

In part, his conversations with the President made him more anxious than ever to visit the Basque region. He wanted to go back, to where his family had originated, and think things through. The President, a polls driven politician, could read the handwriting months before an election. The fact was, pressures were building as his first term ended to dump Vice President Clark.

It wasn't that Clark was dishonest. But now as a second term approached, media investigators were circling. This man would soon be a presidential prospect, after all. Two terms of serving as Vice President guaranteed that. And so, his earlier career as a high priced lawyer for tobacco and gambling interests was now being minutely scrutinized by the press. The President was just sounding Etchevari out, you understand. He had every confidence in Clark, and was sure this would blow away. Unspoken in that confidence, almost muttered as the two men walked away from a photo session of a Rose Garden signing of a bill that Etchevari had bulled through the Senate, was an appraisal, a question and an order. All deniable, of course.

The appraisal was that Etchevari, an old-fashioned generational contrast to both the President and Vice President Clark, would help the ticket more than Clark. The question planted was, "Are you interested? Think it over." The order was to keep it quiet.

On the French side, another preparatory meeting at the *Palais Rohan*, this time chaired directly by the Prefect of Police with Robbie's participation, nailed down security arrangements. These would still be discreet, but now became more extensive. For major stops the uniformed CRS would be on duty, reinforced by numerous plainclothes security officers who throughout the visit would comb the Basque coast and interior regions.

Reversing protocol, and emphasizing his Basque heritage, Etchevari would spend the first two days of his three-day visit in the Basque country, and then finish the trip in St. Emilion, with a courtesy stop in Bordeaux. His first day would be spent on the Basque coast, ending with a gala dinner at the Hotel du Palais in Biarritz. The second day would be spent in the Basque interior, highlighted by his public address at St. Jean Pied de Port. Claudine Auger was already busy handling press requests. Senator Etchevari's initiation as a member of the *Jurade de St. Emilion* would take place on Sunday. That seemed enough activity for one weekend.

Ghislaine bustled about the office and, in connivance with Jean Deplace, made sure that all of Robbie's trips outside the office were in the Consulate General's new armored car, driven by Georges. French security guards assigned on special detail accompanied Robbie to work. They followed in their car while one further guard rode in the front of the armored car with Georges, and also returned with him to his apartment after work.

"Just when I need a little affection, these fellows are playing hell with my social life," Robbie reflected grimly. His mood wasn't improved by the arrival of a copy of Montaigne's *Essays*, a gift from Uncle Seth. What a whimsical gift to send.

The book, however, reminded him of that odd meeting with Claude de Monoury in the library tower at Chateau Montaigne. Robbie determined to bring de Monoury into the investigations chaired by Commissioner Moineau. Following the attack on him, Robbie figured that he was no longer bound by de Monoury's request for silence.

Meanwhile *le tout Bordeaux* continued their leisurely annual round of events, now preparing for the annual *Mai Musicale*. This was a round of concerts, held at chateaux throughout the area. Robbie received tickets to the Saturday afternoon courtyard concert at Chateau d'Yquem in the Sauternes region from Charles de Tourneau. That was unexpected and very welcome.

Ghislaine checked his calendar. It was clear. Robbie accepted de Tourneau's invitation, and was pleased that Sylvie could go with him. Her voice over the phone showed real concern as well as affection. He was pleased to offer her a fine special event to attend with him. Real Holden Caulfield stuff again. Her voice, however, had made it plain that the movies would have been just fine.

On a hunch, remembering something that the Director of the *Renseignements Generaux* in Bayonne had said, Robbie started systematically reviewing the Consulate General's visa files after hours. He didn't expect to find much. Visa files were periodically retired.

Still, he was curious about young Basques who had spent time in the United States, and now, he had a glimpse of a face to go by. It was certainly worth trying.

The Embassy, of course, was kept informed. He was called personally by both Tim Everbright and by Deputy Chief of Mission Elliot Hawkins.

Everbright suggested that Robbie put in for a transfer immediately. "The Front Office wouldn't object, I'm sure. If somebody is after you, why make it easy for them?"

Robbie rather saw the point. For once, he almost agreed with Everbright. Being target practice for some deranged fanatic was not high on his list of inducements for the diplomatic service. But he didn't want to leave Bordeaux and Sylvie. Not now.

Elliot Hawkins called to tell Robbie to upgrade his security. It was not a suggestion.

"Did you get a good look at him?"

"Not really, but I've given the best impression I had to the police artist here."

Robbie gave Hawkins a more detailed rundown on the Etchevari visit plans. Everything seemed to be falling into place. Hawkins was pleased when Robbie confirmed that he would also be included in the membership ceremonies of the *Jurade de St. Emilion* during Senator Etchevari's visit.

"Wouldn't miss it for the world," he said.

Their drive down to Sauternes was pleasant. Georges drove, and the "thunk" of the automatic locking of the car doors gave Sylvie the unpleasant sensation of imprisonment. Robbie rather liked the sound. It was like the new Mercedes that he had once tried in a showroom, pretending that he could afford it.

They drove early, to wander in the car through the Sauternes region, along the meandering *circuit sauternais* that seemed guaranteed to get the tourist lost. In this region, that almost didn't seem to matter.

"What do you think about that attack on you, Robbie?"

"Frankly, it puzzles me. The connection with the ETA is plain. The man had a *makhila*, after all. And now we could say that the message on the Consulate General door was genuine. They just didn't have time to write it in Basque. But why advertise? And why kill an American official? It doesn't make sense."

"Thank heavens you are a trained fencer."

"A swordsman, so to speak." She thought for a minute, blushed and punched his arm.

"Tell me about Sauternes."

"You know there are several different styles," she said. My favorite is the light style of, say, Chateau Coutet. It goes well with *foie gras* and light desserts, and was said to be Maurice Chevalier's favorite wine."

"Why was that?"

"Before his first appearance at the *Folies Bergere* in Paris, he had a glass at a neighborhood bistro to steady his nerves. It seemed to him a good luck charm. Your President Eisenhower also preferred it, according to Alexis Lichine."

"Why is Chateau d'Yquem so expensive?"

"Because it is the best wine of its kind, probably in the world. They pick it only when each grape is absolutely ready. That can be up to eleven different harvest sessions, for as long as six weeks. The selection is so careful that they say that one foot of vineyards produces just one glass of the wine."

"And if you can't afford it?"

Sylvie continued. "What the French Government serves is Chateau Suduiraut. It is a fine rich wine, that comes from a beautiful estate. Le Notre designed the gardens. Chateau Guiraud is on the sweeter side. That is the only first growth wine aside from Yquem to come from the town of Sauternes itself. But there are a number of others. It all depends upon your palate."

"What do you prefer?"

"Chateau Sigalas Rabaud. It is very fine. Aristocratic even. But there are others."

Robbie noticed that Georges was listening to their conversation. "What about you, Georges?"

"On my salary, whatever they are pouring. Perhaps a nice glass of Loupiac, from across the Garonne. I also like a Sainte-Croix-du Mont. I'm from this region. Not all fine wines are expensive. Yes, give me a glass of Loupiac any day."

Georges lapsed into his customary silence, as they drove along the narrow route of the *circuit sauternais*, the car too wide for its side of the road. It was a good thing they met no oncoming traffic.

Robbie asked Sylvie why there were so many harvests at Chateau d'Yquem. "It's a different process, really, from what we were told at Chateau Montmorency in the Graves. Here, the grapes are picked when the normal growing season is over. They ripen at different times, not all at once. What we have here is a combination of over-ripe grapes, and high humidity in the fall. There is a juncture of the little Ciron River with the Garonne in the Sauternes region, and that humidity covers the grapes. It sweetens them, driving up the sugar content. Then the grapes will begin to shrivel. That's why they have to be picked individually, at exactly the right time, when the 'noble rot' has done its work."

"That doesn't sound very appetizing."

"Just taste the result, particularly with a dessert that is not very sweet. You'll be hooked on Sauternes wine too."

"I have all the *douceur* I need right now, thanks," he replied, squeezing her hand.

"Flatterer!" she hissed.

Abruptly they came to Chateau d'Yquem. It rose anonymously on a small hill commanding the region in Sauternes. It was also a residence of flair and distinction, with wine processing and aging facilities and cellars adjoining the chateau. Georges parked the car and they went into the courtyard. They were just in time for the concert. An usher checked their tickets and showed them to their seats. Charles de Tourneau rose, smiled at Sylvie. and shook Robbie's hand.

Robbie looked around. He had not been here before. The courtyard, facing the residential wing of the chateau with its turrets, seemed filled with rosebushes. The musicians, a string quartet from the Czech Republic, began to play. They shared the program with a group of French Renaissance singers.

The music and setting seemed to complement each other. The music was lyrical and graceful, and the singers were a delight. They sang of flirtation and nuance. The courtyard protected the audience from the wind, and the afternoon sun gently warming their faces seemed to make the chateau's light-colored stone glow.

This afternoon alone would be worth a trip to Europe. Robbie wondered, as roses throughout the courtyard scented the performance, how many tourists on their long-awaited trips ever experienced an afternoon this perfect.

Charles de Tourneau approached Robbie during the intermission, drawing him aside. "We need to talk, *Monsieur le Consul*."

"Is something the matter?"

"Very much so."

"Could you come to the Consulate General?"

"No. You are probably being watched, as I am. Chateau Montmorency is not safe either."

"For God's sake, man, what is it?"

Charles de Tourneau made a quick decision, just before Dick Sanderson came over to join them. "I know who killed Yves Crespier. It wasn't a suicide, and Crespier had nothing to do with the Pryor murder." He then walked back to his seat, and ignored his guests for the rest of the concert.

CHAPTER 15

"*La France Profonde*"

Robbie sat with Sylvie near the front section of St. Andre Cathedral, not far from the altar. Tilting his head, he could see the stained-glass windows that flooded the cathedral nave with colored light.

He turned towards Sylvie. Her head was slightly bowed forward, and her eyes were closed. She prayed silently, her lips every now and again moving just a trace. She didn't seem to be imploring or seeking guidance. She was just in a normal sort of communication, a silent one. Her face was calm and relaxed, almost beatific. Her head covering, a scarf, masked most of her quite attractive medium brown hair.

She wore yesterday's dress. There hadn't been time to return to her apartment to change. It wasn't appropriate clothing for church. Maybe that was what she was explaining.

Her features softened and her eyes opened, and she turned, noticing that Robbie was staring at her. Her gaze turned into a stare of its own, and they both smiled. He had thought her beautiful last night. So she was now, in a different sort of way. He could picture her in any setting, even meeting his parents. He hoped they would get along well. One never knew.

It was high mass on Sunday morning. They had risen late after their reception at Chateau d'Yquem, dinner along the way at the Hostellerie du Chateau de Rolland in Barsac, and evening and night together. Sylvie had made breakfast, scrambled eggs with ham, Robbie's favorite, with fresh, warm French bread and Normandy butter with jam. They had drunk their *cafe au lait*, the milk carefully heated, not from cups but from bowls in the traditional way. Coffee had rarely tasted so good.

The music from the choir, and the chants that punctuated the service, were like a time capsule back to when faith and aesthetics combined. In the late morning, the play of colors as the strengthening sun shone through the stained-glass windows became a kaleidoscope, shifting and changing to new patterns, never the same. If you had asked Robbie later what the sermon had been about, he could not have told you.

When she wasn't working at the newspaper office, Sylvie preferred to attend the high mass at St. Andre Cathedral. She liked the formality of it, as she surrendered to its mysteries of faith. She wondered in passing what Robbie thought of it all. He was Protestant, and she knew from television news that the difference was divisive. People still hated because of religion, and for a long time in Northern Ireland, also killed.

She was sorry to have missed confession. She would make up for that as soon as she could, after her day with Robbie was over. Perhaps tomorrow morning then. It seemed somehow odd to confess something so fine and loving. Repentance would be a problem. She didn't feel sinful, and she didn't do things for form's sake. It was a jumble. Anyway, she just couldn't have gone to confession with Robbie there. So she had not. And now she stayed with him while others went forward for communion.

She wondered how serious he was. She didn't really know him. What she did know seemed nice. But she would have her career. That she had decided long ago. What would other women she admired have done in her place?

She remembered that it was in this cathedral that her heroine Eleanor, Duchess of Aquitaine, had married Prince Louis. She had known her own mind, marrying at 15. Did Sylvie? They had become King and Queen of France, before she had discarded Louis VII to marry the dashing Duke of Normandy, who founded the dynasty of Plantagenet Kings of England, ruling there as Henry II with Eleanor as Queen of England. Sylvie smiled at her sudden decision, making one while deferring another. She would also be married in this cathedral.

She then remembered her own girlhood. There were the sisters of her early education, who had later seemed to her a bulwark when she was at the university. So many had seemed quite lost there. The lessons hadn't troubled her. She had rather enjoyed them. The sisters had probably spoiled her a bit.

She imagined the evening torchlight parades at the little parish church of Uzeste south of Bordeaux, where Pope Clement V was buried. In particular, she saw the lovely early medieval statue of the Virgin which Clement himself had admired. There were, of course, grander ceremonies at the cathedral at Bazas. Sylvie had had her own first communion there. But the parish church at Uzeste was closer to her heart.

They stood for the communion. Robbie did so out of respect, since he understood that as a Protestant, he could not take communion there. That was too bad, really. What was the harm? He actually rather looked forward to taking communion from time to time, and did so whenever he attended services at the National Cathedral in Washington.

He wondered what Sylvie would think of the National Cathedral, the latest Gothic cathedral in creation. He hoped that she would marvel, as he did, at the space exploration stained-glass window halfway up the nave, a window shining with festive blues and purples, containing a piece of rock from the moon. He would look forward to showing her the carvings of New England whalers under the capitals of the entranceway, here a harpooner, there a longboat, over there the leviathan itself.

The communion proceeded. Sylvie stood there with him. The rows of communicants going up to the altar rail washed past them. Robbie noticed that they were the only ones standing in the entire congregation who had not gone up to take communion.

He could not, of course. But she remained beside him. Why?

Then the answer came to him. She could not take communion because she had not been to confession. He knew that much, anyway. She had not been to confession because they had spent the morning together, even having breakfast. If she had gone, she would have had to confess that they had been together all last night. She had not done that. Instead, she had stood there with him, alone of the entire congregation.

Robbie couldn't think of their glorious night together in this place. It was not right, beautiful though it had been, as the explosive joy of their first night together had yielded to a loving easiness, a natural, shared intimacy. The desire to give and nurture love had led them on together. It was that afterglow that he remembered now. He still felt it.

He was aware of a new sensation, a mixture of love and pride. Perhaps she was well-known here in this congregation. It was also beginning to be known that they were seeing each other. It wouldn't take a very perceptive observer to understand why they were standing there together, and then, why Sylvie had not taken communion.

Instead, she was standing there with him, by his side, as the bells were rung, as the chants were heard, as the host and the wine were raised, and then shared by every other person in the congregation.

The realization stunned him. Robbie had never felt so loved in his life. She was not ashamed, nor did she try to hide. The contrast with his New England upbringing was startling and even comic. He thought of guilt and the shame and secrecies of *The Scarlet Letter* still imbedded deep in the Puritan culture of his country, and smiled.

This moment of beauty would, he knew, return to him again and again and again, painted in his memory, a private canvas of delight, impossible to share. He could hardly believe that this lovely young woman, in her own church, was openly standing with him, taking her place beside him. This was an affirmation of love, not a shameful hiding from it.

He seemed to breathe the contrast in the liberating fresh air of the cathedral. The coolness of the old stones that May morning added physical refreshment to the spirituality of the service. He became lost in thought and wonder as communion concluded, the music and liturgy ran their course, and the service ended. As they left, he tried to match the stained-glass pictures with his unreliable memory of biblical stories, heroes and villains, but soon gave up. He was sorry to leave this place of beauty.

Neither noticed the man wearing a hat and sunglasses, who sat at the sidewalk cafe near the Jean Moulin Resistance Museum in the corner of the square. Antonio Echurra watched them unobtrusively, over the folds of his sports newspaper. His wound had not been serious physically. It had quickly healed. Now there was time to plan more carefully.

He saw that now, as a matter of routine, Robbie was driving an armored car. That was the inevitable price of his failure at Montsegur. The American Consul's diplomatic superiors would have insisted upon that. But time was still on Antonio's side. And now there was other work to do, near the Consul's apartment. As the armored car pulled out of the square, Antonio paid for his coffee and left the cafe.

Robbie had planned their special day with care. But first, there was a visit that had to be made, to Chateau St. Aubin in St. Emilion.

He had called Claude de Monoury to say that he would be coming, and would bring Sylvie. De Monoury understood that she would keep his confidence. No stories would be written.

"We'll be following Pryor's suggestion again," Robbie said. "We're going to St. Emilion, just like he said to do."

"Maybe this is what he had in mind," she replied.

Following a quick stop at her apartment, they left Bordeaux by the Stone Bridge. Robbie drove on the route from Libourne past Chateau Trottevielle, so named because this St. Emilion first growth had been a coaching station where the old postmistress used to run to deliver the mail to the coach…"*La vielle trotte*"…and then they passed the grand wine estates of the St. Emilion slopes, Chateau La Gaffeliere to the left, and Chateau Pavie to the right. Finally Chateau Ausone, the most artisanal of the eight wines said by Alexis Lichine to be the finest wines of Bordeaux, came into view near the summit, with its neighbors Chateau Belair and Chateau Magdelaine just beyond. Each made superb wine.

On the St. Emilion plateau itself, there were Clos Fourtet, Robbie's particular favorite, rich and flavorful and not well known. "If there were a 'chateau' in the name, Americans would pay more for it," Sylvie teased. Then came the austere and powerful Chateau Canon, which rewarded long cellaring, followed by the two Chateau Beausejours, Becot and Duffau-Lagarosse.

Chateau l'Angelus, newly added to this august list of first growths, was down the slope from the Beausejour properties, on the other side of St. Emilion.

And that, of course, was not counting the many other fine wine estates, such as Chateau St. Aubin itself. Too much exposure to the wind perhaps, or too much (or too little) clay in the subsoil, was enough for a general verdict that a wine was not quite up to first growth standards. That did not imply that such wines were not superb. The best should not be the enemy of the good. But trust the wine writers with their "discoveries" to drive up prices anyway.

Robbie drove through the main gate of Chateau St. Aubin, and parked the armored car on the gravel driveway in front of the three-story residence, a mansion which doubled as a tasting headquarters for the vintage. A somewhat nervous Claude de Monoury met them at the doorway, and ushered them into his elegant study. Paintings with vineyard themes were hung in the entrance hallway.

The study itself was walnut-paneled, and there were books on wines and wine regions in neat stacks on the shelves. They were not coffee table books, for show. They had the sort of information concerning subsoils and plant diseases that a professional wine grower would want to know and have as handy reference aids. Here and there were memorabilia from the *Jurade de St. Emilion.*

Robbie came to the point first. "*Monsieur* de Monoury, we need your help, and we need it badly. I am convinced that you can help the police—and me personally. I have told nobody anything about our discussion at the Montaigne Tower. But now as you know there has been an attempt on my own life. The police are actively pursuing leads. You can help."

De Monoury looked at them both. Well, he had wanted to involve the American Consul. Now matters had gone a step farther. Since the American Consul was himself also a target, now they must pool together what they knew. It would be a sort of protection. He was no longer alone. He looked solemnly at his guests. "I assume that none of this is for publication."

It was a question. Sylvie nodded agreement. "*Monsieur* de Monoury, my editor Jacques Lebrun and I are actively cooperating with the police. We have accepted their condition that nothing will be written about this investigation until it is over."

That reassured de Monoury. At Robbie's request, de Monoury then repeated for Sylvie's benefit the same story that he had confided to Robbie in the Montaigne Tower.

"It is a relief to be able to talk about this. For one thing, I have no idea how far this blackmail may have already spread. Other members of the *Jurade* may also be victims. Perhaps the police may now be able to trace the pattern."

Robbie telephoned Police Commissioner Jacques Moineau. "*Bonjour, Monsieur le Commissaire.* I think that Charles de Tourneau has some information for us." De Monoury was startled. This was news. So he wasn't alone after all. "He and I spoke yesterday, and I'm sure he can shed some light on the Crespier killing. Possibly other matters too. You'll call him and the others? Fine. Yes, tomorrow morning will be fine. Wait a minute." He handed the phone to de Monoury.

He nodded, understanding.

"*Monsieu le Commissaire,* this is Claude de Monoury. I own Chateau St.Aubin in St. Emilion. I too have something to add. At the *Commissariat* tomorrow at ten? Of course. *Je n'y manquerai pas. A demain, Monsieur le Commissaire.*"

"Now we're getting somewhere," Moineau muttered to himself as he put down the phone. He ordered a subordinate to call Jacques Lebrun, and the other participants in their first meeting. He would call Charles de Tourneau personally.

They stayed for luncheon. It was a chance to taste the last three bottled vintages of Chateau St. Aubin, and to talk about something other than attempted murder and extortion. Luncheon was a simple *blanquette de veau,* a traditional French dish, hearty and flavorful. With a salad and some crisp fried potatoes, it was delicious. A *tarte tatin* and cheeses ended the meal.

The Chateau St. Aubin dining room had a picture window that looked out at the vineyards. It was an impressive, beautiful site, there on the St. Emilion plateau. The steeple from the little village church that bordered the Beausejour properties was clearly visible. It had been the bells from that church which had given Chateau l'Angelus on the slope below its name.

Sylvie pointed out the pretty view and the church. "Yes, that is my parish church," de Monoury replied. "But it is only a parish for the living. They stopped conducting burials in the yard a few years ago;

the property was more valuable for growing grapes for St. Emilion wines."

They had some coffee in the adjoining sitting room. No other family members were at home, for Madame de Monoury was in Paris for a shopping expedition and their children were in a private Catholic boarding school. "It had better be a good, salable vintage this year!" he had grumbled good-naturedly in explaining his wife's absence.

"This is our life and our heritage," de Monoury said as he saw them off at his front door. "Generations of my family have planted these vines and tended to the harvests. It is part of our patrimony. We must protect it, or we are rootless, like those who would destroy us."

Their drive into the Black Perigord region of the Dordogne was delightful. Pressed to name a favorite region of France, many travellers would cite the Loire Valley and its castles. For Robbie, it was the Dordogne, which he had first discovered as a college sophomore, bicycling through the region on a camping trip.

There was Bergerac along the way, Cyrano's city. There were great fortifications like Beynac, recalling that this region was for centuries disputed border territory between France and England. There were splendid medieval planned communities, *bastides* like Monpazier, then artificial population centers designed to expand one side's territorial reach, now wonders in stone. There was Sarlat, a magnificent Renaissance city, whose seasonal, bustling Saturday morning market was worth a trip to Dordogne, if not to France by itself. There was Perigueux and its famous cathedral, on which the Sacre Coeur in Montmartre was modelled.

And above all, there was the Valley of the Vezere, verdant, hidden, mysterious, as far away from any confusions of modern civilization as it was humanly possible to get. Here, just a few hours east from St

Emilion, if one drove slowly (and given the scenery, there was no point in doing anything else), was the artistic center of early man.

It seemed that there were caves or shelters everywhere. The lofty rock caves which later became medieval strongholds had in prehistoric times been on the banks of the Vezere River, then one hundred feet higher than today's stream. They had furnished shelter and a form of sanctuary to early man, who had arrived in the valley chasing the herds south as the ice ages had returned.

Discoveries in the last century had created a sensation. The caves, their artifacts and scratchings on the walls were simply far too old and extensive to be dismissed as fakes.

Then in September, 1940, came the discovery of Lascaux near the little town of Montignac. The site had been a sealed time capsule for perhaps sixteen thousand years. Schoolboys in search of their lost dog scooted down a hole that had suddenly been created by storms, and found the cave. The discovery was authenticated after the war. Then the tourists began to come.

The thousands of visitors, the bacteria on their shoes, and the oxygen the visitors needed, started to create lichenous deposits that could destroy the caves. The French Government closed Lascaux in 1963, and then, twenty years later, opened an exact replica nearby. That alone was worth seeing. But it was not their destination today.

Robbie had obtained special permission for them from the Department of Antiquities to visit the original Lascaux. Five visitors a day were allowed, by official arrangement, and he had secured two places. Robbie was sorry that Evalyn could not advance her arrival by twenty-four hours to join him, but he was pleased to share the visit with Sylvie.

Evalyn had realized this was an opportunity that wouldn't come again, but her flight was a charter flight. She couldn't afford to waste the cost of that ticket, much less pay for another one at full price. Too bad the permission had come through so late, but there they were.

"By the way, check your FAX when you get home," Evalyn had said. "Uncle Seth wants to see if you've got the book he sent you."

At Lascaux, they were in dark woods, holm oak, chestnut and walnut trees, shading overgrown, dense vegetation, ferns and tall grasses. It was a forest for secrets, hidden things.

It was mid-afternoon, and they were right on time. The guide greeted them gruffly, and instructed them both to step into a basin of liquid that would kill the bacteria on their shoes. Sylvie hesitated. "If Queen Elizabeth could do it, then so can you, *Mademoiselle*!"

They descended into the cave and came to the first chamber, which then opened into broader miracles of color and representation. Here was a wealth of animals in brown, ochre, red, black, forever charging and turning around the contours of the cave. No wonder an early explorer had referred to Lascaux as "The Sistine Chapel of Early Man."

It was breathtaking, and fresh. One section even seemed luminous and glowing. The guide explained. "You are very lucky. That happens when there has been rain a day or so before. The water coming down gives the paintings a light coat and makes them glisten."

Game of all sorts appeared on the walls, from that long past era. Bison, woolly mammoths, ibex, bulls, galloping horses, stags, even lions and a rhinoceros were there. And these were not just representations. They were skilled works of art by any definition, using the contours of the walls, with precision and elegance.

Light was sparse in the cave, designed to illuminate particular paintings. For the rest, the sensation was one of prehistory and darkness. Robbie held Sylvie close in the darkness as they listened to the guide, wondering at the miracle that had taken place here, grateful for its preservation.

Robbie dropped Sylvie off at her apartment. She refused with mock Victorian dignity his request to come in. "We're going to have a busy day tomorrow, after all. See you, *mon ami*, at our meeting at Commissioner Moineau's office."

He entered his own apartment in the *Chartrons*, turned on the light. and spent a few minutes making amends to Minouette for his long absence. It was one thing, after all, to be unceremoniously dumped from one's accustomed place at the foot of the bed. It added insult to injury to be alone all day, with just a cold breakfast.

Minouette's purring at length told Robbie that he had managed once again to get back into her better graces. He put out some canned salmon catfood for her, and then he retrieved Uncle Seth's message from the FAX machine.

After a brief greeting, it was in groups of numbers. Robbie remembered the old trick that he had learned from Uncle Seth. The numbers referred to pages, lines and words, in reverse order. Each of the three would also be inverted. As a matter of fact, Robbie thought, probably the entire message would be in reverse order. And so it proved. Clearly the copy of Montaigne's *Essays* was the key to deciphering the message. Uncle Seth would be working from his own copy of the same edition.

The groups of numbers varied in size according to the page numbers. The fifteenth word on the twelfth line of page 20, for example, would be 512102. So far, so good. Since only page numbers would go into a third number, a seven-digit group meant that it was a three-digit page number. For example, the group 6022911 referred to the sixth word on the twenty-second line of page 119. Punctuation was left to the recipient. It was a good code, quite unbreakable in its way, unless a third party knew exactly which book was being used as the reference point. That seemed highly unlikely.

Robbie made himself a cup of coffee and arranged the number groups in reverse order. Then he flipped through the pages of the book, noting words on a sheet of paper. Occasionally he would miscount a line or a word, and have to start a word group over again. But on the whole, it proceeded quickly. Robbie read the message.

"I have traveled and spoken at length with friends. They say understanding fanatics is highest intelligence priority." (He meant terrorists, a word presumably unknown to Montaigne.) "That includes groups in your region near the coast and the border with Spain." (Clearly the Basque ETA. This was getting interesting.) "Friends are in secret contact with these people, to gather information. They want revenge for the activities of the government of Spain years ago. One informant even supplies intelligence on current activities in return for such information. Keep this to yourself and be careful. Such people are violent and impossible to control."

It dawned on Robbie that Uncle Seth had not specified which were more dangerous, the ETA or their American contacts. He probably meant both. Robbie hoped he wouldn't find out.

There was an addition, an afterthought. "Extremely confidential. Visitor being mentioned as very close to White House. Visitor smarter and more prominent than he looks."

What was going on here? Clearly some high profile political, behind the scenes maneuvering. Robbie remembered speculation that Vice President Clark was in political trouble, exactly what kind he couldn't recall. He composed a reply message, coded it and FAXed it to Uncle Seth.

"Your message received and understood. Leaving for Paris tomorrow afternoon for short conference. Sister should be safe here. Will return for visit of Senator. Believe fanatics you mentioned may also have a new specialty, intimidation of vineyard owners Bordeaux region for money. I am cooperating with French police."

Tomorrow would be a full day. Robbie looked forward to seeing Evalyn again. He wondered what Evalyn would think of Sylvie, and how well they would get along. Famously, he hoped.

CHAPTER 16

"The Ambassador Requests"

Commissioner Moineau convened the meeting. This time, Robbie thought, there was a more shirt-sleeves atmosphere. There was also an undercurrent, muffled by these police professionals. They were beginning to feel that this was a team, that they were onto something, that the pieces were there or would be, and that they could solve it. There was also an unspoken assumption that they hadn't much time to do so.

Jacques Lebrun and Sylvie were there from *Sud-Ouest*, as well as Claude de Monoury, Robbie, and representatives from the Prefect of Police, the CID, and the *Renseignements Generaux*. Robbie looked for de Tourneau and was surprised by his absence. He glanced at Moineau, eyebrows lifted. "He's on a buying trip. Oak casks. We'll talk with him this afternoon," Moineau said. Robbie was relieved. So, he noticed from a corner of his eye, was Claude de Monoury.

At Robbie's request Sylvie had brought pictures that her newspaper had taken from the Crespier suicide scene and also, for good measure, from the ceremony at the *CND Castille* Resistance memorial. A number of them had already appeared in *Sud-Ouest*. But Robbie had been intrigued by something that Uncle Seth had said, he couldn't remember quite what, about what he had seen in the Crespier photographs.

"Thank you, *Mademoiselle.* Before we all look at these pictures, let us hear what *Monsieur* de Monoury has to say."

"I am somewhat embarrassed, *Monsieur le Commissaire.* Jacques Moineau nodded indifferently, in encouragement for de Monoury to proceed. "Perhaps I should have notified you earlier, *Monsieur le Commissaire*, as the American Consul urged me to do." A few coughs.

"I am being blackmailed by an American, who says that he will have my wine crops destroyed if I do not deliver a monthly payment to him. It is not a large sum. I have been paying it for several months." De Monoury described the collection procedure.

"How do you know that it is an American?"

"When we have spoken, it is always in English. I have spent considerable time in the United States on business visits, and my English is good. His is perfect, and it is American English. That is why I thought that I should notify the American Consul, in hopes he might know something and be able to help."

The *Renseignements Generaux* man took up the questioning. "*Monsieur* de Monoury, can you be more precise about his accent? Is it, for example, an educated man, or a blue-collar worker? Would you be able to estimate a region where the man was from...flat midwest, or southern accent, for example?"

"No, nothing like that. I would have remembered the southern accent, which is so charming." They were silent while de Monoury thought for a moment, then continued. "I have been assuming that he was an educated man. But there really is no reason for me to have assumed that. The vocabulary he used was not extensive. But then, for those calls, it didn't have to be. He was very commanding. Also cold. I remember that. Icy cold. He threatened my family, and I believed what he said."

The CID man joined the questioning. "Describe the voice, please. Was it high-pitched, for example? Did he make an attempt to disguise it?"

"Yes, he did. His calls were muffled. I would say that it was a deep voice, like a baritone, but I am guessing."

Jacques Lebrun added quickly. "The man who called me had a rich baritone voice. I recall thinking afterwards that he could have been a trained singer. But it sounded oddly cold, lacking warmth, no real emotion behind the words, or if there was, buried so deep behind hatred that it didn't come out. The voice of an emotional dead man, I thought."

Moineau observed, "And with you, *Monsieur Lebrun*, he wanted to be clearly understood...if he was the same man. And if he is the same man, he is also something of an egomaniac, preening for the media, I would say."

Lebrun winced.

Robbie leaned forward. He had just remembered something. He addressed the *Renseignements Generaux* man. "When I was in Bayonne, there was talk about the ETA leadership. Two were known. The third was not. But I remember that the third man was called 'the American.' It was a sort of nickname they gave him."

"Well done, *Monsieur le Consul.*" Robbie suspected this was high praise from Moineau. Sylvie, who knew that it was, beamed at him.

On a roll, Robbie continued. "I was in St. Jean Pied de Port recently, preparing for Senator Etchevari's visit." Heads nodded. "While I was there, I asked about the Senator's safety. Nobody seemed alarmed. But I did hear a rumor."

Everyone listened intently, leaning forward.

"What I heard was that the ETA was going to be making some big plans for renewed operations. The rumor was that they had found a new source for money. Perhaps those plans include moving in, Mafia style, on the Bordeaux wine trade. If so, this is not an isolated shakedown for money. It is organized, and furthermore, organized to finance ETA terrorism."

There was a moment of stunned silence.

The representative of the Prefect of Police gasped. Moineau nodded in cautious agreement. "It is worth pursuing," he said. Robbie knew that the Bordeaux mayor, Alain Juppe, would be fully informed within the hour. Commissioner Moineau knew that he would have no trouble now getting budget approval for whatever supplementary police action was needed.

Moineau suggested that the pictures which Sylvie had brought be passed around the table. Robbie didn't notice anything out of the ordinary in the grisly mess that had been the Crespier suicide scene. The others forced themselves to look.

Sylvie was the first to react. "Odd. I hadn't noticed this before. There, by Crespier's arm, on the desk. What is that? It doesn't quite look like anything one would find on a desk."

Magnifying glasses helped somewhat, but the object was still not clear. Jacques Lebrun promised that the pictures would be magnified for their next meeting. "It looks to me like a can used for a spray under pressure, like shaving cream," the CID man said.

Moineau's reaction was acid. "There is no need for guesswork, *Monsieur*," he said, "since everything in that picture is already in the possession of your division. Kindly report back to us not only what the object is, but a full inventory with pictures of everything that was in the room."

The pictures from the Resistance ceremony were then passed around the table. Robbie recalled that he had said at the time, that he had had the feeling of being watched. There were pictures of the ceremony, the placing of wreaths, the brief speeches, a few of the municipal dignitaries and of the surviving former resistance network members themselves, and several of the *vin d'honneur* which had followed. Of all these dozens of photographs, just six pictures had been used for the *Sud-Ouest* article. Had it not been for Lebrun's decision to use the story for the Sunday edition, Robbie suspected that even fewer would have been taken or used.

He studied each photograph with extreme care. He tried to use a cautious, bureaucratic voice, but he fooled nobody. He picked up an enlargement which showed a crowd scene around the memorial. There in the background at the edge of the spectators was a young man. He wore dark glasses and a two-piece grey suit, with a white shirt and conservative tie. He did not seem out of place. But in his hand was the nob of what looked like a Basque *makhila*.

"This looks like the man!" The others left their places and gathered around Robbie's chair. "Yes...I'm sure of that. It isn't a clear picture, but I've seen him once since then . . . lunging at me at Montsegur."

Commissioner Moineau ordered enlargements. The Prefect of Police would make arrangements for them to be sent to all police stations throughout the region, and would immediately coordinate with the neighboring *departements* of Pyrenees-Atlantiques and Dordogne.

"Something else occurs to me," Robbie said. "I have no reason to believe that this man is an American. He may or may not be. But he has obviously lived for a long time in my country, if he is the same man that *Monsieur* de Monoury heard on the telephone. I've already made an informal search of our visa records at the Consulate General here, looking for that face. We don't keep that many records anymore. But if he had been a student in the United States, there might be a record somewhere, either in the field, or back in Washington.

"I'm leaving this afternoon for a conference at our Embassy in Paris," he concluded. "I'd like to take copies of this photograph with me, to show around. Maybe he got his visa at the Embassy."

Moineau grinned and nodded in agreement. "Have a safe relaxing trip, *Monsieur le Consul*. You've earned it. We'll be in touch when you return, you and Senator Etchevari."

Robbie smiled in return. He was pleased with himself, and planned a small indulgence. There wouldn't be enough time to stop off at the *Maison des Antiquites* before leaving for Paris, but once there perhaps he might find a free hour to prowl around the *Louvre des Antiquaires.* He remembered that the cane selection at a shop there was remarkable.

❧ ❧ ❧

"So this is Bordeaux!"

Evalyn emerged from the Air Inter plane and gave her brother a big hug. Robbie was standing at the tarmac by dint of having flashed his consular identification card at Merignac Airport officials. So was Sylvie, but farther back.

"You look great, Evvie," Robbie said, and so she did. "Nice flights, I hope?"

He didn't wait for an answer before introducing Evalyn to "Sylvie Marceau, dashing journalist from *Sud-Ouest* who is going to keep an eye on you while I pop off to Paris for this conference." Sylvie and Evalyn, who had each rehearsed their meeting, smiled and shook hands without any appraising glances. The moment was so spontaneous that it seemed unnatural. Then they laughed. Robbie, a quizzical glance on his face, didn't get it. It would take too long to explain, Evalyn thought, and then chances are that he still wouldn't get it. She smiled conspiratorially at Sylvie, who did get it. They were going to be friends.

There was just time enough for some coffee together, while Georges secured Evalyn's luggage. Then Robbie checked into his flight for Orly Airport. "See you Wednesday night, Sis," he said, giving her another peck on the cheek before leaving.

Evalyn and Sylvie settled into the armored car while Georges drove back to Bordeaux. Evalyn had liked Sylvie on sight. Just her age, well, maybe a year or two older, and making a career on her own, from what she had gathered from Robbie's infrequent correspondence. That Sylvie had been mentioned at all was significant.

"So tell me, how is Robbie doing in Bordeaux?"

Sylvie smiled. This might be more relaxed than she had thought. This open, smiling young woman might well pass for a less reserved version of herself.

"He is well liked. Beyond that, what is difficult for an American, he is accepted. This is a closed city and society. Your brother has opened it."

Evalyn was pleased, and quickly moved on. "All but one, I gather. Robbie didn't tell us much, but we did hear that he has been attacked and has police protection."

So the family didn't know the whole story. Well, it was not Sylvie's place to volunteer more than Robbie had confided. "Yes. He has been officially looking into the Basque terrorist ETA group. I gather that all recent American Consuls in Bordeaux have had that task as part of their regular responsibilities. Apparently your brother is learning more than the terrorists want him to know."

Better conclude this on a reassuring note. Evalyn surely would be reporting back to their worried parents. after all. "But you are right. He has special police protection at all times now. Even his apartment, where you are staying, is under police surveillance. They won't bother you. But it may be reassuring to know that they are there."

There was a lot that Sylvie in turn wanted to know. But she didn't think that it was wise to ask too much too soon. Better to build step by step on the confidence that she felt with her new friend than force matters.

"I recognized you immediately from your picture," she said. "Robbie has it in his living room, along with your parents and his uncle."

"Great-uncle, actually. 'Uncle Seth,' we call him. He has no young family of his own. Wonderful man." She left it there.

Sylvie amplified her response to Evalyn's previous question. Perhaps she could draw Evalyn out. "Robbie and I have been working together with the police on this Basque ETA matter. What is so interesting is that he seems to have a flair for pulling an investigation together. He does it something like a journalist, but really more like a detective."

She paused, remembering. "He said something interesting just yesterday, that a diplomat has access to all sorts of people, official and not. The trick is to be able to weave together what they are saying. One almost forgets that your brother is doing it in what is for him, a foreign country."

That was a nice compliment for Evalyn to hear. "He'd be very pleased to hear you say that. Robbie has always been interested in putting things together, something like a detective, I suppose. There was that little business in his first post, the Embassy in Singapore. But he is really proud of what happened while he was a college student."

"What was that?"

"While he was downtown shopping in a jewelry store, a robbery took place. The robbers panicked, and began shooting. Robbie kept calm. Afterwards he helped the police investigators, and then testified at the trial so accurately that the prosecutors relied heavily on him. Later they said that without his help, there would have been no conviction."

"That must have taken a lot of courage."

"Yes. Furthermore, Robbie has told me several times how he really enjoyed that experience. He once said it was the most satisfying work he'd ever done. By that, I think he meant that he had done something demanding that took a lot of hard work and concentration, and was full of personal risk. He liked the detection part in particular, like putting a puzzle together, he said. But don't misunderstand. He has always aimed at being a diplomat. Father was also in the career Foreign Service, as perhaps Robbie has told you."

Sylvie shook her head. No, he hadn't.

"So we are both a bit used to the overseas life," Evalyn went on, "Robbie more than me, and he always liked puzzles, figuring them out. If he had not been a diplomat, then I think he might have been a detective of some sort. Maybe FBI. Maybe even CIA."

That was a lot of background, and more confidences than Sylvie had any right to expect. So Robbie wasn't CIA, and Evalyn wanted her to know that. It had to be true. There was every reason for Evalyn not to volunteer information that was not true, after all. Sylvie decided to hold for a while her curiosity about Robbie's personal life. Like, what was he doing in that jewelry store in the first place?

Robbie glanced at the ornate carriage portal and gatehouse and crossed the courtyard to the entrance of the official residence of the American Ambassador to France, 41 Rue de Faubourg St. Honore. The door to the entrance hall swung open, and he walked into the reception room to his left to check his coat and sign the official guest book. Then Robbie proceeded to the connecting salon where Ambassador and Mrs. Ronald Adams were receiving their guests.

"Ah, there you are, Robbie," said the Ambassador, breaking into an unreadable smile of affability that cajoled a similar response. The Ambassador led Robbie slightly aside, before returning to introduce his guest to his wife.

"I just got a phone call this afternoon from the Under Secretary. It might be well for us to have a talk about this Basque business after dinner. Expect you'll be able to join me upstairs in the library for a cognac then?"

Robbie thought that this was an advantage that the Foreign Service had over the military. He had just received an order, in the politest possible way. Actually, the Ambassador's initiative resolved a difficult problem of tactics. How otherwise would he, a rather junior officer in the heirarchy, have approached the Ambassador? He nodded acceptance with a smile, and shook hands with a radiant Pamela Adams.

She matched her husband's charm, and then some. Together, they had risen through state politics to his seat in the United States Senate, and an influential voice on the Foreign Relations Committee. Pamela Adams became Georgetown's leading hostess, her invitations coveted occasions to meet Washington's A-list. The talking heads on Washington Sunday talk shows had it that during the next Administration, should the White House not change hands, Ronald Adams would be on the short list for Secretary of State. Clearly they were good allies to have for the battles to come.

Robbie walked through the connecting salon to an elegant, spacious reception room in light colors, blues and cream, with *boiseries* throughout that were mirrored in the borders of the immense rug, also in cream and blue. He was early, a diplomatic custom for junior officers. You were a guest, but also expected to earn your invitation by helping your host. Robbie took a glass of white wine from a waiter, nibbled at an *hors d'oeuvre* or two, and waited for someone he knew to enter the room.

This reception was the beginning of the semi-annual conference of the American consular missions in France: Marseilles, Strasbourg, Bordeaux, and Martinique in the Caribbean. Lyons and Nice used to be on the list, but those consular missions had been cut for budgetary reasons. Martinique counted under French law with other French islands in the Caribbean as an overseas department of Metropolitan France. The Consulate General in Bordeaux, founded in 1790, was the oldest American consular mission in the world.

Robbie had checked in that afternoon with Marge Hawkins. A note from Elliot told him to take a couple of hours off, and wander around the city if he cared to (he did). They could meet at the Ambassador's residence that evening and drive back together. Elliot's note had included the full schedule of events at the Embassy for the next two days.

The invitation from his host and hostess, Elliot and Marge Hawkins, for a Tuesday night dinner for the visiting consular officers, would also be a nice social occasion. Robbie was less sure about Consul General Tim Everbright's Dutch treat restaurant invitation for Wednesday evening. Fortunately, Robbie already had his confirmed reservation back to Bordeaux on an Air Inter flight late Wednesday afternoon. Evalyn's visit furnished him with a welcome escape. He hoped that she and Sylvie had gotten along well.

The guests were beginning to arrive. It seemed that half the National Assembly was there. The occasion, Robbie recalled, was a visit by several of the Ambassador's former colleagues on the Senate Foreign Relations Committee. They had now arrived as well, in time for the Chairman and the Ranking Minority Member to join Ambassador and Mrs. Adams in the receiving line.

And there, being pointed towards him by Ambassador Adams, was Senator William J. Etchevari.

Robbie went over briskly and was introduced to the Senator. "I guess you are the man I have to thank for my schedule, Mr. Cutler," the Senator began.

"Call me Robbie, Senator. Everyone else does. Everyone is looking forward to your visit. That made it easy to arrange. The only problem was putting in place all of the people who wanted to see you. No knocking on doors was needed. Your visit is looked forward to by all of the Basque people, and not just by them. Beginning Friday, you should have quite a visit."

"Tell me about the ETA now. I've seen the written reports. As you probably know, I'm also on the Select Committee on Intelligence." In other words, no bull please, Robbie thought. He led Robbie by the arm off to the side of the growing crowd, smiling selectively at passersby as he did so.

"They are up to something. As you know, they've tended to shy away from Al Qaeda, in part I suppose for self-preservation. But they are not standing down. Quite the contrary. That doesn't mean that you, personally, will be in danger, Senator. Our best estimate, and that of the French police as well, including their FBI, the *Renseignements Generaux*"—Etchevari nodded in understanding—"is that you are not in danger. They would have to be really stupid to alienate their own people by putting you at risk." Etchevari nodded again, agreeing with the assessment.

"There is some concern about your public address at St. Jean Pied de Port, or possible reactions to it." Robbie tried to remember and then summarize his talk with Prefect Jean-Claude Mauret in Pau. "French officials are aware of your position on terrorism. They admire that."

Robbie segued into broader territory. "They are also antsy on the question of separatism. Looking at Corsica over the past few years, I guess they would have to be. But realistically, they just don't see Basque separatism evolving as a serious option, with or without the ETA. They do, however, privately concede that more should be done to 'reassure the Basque people that we respect their culture,' as the Prefect of the Basque region put it to me. Also, there is increasing sentiment for a separate Basque *departement*. After all, that was part of Mitterrand's election platform as far back as 1981."

Senator Etchevari chewed that over.

"And there is something else, Senator." Etchevari raised his bushy eyebrows. This young man was a cut above most diplomats of his age and grade. Less bureaucratic surely, and in his approach to political issues, more broadgauged. He would remember Robbie Cutler.

"I called on your cousin and his wife, Mr. and Mrs. Jaime Etchevari, at St. Jean Pied de Port. They hope to meet you personally, and if time permits, they would be honored if you could stop by their home. I've been there, and met them. If time doesn't permit, they will meet you publicly when you give your address."

Etchevari nodded in agreement. It would make a nice photograph for the voters back home.

"But one thing that Jaime Etchevari said to me was surprising. He said that he had heard that the ETA was getting more money, and he clearly thought it would become more dangerous in the future. He seemed to me to have an ear to the ground, and he is a man of judgment."

Robbie stopped there. There was no reason to brief the Senator further, nor was he authorized to go beyond what he actually knew, into the realm of speculation. Senator Etchevari now had something to pursue with the American intelligence community.

It was time to go into the State Dining Room for dinner. Robbie was pleased to note that like his fellow consular officers from Marseilles, Strasbourg and Martinique, and ranking officers from the Embassy including Elliot Hawkins and Tim Everbright, he had a round table for twelve to co-host. That was a nice gesture.

There were a dozen such tables in the tapestried west wing room. Elaborate candelabra at each table provided some light. The glow from their candles complemented the light from the ornate chandeliers, that was reflected throughout the room by its gilded antique mirrors. The *boiseries* and the pale gold damask window curtains were exquisite. The eighteenth-century effect was like the formal reception rooms at the Stock Exchange in Bordeaux, formerly the Place Royale, where the consular corps was formally received at dinner each New Year.

Robbie introduced himself to the guests at his table, and the evening passed pleasantly. The wines that evening were from Bordeaux, and their appearance, like old friends, dominated the conversation, as the French guests understood that their young host was from the American Consulate General in Bordeaux.

After dinner, some witty welcome remarks from Ambassador Adams were well received, as was the charming attempt of his ranking guest to deliver a memorized, short message in French. The Senator finally gave up and simply said in English, "I apologize for my failure to learn your fine language. When I was here before, in 1944, there was neither the time nor the opportunity. And I never thought, as a scared private soldier, that I would ever have the opportunity to spend such a fine evening in Paris with so many elegant people."

He raised his glass and shouted the one French phrase he could remember. "*Vive La France*!" The words may have been planned, but they were heartfelt, and the dinner guests knew it. There was a prolonged standing ovation, and a moment which the guests would long remember, which would go to some inner place where treasures of feeling were safeguarded and cynicism could not reach.

After dinner, as the guests filed back into the reception rooms for cordials and coffee, Robbie followed Ambassador Adams to the oak-panelled library on the floor upstairs. Cognac was poured, and the waiter left the two men and closed the door.

"We were all worried about you, Robbie. Sure you are all right? It was a close call down at Montsegur, I heard."

"Yes, sir. Good thing I am a trained fencer. He wasn't. That made the difference. But I'm sure that he was a Basque terrorist from the ETA. Who else would use a poisoned Basque cane, a *makhila*, for an attempted murder?"

Ambassador Adams nodded in agreement. Then he then picked up just where he had left off when Robbie had arrived. "The Under Secretary called to say that there was more to the Basque situation than meets the eye. He said specifically to have a private talk with you. What's going on, Robbie? What have you been hearing?"

So Uncle Seth had carried matters one step further. That made matters easier. It had gotten him this private meeting. But there was every reason not to refer to Uncle Seth now. He was on his own.

"Mr. Ambassador, I have heard that the Basque terrorists are about to expand. To do so, they need a great deal of money. In the past, they had collected funds through a system of enforced taxes on Basques living in the region, both on the coast and in the interior. There is now evidence that they have been branching out, like the Mafia. I can't quite prove it yet, but I believe that they are trying to blackmail the Bordeaux wine industry into paying them protection money."

"How could they do that?"

"It wouldn't be difficult, provided they chose their targets selectively. Everyone forgets that wine is a delicate agricultural product. Open a cooling valve too soon, or forget to open it at all during the fermentation process, and an entire year's crop can be destroyed. The wrong chemicals applied…" He let the thought trail off, as the Ambassador was nodding his head in agreement.

"Ingenious. You say there isn't much proof of this?"

"Actually there is direct testimony of the shakedowns, but not of the ETA connection. I was told of the shakedown directly by one of the victims, a reputable wine estate owner from St. Emilion. I have encouraged the man to go to the police. He has now done so."

"Why did he go to you in the first place?"

"He thought that the man shaking him down was an American. His contacts were all by telephone, and the man spoke flawless American English."

"I see. You did well to get him to go to the police."

"It doesn't end there, Mr. Ambassador.

"I thought not. What is the official concern?"

Robbie swallowed some cognac. It was a single vineyard *fin bois*, delicious, rich and flavorful, mellow and strong, without bite. He was overdue for a visit to Cognac, within the Bordeaux consular district. "Since 9/11 we have a new national intelligence priority, the penetration of terrorist movements, whether or not they directly target the United States."

The Ambassador nodded.

"That of course creates problems. If a terrorist knows he is in touch with the CIA, what is the price of his cooperation? And what if we learn about a terrorist operation? Do we step in and try to stop it? How do we keep the contact without tipping our hand? It's a nice moral dilemma. Be that as it may, it seems that we have a highly-placed informant within the Basque ETA. I assume that the French Government does not know this."

"It's certainly news to me too. Why would he work for us?"

"There are others that the informant hates even more than he hates the United States. Do you remember the GAL, or '*Groupe Anti-Terroriste de Liberation?*'"

"Never heard of it. Tell me about it."

Robbie explained. "That was an armed, organized group of thugs that operated in the French Basque region in the mid-eighties. They specialized in killing ETA operatives. The word put out was that they had been hired by the Basque people themselves, who were tired of paying the ETA taxes. Actually, they were probably working with the connivance of the Spanish Government of the time."

"Yes. I've heard something about that, come to think of it." Ambassador Adams refreshed their glasses of cognac.

"Thank you, sir. This is delicious, by the way. It is possible that our ETA informant, who supplies the CIA with information about Basque terrorist activities, is doing so in order to learn what we know about the GAL. Why I'm not sure. Possibly he lost somebody in his family to the GAL hit squads. In any event, there now seems to be some sort of American link to terrorism in the Bordeaux region."

"How do you combine the two? The ETA's attempt to get more money, and this terrorist?"

"Again, I cannot do so yet with mathematical certainty. But the fact that the blackmailer speaks perfect American English gives us an opportunity to find out.

"There is something else. At a ceremony in the Dordogne, I was watched closely, as I have been for some time. The photographs taken of that event have just been enlarged. It is a little grainy, but I am convinced that I can identify in one crowd picture, the same man who attacked me at Montsegur. He even carries a Basque cane, a *makhila*, which nobody in the Dordogne would have any reason to possess. It would just be out of place.

"I think he may be our man," Robbie concluded. "Find him, and we have found the ETA's assassin. Oh yes, another thing: The *Renseignements Generaux* are only sure of two of the three members of the ETA's ruling Executive Committee. A third man should have been picked to replace the man who was arrested a while back. This man may even be the shadowy new member of their Executive Committee who has not yet been identified."

"Why would he have tried to kill you?"

"I just don't know, Mr. Ambassador. He must have learned that I was investigating shakedowns on the wine estate owners. But how he learned that is beyond me. There are only a few people that know that."

"Was he following through on the threat the ETA had made a while back at the Consulate General?"

"Again, I don't really know, sir. That part of it doesn't make any sense to me, particularly since 9/11. Why bring in the American Government as an enemy? The local police assumed that the ETA hadn't left that message. Until Montsegur, I'd tended to agree with them."

Ambassador Adams nodded, trying to put the pieces together. "Do you have a copy of the photograph with you?"

"Yes. Furthermore, since Montsegur, I have been going through the visa files that we still have at the Consulate General. To speak American English that well, he must have spent years in the United States, possibly as a student. The logical places where a Basque would apply for a student visa would be either in Bordeaux, where nothing has turned up in our files, or at the Consulate at Bilbao, in Spain."

"Which, of course, the budget cutters have now closed."

"Yes, sir. I don't know whether their records would have gone to the Embassy in Madrid, or directly back to the Department of State. In any event, we need an urgent search of records, here and in Madrid, and in Washington, as well as at our other consulates. I've brought enough copies of the photograph for that. They'll have to make allowances for the beard. Maybe he didn't have it in his student days. Meanwhile, in view of Senator Etchevari's visit, the French police are already distributing the photograph throughout the French Basque region."

"I'll have my aide draft an urgent message tomorrow. Give him copies of the photograph. We'll have those records checked in Washington and throughout the region. You bring up the matter at your meetings tomorrow. I'll have an early morning word with Tim Everbright. Put it in the context of cooperating with the French police. This is, after all, the man who attacked you. But I wouldn't say anything about the intelligence connection. And Robbie…well done. Anything else?"

"Yes, sir. Stan Bartlett has been doing a great job. He's a take charge guy. That doesn't always sit well with the bureaucracy, but he's a good man. Rough edges, like Dick Holbrooke or Phil Habib, but solid, with good judgment. When the bureaucrats run for cover, he'll be the one that takes charge."

"I appreciate that, Robbie. Integrity seems to run in your family. There may be a good spot for Stan Bartlett in my future plans. We'll see. In the meantime, keep at it, but for God's sake, be careful."

Robbie took that as a go-ahead to continue his active cooperation with the police. He left the library to rejoin the cognac sippers in the reception room as Ambassador Adams placed his call to the Under Secretary in Washington.

CHAPTER 17

Emily Saves A Vacation

Robbie usually saw breakfast as a grim duty. Here, in the sunlit kitchen of Marge and Elliot's official residence overlooking the Bois de Boulogne, it was a pleasure. The ringing telephone was an unwanted intrusion, interrupting their sleepy conversation over toasted *brioches* and scrambled eggs with ham. "Probably the duty officer again," Elliot grumbled. "They never seem to be able to handle anything by themselves." He picked up his portable phone and then, with a surprised grin, handed it to Robbie. "It's for you."

"Sorry to call so early, Big Brother." Clearly Evalyn was over her jet lag, and anxious to begin touring. "How was the reception?"

"Great. I checked out the Ambassador's residence. Give me a few years, a few more million, the right political credentials, and it's all mine. How did your day go?"

"Fine. I had a long nap, then Sylvie took me to a reception. She's quite nice. Much too good for you, I suspect. I met just everybody. Lots of wine people, diplomats and presidents of this and that. Everyone seemed to like you. Can't imagine why. Had a wonderful talk with Suzel Latouraine, who promised to show me around the shopping areas downtown this morning. I really liked Emily Sanderson, the British Consul General's wife. She's just priceless. Those hats! I'm meeting her for luncheon."

"Terrific. Then, what's on tap for this afternoon?"

"That's why I called. Where is that Ford of yours? I found the keys on your desk, but I don't know where your garage is. Mind if I take it out? You know I'm a good driver." That was certainly true. She was probably more careful than he was, if he had to admit the truth.

"No problem. But it may need some gas. It goes by the liter here and it's expensive. Keep track and I'll reimburse you. I don't know because I didn't drive it last…"

His voice trailed off, and he remembered. When Georges had picked him up in the armored car at Foix, Jean Deplace had come along to drive Robbie's Ford back to Bordeaux. Nice of him.

But nobody had ever taken a close look at the Ford since then. He had not driven it. Nobody should until it was cleared.

"Wait a second, Evvie. I've changed my mind. The Ford really ought to be checked out before it is driven. I was having some problems with it earlier, and wouldn't want you to be stuck somewhere. I'll call the Consulate and see that that is done. You stop off on your way downtown and leave the keys with Ghislaine. She'll call you when it is okay to drive. Meanwhile, have a great day. Shopping is a treat in Bordeaux, and Suzel and Emily will be great company. 'Bye."

His next call was to Vice Consul Stan Bartlett. Stan as usual was in the office early, setting up for the morning visa crunch. "Hi Stan, Robbie. Any messages from yesterday afternoon?"

Charles de Tourneau had called. Robbie felt relieved at that. "Look, Stan, my sister Evalyn just called and asked to drive my Ford. I said yes, but then remembered that it hasn't been checked out since that day at Montsegur. Would you call the *Commissariat*, or ask Jean Deplace to do so? I'd feel better knowing that security experts had been over it.

"Yes, the reception was nice. Ambassador Adams knows you are really running things in Bordeaux. Got to run or I'll make Elliot late.

Ghislaine has my schedule, and I'll be at the Embassy if you need me. Many thanks."

They sipped their steaming coffee, too hot still to finish, and Elliot and Robbie drove to the Embassy, just off the Place de la Concorde on the right bank. The driver let them off, and they walked briskly past the Marine security guard, who saluted Elliot, then they strode into the large entrance hall and up the staircase. The consular conference was being held in a conference room on the second floor of the Embassy. There was just time to grab a cup of coffee and greet colleagues from the other consular missions before Ambassador Adams and his aide appeared, to open the conference.

The Ambassador gave a brief and cheerful welcome. His observation that rank aside, in their jurisdictions they represented the United States every bit as much as he did here in Paris, may not have been strictly speaking true, but it was what the conferees wanted to hear and believe, and it marked Adams as a regular guy.

As Adams left, his aide came over to Robbie, who handed him several copies of the photograph taken at the Resistance ceremony, plus a copy of his overview of the ETA, which excluded intelligence details. This was the report that Robbie would be presenting later in the morning.

Then Elliot gave an overview of Franco-American relations. Like Hawkins himself it was witty, perceptive and broad brush. Robbie thought, I'd like to be able to do that in a few years. Then Elliot turned the meeting over to the conference host, Consul General Tim Everbright.

Listening to old Everbright drone on was like watching a rerun of a television show that you hadn't liked as much as you had remembered. In his hands, the interesting became pedestrian, and the mundane deadly dull. But he did know his stuff, and he judged other consular officers accordingly. You'd better know immigration and visa law and procedures, missing persons, repatriation and emergency help to American citizens when you were dealing with Everbright.

Which was exactly the way it should be, Robbie realized.

There was an overview of political events as seen from the consulates. Arnie Jones gave a view of Marseilles political and economic events that was current and salty. The right wing National Front was slipping badly from the stronghold in the region it had once enjoyed. He took some kidding from his colleagues about the Marseilles soccer team, once the region's pride, and now dragging in the national standings He's ripe for a side bet against the Bordeaux Girondins, Robbie thought.

Joelle Evans talked about the European communities, whose parliament is located at Strasbourg—along with three, three-star Michelin restaurants, Robbie recalled. Christiane Rodriguez spoke about Martinique, and a general conversation developed about France's relationship with its overseas metropolitan *departements* and possessions. Robbie held forth on the French southwest and its importance to both the French and American economies, as more and more American companies, from Motorola to Ford, headquartered their European or French manufacturing operations there. It was, he said, a powerhouse in the making.

Consular operations were next on the agenda. With Consulate General Lyons and Consulate Nice both now history, and Strasbourg and Bordeaux both on the tentative list of posts to be closed, belt tightening was the fashionable topic.

"Sure," Arnie Jones said, "redraw the consular organizational lines, so that everything that Bordeaux does is split between my Consulate General in Marseilles and the Consulate General here in Paris. That will be a great comfort to the first elderly American tourist whose husband has a heart attack in Toulouse and then finds out that there is no American consul to run interference with the local hospital—or coroner, for that matter.

"Don't those budget cutters ever look at a map?" he grumpily concluded, to an audience shaking their heads in agreement.

Everyone was sure that more consular post closings were inevitable. That didn't make them right. And when, inevitably, closed consular posts were reopened a dozen years down the line, and property had to be leased once again, and new employees located and trained, and physical security reinstalled, the outlay would be many times whatever pittance had been saved by closing them in the first place.

Then came the semi-annual fight over fellowship grants. For this set piece, Elliot Hawkins returned to chair the meeting. There was a diminishing amount of resources left to offer travel fellowship grants to those who might lead France in future years. Whether young politicians, media personalities, or mid-level government overachievers, the program had paid dividends in the past. Now, each consulate had its list of potential grantees. So had the Embassy, but it was a longer list, one surer to be realized.

Robbie's list included several young mayors who had never visited the United States. He had hoped to nail a fellowship grant for each of them, but at meeting's end, only his leading candidate had been accepted. Odd sort of procedure, Robbie thought, where each member of the jury has an interest in the outcome and a vote. Of course the chair being the Deputy Chief of Mission, most of the Embassy's candidates won grants. The only consensus was that this program, a survivor from the days when USIA was a separate agency, was a good one that must continue.

Security was the first topic after the luncheon break. Nobody needed reminding of the sad milestones of the past, the murder of Embassy officers, and attempted murder of the Consul General in Strasbourg years earlier. Robbie's presentation was scheduled first.

"You probably know most of what I have to say through the written reports, but there are a few new things. First, the Basque ETA is becoming more active once again. They have also targeted me." He gave an unvarnished account of the attack at Montsegur, and the

ETA spray paint episode at the Consulate General. "I can't explain that one. It's not like them, and it's probably not in their interests to target an official American," he noted.

Joelle Evans asked about the pouch incident. "The police tell me that that was unrelated. That seems right, since they have caught the man who did it, a small time drifter, but you still have to wonder."

Robbie continued. "There is a broader aspect to this right now. The French authorities have asked for our assistance, and the Ambassador has given the go-ahead." Everbright snorted a bit, but he was outmaneuvered and knew it. "They have reason to believe that the ETA man who tried to kill me may have been a student or long-time resident of the United States. There is a witness that he has talked with, and that witness swears that our man's American English is flawless."

Arnie Jones's bushy eyebrows peaked. "Any regional accent?"

"No, nothing that the witness, who has himself lived in the States by the way, could place. I've been cooperating with our regional newspaper *Sud-Ouest* in trying to identify the man, and they are holding back from publication what they already know, at the request of the police.

"We've located a picture, not exactly clear but not bad either, of the man who attacked me." Robbie passed out copies of the enlarged photo from *Sud-Ouest*. "We need a crash effort to see if he registers in any of the visa application files, particularly here in Paris. Also, try to picture him clean-shaven.

"Another thing. Senator William J. Etchevari will be beginning a three-day visit to the Basque region on Friday. This photograph is already circulating throughout the southwest as security preparation for that visit. But if we were able to put a name to the face, that would help a lot.

"Now let me tell you more about the ETA." He took out his report, and took a sip from his glass of water before summarizing it for them. At that moment the Ambassador's aide ran in and tapped

Robbie on the shoulder. "Come up to the office at once. There is an urgent call from Bordeaux."

Robbie mumbled his excuses, handed his report to Joelle Evans to read to the group, and bounded out of the room and up the stairs at the aide's heels.

On the phone was a glum Vice Consul Stan Bartlett. "Robbie, Evalyn is okay, not hurt. But your instincts were right on target. I called Commissioner Moineau as you requested and got right through. He sent out some demolition experts to check out your Ford at the garage. Apparently they didn't take it quite seriously enough, or there is some new technology here. As they were unlocking the driver's door there was an explosion. They were both killed instantly. The impact leveled everything.

"I suggest (the word probably cost him something, Robbie realized) you get right back to Bordeaux. I've confirmed your return flight at three o'clock from Orly. Police Commissioner Moineau wants to see you as soon as you get back."

"Where is Evalyn?"

"She was having luncheon with Emily Sanderson when it happened, and she's at the Sanderson residence at Avenue Carnot in Cauderon." He gave Robbie the telephone number.

"Well done, Stan. One other thing. Please call Moineau back. He should make sure that Charles de Tourneau is present as well as the others when I return. This business is coming together. I think that de Tourneau may have one of the missing pieces of the puzzle. Anyway, we'll see this afternoon."

"Check."

Robbie called Evalyn, and spoke with Emily Sanderson first. "Robbie," she said, "I'm not going to take any argument. This nice young lady isn't going to be in any danger here with us, and you need to concentrate on whatever it is you are doing. Evalyn is going to be our houseguest through the weekend. It's all decided. Now here is your sister."

That made sense. That's what everybody missed when they tried to understand the British and Americans getting along. It wasn't just the language. You could count on the Brits when it really mattered. Evalyn's voice sputtered on the phone. "What a super lady. We're getting along famously. Don't worry about me."

Robbie checked with the aide, who told him that Ambassador Adams's message had already been sent to Embassy Madrid and to Washington. An Embassy car took him back to the Hawkins residence, where Marge had already repacked his luggage, and then to Orly Airport, where he had just enough time to catch the three o'clock flight back to Merignac Airport in Bordeaux.

Stan Bartlett met the plane, and Robbie was whisked around airport security and into the waiting armored car that Georges was idling, blocking traffic in front of the airport's arrival entrance, to the great distress of the taxi fleet. It dawned on Robbie that he hadn't any idea whether terrorist action was covered by his automobile insurance policy, or whether he would have to bear the total loss of his Ford. Cheery thought. He'd ask Jean Deplace to look into his coverage later.

Georges dropped Stan off at the Consulate General, and then at Robbie's request drove past the smouldering ruin that had been his parking garage. Robbie's security escort had picked him up at the Consulate General, and now stood guard as he brought his suitcase into his apartment.

Evalyn had tidily packed her things and picked up, and left a note for him. "Off with the Sandersons, as you'll hear from Stan Bartlett. Look forward to joining you when your visitor leaves. You never told me that Bordeaux was this exciting! Don't forget to check in with Uncle Seth. This sounds like his sort of problem too. Haven't called the parents. Love, Evvie."

Minouette curled around his ankles. Doing his best Bogart imitation, Robbie picked up the animal and said, "Well, I guess it's just you and me now, sweetheart." He poured her a fresh saucer of milk, mixing it with a little sugar to better resemble mother's own, then he stashed his unpacked suitcase in his bedroom, and left the apartment for the *Commissariat.*

They were all waiting for him. Robbie noticed that the cast was now enlarged. He was greeted by Commissioner Moineau and looked around the conference table. There sat Charles de Tourneau and Claude de Monoury, and then Sylvie Marceau, in the chair next to his own, who said that Jacques Lebrun had been detained at the newspaper.

Directly across from Commissioner Moineau, however, sat the Prefect of Police, Jean-Luc Charasson. The placement was interesting. Charasson was the ranking official in police matters for the entire region, Moineau's direct superior, and responsible in theory only to the Minister of the Interior. He was letting Moineau take the operational lead, for now, anyway. Next to him was the Director of *Renseignements Generaux*, whom Robbie had last seen at Bayonne. There was the Criminal Investigations Division Inspector and his deputy, who had lead responsibility in murder investigations.

There were also a number of uniformed officials. Robbie took stock. There was an officer of the CRS. This was a paramilitary group under the Army which furnished security in matters of national importance, Robbie recalled. He supposed a rough American equivalent would be the National Guard. There were several uniformed *agents de police.* There was also a new player in a uniform that Robbie had last seen when he had driven over the Spanish border at St. Jean Pied de Port. Of course, he was from Border Security, the DST, which handled border and customs security. They were also answerable ultimately to the Minister of the Interior.

This was the first team. Quite an impressive group.

Some introductions were made. It was Commissioner Moineau's meeting, but Robbie thought it best to begin. "*Monsieur le Prefet, Monsieur le Commissaire,* on behalf of myself and Ambassador Ronald Adams, allow me to express our sadness on the death of members of your security force. We are deeply grateful, and I will pay my condolences personally to their families."

The meeting then began with an account of the car bombing. The garage owner and employees were all being interrogated by the CID to see what each might know, and in particular, whether anyone could recognize the newspaper photograph of the ETA man.

Then Commissoner Moineau gave an overview of the investigation to date. He asked Claude de Monoury to repeat his account of blackmail against his wine estate, calculating that this would encourage de Tourneau to tell what he knew fully.

De Monoury's account of the American voice prompted Robbie to state that, in addition to checking his own visa files, he had asked his fellow consular officers that morning in Paris to search for an applicant who matched the *Sud-Ouest* picture, bearded or clean-shaven. He added that Ambassador Adams had pledged active cooperation in the search, which now extended to Washington and Embassy Madrid. Moineau asked the DST officer to check their files, and in particular, circulate the photograph at all border stations with Spain. Heads nodded approvingly.

Charles de Tourneau then added his account. It closely matched what de Monoury had already said. There was, however, one important addition. De Tourneau had actually seen the man. Listening to de Tourneau, Robbie thought that his physical description could have been the assailant at Montsegur. De Tourneau studied the picture in *Sud-Ouest*. "It isn't all that clear, but definitely it is the same man." He thought for a moment. "Yes, the same man. I'd stake my life on it." He swallowed hard as he realized that he had just done so.

That was it. The link between the shakedown, and the attempted murder of Robbie Cutler was now established, by an eyewitness. There was collective excitement: now we're getting somewhere.

Robbie asked the first question. "You told me that you doubted that Yves Crespier committed suicide. Why did you say that?"

"Crespier and I have known each other since childhood. Our fathers fought together in the Resistance; we wouldn't keep even this a secret. I approached Yves, and he told me that he had also been blackmailed, by the same man surely. He intended not to give in. That was like him."

"What happened?" The CID Inspector leaned forward.

"I'm sure he was murdered. He had told me about the ETA. Either he had figured out the ETA connection, or they had told him, in an attempt to intimidate him. But they tried to intimidate the wrong man. I can't explain that note. Maybe he meant something else, I can't say. But nobody was less likely to commit suicide than Yves Crespier. His religion forbade it, and he was devout. Also, he was brave, like his father."

Exactly what Uncle Seth had said, Robbie remembered. Commissioner Moineau lit his pipe. "Nobody writes a typed suicide note," he said. "Also, his signature appears normal. That is not my experience with such cases. They are always handwritten, and do not look anything like the suicide's usual handwriting. Too much stress, of course."

Robbie noted an appreciative glint in the Prefect of Police's eye. Commissioner Moineau then asked the CID man for a report on the contents of Crespier's office, as Sylvie passed around enlargements of the picture of that murder scene that had appeared in the newspaper.

The CID man then focused on "the object that *Mademoiselle* Marceau mentioned last time. It is a can of spray paint," he said.

"Look at Crespier's outstretched hand, trying to reach it," Robbie interjected. "As he was dying, Yves Crespier was trying to tell us something. What color was the spray paint?"

"Bright red."

"I thought so." Robbie couldn't conceal his excitement. "You'll find, I'm sure, that it is the same color that was sprayed on the door of the Consulate General. It wasn't the ETA who did that. It was Yves Crespier, or people working for him. He was trying to signal us then…and at the hour of his death. The odd thing is, that by confiding in you, *Monsieur* de Tourneau, he also told all of us that it was the ETA. Now we know the real enemy."

The Prefect of Police asked, "Anything further to add, Monsieur de Tourneau?"

"Yes." De Tourneau described what the ETA man was like. "He was very sure of himself. I had the feeling that I may have been the first, or one of the first, estate owners he approached. He told me that he had protection everywhere. I thought that meant there was nothing I could do but go along with him, for a while. But I made one mistake, it seems."

"What was that?" The entire roomful of people leaned forward at the same time.

"I confided my suspicions to Douglas Pryor during his last visit to Bordeaux."

After the meeting, Georges drove Robbie arid Sylvie back to Robbie's apartment. There would be enough time to worry about getting her car later, much later.

Sylvie volunteered to make some dinner while Robbie composed his message to Uncle Seth. The meal would be a simple affair. His food supply tended towards the uncomplicated, meats that he could broil, and canned soups and vegetables that he could heat. The wine selection, she was amused to see, was more elaborate. Leave him to his own devices, and he would be drinking fine wines with hamburger or meatloaf.

Robbie coded his message. He told about the bombing of his car ("coach," according to Montaigne), and Evalyn's safety. Then he summarized de Tourneau's story, and his own talk with Ambassador Adams. He asked whether the investigation of the Pryor murder had made any progress. Then he ended the FAX message by sending a copy of the picture of the terrorist that had been taken at the Resistance memorial.

The reply message came as they were finishing dinner. It was short and to the point: “New suicide explanation seems accurate. Friends say fanatics confirm safety Senator trip. Never rely on them.”

Robbie knew he couldn’t let his guard down. For now, though, he had done all he could, and it was time to relax. Then he remembered his suitcase, and went upstairs to unpack it.

Marge had been thoughtful, and thorough as well. His clothes were all neatly folded. On top of them was a note regretting his short stay, and hoping that his sister was now safe. A gift was enclosed as well, a gift that made Robbie call downstairs.

“Sylvie…Come take a look at this!”

It was the latest edition of *Pryor On Bordeaux Wines* and it had been personally inscribed by the author to “my old colleague and friend, Elliot Hawkins,” during Pryor’s last trip to Paris.

CHAPTER 18

Dinner In Biarritz

"Let's set a trap for the ETA," Robbie said. "It's just an idea. Perhaps you'll have a better one. But I've been a target myself, and now I'm pretty sick of waiting for them to act. Let's surprise them. Let's force their hand."

"*Eh bien, Monsieur le Consul*, just what do you have in mind?" Inspector Moineau cradled the phone in his hand while he lit a cigarette. Then he perked up, his curiosity aroused, then his sense of humor, then his professional interest and finally, his agreement. "I like your idea. I like it very much. You can make the arrangements, from the Consulate? Fine. We can step in if you have any problems with the hotel. I know the manager will cooperate."

The dinner in Biarritz would be a sumptuous beginning for Senator Etchevari's three-day visit. It would be held at the *Hotel du Palais*, a dowager deluxe beachfront hotel whose very address, 1 Avenue de l'Imperatrice, announced its regal past. First called the *Villa Eugenie*, it was built by Emperor Napoleon III for his Empress Eugenie. As a Spanish Countess she had vacationed in Biarritz when it was just a fishing village. Their former summer residence now regally anchors its end of the beach with three broad stories of rooms, outlined by individual pilasters, the whole topped by extensive mansard roofing.

By imperial whim the Villa Eugenie had become a palace, and Biarritz evolved from an annual seaside vacation spot to a European destination. Even the fall of Napoleon III and the burning of the building itself had not seemed to matter. Quickly rebuilt as a luxury hotel, the *Hotel du Palais* with its oceanview suites, air of luxury, prime location and fine wine cellar became host to Europe. From Otto von Bismarck, who nearly drowned in a swimming accident in the treacherous undertow off its beach, to Sarah Bernhardt, they all came. King Edward VII, a seasonal guest year after year, here named Asquith Prime Minister of England in April, 1908.

The *Hotel du Palais*, Robbie thought, was the place that he would take his grandparents, if he had grandparents living, that is. It had a wonderful sense of sinning decorum about it. "You could just imagine," he had said to Sylvie as they were driven over from Bordeaux, "what went on here, all those European rulers far from home."

Sylvie smiled indulgently at him. "What makes you think it doesn't now?"

What hadn't changed was the magnificence of the location, perched on the edge of the *Grande Plage*, Biarritz's most extensive beach. Surfing became a European fad here, despite the rather dangerous undertow and currents. Also maintained was the tradition of treating guests as welcome visitors. There remains an opulence about the main dining room, with its ocean views, that recalls the last century. Here you may dine and relax and leave cares behind, if your plastic is good.

Well, perhaps not tonight.

The Friday dinner for Senator William J. Etchevari had been planned with meticulous care. The guest list had posed problems, and Robbie off and on had spent days compiling it. It seemed that every political dignitary from the entire Basque region wanted to be included. Some, like the Mayor of St. Jean de Luz, obviously would be. Then there were prominent Basques from all walks of life; sports, the arts, writing, to name a few. One had to take a broad view of the visit itself as a series of events. Everyone couldn't be included the first evening.

Robbie, with Ghislaine's patient help, kept that in mind, so that people who were important enough to be considered for this dinner invitation would probably get a consolation prize if they hadn't made the final cut. They could be included in other events. And then, of course, there was the public address at St. Jean Pied de Port, where all were welcome. All in all, the planning seemed to be coming together, Robbie thought.

For this dinner, they would use the entire main dining room. The expense was in part underwritten by the City of Biarritz, and in part by the *Hotel du Palais* itself. Senator Etchevari's presence was felt to more than justitify the expense, for in reality this once fashionable, indeed ultimate destination now had many trendier competitors.

The town fathers understood that it was wise, from time to time, to put on a big splash. Anything to signal to potential moneyed clientele that this was a vacation destination worth considering. Those who could afford it had so many other choices now, from the big island of Hawaii to cruises. Hence the heated saltwater pool, which overlooked the public *Grande Plage* and the ocean itself.

Georges drove up to the hotel, past the small group of people in Basque traditional clothing who were, it turned out, handing out leaflets, and let Robbie and Sylvie off at the front entrance. In the manager's office, they checked the guest list for any last minute cancellations or substitutions, and went over the menu once again. The idea had been to intersperse traditional Basque dishes with seasonal French cuisine. Champagne would be served as Bayonne ham and Basque miniature garlic sausages, or *loukinkos*, were passed for starters.

"I still don't understand the changes in the wine menu," the manager said. "Why it should make any difference is beyond me. But we will be serving the wines you requested. Fortunately, your Commercial Officer at the Consulate, Guy Leblanc, was most helpful. Without him, and his contacts in the market, we wouldn't have been able to substitute the wines in time.

Dinner would begin with grilled salmon from the Adour River, which flowed to the coast at Bayonne through the Landes district. They would have a white *Graves*, a Chateau Montmorency, with the salmon. Next would come broiled muscovy duck with early vegetables, set off in the Basque colors of red, green and white. The red wine would be 1985 Chateau St. Aubin, donated by Claude de Monoury.

Sylvie gasped at the menu, and blurted out, "Where did you get these wines? They're all connected with the ETA's extortions, every single one of them."

"That's the reaction I want, from somebody else…if he shows up," Robbie said.

An extensive platter of local cheeses would then be accompanied by a 1975 Chateau La Source from the *Medoc*. Then fruit compote lightly soaked in armagnac would conclude the dinner, as coffee and armagnac were served. The unavoidable welcoming speeches, and Senator Etchevari's reply, which Robbie would translate into French, would follow. Then there would be a brief floor show, featuring Basque dances, before general dance music would begin. All in all it should be a memorable occasion.

Certainly the hotel management thought so. They had augmented their regular staff with more waiters and serving personnel, and had even supplemented their kitchen staff with a Basque chef and his helper. Basque decorations filled the main dining room, and complemented the French tricolor and the American stars and stripes at the rostrom from which the dignitaries would speak. Everything seemed to have been anticipated in order to create an evening that would start the visit well.

There was, of course, the matter of security. Armed CRS guards in uniform were posted outside the hotel, enough to respond quickly and in force if needed, but not enough to cause alarm. After much internal discussion, metal detectors were ruled out. After all, this was a crowded evening, and the Senator would be making public appearances the next day in any event. This wouldn't be the right time and place for the ETA to create a security problem, went the prevailing view.

Several groups of hand-picked security agents, sprinkled around the hotel in twos and threes, were dressed as guests of the hotel. A scattering of *gendarmes* from the Bordeaux *Commissariat* stationed in the hotel lobby with their uniformed colleagues from the coast were a more conspicuous presence. Officers from the *Renseignements Generaux* were extra waiters around the main ballroom. Like a spider, Police Commissioner Moineau oversaw the lot from a mobile command post that featured closed circuit television throughout the public areas of the hotel.

Meanwhile Robbie made final the protocol arrangements. The Senator's head table would include Police Prefect Charasson, Prefect of the Pyrenees Atlantiques Jean-Claude Mauret, Sub Prefect Georges Armand, the Mayors of Biarritz, St. Jean de Luz and St. Jean Pied de Port, Robbie Cutler, a Basque film star, and a champion of the national game, *jai alai* or *pelota.* All were there with their spouses except three bachelors: the *jai alai* champion, Robbie, and the Senator. The event looked like a success in the making.

The last ETA Executive Committee meeting was reassuring, concentrating on last- minute plans for the Etchevari visit. Antonio deferred until later a report on his financing receipts. Then they could assess the ETA's position in the light of both those receipts and Senator Etchevari's visit. It all seemed reasonable. Still, Raul felt troubled. It was a sixth sense.

Raul thought he was right to be suspicious. He had said as much to Alberto yesterday, when they were waiting for Antonio to arrive for the Executive Committee meeting. True, they had no direct knowledge of the matter, but word had leaked out from a well-placed informant that a *makhila* had been found after an attack on the American Consul. And then there was that business of the suicide of the wine estate owner. Perhaps that was a lucky coincidence, perhaps not. It all sounded a little convenient. After all, Antonio had been moving in on the wine estate owners, one-by-one he had said, and with the approval of the Executive Committee, after all.

The receipts were good and they were growing, they had to admit that. But this was becoming risky. And when a valued courier was knifed in a French prison during a scuffle in the prison yard, they had to wonder. They had never understood why he had been picked up in the first place. Something about a diplomatic pouch. That was hardly the ETA's business, after all. And now there was the matter of the Etchevari visit.

They had gone over final plans for the visit in detail. Coordination seemed tight, but you never knew. The emphasis was to be on a low-keyed telling of their Basque story. Leaflets would be passed out, that sort of thing. In essence, Antonio's plan was to co-opt the visit by welcoming it. They had agreed. It seemed reasonable. Any overreaction would then be blamed on the French authorities.

Still, Raul was uneasy. That is why he had stationed his nephew, with Alberto's grudging approval, at the dinner tonight. Better that they not personally attend a function in a closed area, surely crawling with police. The funny thing was that the young man really was studying to be a chef. He had even worked odd jobs, as a waiter and salad chef, in hotels in the United States when he had been in training. He could be counted on later to give them a first hand impression of Senator Etchevari.

Alberto and Raul would be at St. Jean Pied de Port the next afternoon, to hear Senator Etchevari's speech there. They were known of course, but it seemed worth the risk. There would be a huge crowd, and besides, a personal impression of this famous American would be worth having. It was an event not to be missed, important for the Basque people, who would know they had been there, and for the ETA.

Intelligence and security, those were the important factors. The call from Raul's nephew from a public phone a block from the *Hotel du Palais* was a warning. "The wines, Antonio, this is no accident." This provocation required an immediate and a public response. Good thing he had made careful contingency plans. Everyone drinks off duty, and tries to magnify his importance, and CRS troops were no exception. They talked more than police *gendarmes* would have done, and Antonio's loyal friends had heard and encouraged every word.

After one such drinking session, one of Antonio's girls had ensnared a CRS trooper who hadn't needed much encouragement. The man had awakened alone in a hotel bedroom the next morning, dizzy with a hangover, and eager to sneak back into his barracks from his overnight pass, wearing the coveralls he had found in the room. There was no chance that he would report the theft of his CRS uniform, with insignia and unit designations. He had a spare uniform anyway.

Antonio suspected that the real action for the visit of Senator Etchevari would be the public address at St. Jean Pied de Port, rather than this stuffy dinner exercise at Biarritz, or that wine ceremony at St. Emilion. Meanwhile, the cause could be helped along somewhat if there were a few arrests tonight. He would have been willing to bet that there would be.

❧ ❧ ❧

Robbie had picked up Senator Etchevari at the coastal airport in plenty of time. While Georges drove them back to Biarritz, they went over the final schedule for the visit. "I had a good series of meetings in Paris, of course, but this is the highpoint of my trip," Etchevari said. He absolutely glistened with anticipation at seeing his family's homeland.

"When were you last here, Senator?"

"It was a number of years ago, when I was in private business, before the political bug struck." He started to reminisce. "Before that, I once came on a bicycle tour with a group of Americans and French young people. We camped out in the Basque region. Worst night of my life. We camped in the remnants of a concrete German bunker along the coast a few miles south of Biarritz." He winced at the painful memory. "I never thought then that I would be coming back for a dinner at the *Hotel du Palais*, much less one given in my honor."

"Tonight should be largely ceremonial," Robbie offered. "There will be a nice dinner with French and Basque special dishes, and good Bordeaux wines to match."

"Sounds good."

"There are just too many people for a real receiving line."

Senator Etchevari smiled. "Robbie, you haven't spent any time in politics. That's for sure. How many guests will there be?"

"One hundred and eighty."

"That's exactly one hundred and eighty people who will get mad at me if I don't greet them personally. It's either that, or I'll have to spend the entire dinner table hopping. Which should it be?"

"Greet them at the beginning, I'd say."

"Good. Please set it up with the security people. Who should be with me in the receiving line?"

That took a moment's reflection. "I'd say the Prefect of the *departement*, Jean-Claude Mauret, and the Mayor of Biarritz, both with wives."

"Fine. Put the Mayor and his wife first. They will know most everybody anyway, and will be able to introduce them to the Prefect and me. Should you be in the receiving line, too?"

"No. And the Prefect speaks fluent English. He'll be able to handle the introductions to you from the Mayor."

"Sounds good."

"That order continues after dinner. The Mayor will give a brief welcome, followed by the Prefect. He will present you with a certificate from this region in honor of your public service. Then will come your remarks."

"Will a translator be necessary?"

"I've been thinking about that. Most people here will speak enough English, but it is still a compliment to your audience to have a translation. I'd be glad to volunteer."

"Fine."

"Just one thing, Senator. A couple of sentences at a time, please. Otherwise I'll get lost."

The Senator relaxed in a broad grin. "Don't worry. It'll be just fine. The important speech is tomorrow anyway."

Robbie was about to ask about translating for that speech, when the Senator added, "My staff made arrangements directly with the Mayor of St. Jean Pied de Port. She will have a Basque translator present. I'll try a few words, but you never know what the folks in the old country will think of the accent that you learned as a child from your grandparents. However, I've found that people always appreciate it when you try to speak their language, even if it is just a few phrases here and there."

Of course. The speech would be translated into Basque, not French. That was the entire point, after all.

The armored car lumbered up into the driveway of the *Hotel du Palais*. Senator Etchevari was a little disconcerted to see the group of Basque demonstrators handing out leaflets, and mulled that over for a moment. But since the police were present, better not to risk some scene over a local situation that probably didn't concern him in the first place.

Senator Etchevari checked in and was greeted by the manager, while Robbie went off to make the requested arrangements for the receiving line that evening. He was pleased to see Sylvie waiting for him in the lobby.

Commissioner Moineau had a quick decision to make, and he made it. Robbie's first call had been to him. Moineau decided that he couldn't take any chances, now that this visiting American Senator had decided to play politician with everybody on the guest list. That meant, what, upwards of two hundred people, well, one hundred seventy-five anyway, who would have immediate physical access to Senator Etchevari. That was a far cry from the dozen or so carefully screened dignitaries that Moineau had counted on.

Moineau ordered the installation of metal detectors near the entrance to the main dining room, far enough away so that they would not be an inconvenience to the receiving line itself. The trick was to funnel people through the metal detectors. Well, Moineau would entrust that sticky detail to a trusted senior lieutenant. "But nobody…I mean NOBODY…is to go into that dining room who has not first been through the metal detectors."

This change of plan, and Senator Etchevari's decision to greet everyone personally, was reported by the chef's helper to his uncle Raul, who shared the infomation with Alberto and Antonio. Antonio smiled. It was all working out rather well. He only had two calls to make, and he did so at once.

Meanwhile Robbie also made two calls, to the Mayor of Biarritz and to Prefect Mauret, informing them of the change of plan, in the guise of seeking concurrence. All was back in order shortly.

Commissioner Moineau's lieutenant had done well. Metal detectors cannot be unobtrusive, but they were placed with the minimum of likely disruption. And Robbie had to admit that their presence, for many guests, added both reassurance and an air of spice to the evening.

Some newspeople had showed up, with video cameras. They were local television stringers representing the French national news studios. Robbie had thought that the three interviews Senator Etchevari had granted that afternoon, quickly arranged by Claudine Auger, to Sylvie for *Sud-Ouest,* to a stringer from the Paris *Herald-Tribune,* and to a pool reporter from the small coastal papers, would have been enough coverage, but they had probably just stimulated more media interest.

Robbie knew one of the reporters and approached her to ask what was going on, so he could brief Senator Etchevari. Her reply was startling. "We got a tip that some news would be made here tonight," she said.

By six-thirty the receiving line had formed, and the early guests were through the metal detectors. The Mayor of Biarritz seemed to know everybody, and his introductions to Prefect Mauret and his wife went smoothly. So did Prefect Mauret's graceful handoffs to Senator Etchevari. Behind them, a small orchestra had begun to play some background music.

Within twenty minutes, the line was full, extending from the metal detectors through the length of the lobby to the receiving line. Everyone remained in a good humor. Robbie suspected that the backup was probably due more to the desire of two elected politicians, the Mayor of Biarritz and Senator Etchevari, who had hit it off perfectly, to greet each guest individually, than it was to police inefficiency.

Then it happened.

The Mayor greeted the widow of a former Mayor of Ciboure on the Basque coast. She gave a formal nod to Prefect Mauret, who was introducing her to Senator Etchevari, when the woman broke into a shout.

Thrusting a list of prominent ETA members detained by the French Government or extradited by France to Spain, she screamed, "If you are really a Basque patriot, Senator Etchevari, take up our cause! Urge the release of these men now!"

The television video cameras caught her outburst in full, together with Etchevari's astonished reaction, and then the police jumping forth to drag her away from the receiving line as she went limp. The videos reached Paris via satellite hookups from their local affiliates just in time to hit the evening news on all three national French television stations.

CHAPTER 19

Three Telephone Calls

Antonio had every reason to be pleased with himself. He recalled the Biarritz dinner with a sardonic grin. That was a lesson he'd learned about American politics during his years at Wharton; media creates its own reality.

Last night's dinner for Senator Etchevari, for example, was supposed to center on speeches, the presentation of a meaningless award, and the stroking of local politicians, including Basque region officials who were playing into the hands of the French Government.

All that was now irrelevant. Everyone had seen the new reality of the event, the protest list given to Senator Etchevari by the widow of the Mayor of Ciboure. A long fighter for Basque causes, Raul and Alberto would tend to believe that she had acted on her own.

Well, in a sense, she had. Her going limp was an inspired improvisation, and it was great theater. Antonio knew that French television was playing to the fears of their viewers. His staged media show would build on terrorist activity in France by Islamic fundamentalists and Corsican nationalists.

Predictably, correspondents would now write about the Basque movement and the ETA. The news event had not been the actual event, but that was irrelevant. The news event became the actual event. That was all that counted.

There would now be even heavier coverage for Senator Etchevari's speech at St. Jean Pied de Port. That meant that there was no need for disruptive activities there. The media speculation that there might be would feed on itself, creating a wider audience. That in turn would produce new recruits for the ETA. Possibly Senator Etchevari might play into his hands and overreact, creating new opportunities that might be exploited.

Antonio looked forward to his afternoon at St Jean Pied de Port.

He was right about media coverage in St. Jean Pied de Port. What Antonio could not have known was that it had also been a slow news day on the other side of the Atlantic. With a five hour time difference, and a prominent American Senator involved, the events at Biarritz had also made two American morning national television talk shows, one helpfully generated by the Senator's press office in Washington. Of the print media, only the New York *Times* had covered what was known, but that was a start. Admiring follow-up calls from the White House press office to contacts around the nation would do the rest.

Stringers from the American wire services, BBC, Reuters, and *Deutsche Welle* all converged on St. Jean Pied de Port. The presence of NBC's chief foreign correspondent, in the region for a long delayed vacation, added to the clamor.

None of this was lost on Senator William J. Etchevari. He more than anyone else looked forward to this afternoon in the full glare of the media, in the homeland of his people. It wouldn't hurt his reelection prospects the following year, either. With any luck, the reelection committee's fundraisers planned for early fall would get a needed boost, scaring off any potential challengers in the primaries. After that, the seat would be his for another six years, assuming that Vice President Clark stayed on the ticket. Chances like this one did not come very often, in Etchevari's experience.

Accompanied by Mayor Jeanne Lhosmette and by Robbie, and tracked by the media, the Senator called on his cousin Jaime Etchevari and his wife Julie. They bowed their heads at the low door, entered the immaculate little home, and sat down in carved wooden chairs around the dining room table. Julie proudly served homemade pastries and strong coffee while they compared notes.

"The American Consul tells me that you say that Basque nationalism is on the rise," Senator Etchevari began. There wasn't any need for Robbie to correct him. His cousin did so.

"No, that isn't quite it. What seems to be going on is a feeling that there will be more activity. People know that the time of safe-haven in France for the ETA is over. Also, the ETA has lost ground since those murders of municipal counselors in Spain. There was a cease-fire, but their recruiting hasn't stopped. Maybe they're split. I don't know. But there seems to be a new vitality. They've not marking time any more. For one thing, we hear that the ETA has found new sources of money."

Mayor Lhosmette nodded agreement. "I hear that, too."

"What is the point of all this? Do they really think that Basque independence is possible?"

Mayor Lhosmette answered. "Fanatics create their own logic. For a start, their movement"—Senator Etchevari and Robbie noted the careful use of 'their' by the Mayor—"has had many reverses in recent years. Their momentum has been lost. Many former militants now want to stop the struggle, or just leave it to legal means, such as a referendum. Hundreds of their most committed followers are in Spanish prisons. So is virtually all of the old leadership. And with the French Government now denying this area as a safe haven, they must be getting pretty desperate. They have to replace their recruits, maybe even spring some of their followers from prison, and come up with some fairly serious money, or they will not survive what has become a war of attrition against Spain and France. They must somehow move forward or their movement will collapse."

She had thought it all through. Her host shook his head, agreeing. So did Julie. Senator Etchevari followed up logically.

"What do you think needs to be done for the Basque people?"

"Understand, Senator, I am a mayor. You think about the bigger things. I think about local schools and public safety and health care and transportation. Those are my priorities. So I would love to see some emphasis in the schools on the Basque heritage, some courses in our language and even know how some talented youngster is going to go to a university someday."

"That is a worthwhile agenda," Etchevari commented. "I am sorry that in their haste to assimilate, my family never passed on the Basque language to me. I feel that as a great loss." He seemed lost in thought for a moment.

After the meeting, Robbie met Claudine Auger and together they checked out arrangements for the speech. The microphones were raised to match Etchevari's height. The podium commanded the scene, with a fine photogenic backdrop of the half-timbered Basque houses along the river that bisected the town.

Claudine had scheduled and cleared with Senator Etchevari several more background interviews, including one with NBC's chief foreign correspondent, who was cavalierly outfitted in a safari jacket. Claudine promised him the full text of the Senator's speech, which he would later analyze on-camera. Too bad he isn't wearing a pith helmet, she thought.

Robbie was now ferrying the Senator around introducing local officials, so his time with Sylvie was limited. Since Sylvie was covering the visit for *Sud-Ouest*, probing here and there for a story, their interests in the visit were not identical anyway. That was worrisome. She also seemed aware of this divergence, but it didn't seem to bother her. She seemed to like it. That also was worrisome.

She seemed so intense. He found himself absurdly wishing, as she took notes with other journalists whenever the Senator spoke, that she would wink at him. Just one wink. That would say that they had their own world after all, beyond this. This was ridiculous. He was thinking like a cartoon character. Next he'd be checking his horoscope. What page was it on, anyway?

Then he found her, and they shared coffee at a sidewalk cafe by the river, comparing notes of the dinner in Biarritz.

"Was it as bad as I think?" he asked.

"Probably worse," she said. "The only good part, from my point of view, if you saw *Sud-Ouest* this morning, is that my story on Etchevari became the first-page lead, with rewrite melding in details of the protest to my afternoon story."

He sipped his coffee. "The great question, of course, is what the ETA will do now. Will they leave it alone, or go for more news today?"

"You aren't the only one wondering that," she said. "That is why this little town is getting a media invasion. Everyone seems to believe, no, feel that there is far more about to happen than we have seen already. And believe me Robbie, nobody in the media, whether print or television, ever wants to miss a breaking story. They—we—would all rather cover something unnecessarily than miss a real story."

She thought for a moment. "As a matter of fact, that is what I spend most of my time doing. Jacques Lebrun would never understand, believe me, if this Basque business developed into something important, and our newspaper, with the biggest overall circulation in the region, and special editions for the Basque region, was the only one that missed it."

"So you'll be covering Etchevari throughout his visit?"

"The reporting end, yes. Lebrun himself will write whatever editorials will be run after it is over. He's looking forward to that. But I'll do the rest."

"I'm looking forward to the *Jurade* luncheon tomorrow afternoon after their ceremony. Don't forget that you promised to be my luncheon date. So finish your stories by then."

She smiled. "*Oui, bien sur, Monsieur le Consul.*" She checked her watch and frowned. "But now I've got to go."

He put some coins on the table as she left the cafe, pursuing another story lead. Robbie looked up and saw her leaving. Abruptly she turned around, smiled, and gave him a wink before vanishing into the crowd.

The afternoon warming sunshine was pleasant, and the growing crowd at the St. Jean Pied de Port market area, the Place Charles de Gaulle, was in a festive mood. Beyond the Nive River and its half-timbered houses was the Upper Town, with ramparts designed centuries earlier for the town's protection.

Many of those who had arrived in the town early enough had spent the morning exploring the scenery of the Upper Town, where pilgrims in past centuries, and the historically minded in this one, had climbed the Rue de la Citadelle, or the Rue d'Espagne which led to the medieval Porte d'Espagne, and the pilgrim route in Spain. "If I get through this ETA mess," Robbie silently promised his New England God, "someday I'll make that journey, first to Roncevaux, and then to Santiago de Compostela beyond."

Now the crowd slowly increased. It seemed that young people in traditional Basque clothing were all over the Place Charles de Gaulle, handing out leaflets on Basque culture and history and customs. The leaflets were politically unexceptionable, but informative. More than one televised report, filed by an earnest-looking twentysomething on a first visit to the region, was based entirely on the information they contained.

As agreed in Bordeaux earlier, security was heavy, but not heavy-handed. Police made repeated checks of suspicious-looking characters, and known drunks and prostitutes were stashed in adjoining cells in the local police station. Now Prefect of Police Jean-Luc Charasson was worrying. After that incident in Biarritz, with all these media people present, the stage was set for trouble. He would tighten security at St. Emilion.

One CRS trooper gave Alberto Aguilar and Raul Izquierda hard looks before letting them pass. The trooper then had given Raul an amused, conspiratorial poke in the ribs. Raul looked past the uniform and suddenly recognized Antonio. They had gone several paces into the crowd before Raul muttered his discovery to Alberto.

Then Mayor Jeanne Lhosmette, speaking in Basque and then in French, welcomed Senator William J. Etchevari back to his Basque homeland. It was a great day for the Basque people to welcome him back, went the theme. The descendant of sheepherders from this very region was now a United States Senator, a member of the inner circles of the greatest power on earth. Well, he might be if he voted with the President more often, Robbie thought.

The small army of journalists, annoyed at only receiving advance summaries of Etchevari's speech, scribbled background notes and practiced posing for their cameramen.

It was impossible to say where the polite applause for Mayor Lhosmette's remarks blended into the tumultuous ovation that the crowd gave Senator Etchevari as he stood up and walked over to the rostrum. All peered forward except the trained police and uniformed CRS sprinkled throughout the crowd and on the nearby rooftops. They continued to scan the crowd.

Senator Etchevari looked at his audience for a long moment, letting the suspense build. Then he began. He spoke with a slow, building cadence, a cadence that was matched by his Basque language interpreter, who translated Etchevari's remarks sentence by sentence. The effect was nearly hypnotic.

"Our Basque nation has a proud and glorious history...Beginning in this beautiful land, we have remained loyal to our culture and our heritage...Many, like myself, now live beyond the seas...But always, this Basque region is our homeland..."

Etchevari had his audience and the media transfixed. For several minutes, there was no applause as he spoke. People were afraid of missing what he might say. But gradually, with the excellent accoustics and precise translation, the crowd grew comfortable with the speaker, and a rhythm developed. Sentence, translation, applause. Sentence, translation, applause.

Now Etchevari, having established rapport with his audience, carefully shifted his theme.

"In Washington, I always remember the Basque people, and am proud to be a Basque." Applause. "In the Senate, I am proud to uphold the heritage that you and I share." More applause. "From the White House to the Capitol, and throughout our America, all people know that a son of sheepherders from this very region now sits in the counsels of power." Sustained applause.

"More of our people should have the opportunities which I have had. To make that possible I announce today the creation of a scholarship foundation for young men and women from the seven Basque regions. Beginning next year, awards will go each year to seven young men and to an equal number of young women to pursue higher education at the universities of their choice." Measured, prolonged applause.

Having set forth his introduction. and created a link with his audience, Etchevari now began to touch on his main theme. As he did so Robbie joined those who were looking through the crowd. He knew what Etchevari was about to say. It had been added following last night's disruption in Biarritz.

"We have not always been treated with justice in the past." Silence. Where was he going with this? "Some do not understand our strength in fortitude. Others mistake our unity and aspirations as mere folklore, like a costume to be put on or taken off on feast days." Affirming nods throughout the crowd, as people turned to one another in agreement with his words.

"We should do much more to make certain that our unique culture is not lost. We must also never yield to the counsels of those who seek, for their own purposes, extremism and terrorism. They do not speak for you and me. They do not speak for our history and our people. They would tear us apart and make progress impossible. They usurp the language of patriots, but they are gangsters.

"Our Basque way is the path of honor and tradition and achievement. Today, for the first time, the attention of a fickle world is upon us, you and me. Let us resolve together to strengthen our Basque heritage, to reject terrorists and their false promises, and to move forward together as a proud people."

He ended in Basque, appropriating the nationalists' motto, *"Zaspiak-bat!"*—"The seven are one!" It was inspired by John F. Kennedy's *"Ich bin ein Berliner"* at the Berlin Wall, and it worked perfectly. He was speaking to people in their own language. Let the Basque language be the one translated!

The crowd rose to its feet in an approving roar, drowning out the French translation given by the Basque translator. The media crowd reached for their cellular phones to describe the tumult as Senator Etchevari smiled approvingly at Robbie.

"It's a decision only you can make, Mr. President."

The President smiled at his Political Adviser as they turned off the television. It was nice not having to rely on CNN, or on split screens, the way that Lyndon Johnson had done. With special satellite dishes, the White House could, and did, have access to virtually any television coverage in the world.

"Sure," the President agreed. "What's the latest on Clark?"

"Bad to worse. It looks like a Grisham novel. His law firm wasn't just defending gamblers. Nobody would care much about that. It's beginning to look like his clients were fronts for the Mafia. The Russian Mafia. Clark was Managing Partner at the time. He must have known, which may make him a crook. Or he didn't know, which makes him a fool."

The President nodded dismissal to his Political Adviser. Then he picked up the phone and his call was placed to Senator Etchevari at the Mayor's office in St. Jean Pied de Port.

Antonio was outraged This politician in one speech had threatened everything the ETA had built, all the struggles they had made while he, Etchevari, was safely building his own personal fortune and his political career. He stumbled out with the crowd and changed his clothes in the safe house, keeping the CRS uniform pressed. He would need it in St. Emilion.

An hour later he placed a telephone call to Jacques Lebrun, at his *Sud-Ouest* office. "Hello, *Monsieur* Lebrun. This is the ETA calling. The code word is 'Navarre.' I repeat, '*Navarre*.' The traitor Etchevari will not survive his trip to our Basque nation, which he has dishonored." Antonio repeated his message more deliberately and then hung up the receiver.

Robbie dropped the Senator off at the Hostellerie de Plaisance in St. Emilion, on his way back to Bordeaux. Etchevari was in a sunny frame of mind. "It's always good news when the White House takes favorable notice, Robbie," he said cryptically.

Robbie was pleased to see Marge and Elliot Hawkins in the hotel lobby. They had arranged to be with Etchevari for a quiet dinner and early night before tomorrow's induction ceremony by the *Jurade de St. Emilion*.

To say that it had been an exciting day would be an understatement. Robbie felt caught up in a great event. So that was what it was like to be in politics, and to make a difference. Robbie wondered if the ETA would take that lying down; he rather doubted that they would. He would compare notes with Commissioner Moineau in the morning. He looked forward to luncheon after the *Jurade* ceremony with Sylvie. He would call her and Evalyn as soon as he checked his messages. Georges let him off at his apartment, and security officers went with him to the door.

Minouette curled around his ankle as he played the tape. There were two messages. The first was a chatty one from Evalyn, who was enjoying her stay with the Sandersons to the hilt. She said that Emily would be taking her to the *Jurade* luncheon the next day. Dick was stuck with a last-minute delegation of VIPs. Robbie smiled. So that happened to others, too.

The second message made him sit up. It was from Ambassador Adams in Paris. "Call me as soon as you return," the Ambassador had said, giving a private number.

Robbie did so. Mrs. Adams answered the telephone, and immediately passed the receiver to her husband.

"Hello, Robbie." There were no preliminaries. "I've had a call from Joan Pearson." She was the Assistant Secretary of State for Consular Affairs, "CA" in State Department jargon.

"Her people have finished the search of student visa records that I requested. They are positive that your man is one Antonio Echurra, a Basque now in his thirties. He spent six years in the United States, and has an MBA from Wharton. She's sending you his file directly. It should already be on your FAX machine." Robbie looked over. Some papers were there.

"Something else. I want you out of Bordeaux, as soon as Senator Etchevari leaves. It's become too dangerous, and nobody can assure me that picking up Echurra will solve your safety problem. Anyway, I have some good news for you. You're locked-in now for Political Officer in our Embassy in Budapest, after language training. That's what you wanted, isn't it?"

"Yes, sir." Robbie's voice sounded flat even to himself. He'd wanted this for years. Why wasn't he delighted?

"Another thing, Robbie. This further detail must be kept under wraps until Diplomatic Security checks it out, and the Bureau if necessary. They'll be here on Monday."

"What's that, Mr. Ambassador?"

"It was a contested visa case. Echurra had a history of agitation with the Spanish police. He was then living in Pamplona. The visa was granted despite his record after a persuasive argument was made in his favor by the American Consul in Embassy Madrid who eventually issued the visa."

Ambassador Adams paused. "That Consul was Elliot Hawkins."

CHAPTER 20

Au Revoir, Bordeaux

Three more telephone calls followed immediately. Lebrun had called Commissioner Moineau and told him about the ETA threat. Moments later, after his call from Ambassador Adams, Robbie also called Moineau. "We've identified our ETA man," he said. Robbie FAXed him Echurra's visa application photo, which showed a younger, thinner faced version of the same man Robbie had seen.

"*Eh bien, Monsieur le Consul,*" Moineau began. "This is our night for breakthroughs. I've just had a call from Lebrun. The ETA has signalled that they will kill Senator Etchevari. Don't worry. I've tripled his security immediately. Nobody can get through."

"Have you warned Senator Etchevari?"

Silence. Robbie began to argue. "*Monsieur le Commissaire,* he's got a right to know."

Moineau shrugged his shoulders. If he didn't call, then Cutler surely would. They might as well do it together. Their conference call went through immmediately. "Senator, this is Robbie Cutler. I'm on the line with Police Commissioner Moineau."

"What's up, Robbie?"

Moineau spoke. "*Monsieur le Senateur,* a credible threat on your life has been issued from the ETA. We are sure of the source. Your personal protection has been tripled. However, I believe that you must reassess the public ceremony tomorrow. Nobody can absolutely guarantee your safety."

Etchevari thought for a moment. What would the White House make of his cancelling the appearance? It certainly wouldn't be a plus. It might even make the President reconsider. "I can't hide, and I don't want to. I appreciate your call. Let's go ahead. To hell with the ETA."

Commissioner Moineau's meeting the next morning was brief, more touching base with latest developments than anything else. Antonio Echurra's photograph had been run off by the thousands and distributed overnight throughout the region, to every police departrnent, CRS barracks, and border station.

Antonio Echurra was now a wanted man by name, and the police had arrest warrants in hand. He was so hot that none of the usual marginal defense lawyers had nosed around to pick up a new client. If taken alive he would be represented by top-flight talent, Robbie was sure of that.

Jacques Lebrun coldly recited the chilling story of his telephone call, imitating the inflections of his caller, surely Echurra, as best he could.

Charles de Tourneau confirmed that he had dealt with the man in the photograph, "although I never knew his name. It's the same man."

Claude de Monoury understood that his own life was now also at risk, as Echurra might connect him with this manhunt. And de Monoury would today, as *Premier Jurat* of the *Jurade de St. Emilion*, be on very public display.

And so will all of us, Robbie thought glumly.

As the meeting broke up, Charles de Tourneau caught up with Robbie. He was about to launch into something, when he spotted

Sylvie on Robbie's arm. "We never had our meeting, *Monsieur le Consul*," he chided. "Let's talk after the ceremony in St. Emilion."

Robbie wondered what else de Tourneau had in mind, as he spotted Georges waiting in the armored car. He and Sylvie drove over to St. Emilion in apprehensive silence, holding hands. Sylvie had her mind on what might happen that day to Robbie She didn't believe for a moment that the ETA's death threat was only for Etchevari. Robbie wondered what might happen that evening, when he told her that he was leaving Bordeaux.

By mid-morning, the lower town's market place square, or Place du Marche in the hilly village of St. Emilion was teeming with people. It seemed that every journalist that had been present at St. Jean Pied de Port was there. Only two pool print journalists, another from French television, and Sylvie Marceau from *Sud-Ouest*, were allowed into the Monolithic Church for the *Jurade* ceremony itself.

Claudine Auger had coordinated the media arrangements with the *Jurade* and the police. She did not know, Robbie reflected, that there had been a threat on Senator Etchevari's life. That had not been made public. Sylvie was the only journalist present who was aware of last night's ETA death threat on Senator Etchevari. The other jounalists were there by instinct. For once, that predatory journalistic instinct was on target.

Police, both uniformed and plainclothes, were everywhere. Security officials had scoured the interior of the Monolithic Church repeatedly. Metal detectors were installed at every entrance to the market square, and to the church itself. This was far from the festive, opulent mood that usually marked the ceremonies of the *Jurade de St. Emilion*. Perhaps the luncheon to follow would restore that mood.

Robbie thought that the *Jurade* was a wine organization in which the entire Bordeaux region could take pride. Their ceremonial activities, such as setting the beginning of the grape harvest, were carried out each year with fanfare and dignity.

A glimpse of the *Jurade's* members ambling into the square to take their places within the church proved that it was one of the most colorful wine societies as well. They had on long scarlet robes, with silk caps to match, and their robes were bordered with ermine.

And the setting for their initiations was spectacular.

The Monolithic Church had been carved out of solid rock, its entrance being from the lower town's market square. Overhead was the upper town, with small bustling stores and restaurants resting literally on top of this vast hollowed out edifice.

Originally, tunnels and crevices in the porous limestone rock had served as shelter for medieval monks or mystics, including surely the monk Emilion, for whom the town was named. Then the enlargement had begun, over four centuries. It had become one of the largest such churches in Europe. Robbie wondered whether just possibly the Lascaux cave instinct was still at work, now uniting faith and history through wine.

Robbie found Emily Sanderson and Evalyn at a cafe enjoying cups of *cafe au lait* in the morning sunshine. Then they scooped up Marge Hawkins, emerging into the Place du Marche from the upper town as Elliot disappeared into a holding area near the church to await the ceremony. There was no time to talk with him now, even if Robbie could have thought through what to say. With a last look around the Place du Marche, Robbie and the women entered the church, passed through the metal detectors, and took their places for the ceremony.

The morning sunshine poured through three large windows above the main doorway to light the interior of the underground church with soft splendor, an aide to faith, Robbie was sure. Throughout the church, massive candles set on tall iron stands also provided flickering illumination. The effect was one of solemnity and celebration.

Towards the front, several rows were reserved for members of the *Jurade*, and after the church had filled with spectators in they came, led in file by the *Premier Jurat*, Claude de Monoury. If he were nervous about this ceremony, he wasn't showing it. The music of trumpets and hunting horns filled the church, as all rose, and the *Jurade* members made their entrance.

The ceremony was a mixture of tradition and humor. Claude de Monoury tried to maintain that tone, but all he could think of was the possibility of an assassination, at any moment. Thank heavens for all of this police protection. He hoped that Echurra would be caught soon. If not, he had no doubts that he would be on the list of victims before long.

Armed CRS troopers lined the walls of the church on both sides. They faced the altar but scanned the seated audience. So did the undercover police and the *Renseignements Generaux* agents that peppered the audience.

Claude de Monoury stepped forth and began the initiations, or "*intronisations*" of new members. There were fifteen this year, rather more than usual. However, with a fine vintage from last year now blending in the cellars, the *Jurade* had thought to capitalize on that vintage to increase its publicity through this ceremony. Each initiate stepped forth in turn.

The Swedish Minister of Transportation was the first. An elderly man, he barely heard what Claude was saying, but knew when to take a long sip from the goblet that was offered to him. Then as some chanting began from a choir at the rear of the church, he ad-libbed "*C'est delicieux*!" and the ice was broken. Everyone smiled and began to relax as Claude de Monoury put the ceremonial ermine shawl of the *Jurade* over the man's shoulders.

The others proceeded with similar smiling dignity. Senator Etchevari would be the last initiate, and seated at his side was Elliot Hawkins. Elliot seemed to smile wanly, right at Robbie. Robbie realized suddenly that informing Senator Etchevari of the death threat meant that he would surely have told Elliot.

It stood to reason. So did something else.

Elliot hadn't become Deputy Chief of Mission at Embassy Paris by being slow on the uptake. He would also realize that he had not been personally informed by Robbie of the threat, as he should have been. That meant that Robbie hadn't known what to say. People usually avoided conversations when they were embarrassed. So Elliot's Foreign Service cover surely had been blown. His wan smile was testimony to that.

Claude de Monoury paused to refill the ceremonial goblet with wine. It wasn't possible to see which wine was being used, but Robbie was sure that it was some of de Monoury's own Chateau St. Aubin. That was also a tradition with the *Jurade de St. Emilion*. One served one's best, and generously.

Elliot Hawkins stood up and moved over towards the altar, facing Claude de Monoury and the seated audience. He smiled with anticipation, as Claude picked up the brimming goblet and leaned towards him. Elliot's right hand reached forward to take the goblet. Elliot scanned the crowd and his eyes caught something unexpected to his right.

The moment seemed frozen in time.

This was really too much, Elliot thought. He could rationalize many things. He had had to do so, in order to serve his nation. He had had to be aware of things that people safe in their beds wouldn't want to know. It had aged him and made him wrestle with his conscience, ever more elastic, more than once.

How did one keep a terrorist contact without slipping over the line? Perhaps it wasn't possible. But he had tried. He was sorry about Pryor, and would have saved him if he could. But that had happened without his knowledge. It had not, however, been difficult to figure out the truth. After he had done so, he had really had no choice but to try to save Echurra, letting him know about the pouch containing the Pryor letter. He could not, after all, bring Pryor back to life.

As he had done so often during his professional life, Elliot had taken a calculated risk. The pouch might have contained important evidence, after all. Thank heavens it had not. He had tried to let speculation about Pryor's murderer being a wine estate owner play itself out. Too bad that Robbie Cutler had insisted on playing detective.

Yes, he had had to put Echurra on Cutler's trail. He felt badly about that. But he had, after all, also arranged extra security for Robbie, including that armored car. He had also pulled strings to get Robbie reassigned out of Bordeaux a year early, and even to the assignment that Robbie wanted most.

Despite all the false steps, the result had been worth it. Elliot had been on the verge of cracking the entire Basque ETA terrorist organization. It was the culmination of his best agent operation. The gambles had paid off. It only remained to pass the bundle onto French contacts, and see what the future held. Then with any luck it would be Ambassador Hawkins next, consistent with his Foreign Service cover, and a welcome end to this intrigue.

The seconds passed. Claude de Monoury held the goblet towards him, with a stage whisper: "It's your turn, *Monsieur le Ministre.*"

Elliot didn't hear him. Staring to his right, he saw that Echurra was clearly out of control. The GAL handle no longer worked to muzzle him. Elliot saw through the CRS uniform. He had been appalled by the ETA death threat that he had heard last night from Etchevari. So Echurra was even ready to add the murder of Senator Etchevari to his list of crimes.

For an odd moment, Elliot saw it all in slow motion, his contact, terrorism, murder, the gun, while he tried to understand it all, like Alec Guinness in *Bridge On The River Quai*. Was he just helping the enemy, after all? Or was he serving his nation?

He glanced at the man behind him. Etchevari was a good man. Maybe a potential President. He didn't deserve this. And in the aftermath, his own connection with Echurra wouldn't be kept hidden. It was all unravelling. Well, maybe there was one more service that Hawkins could perform for his nation. He hoped Marge would understand.

There was a sudden scream from Marge Hawkins as she saw the expression on her husband's face. Robbie stood. So did Police Commissioner Moineau and a few others

"There he is! That's the man you're after! *GET HIM*!" Elliot Hawkins yelled over and over while pointing straight at the CRS trooper on his right near the front of the church.

"You bastard! *Salopard*!" screamed the trooper.

Antonio Echurra had just time enough to draw his gun and get off one well-aimed shot at Hawkins before the two plainclothes officers flanking Senator Etchevari shot him. It was all over in seconds.

* * *

Commissioner Moineau, Jacques Lebrun, Charles de Tourneau and Robbie sat together at a cafe in the Place du Marche and drank cognac The church had quickly emptied and so, finally, had the square. Charles de Monoury had left to salvage the *Jurade* luncheon in the upper city. A police ambulance had taken away the bodies of Hawkins and Echurra. Senator Etchevari's security escort had bustled him away from the scene. Whether or not the danger was entirely over, nobody could be entirely sure. It was better to be safe.

Robbie led off "You told us, *Monsieur* de Tourneau, that you had told Douglas Pryor of the extortion of wine estate owners. I think he was going to announce it publicly at the Vintage Dinner in Washington. He'd somehow gotten enough confirmation to go public. And then, as the savior of Bordeaux wines from terrorism, his reputation would be secure for life. But once he put out that word, it got back to the ETA. They couldn't let that happen."

"How do you explain his letter to the Consulate General?"

"*Monsieur le Commissaire*, Pryor was a cautious man. He wanted confirmation of what he had been told. His letter requesting a briefing on the political situation here really meant an analysis of the Basque terrorist threat, that de Tourneau had mentioned to him. It was after the letter was sent that he decided to go public first, instead of waiting. Maybe he had some other confirmation of the ETA's extortion scheme. Maybe he was threatened in some way. Something seems to have forced his hand.We may never know for sure. It seems clear that somehow the ETA found out, and then pursued him to Washington for this public event. One pill was found in his pillbox, poisoned. That had been planted beforehand. They could just have relied on that to do the job, probably when Pryor was far from Bordeaux. But now, Pryor had to be stopped. So they moved up his death.

"The irony is that he might have thought that by going public, he would be safer. He never got the chance to make his announcement. Meanwhile, his letter had already been sent."

De Tourneau nodded in agreement. Robbie went on.

"Antonio Echurra was, clearly, a key member of the ETA, probably the new Executive Committee member that hadn't been identified. It all seems to fit, from the 'American accent' that *Monsieur* de Monoury had noticed, to his extended residence in the United States. As you know, that has now been confirmed by official visa records."

Jacques Lebrun had a question. "What was all that about 'Pryor casks' and special wine samples for Douglas Pryor?"

De Tourneau was embarrassed and looked it. "That's what I was going to tell you, *Monsieur le Consul*. Pryor's murder meant that the ETA was onto him. Next they would go after whoever had told him about the ETA shakedown of wine estate owners. I decided that the best defense, as you Americans say, was a good offense. If I was impugning his integrity as a wine critic, I hardly would have been confiding in him. I'm ashamed of myself now, but there you have it."

Lebrun nodded. That vindicated his judgment not to run the "Pryor cask" story in *Sud-Ouest* without confirmation. He ran a newspaper, after all, not a scurrilous gossip sheet.

Robbie sipped his cognac again. "I should have taken one piece of evidence to the next step earlier than I did. The *Sud-Ouest* photograph of Crespier's body shows his hand stretched towards the can of spray paint. In his last conscious moment, he was trying to tell us something. It's clear now that Echurra killed him, or had him killed. Such a man was also capable of murdering Pryor. But the suicide letter still puzzles me a bit."

Commissioner Moineau smiled. "That was what put me on the track in the first place. As I said before at our meeting in my office, suicide letters are rarely typed. Also, Crespier's signature showed no particular strain. It was a normal signature.

"But beyond that, I could not understand why the letter had been folded. A suicide letter would just be signed, to be found with the body. The fact that it had been folded meant that it had been sent to someone, surely Echurra who then realized his opportunity to *add* a sentence and change its meaning.

"You see, it was really two letters not one. The first was Crespier's letter to Echurra. The second was Echurra's addition to make us believe that Crespier committed suicide."

Lebrun followed up with a question to Robbie. "How do you explain the attack on you?"

"Clearly there was no connection between that attack and the earlier threat that was spray-painted on the Consulate General door. No," Robbie concluded, "Echurra had to be directed towards me. He must have become aware of the letter from Pryor that was in the stolen diplomatic pouch. He put two and two together, and decided to stop my investigation."

Robbie took another sip of cognac. "Of course, that didn't succeed. Moving right along, he decided to plant a car bomb on my Ford afterwards. Persistent fellow."

"You Anglo Saxons! I'll never understand your sense of humor," Moineau said. Then he added, "Please continue, *Monsieur le Consul.* How does this all tie in with the Pryor murder?"

"Remember that the letter from Pryor mentioned a trip that he had taken to the Basque coast. Pryor must have asked too many questions in Biarritz. Clearly the word got back to the ETA, and Echurra decided to kill Pryor. That must have been when Echurra arranged his poisoning, to take place when he was far away."

Lebrun rose to leave. "It was a lucky thing for Senator Etchevari that your man Hawkins saw Echurra pull out his weapon. What a brave sacrifice that was." Their questions answered, Lebrun and de Tourneau finished their drinks and left the table.

Commissioner Moineau turned to Robbie. "I think you have more to tell me, *Monsieur le Consul,*" he said softly. "For one thing, you and I were both standing. I am sure that you saw, as I did, that Echurra had not pulled out his revolver until after Hawkins screamed at him, not before. The sequence is interesting."

"Yes." Might as well come out with it all now.

"This is theory, and there is nothing that would stand up in court. Furthermore, those who could confirm it are both dead. But I think I can piece together what happened. For your information only, of course, *mon ami.*"

Moineau nodded. "*D'accord.*"

Robbie swallowed some cognac. It was good and warming. Funny he hadn't visited Cognac yet. It wasn't that far from Bordeaux, after all.

"Elliot Hawkins, the Deputy Chief of Mission at our Embassy, and Antonio Echurra had known each other for years. Echurra even went to the United States with his help, many years ago. But Echurra was a very twisted individual, motivated by a number of things besides misguided ethnic patriotism. I'm betting that the records, both police and newspaper records, will show that he had relatives murdered in the GAL killings in the Basque region some dozen years ago."

Moineau stroked his chin. "The name does sound somewhat familiar, come to think of it. That would probably be reflected in our police files. So Echurra's motivation was vengeance?"

"I think so, both personal and for his people. He probably understood that the nationalist movement was just spinning its wheels, and needed a new infusion of money and goals. That would have been his Wharton training, I suspect. He took the Basque movement as some kind of case study and went on from there."

"A chilling thought."

"And on the personal side, he had vengeance in mind. He was after those in the GAL who he thought had murdered his family. That is the connection that is the thinnest of all. Let me try to construct the hypothesis. It will have to remain just that, but perhaps it will help you close your books on the matter, *Monsieur le Commissaire.*

"We have all known that until yesterday, this visit by Senator Etchevari was not supposed to pose a real security threat. I suspect that information came from Echurra himself. It was either disinformation, designed to throw us off the track, or perhaps he changed his mind after the Senator's speech at St. Jean Pied de Port yesterday afternoon. The *quid pro quo* for Echurra's cooperation may even have been information, real or concocted, passed to him on the GAL killers."

"So you think that there was a devil's bargain for information from Echurra?"

"Yes. Hawkins had served in Madrid. That is surely where he first met Echurra. Perhaps Hawkins was even running Echurra as an intelligence agent. Echurra's problem was that Pryor might expose him. Hawkins's dilemma was probably that of an honorable man enmeshed in the world of terrorism, step by step.

"After a while," Robbie continued, "Hawkins became aware that he was dealing with a fanatic who couldn't, in the end, be controlled. And so he made this sacrifice. He was a man of honor, after all."

Moineau glinted at Robbie. "*Monsieur le Consul,* it's appropriate that wine helped solve the case. As you suspected, putting those wines on the menu at the Etchevari dinner in Biarritz was a clear signal to the ETA that we were on to them. They tried to use Bordeaux wines...but it was those same Bordeaux wines that drove them into the open at last."

Robbie nodded. "Yes. *In vino veritas*, after all."

"One last point," Moineau continued. "Your theory about Hawkins explains a great deal. It will go no farther. But one thing still puzzles me and that is that fairy tale that you just told Lebrun. You gave me a copy of the letter from Pryor too. It was sent to former Consul General Johnston, and it doesn't mention you at all. It certainly wouldn't give Echurra a reason to kill you."

Robbie pondered answering for a moment. Not everything could be explained by his hypothesis. But Hawkins had just sacrificed his own life. That was redemption. There was nothing to add.

"Matters are best left that way," he said.

Moineau agreed.

They finished their cognacs and left the cafe.

Robbie and Sylvie took their places at Claude de Monoury's table and prepared for the feast of a lifetime. The *Jurade* luncheons were famous, and the *Premier Jurat* had outdone himself. Wine glasses in profusion, and waiters by the dozen lined up to serve a rich assortment of every good thing they could imagine.

The courses and wines followed each other lazily. It was not possible to imagine a more sumptuous meal, or finer wines. The scenery was spectacular, as vineyards in the background framed chapel walls in the bright sunshine.

"More wine, *Monsieur le Consul*?" It was a solicitous waiter, but an odd question. Wines were simply poured in the right glasses. Seconds were not offered. They didn't have to be, and might spoil the taste for the next glass. Come to think of it, how did the fellow know that he was the American Consul? The nameplate didn't say that.

Robbie looked closely at the waiter, who then made his mistake. He looked startled and, yes, guilty. Robbie had seen the man before, on the sidelines at the *Hotel du Palais*, in some kind of chef's uniform as the guests arrived. Then Robbie remembered seeing him before that, getting into the cab as Robbie arrived at the Willard Hotel for the Vintage Dinner, with that same guilty look. The man dropped his carafe of wine and started to run. Not soon enough. A shout to the *gendarmes*, and he was caught.

❧ ❧ ❧

This was the moment that Robbie had been dreading. He was with Sylvie that evening back at his apartment in Bordeaux. She was full of the day's excitement, the murders, the *Jurade* luncheon and her article, and he had to tell her his own news.

There was no good way to do so. Finally he poured two glasses of champagne and came and sat with her on the couch.

He looked unhappy. That expression stopped her chatter.

"Sylvie, I have something to tell you." She looked at him anxiously. He looked like a big, mournful puppy. She hoped that he wasn't going to do something foolish. She liked him very, very much. But there was her career to think of, and they really had to sort out their views on religion. It might work, and she hoped that it would. But not now, not yet.

He continued. "I had a call from Ambassador Adams in Paris last night. He has been concerned about this Basque business, the terrorists and so on. He has ordered me out of Bordeaux. Now. I'll be assigned after some language training back to Europe, but to the American Embassy in Budapest. I've always wanted that," he confided. "But now I'll have to leave Bordeaux, and I don't want to leave you. I don't think that I can."

Her own voice softened. "I wouldn't mind waiting a bit if you are really serious about us, Robbie. We do have things to work out. But you have never even said that you loved me."

He made up for that omission then and there.

About the Author

William S. Shepard served as Consul General in Bordeaux, and travelled throughout the four regions, including the Basque country, that the Consulate General then served. His nonfiction writings include articles on the Basque ETA organization, the status of the career diplomatic service, and other national security topics. He is a member of the *Jurade de St. Emilion*, the *Commanderie de Bordeaux*, and other wine societies.

0-595-22413-X

Breinigsville, PA USA
20 May 2010
238443BV00002B/39/A